ISIS TRILOGY

BOOK ONE

THE
RED
MIRROR

ONE LIFE IS NOT ENOUGH

S. L. GORE

2018.04.06 Edition

ISBN 978-1-940304-00-7

Published by Tajine Publishing, Las Vegas NV
This book is also available in eVersion.

Author website: www.SLGore.com

AUTHOR'S NOTE
This book is a work of fiction. Names, characters, places and incidents are the product of the author's imagination or are used fictitiously, and any resemblance to actual persons, living or dead, or events is entirely coincidental.

*I dedicate this flight of fancy to Egyptologists,
especially Willeke, Hans, Monica, Anna and Katya.
Mental giants all, with great physical stamina and
deep sensitivity for literature, language and art,
they are my heroes.*

*Thank you to my three muses, Jesper, Carol and David,
for traveling the Isis journey with me every step of the way.*

And to the Writers Bench.

TABLE OF CONTENTS

Map of Ancient Egypt 500 BC

Part One   The Red Mirror

Chapter 1	Obsession	1
Chapter 2	River God	7
Chapter 3	The Temple	12
Chapter 4	Summons	19
Chapter 5	Sit-hathor	22
Chapter 6	Preparation	27
Chapter 7	The Bath	31
Chapter 8	Encounter	35
Chapter 9	Eiffel Tower	39
Chapter 10	The Wynn	43
Chapter 11	Return	48
Chapter 12	The Nile	50
Chapter 13	Abydos	54
Chapter 14	The Wizard	59
Chapter 15	Khent-min	62
Chapter 16	Temple of Min	68
Chapter 17	The Poem	73
Chapter 18	Hermopolis	77
Chapter 19	The Amulet	82

Part Two   Hathor Power

Chapter 20	The Hunt	89
Chapter 21	Lion	95
Chapter 22	The General	100
Chapter 23	Ishtar	105
Chapter 24	The Test	110
Chapter 25	Search	114
Chapter 26	The Sash	120
Chapter 27	A Plan	124
Chapter 28	Decision	129
Chapter 29	The Bite	133
Chapter 30	Discovery	139

Chapter 31   Transfer of Power   144
Chapter 32   Brothers   149
Chapter 33   Echo   155
Chapter 34   Cobra   159
Chapter 35   Rescue   164
Chapter 36   Confession   169
Chapter 37   Barb   174
Chapter 38   The Boyfriend   178
Chapter 39   Fortune-Teller   183
Chapter 40   Hector   188
Chapter 41   Truth   192

Part Three   The Great Green
Chapter 42   Saïs   199
Chapter 43   Qeb-ha   203
Chapter 44   Red Door   206
Chapter 45   Hermes Trismegistus   211
Chapter 46   Chosen One   216
Chapter 47   Isidora   222
Chapter 48   Antinous   227
Chapter 49   Invitation   232
Chapter 50   Night Visit   236
Chapter 51   The Seed   240
Chapter 52   Red Turban   245
Chapter 53   The Ship   251
Chapter 54   The Great Green   257
Chapter 55   Thrice-Greatest   262
Chapter 56   Phone Call   267
Chapter 57   Cleopatra's Barge   272
Chapter 58   Revenge   279
Chapter 59   Full Circle   284
Epilogue   289

Author's Comments & Glossary   291
Cast of Characters   299

Map of Ancient Egypt – 500 BC

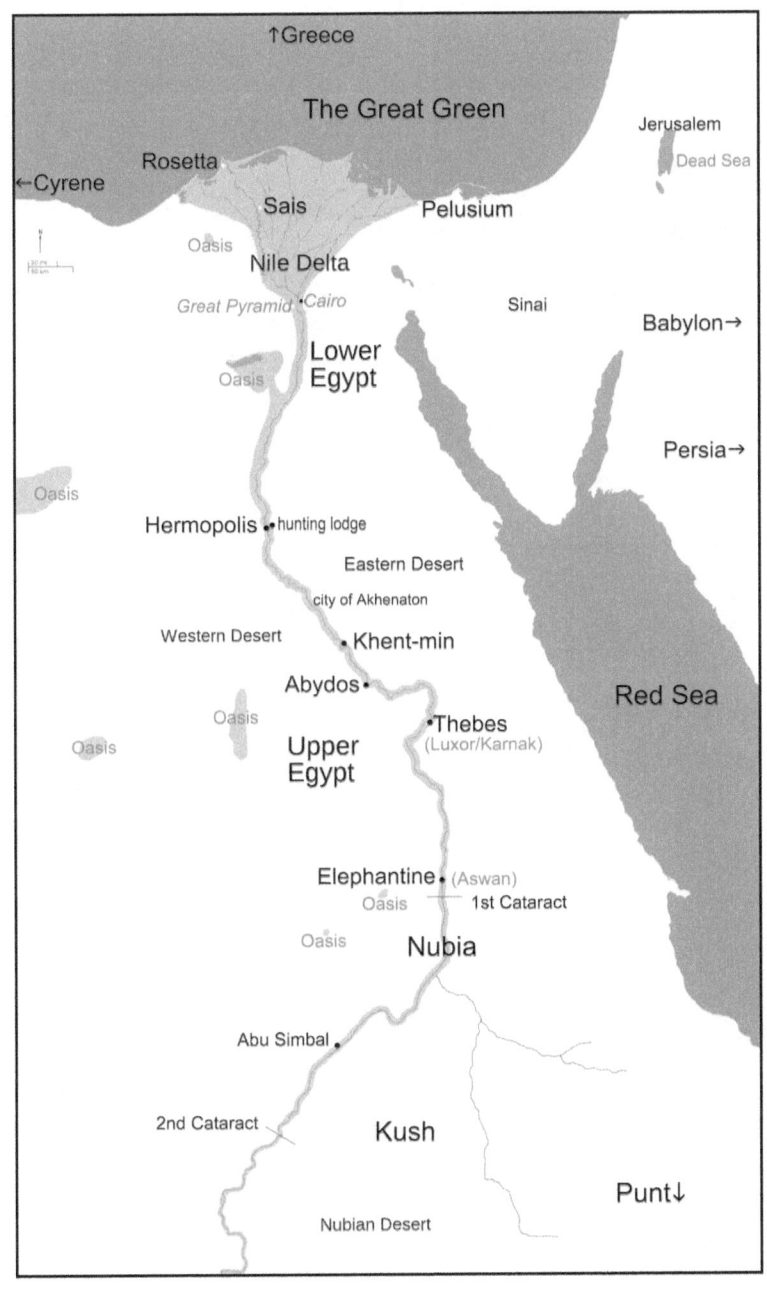

↑Greece

The Great Green

Jerusalem

Dead Sea

Rosetta

←Cyrene

Sais

Pelusium

Oasis

Nile Delta

Great Pyramid •Cairo

Sinai

Babylon→

Lower
Egypt

Oasis

Persia→

Oasis

Hermopolis •hunting lodge

Eastern Desert

city of Akhenaton

Western Desert • Khent-min

Abydos•

Oasis

Red Sea

•Thebes
(Luxor/Karnak)

Oasis

Upper
Egypt

Elephantine• (Aswan)

Oasis   1st Cataract

Oasis

Nubia

Abu Simbal •

2nd Cataract

Kush

Punt↓

Nubian Desert

PART ONE
THE RED MIRROR

CHAPTER 1 OBSESSION

Sheets tangled between my thighs, pillows tossed all around, I woke in a sweat in my wide, lonely bed. I had dreamed again of the Red Mirror. The vivid images were still playing in my mind when sunlight shattered the glass and the lush tapestry of my dream unraveled. Finally, all that remained was a crimson glow.

It was a rainy afternoon, an ordinary Tuesday, when the red aura first lured me into the shadows deep in the antique mall. There at the end of a long maze of neon signs, crystal goblets and sequined dinner jackets was a dark, dusty stall choked with jumbled figurines and castoff books.

The mirror whispered, and I paused. Warm phantom fingers caressed my shoulders and trailed across the base of my throat.

Almost breast high, slightly taller than wide, the old mirror leaned backward against a Chinese screen aflame with yellow chrysanthemums and orange-crested songbirds. Faint traces of blue and white flowers with glints of silver here and there peeked through layers of grime.

I stepped around fragile vases and toppled statues until I stood just in front of the red lacquered frame. The faint aura was subtle, but glowed brighter as I drew near.

I could see that once cleaned, the frame could be beautiful, but it wasn't the artistry that bewitched me.

"Come," the Red Mirror beckoned. "Taste of a life more sensuous than any dream."

A love affair with an object isn't unusual for me, but most of the time the attraction is like a one-night stand, the thrill forgotten as soon as out of sight. Now and then, I'm seized hard and buy right away. My condo is full of treasures that grabbed me and wouldn't let go.

I walked away that day, though. I was strong and refused to surrender to temptation. I'd promised myself no more impulse buys. I'd promised Barb to be good.

But the old mirror was special. It became an obsession. Haunting my dreams. Plaguing my days. Like a wild mating call in the jungle, it drew me back.

Of course, the mirror hadn't sold when I brought Barb for her approval. It waited patiently for me, knowing I would come.

The mirror pulsed slightly—in and out, in and out. My own pulse sped faster, and the mirror throbbed brighter, then dim, then bright again. The red aura glowed.

I looked expectantly at Barb.

"Well, what do you think?"

"Mexican," she declared, dismissing its value without a second glance.

"Do you see anything...unusual?"

"I see a dirty old mirror. Let's have lunch."

Barb and I settled at a window table covered in a cloth splashed with yellow daisies. A blue vase of white baby's breath and pink rosebuds stood in the center. Country prints in painted frames covered the lemon walls.

Sunshine poured in a narrow window, warming my back, shimmering on Barb's smooth, wheat-colored hair. Her latest cut was chin-length with long bangs past her eyebrows. She wasn't wearing her contacts today. Hot pink rectangles framed her sharp blue, never-miss-anything eyes.

"Let's order the high tea," I suggested hopefully.

"No sweets for me," Barb declined. "I've gained two pounds." To the server, she said politely, "The minestrone, please. No bread."

I sighed and surrendered to a salad, when I secretly craved a fresh scone with thick Devonshire cream and tart raspberry jam.

Our tea arrived in a white porcelain pot with a green cozy. Barb's cup flaunted red roses; violets sprinkled mine. Both sets were edged with gold. Holding her angular arms close to her sides, she expertly poured the tea without spilling a drop.

"How was your date?" she asked, although she already knew the answer. She'd be the first to hear good news.

"I don't think I'm going to see him again."

"Another one who's not perfect?"

"He was a bore. You know everyone in Vegas is trying to sell you something."

"I admit my love life's not all that great, but surely there are *some* good men around."

"He *is* around. I just haven't met him yet."

"Don't you think this 'Mr. Right' stuff is a little tired?"

"It's called a soul mate, Barb," I said a little defensively. This was non-negotiable territory that we'd covered many times.

"You could do anything, you know. You've got brains—if you'd just use them. But you're fixated on some white knight who'll make everything good. Did you ever consider that knights don't want party girls."

Party girl? *Thanks, Barb.* I stared at her, thinking, *And what's wrong with white knights?*

I bit my tongue, of course. She'd earned the right to talk to me like this; she listened to my complaints on a daily basis.

"Look, you hate your job," she plowed on. "And you should. You're capable of so much more. Yes, Ed is a jerk. Most bosses are. Stop feeling sorry for yourself. Do something about it."

I sighed. Barb was right about one thing. I did feel a little sorry for myself.

"I should go somewhere…have some adventure…meet some new men."

"Where would you go?"

"Some place exotic…far away…nothing like here."

I bought the mirror after Barb left. When the dealer came down with almost no haggling, I took it as a sign that the Universe had put the mirror in the antique stall especially for me.

The bulky rectangular frame was too big for the trunk of my little white convertible and too wide to fit through the doors. So I put the top down and drove the mirror home like a passenger in the back seat, the tall red frame standing behind me, secured by seat belts.

I pushed a couple of iffy yellow lights—okay, maybe one was red—in my hurry to get home. Somewhere along Eastern Avenue between Tropicana and Flamingo, the dirty old thing from the rejects of an estate sale was christened "The Red Mirror."

Heaving the mirror onto the top of a shopping cart, I rolled it through the parking garage, up the elevator to the third floor, into my condo, and finally leaned it against the white wall. Aisha, black fur gleaming, purred round my ankles.

"Say hello to the Red Mirror, Aisha."

I poured a glass of Merlot, slipped out of my leather pants, settled into my gray leather armchair with Aisha in my lap and faced the mirror. Three fat ivory candles on the round, glass coffee table spread a halo of buttery light. The rest of the room was in shadow. Aisha's deep, vibrating purrs were the only sound.

"Okay, Red. You can start to glow now. You can start to make *me* glow."

I waited. Nothing happened. No red aura. No phantom caress. No warmth. I felt nothing at all, except doubt. I hate doubt. I never know what to do with it.

Please don't let this be another fantasy.

I could hear Barb saying, *You bought that old mirror because it turned you on?*

Yes, Barb, the mirror first baited me, and then enticed me, but when the seduction was complete, it went cold. Having made me an addict, the mirror refused to give me a fix.

Robbed. I felt robbed.

I took another sip of Merlot and closed my eyes, emptying my mind of all thought, breathing slowly and rhythmically, almost in tune with Aisha's purrs. My eardrums sang. A swirling fluid mass of minute glowing flecks formed behind my eyelids. I let it grow. The longer I focused, the faster the flecks swirled. The spiral deepened. If I let myself slide through the center, I could end up in another universe.

When I opened my eyes, I saw a flash of silver in the frame. It wasn't particularly bright, but definitely there. Then came another tiny spark, and then another. Moving Aisha aside, I went over to stand in front of the mirror.

I counted sixteen dull metal struts around the four sides of the red-lacquered frame; a metal, star-like pattern anchored each corner.

The top right strut, black with years of grime, was cool to my fingertip. I rubbed, and the dirt came off easily, exposing untarnished silver. The metal gleamed in the candlelight. I rubbed more black residue away, and more silver shone.

Then the mirror breathed. Inhale. Exhale. My heart stopped. I stepped back. As I watched, the faint red aura grew brighter and brighter, until finally, the mirror pulsed exactly as in the antique stall. It glowed.

I felt the warmth. I felt the caress. I hadn't imagined the mystery. This was real. The magic was back.

Settling cross-legged on the white marble floor, I massaged the silver strut slowly and gently with my index finger wrapped in an olive oil-soaked cloth. Aisha vibrated against my bare thigh, and then she was gone.

The temperature in the room rose, first markedly warm before turning hot. Viscous air pressed heavily on my damp skin. I breathed in an overwhelming fragrance of smoky incense, both pungent and sweet. The slight buzz in my ears grew to a hum.

My living room with the red sofa and familiar oil paintings disappeared. Vague shapes moved in the shadows of a cavernous room. The flames of torches flickered on far walls.

Drifting outside of time in a velvet sea, I no longer felt the cool, hard marble under me. I felt nothing through my thin panties. Nothing at all.

The woman stared straight at me when I looked back to the mirror. Her green eyes were remarkably like mine, except hers were bolder—so bold—and heavily outlined in black. I had the impression her bold eyes could see right to my soul.

Panic rose first in my chest and then settled in my throat; I could scarcely swallow. The buzzing in my ears vibrated like a thousand bees swarming in my head.

Forcing myself to breathe slowly, I leaned closer and whispered, "Who are you?"

I barely recognized my own voice. I might have been talking from the bottom of the sea. My distorted words, spoken so softly, ballooned to fill the room.

There was no response from the green-eyed woman in the mirror. I tried again.

"Can you see me?"

Apparently, sound couldn't cross the glass, because she gave no sign of having heard. Her hand came up and adjusted a stray lock of unnaturally thick, jet black hair.

She was exotic, foreign-looking, yet her face was familiar, like someone I knew from a dream. She lifted her chin and angled her head slightly, looking straight into my eyes.

It was in the way she tilted her face, and the satisfaction in her look, that gave it away. She wasn't studying me but admiring her own reflection.

I saw her, but she didn't see me—a strategic advantage. My fears melted away. Something magical, an *adventure*, presented itself. Having come this far without harm, I dared to imagine possibilities. The Universe opened a door. It was my choice to step through.

CHAPTER 2   RIVER GOD

A chorus of a thousand songbirds shattered the silence, and I opened my eyes to a new world. I don't know how it happened. I can't explain the mechanics. My first sight was a flock of sparrows darting in and out of nests tucked into the tops of ornate Egyptian columns. Yellow finches and iridescent blue warblers swooped from lacy trees to the ground and up again. I'd never seen so many birds. I couldn't begin to know all their names. Their constant song chimed in my ears and echoed through the stone buildings close by.

After sound and sight came feeling and smell. I was incarnate again but had no memory of the transition through the mirror to this garden.

Green grass, soft and moist, cushioned me. The air was heady with the perfume of flowers mingled with the earthy fragrance of loam. A bare whisper of a breeze kissed my skin. I was at one with the warmth, dissolving into balmy air.

A long grassy lawn bordered by pink oleander bushes ended at the bank of a wide river; green-brown water flowed past. Beyond the river, in the distance, steep dun-colored cliffs rose under a cloudless blue sky. Lush green fields lined the far shore.

I stretched out my legs and wiggled my toes. The nails were stained rust red; tiny geometric designs trailed across the tops of narrow feet. A crisscross pattern encircled my ankles. At first I thought the designs were tattoos but then recognized *henna* from photos of Berbers in an old issue of National Geographic.

By the look of my well-toned muscles and firm thighs, this body walked a lot. I felt very fit. I liked the new me.

A ring with twin golden horns holding a grape-sized lapis lazuli stone gleamed from the middle finger of my right hand. Two gold bands, heavy and flat, coiled around my upper arms, molding to my flesh. A gold collar necklace at the base of my throat fastened with a short length of chain falling down my back, under my hair.

Only it wasn't my hair, but a wig. My head prickled under the heavy mass that fell to my shoulders. I pulled it off. Warm air rushed around my ears. I scratched my shaved scalp, but not hard, still a little timid to touch this new body.

I suppose I should have been terrified, but I didn't feel anxious at all. In fact, I was more relaxed than I could ever remember. The tepid air, filled with birdsong and the gentle rustling of palm leaves in the warm breeze, lulled me—even the flow of the river had a narcotic effect.

The shape of my breasts, high and firm with dark roses around the nipples, was clearly visible through the sheer cloth of wide linen straps. I didn't wear a bra.

My arms and shoulders were bare. A band of linen encircled my rib cage. From there, the ankle-length white linen dress fell in tiny pleats, clinging to the rise of my belly and the slope of my thighs, hugging the curve of my impossibly slim hips.

My pubic hair was gone; my shaved mound rose under the filmy fabric. No underwear at all. Did everyone walk around like this?

"Isis!"

I had a name, the name of a goddess. I also had a man. At least, I saw one coming right at me. And what a man he was—a River God of bronzed flesh and white linen.

A snowy stiff kilt wrapped tightly around his narrow waist and ended above his knees. I caught a glimpse of the taut, elongated thighs of a runner.

Broad, straight shoulders tapered in a triangle to muscular, lean hips. He wore nothing above the waist except a wide, beaded collar. In the sun, his chest glowed like burnished stone. I wondered if he also was without underwear.

He held out his hand to help me up, and I rose to my feet. His exotic scent went straight to my head. One step forward and we would be touching, his bare chest, hard and smooth, on my gauze-covered breasts. I stopped myself just before I reached out to run my fingers down his flat belly and under the kilt.

I was never this bold on the other side of the mirror. I wanted to touch him, to fondle him, to make him quake with desire.

His angular features, framed by a blue and white striped headdress, might have been too sharp on another man, but not River God. There was nothing about him that didn't sear me. I felt his heat right down to my bones.

Thick, black *kohl* lines around his dark eyes stretched to the temples. His mouth, exquisitely carved in softer stone by a master sculptor, was at the same time sensuous and hard. I willed the perfection of those lips to explore every inch of my body, yet he made no move. Could he not feel the waves of my desire crashing on his shore?

My fingertips, light as the wings of a butterfly, stroked across his chest and along his shoulder. I barely touched him, but I know he felt the spark. I saw it in his eyes. I saw it in the subtle upturn of his lips.

I was too mesmerized to appreciate what that combination of cool half-smile and smoldering eyes might mean. The omens of my heartbreak were there from the beginning, but I chose not to see.

Slowly trailing my fingers down his biceps and along his forearms to the wide gold bracelets at his wrists, I watched the tiny hairs rise. Gooseflesh rose on my own skin, like a chill across my shoulders in spite of the heat.

He took my hand from his wrist and raised it slowly to his lips, wetting my fingertips with his tongue.

"Not here, Isis," he whispered, his breath hot and moist in my ear. "Not now."

He stroked once across the hollow of my throat. His touch was utterly real; I couldn't be dreaming.

With his lips at the curve of my neck on the magic spot that opens all doors, he breathed, "I shall come to you later and taste of your nectar. You shall fly to the stars with my tongue on your lotus."

He stepped back then, his body morphing into a kind of military posture with arms a bit rigid at his sides. Even his voice took on a commanding tone.

"Where is your slave? You are expected at the Temple."

Temple?

I scurried around in my mind, frantic and desperate for direction.

What temple? What would I do when I got there?

Inhale. Exhale. I concentrated on keeping the panic from my eyes. My first test was River God. If he sensed anything was amiss, he didn't show it.

"Do not forget your wig." He picked up the mass of thick black waves, placed it on my shaved head and then ran his thumb around the curve of my lips.

There was plenty of promise in his eyes and half-smile, but no hint of suspicion. He didn't see me at all; he saw only Isis. And he very much liked what he saw.

We walked side by side, close but not touching, along a narrow stone path just wide enough for two. It ran perfectly straight through flowering gardens shaded by tall date palms, stately sycamores, and groves of pomegranate and fig. A square field of red poppies swayed in the light wind.

He was silent and didn't look for conversation, and for that I was grateful. Whatever language he spoke, I understood every word, but what would happen when I tried to speak? I glanced sideways up at him. He held himself exceedingly erect; his eyes focused ahead in a face expressionless as a granite carving. But I could still feel his heat.

We passed under trellises laden with grapevines. Fountains gurgled like natural springs into vast rectangular pools covered with deep green lotus pads; tall white blooms trembled on slender stalks. Everywhere there were birds, hundreds of them, of all colors and sizes, each with its own song.

The narrow path joined a wide avenue with stone sphinxes marching down each side. A sea of foot traffic flowed in both directions, but no one hurried. In the distance, metal clanged against stone, repetitive, rhythmic and without pause—the sounds of construction.

River God stopped at a tall, carved obelisk tipped with gold where a giant with oiled ebony skin stood statue-still.

His biceps were like ripe melons; thick thighs bulged. Striated scars from some age-old tribal ceremony covered his cheeks. His onyx eyes were careful not to look directly at me when we joined him.

River God leaned slightly into me, but not enough to show intimacy, saying quietly, "Look for me in the heat of the afternoon, Isis. I shall come when the others are sleeping."

Look for him *where* in the afternoon? What others? I wanted to grab his arm and beg him not to leave me. I felt the panic again, this time closing my throat. The taste in my mouth was as bitter as espresso.

Heat rose off the hewn stone roadway in shimmering waves. The soft, cool morning breeze coming off the river had died. Overhead, the sun was white-hot.

River God didn't touch me again before joining the current of brown bodies and white linen blazing in the sun. My eyes followed until his blue and white headdress disappeared in the crowd, and I was left with Goliath, my Nubian slave.

Almost every eye followed me as we headed down the avenue. Many inclined their heads in a gesture of reverence when I passed. A group of bald men in long white kilts stopped and bowed from the waist. Although no one spoke directly to me or called out a greeting, every gesture told me that they saw someone they knew and not a stranger.

The diaphanous pleats of my gown flowed pleasantly along my thighs as I glided smoothly and gracefully on the slightly uneven paving stones. Light on my feet, comfortable with my erect posture and at ease with my body, I decided I might be a dancer.

I took long strides in fine-tooled leather sandals, pointed at the tips. I couldn't remember putting them on. Panic gripped my throat again; I touched my head and felt the wig. Relief. Thank you, River God. The only bare heads I saw belonged to men.

We didn't go far on the wide, paved boulevard before turning into a rose granite temple with carved painted pillars. Goliath stopped under a lintel decorated with outstretched orange and green vulture wings, and I crossed alone from day into dusk.

CHAPTER 3 THE TEMPLE

Soft hazy sunbeams streamed down through square openings at the high roofline, piercing the deep shadow. Clouds of incense drifted among jewel-colored columns with a cow-eared goddess carved at the tops. The only sound was the mystic murmur of chanting.

Coalescing from nowhere, a fragile young girl with skin as flawless as fine ivory glided without a whisper to stand before me. Never looking into my eyes, she draped a garland of olive leaves mixed with cornflowers and lotus petals around my neck. My eyes stung; the floral scent softened the tang of burning aromatic woods. The air was hot and still.

Shimmering hieroglyphs in colors bright as neon exploded from every surface. Giants with mystical crowns or the heads of animals performed strange rituals in soaring murals painted in vibrant red, yellow and blue.

I resisted leaning my head back to take in the vast ceiling with its elaborate geometric designs, absorbing as much as possible without being obvious. But I couldn't stop my eyes from traveling everywhere at once.

The young girl led me to a windowless chamber fogged with frankincense and lit by hundreds of alabaster lamps.

Women as graceful as sea nymphs moved about in long gowns, the glide of their sandals silent on the stone. Sheer, glowing white linen caressed their lean thighs and clung to the slim curve of their hips. No one else wore a flower garland.

A hush stilled the room. One after another, the women went silently to their knees to place their foreheads on the stone floor with arms stretched out toward me. Then they rose all together in one liquid movement to their feet. Aware of every cell in my body, I vibrated from deep within.

I don't remember crossing the room but found myself standing on a low dais. One after another, the priestesses approached me, each with offerings of blue lotus and woven baskets filled with figs, dates and pomegranates. When my arms could hold no more, two Ancient Ones wearing elaborate headdresses with golden horns murmured an incantation and took everything from me.

The first Ancient One was so thin and wrinkled, she might have been a mummy. The second had cheeks scarred from the pox. They both studied me for a long moment with all-knowing eyes, but I sensed they saw only Isis. The pockmarked old crone waved a tiny incense burner close to my face; I inhaled a sweet perfume that made my pulse race even faster. Heat rushed through me; my nipples hardened.

I stood very still and never spoke. I didn't feel any danger; every touch on my body was reverent.

Warm fingers loosened the ties of my gown, and within seconds, I stood naked, the folds of gossamer linen caressing my ankles.

The two Ancient Ones painted hieroglyphs on my arms and thighs with a kind of black ink. With each design, they chanted a new incantation.

My heart drummed so hard I thought they surely could see it pound in my chest. Tiny beads of perspiration rose on my flushed skin for a brief moment before evaporating into the arid air. My mouth was cotton-dry, but not my secret valley. My nipples rose to aching peaks.

The two women paid no attention to the changes in my body but continued to draw mystic symbols, all the time murmuring spells under their breath.

Drawings finished, the Ancient Ones exchanged my own necklace and garland for a heavy, beaded collar ending in a counterpoise down my back.

As if one body, the roomful of priestesses flowed around me, slowly and sensuously circling, their white robes shimmering in the lamplight. They sang praises, chanting the word *menit* over and over. I knew, without knowing how, that they sang to the collar, summoning its power. Thousands of tiny glass and gem beads burned into my flesh. I was a furnace of raging heat.

When the chanting stopped, the chamber was silent as a tomb.

The first sound of the finger cymbals was a distant tinkle of tiny bells. The jingling grew louder and louder but never brassy. Golden rain tickled my ears and washed away my fear.

Through a fog of incense, a woman with the yellow-green eyes of a cat drifted toward me. In her outstretched hands, she carried a tall headdress with twin ostrich feathers and two shiny ox horns holding a gold disk. With each swaying step, the white feathers fluttered, the gold sparkled.

The room of priestesses began chanting again as four hands balanced the solar disk headdress on my wig. I imagined myself as a figure in one of the vividly painted murals, but how would I walk?

Anet-hra-k Hathor! (Hail to Thee, Hathor!)
Auksh satet-v en Amenta (O daughter of Heaven)
un uat er Isenkhebe Nefrusobek (open a way to Isenkhebe Nefrusobek)
Anet-hra-k Hathor! (Hail to Thee, Hathor!)

I knew they were singing about me, though they chanted "Isenkhebe Nefrusobek" and not Isis.

Finally, the Ancient Ones anointed my shoulders, breasts and belly with musk and led me by both hands to massive, gilt double doors.

The doors opened, and I walked through alone.

Watching me from the shadows were two men. I could just make out the whites of their eyes. I felt their heat and smelled their scented sweat. In the low lamplight, my own body, oiled and naked, gleamed.

There was a new, heavy fragrance here with a narcotic smoke that blurred my vision and made air rush in my ears. My head pounded. I felt dizzy, and for a brief moment, I was afraid I would faint.

The sanctum shimmered in gold around a white alabaster statue of a seated Goddess wearing a solar disk headdress identical to mine. Her right hand resting on her thigh held a large, glittering ankh.

Without any conscious direction on my part, my hand moved to a musical instrument in a wooden case atop a black marble pedestal. A graceful silver loop held three delicate rods, each one mounted with dozens of small metal disks. The gleaming silver handle formed into twin heads of Hathor, the cow-eared goddess sitting on the altar throne.

High, chiming notes teased as I lifted the sacred *sistrum* from its ebony box inlaid with ivory. The men stirred when the seductive music broke the silence. The chamber was electric and so still, I could hear them inhale and exhale, together as one person.

Every action was as natural to me as breathing. I held the necklace out from my throat toward Hathor, shaking the *sistrum* in a slow, even rhythm that grew more and more feverish. When I opened my lips to sing, the words flowed from me without effort.

"O Hathor, O Divine Cow and giver of milk,
O Goddess of Fertility,
O Goddess of Wine, Music and Dance,
O Goddess of Love.
We adore you.
We ask your blessings for this Son of the Pharaoh,
this First Prince of Egypt."

The alabaster lamps cast a steady light that barely flickered. My voice, strong and husky, vibrated in my throat. The crown of my head pulsed. I no longer felt the weight of the headdress—or the ground under my feet. I felt light as air, floating again in a velvet sea.

"This Royal Prince, beloved of Horus,
comes to dance.
He comes to sing;
His bag is full of great offerings,
His sistrum is of gold,
His necklace of malachite.
His feet hurry to the Mistress of Music,
He dances for her;
She loves his doing."

The two men moved right next to me, one on each side. The tall one took the *sistrum* from my hand and returned it carefully to its wooden case. The slighter one, the royal insignia hanging from a thick gold chain around his thin neck, removed my headdress and set it on the altar at the Goddess Hathor's feet.

My heart pounded in my chest; the heavy scent of musk filled my shallow breath. Half of me was in a trance, the other half terrified.

I stood stock still while they each stroked my body, four hands caressing my breasts, my buttocks, my thighs.

They led me together to a divan and laid me down on soft fur. They started at my feet and sucked one toe, then the next, in perfect unison. Their thick, wet tongues moved to my slim ankles and then up my calves and along the inside of my loins. Licking and sucking, they lingered like preening cats, tormenting me.

They nibbled at the tender skin, edging closer to my dark and yearning valley of desire, taking their time, teasing me, enjoying the straining of my hips and my low cries when they came near, then moved away. I was overcome with need; my womanhood begged for their mouths.

But before their lips and tongues found my sacred lotus, they rolled back on their heels and chanted in unison.

"O beauteous one, O great one,
O great magician, O splendid lady.
The Pharaoh reveres you;
give that his Son may live!
Behold him, Hathor, flaming one,
His manhood is straight,
The Son of Pharaoh reveres you,
O Gold of Gods,
Give of your milk that he live!"

With that they came to me again, each suckling my breasts, hands kneading like babes at their mother's teats. I lay on the divan, electric shocks rolling through me, moans reverberating in my throat and chest.

The Royal One mounted me while the other licked my open lips with his broad tongue. He did not kiss me, though.

Rocking slowly, thin chest rising each time his hips moved forward, the son of the Pharaoh thrust again and again, never looking at my face, but only at his companion.

The pendant insignia on the heavy chain swung toward me and back, toward me and back. *Would he spill his royal seed in me?*

As if on cue, he rose up and lay his manhood on my stomach as a flood of white milk spewed. The taller one quickly bent and lapped it up with his tongue. Then they leaned forward and kissed each other, the Royal One taking back the semen with an open mouth.

"They have come from the Prince of Egypt," they chanted together.
"His gifts to Her, cleansed by Her, accepted by Her for the glory of All."

The two knelt before the statue of Hathor, and the tall one placed a carved gilt chest on the altar. It was over. I realized that they had never removed their kilts.

Not looking back, they opened the heavy golden doors and disappeared into the antechamber.

I lay stunned on the low sofa, aching and throbbing. *What kind of a priestess was I, anyway?*

The doors opened again, and the Ancient Ones entered, wearing braided, shoulder-length wigs with twinkling gold chains. Not saying a word, moving silently across the basalt floor, they came straight for me.

With the tender hands of a mother on a child, they cleaned me everywhere with lotus-scented water. They washed away the symbols and all trace of fluids. I relaxed into the deep fur of the divan and let them cool my fire.

"The Goddess is pleased," the old woman with scarred cheeks assured me. "The Pharaoh shall be pleased. The spell of Set the Destroyer on the First Son of Egypt, the son-of-Horus, has been broken. The Golden One has given the Crown Prince back his manhood."

"Not very likely," I muttered under my breath, deciding it best to keep my doubts to myself.

🔖

When the two men exited the night of the inner sanctum and came out into the bright of the day, one was elated, the other somber and pensive.

"What is it, Setne? Why this glum face? Have we not accomplished our task? I shall be Pharaoh! Where is your joy?"

"Perhaps it was not wise for me to participate, my Liege. There was something odd about the priestess."

"Nonsense. She seemed like any woman, stupid and insipid. She had lovely teats, though. I did enjoy that."

"I cannot say what it is, Sire. It is only a feeling. A feeling that she is different."

"You see enemies behind every column, Setne. Surely you do not fear some whore priestess? She is nothing. Did you not say that her life is the Temple and nothing more?"

"It is not a real fear, my Prince, but an unease."

"I have only one unease. That we have travelled all this way to sanctimonious Thebes for naught. You promised me this absurd ritual would put an end to the old man's incessant nagging. That it would silence my dog brothers. And now you suggest there is risk that they shall not be satisfied?"

"No, Sire! Of course not. You may trust, as always, in my counsel."

"Then we have nothing to regret. Hide that grave face from me and do not spoil my day. I was so looking forward to a celebration."

He snapped the back of his fingers into his left palm, and a slave ran over with a chalice of wine.

"Tell me that you have a plan to amuse me, Setne. Do not keep me waiting in this wretched heat. Where is my reward?"

"I do have a celebratory gift, my Prince. Twins. Just the age you like. I believe the boys shall not disappoint."

"Good! Let us have a look at them. And tomorrow I wish to leave this holier-than-thou city and go where they understand pleasure."

Eager to see his new playthings, Psamtik, Crown Prince of the Two Lands, stepped quickly and lightly along the stone path leading to the Royal Barge. Setne the Scribe followed six ceremonial paces behind. In his mind, he replayed the scene in the inner sanctum. What *was* there about that woman?

Before and after them marched the Royal Guard in blue and white striped headdresses and blazing white kilts, the polished bronze tips of their spears flashing in the sun.

CHAPTER 4 SUMMONS

Oil of jasmine from a metal urn set with turquoise ankhs and eyes of Horus spilled into my bath. The tepid water lulled me; I floated on a perfumed cloud. Hammers clanged on stone in the distance, and palm fronds rustled in a high breeze. Birds sang—always the birds. The air chimed with their constant song.

"Isenkhebe Nefrusobek."

Spoken in a quiet voice scarcely more than a murmur, the sound of my formal name brought me back.

I opened my eyes to a young girl kneeling with her forehead to the tiles, palms down, delicate arms stretched out along the bright-colored mosaic of wild geese flying above marsh grass. Tiny silver bands secured scores of plaits in her glossy black wig. She held herself so perfectly still, I wondered if she breathed.

"What is it, Maia?" My voice played low and luxurious to my ears, a new tone, a new languid me.

"She who is blessed-of-blessed, the Highest-of-High, the one whose name I am not worthy to utter, the High-Priestess, commands your presence in the Temple."

"Did she say why?" After this morning, I wasn't sure if I wanted to go back there. Besides, I was waiting for River God.

By Maia's sharp breath, I understood that the wishes of the Highest-of-High were not to be questioned.

A flock of twittering young girls swooped down and drew me from the bath. They first dried me from bare scalp to hennaed toe with towels of linen and then massaged my skin with fragrant oils. They doused me all over with a heavy gardenia perfume, concentrating on my armpits, the base of my throat and my sacred mound. I had been shaved everywhere. My flesh was smooth as polished alabaster.

Out of a carved and painted chest came a wide, beaded necklace of turquoise, carnelian and garnet strands mingled with golden ankhs and hippopotamus charms. Large matching earrings were looped through my earlobes. The girls quickly wrapped the heavy gold bands back on my upper arms and slipped the massive lapis lazuli ring on the middle finger of my right hand.

The fine weave of my sheer linen gown lay like a spider web on my oiled skin.

Turquoise and gold beaded sandals were placed on my feet, and I was ready. The faces of my household beamed with satisfaction and pride.

A bird-like old woman called Kiya solemnly led the way down a straight path through red oleander bushes. The fragile gold bells in my shoulder-length wig of black braids chimed in my ears with each step.

We went directly to a green gate in the white wall of the compound where Goliath waited, his ebony skin glistening. He really was a magnificent creature. My eyes traveled from the white triangle of his headdress to the white triangle of his kilt, lingering on his broad shoulders, massive chest and muscled abdomen. I caught myself daydreaming of secret places I would taste if we were alone.

We didn't go to the same temple as this morning. Goliath and I were mere specks before this massive pylon plastered in vivid murals of Pharaohs and Gods. The walls slanted slightly inward toward a high colorful cornice where great red and yellow flags on wooden poles snapped in the hot wind.

Passing through a gate built for giants, we entered another forest of slender limestone columns with capitals of carved, cow-eared Hathor heads. Narrow shafts of sunlight, filled with golden flecks of dust, slanted from the stone roof through shadow to the travertine floor.

Goliath stayed at the entry when I crossed under yet another granite lintel painted with outstretched wings into a hive swarming with priests, their heads shaven and chests bare, ankle-length white cloths wrapped around their hips.

I had no sooner entered than an old, pudgy priest stepped into my path and bowed at the waist.

"Welcome, Isenkhebe Nefrusobek," he greeted me with my formal name in a voice with an unnatural high pitch.

A soft leopard skin draped his fleshy shoulder. The magnificent amethyst dangling from his earlobe cast purple sparks in the filtered light. There was something odd about him that I couldn't quite place; I sensed no sexual energy at all.

"The Highest-of-Highest, Golden-of-the-Golden One, Supreme High-Priestess of the Two Lands awaits you in her private audience hall."

I bent my head so that he could place a wreath of blue lotus petals around my neck and sprinkle jasmine-scented water from a green faience bottle on the crown of my wig.

His next words were those of caution. "If you come to say something to your Mistress, count in your mind until ten."

He meant to be solemn, but his irritating, squeaky voice made it difficult to take his warning seriously. I tried to keep my face a mask and hoped my eyes hid the ridicule behind them. Instead of my normal pity or sympathy—much less compassion—I felt the most irrational revulsion for the man. Isis had no patience with this priest and no tolerance for eunuchs.

Soft echoes of chanting resonated along a gleaming stone corridor lit by flaming torches in deep alcoves. We finally reached tall double cedar doors mounted with golden lion head doorknobs. The old priest put his hands on the lion heads and leaned with all his weight.

Suddenly, the doors swung wide open into the blaze of a thousand brass lamps. A wild chorus of shrill male voices stopped in mid-note. The chamber was so still, I could hear the lanterns consume oil.

The eunuch priest stepped to the side and inclined his head toward me, his massive amethyst earring swinging back and forth, splintering the rays of light.

"*Enter,*" his silence commanded me. "*Sit-hathor awaits you.*"

He had not spoken out loud, yet I understood each word. The shock of it rocked me. If he could speak directly to my mind, could he also read my thoughts?

If he perceived my secret, he gave no sign. He closed the doors behind him when he exited, leaving me alone in a room full of staring eyes.

CHAPTER 5 SIT-HATHOR

Isenkhebe Nefrusobek, my child, come nearer that we may look upon you and feast on your beauty."

The voice of liquid gold belonged to a striking woman in her forties seated on a dais covered with a carpet of richly-dyed wool. The four legs of her chair were carved limbs of a lion ending in massive claws at the feet; the chair's arms were capped by lion heads. She might have had an iron spine, she sat so straight against the low back. Her forearms rested on her thighs, like the statue of Hathor in the inner sanctum this morning, but she didn't hold an ankh. I could see nothing in her hands.

"Come closer," she repeated, holding out her right hand to me.

I sank to my knees, brushing my lips to the ring on her middle finger, a giant lapis lazuli set in gold horns, identical to mine.

"It has been too long, my daughter. Our duties are many; the hours are few. We have reports of your superior talents. You have trained well. You bring us great pride."

She placed her hand on my bowed head. The affection flowed from her heart through her palm into my tingling crown. This woman loved me. The power of that love moved like a nourishing current from my head down my spine to the tips of my toes.

With each moment, the obscure layers of my consciousness revealed more and more, like the thousand veils of a dance falling away. My nerve endings buzzed.

Her long, slender fingers slid beneath my chin and lifted my face upward; her dark eyes bored into mine, compelling me to stare straight into hers.

"I have a mission for you, Isis," she whispered. "The time is full, the need is great, and you are ready."

My head jerked back slightly. She held firmly to my chin, while her eyes lined in *kohl* probed deeper.

"You are ready, my daughter. Do not doubt. Fate and Fortune come and go when the Goddess commands them. The Goddess commands you now. Do not neglect to serve Her."

What more might a goddess command than the ritual with the two men? My mouth opened, and words came out without my thinking.

"Dearest blessed Mother, giver of my life, it is said that the work of the Goddess Hathor is what acts upon women. I pray that the task you require is in alignment with the path She has set for me."

Sit-hathor's face hardened in an instant. Harsh lines creased her lush lips. She dropped her hand, sat even more straight in her chair and stared down at me. Her eyes glinted like obsidian; I saw both fire and ice. The silence in the room deepened.

"Fruit of my womb that was forbidden to bear fruit," she said with no trace of affection in her cold tone, "heed well that pride and arrogance are the ruin of its owner. Would you doubt that I, Sit-hathor, Supreme High-Priestess, know the true will of the Queen of Gods? She has spoken to me as I now speak to you."

My loving mother or not, Sit-hathor was not a woman accustomed to her will being questioned.

The murmuring in the chamber that had started as a buzz now roared in my ears. This was not going well. Remembering the advice of the old priest, I counted slowly to ten. When I next spoke, I was careful that my words would please.

"The fault in every kind of character comes from not listening, my Mistress and Blessed Mother. My ears are fully open to receive your words. My heart is fully open to fulfill your wishes. I shall trust in the words of the Great Goddess as spoken through you. There is no protector save the work of the Gods."

Satisfied with my response, Sit-hathor relaxed her shoulders, nodding her head, breathing out a long exhale that came from deep within. With her breath flowed a seductive aura that swirled around her, spreading outward, drawing everyone in the chamber to her as a queen does the hive.

I again saw fondness in her dark eyes. She smiled ever so slightly, but not enough to show her teeth. The tension in the room eased in a great collective sigh.

"You are indeed of my womb," she said warmly while pressing a gold charm into my hand.

Smaller glyphs spelling 'one-who-has-entered-the-heart' made up a larger hieroglyph for 'heart.' This talisman was exchanged only between the closest of friends—or lovers.

Her fingers under my chin again, she drew my face up to hers. Her flashing dark eyes warned me not to speak.

"The man you meet shall know you by this amulet." She whispered so quietly, I strained to hear. "He shall know you to be his daughter."

Daughter! A profound jolt shook my core. Isis had no father. The Highest-of-Highest of Hathor's cult is forbidden to bear children with a mortal, even a Pharaoh. All my life I'd believed I was sired by a God. Everyone believed it.

"Yes, your father," she confessed directly in my ear. "You are, at last, to meet your destiny."

She settled back in her chair again and smiled at me benignly, aware no doubt of my shock and perhaps a little amused. She had kept this secret for many years.

"Prepare for a river voyage, my daughter. Put your trust in the priest Qeb-ha."

Qeb-ha! No! Not that half-man with the power to read my thoughts!

In the same raging moment, I was both a woman stunned at the news of a father who wasn't a God—and me, terrified of a voyage with a eunuch who could speak without words and whose probing eyes might see me hiding inside. What would he do if he sensed me there? What would anyone do?

My head spun. I panicked at the thought of being trapped on a boat with that wretched creature. I couldn't empty my mind of the image of his pathetic member hanging alone, his scrotum ripped away in some terrible ritual.

"Be wise, my daughter," Sit-hathor was crooning. "You shall learn with each day the task before you. Put aside your foolishness. Allow the whisperings of the Goddess to enter your heart. Even a fool acts wisely if he follows his heart."

I couldn't help but wonder why she would send me anywhere, if I were so foolish, but had the sense this time to keep my thoughts to myself.

"Fate and Fortune," I intoned, "come from the Gods."

Sit-hathor's blessing with her fingers on my crown signalled the audience was over. But she had final parting words before I stepped away.

"You are the flesh of my body. You are a piece of my *Ka*. Remember, my daughter, there is nothing left but the doing."

The massive doors opened for me, and I backed out past lion heads flashing in the light. As soon as I exited, the doors clanged shut, leaving me alone in the dim, silent corridor.

I had forgotten that it was day when I re-entered the courtyard with columns topped by carved heads of Hathor. The sun was an unrelenting white disk in the washed-out sky. I blinked and shielded my eyes against the harsh light.

He startled me, the fat old eunuch Qeb-ha, coming from nowhere to stand in my path again. He had been waiting for me in the shadow of a wall covered in elaborate hieroglyphs telling yet more tales of Pharaohs and Gods. I tried to hurry past him, to get away from Sit-hathor, to get back to my villa where River God had promised to come.

"Do not resist. You are chosen. It is the will of the Goddess."

Qeb-ha spoke again without speaking. Despite the oppressive heat, a chill came over my body. All the air in the open courtyard had been sucked away; I struggled to breathe.

"I do not understand what I am supposed to do! No one has told me anything!" As hard as I tried to calm my growing panic, my voice grew more anxious and strident with each word.

How would I ever get home without the Mirror? I couldn't bear the thought of being stuck here, that there might be no going back.

I had the sense of being rushed to some unknown and inevitable conclusion, with no hope to slow down events or alter their course.

The priest didn't actually touch me, yet it was as if his hand grazed my arm. A bewildering energy, somewhere between calming and controlling, flowed through my frazzled nerves. Blood throbbed in my temples; I felt myself sway slightly under the weight of the sun.

"The barge sails at first light, Isenkhebe."

Thank Hathor, he talked out loud in that voice as irritating as the screech of a marsh bird. He was a vile, genderless little creature, pathetic and frightening at the same time.

"Do not belittle an old man in your heart. Remember the wealth of a Temple is its priest." He'd read my thoughts.

I tried to blank my spinning mind, not to think anything, but it was impossible. A thousand emotions raged. I struggled to distinguish my feelings from those of Isis, but I was losing myself in her.

Qeb-ha's expression, calm and all-knowing like a Buddha, was one of patience, as if dealing with a child. I searched his eyes, but they were as fathomless as a deep well in the desert. I sensed that although he read my turmoil, he saw only Isis—at least for now—and not the real me. If there still was a real me.

"Do not be discouraged, Isenkhebe," he squeaked. "The voyage is long. We shall come to know each other's worth."

Long? How long? Was I expected to obey blindly? Did Egyptians actually follow such demands without question?

Goliath stood at attention, skin gleaming, where I had left him under the lintel adorned with outstretched, green and orange vulture wings. I wasn't certain how much time had passed. The sun had moved several degrees toward the Western cliffs. Surely River God waited for me with his promise of the stars.

River God. My anchor in this storm. I longed to feel my way down his smooth chest and across his flat belly to settle on his undamaged manhood. After the sordid ritual with the Crown Prince and his slimy Scribe, and then the unnerving encounter with a freak eunuch, I wanted a real man.

I found myself consumed with an overwhelming need to caress an unquestionably male body, to feed off its power.

Goliath stirred. Sunlight glistened on his massive forearms. I imagined I saw his mound rising under his white kilt.

If I returned to my villa to find River God had come and gone, I would command the Nubian to give me his strength. Yes, Goliath would do just fine.

CHAPTER 6 PREPARATION

Chaos greeted me at my graceful villa set in a verdant garden behind white walls. High-pitched voices, all talking at once, bounced off polished stone. Gesturing wildly with both hands, Kiya, so solemn this afternoon as she led me down the oleander path, waved lists written on papyrus and shouted at everyone. Her legs were thin as a sparrow's. Her eyes bulged. An electric field surrounded her; sparks flew in the air in all directions. Egyptians were not always so calm, after all.

"The kitchen has prepared jugs of wine, beer, olive oil and salted meats. The gardeners are packing baskets of dates and figs. Now you must remember, Isenkhebe, to keep the butter and cheese cool in the Nile—"

I shut out her voice. There seemed no chance now for a stolen afternoon with River God. Even Goliath was out of the question, certainly not here, not now in these frenzied chambers.

Maia, sorting wigs and gowns in my bedchamber, immediately prostrated herself when I entered.

"Rise up," I said impatiently. "Did he come?"

She blushed and lowered her eyes.

With her head slightly bowed, avoiding to look at me, she answered, "Yes, Isenkhebe Nefrusobek. He came after the second meal."

Mica sparkled on her lids. Thick lines of *kohl* extended toward her temples. Her black wig had tiny braids twisted with white and blue linen cords. She kept her face averted to hide her disapproval, but I knew.

"Well?" I demanded. "Did he leave a message?"

"He did not speak to me, Mistress. He entered through the hidden door but left when he saw the preparations for our sacred journey."

At least River God knew I was leaving; my guess was he'd be back. The thought made me lighter, more hopeful. I even felt hungry. I didn't remember the last time I'd eaten.

"Send for sweet wine, black dates and barley bread. And see if there is any roasted duck or pigeon left from the meal. I am starving."

I settled on a mound of pillows, deciding that, all things considered, I could get used to this life. Maia handed me a black purring cat.

"Does Isenkhebe Nefrusobek plan to take Pehtes on the voyage?"

"Oh course. Who else shall I caress on the long nights?"

Pehtes settled between my thighs, like Aisha.

"Is that not right, Pehtes? I believe you shall be stroked on this journey more than I."

"Kiya!" I called as soon as she entered my bedchamber. "Make certain my bow, the arrows and my steel dagger with the jeweled hilt are packed."

She scurried over to me, upper lip curled back, tongue clicking against teeth yellowed by age and chewing herbs.

"No more hunts! It displeases the Goddess for you to kill."

"Would you deny me such a simple pleasure, if Hathor is not so displeased as to forbid it? Think of the horses and the chariots flying over the stones. Picture the great fire and the desert night filled with the scent of roasting game."

A scene in a desert flashed through my mind, a secret scene with a slain lion. To kill a lion is forbidden to a priestess. Only my chariot driver knew the truth of that afternoon in the Western Desert. And Neith, goddess of the hunt. She knew.

I might have had the driver's tongue cut out but instead took pity on him.

"If you value the life of your wife and child," I had menaced, "you will speak of this to no one."

I'd fantasized that afternoon in the Western Desert of returning to camp with the lion skin mounted to the front of my chariot, a trophy to prove I could hunt as well as any man. The hunting party would have gathered around the chariot and cheered wildly, "Isenkhebe, Isenkhebe,

Queen of the Hunt!"

But instead, I left the carcass to rot in the desert and be devoured by jackals. Neith the hunter goddess had not yet named her price for my transgression.

I spent the next hours sorting through scrolls and overseeing the packing. Maia put a stone palette, pens, brushes, a pigment bag and a water jar in a painted chest with blank papyri.

She carefully wrapped alabaster bowls in soft linen and stored bathing oils and perfumes in ornate wooden cases. An ebony cosmetic spoon carved in the shape of a nude woman with obsidian and ivory eyes went in her own box crafted of Lebanese cedar and painted with secret spells promising eternal beauty.

The medicine chest was stocked with fresh herbs, powdered draughts and vials of potions accompanied by tiny scrolls of incantations carefully recorded in miniature script drawn with brushes as fine as one bristle.

Kiya clapped her hands, and two initiates appeared, one with a large chest and one with a small.

"The amulets have all been properly blessed in the Temples. I am giving the chests over to the care of Qeb-ha, Isenkhebe. He is more experienced in these things."

Qeb-ha. I supposed I would have to ask his permission for every expenditure.

The larger chest contained tiny vultures and *tiet* knots for protection, crocodiles for power, frogs for fertility and scarabs to ensure rebirth. The figurines were made of blue or green faience, not quite ceramic and not quite glass, an Egyptian specialty for thousands of years.

The smaller treasury held amulets crafted of gold, rare silver and lapis lazuli carried by caravan from a land that one day would be Afghanistan.

"These are for gifts to noblemen and priests. To ease your journey. Not for foolish things."

Foolish. Why was everyone always accusing me of being foolish?

The sun god Re disappeared behind the golden cliffs across the Nile. The nightly battle in the Underground with *Apep* the serpent had begun. Tomorrow the struggle would end once more with a victorious Re rising as the new dawn.

The villa was quiet; an anxious silence had replaced the earlier chaos.

Who would sail with me at dawn? Surrounded by lush gardens, sweet scents and quiet nights, my household lived in peace and tranquility. The high walls of the compound protected them from the real world. No one wanted to leave. I didn't want to leave.

A soft breeze had come up; the blue and gold ankh-embroidered curtains around my bed billowed like sails. Above the pink marble bathing pool draped a heavenly cloud of sheer, rose-colored linen.

Maia floated white lotus blossoms on the clear water and lighted white alabaster lamps filled with gardenia-scented oil. Without a sound, she placed on the edge of the pool a silver tray of multicolored glass bottles holding virgin olive oil mixed with powdered limestone to cleanse my skin.

"I wish to bathe in private. See that I am not disturbed. I shall consult the Goddess that I might choose well those who journey with me."

"Good night, Mistress. May the Goddess bless this sleep."

The unwatered wine relaxed me. I refused to think of the voyage or my destiny with a father I had never seen. Instead, I chose to summon River God to my daydream, to feel his touch on my throat, to hear his moist promise in my ear.

I would do my duty to the Goddess but feed my own hunger first. Hathor created me. I am who I am because of her. The plans of a God are one thing; the thoughts of men—and women—are another.

I slipped into liquid velvet and closed my eyes. The water was the same temperature as my body and the evening air. We were one.

A nightingale, the only sound in the stillness of the new night, sang outside my bedchamber in the darkening garden. The perfume of gardenia and jasmine drifted on the mild evening air.

He was silent. I sensed his presence rather than heard him. My first sight was bare feet and sturdy ankles. My eyes traveled up straight runner's legs past the engorged penis, head glistening in the lamplight, into the face of River God.

O Hathor! You are indeed the Highest-of-High!

CHAPTER 7 THE BATH

He was in the water before I could move, straddling me, pushing me into the unyielding stone of the pool wall. I didn't complain. With my fingertips, with my mouth, I tried to reach him, but he teased me and held my hands, not letting me touch him.

He eased down into the water on top of me, the nape of my neck on the edge of the pool, his hardness pushing against the softness of my belly. I stretched to reach his sculptured lips with mine, but his mouth was at my ear.

"Do not move, Isis," he breathed, "or my seed will issue. I want it to last."

The scent of myrrh in his breath wafted around us.

Releasing my hands, he pulled me full into the pool. I floated on my back, white lotus blossoms with dazzling yellow centers swirling in eddies around us. My nipples rose from the water; the areolas of my breasts were dark circles at the surface. On his knees beside me, his erection pierced the clear water.

He started with my closed eyes, then my open lips, never touching me but exhaling like a gentle wind across my flesh, blowing softly in my ear, down the side of my neck and across my throat.

The water was warm on my back, and the air warm on my face. His breath was warmer still on my breasts.

I felt his hand slide between my thighs. I opened, relaxing into his touch, content to do nothing, to exert nothing, to have no will of my own. Languid, not in a hurry, he stroked my swollen bud in tiny circular movements without pressure. I drifted in sheer pleasure, floating among sweet-scented blossoms.

With his hands around my ankles, he pulled my knees to drape on his shoulders. He cupped my buttocks, raising me to his lips, his tongue swirling my throbbing lotus. He sucked and then played with his tongue and then sucked again.

The orgasm cascaded through my womb, muscles rolling in contraction after contraction. A long, pitched cry escaped my throat.

River God's mouth was on mine in an instant.

"Sh-h-h, Isis. Your household is awake and nearby."

Too late for that. By now, every eye looked to my rooms. Every ear strained to hear more.

He stood up in the pool with the water coming to mid-thigh. He had gone tense and his erection slack.

My hands in his, he drew me slowly to my feet. My breasts rose and fell with each breath. We stood inches apart, water streaming off, our skin glowing in the mellow light of the white lamps, the air sweet with their perfumed oil.

He was like an animal alert to danger, every nerve in his body taut. River God knew he tasted forbidden fruit; the charms of a High-Priestess are for the Temple only.

But not this priestess.

"They will stay away," I promised. "I have given orders to be alone."

He stared hard at me for a moment. His eyes were so black, I couldn't see the pupils. Then they softened to a smoky charcoal, and the hint of a smile shone through his caution. He was mine again.

His lips were full and dry and covered mine with ease. Taking his time, his tongue explored. He sucked gently on my tongue and drew me to him, pressing my breasts into his chest. His erection was back.

I found myself outside of the pool, gliding backward, two bodies moving as one as he guided us to the bed with billowing sails. The curtains brushed our bare flesh but didn't cling; our skin had dried in the desert night air.

We sank together onto the plush cushions of a bed designed more for pleasure than sleep. Smelling the mating scent, Pehtes purred round my ears.

I lay spread on soft linen, my shaved head sinking into cool silk pillows and warm cat fur. River God's mouth was on mine again in a deep, lingering kiss probing with his tongue. His touch was more sensual than sexual; he savored me as one does a fine wine, something precious you loathe to finish.

"Sail with me tomorrow," I blurted impulsively. "With you in my bed by night, I can face anything by day."

Startled, River God stopped his caress.

"I cannot do that." His voice was incredulous. I might have asked him to fly. "I am as bound to my duty as you are to yours."

Like a fool, I didn't have the sense to stop.

"I am the daughter of Sit-hathor," I insisted in a tone that sounded, even to me, petulant and spoiled. "I am in need of protection. You can appeal to the governor. Who better to protect me than you?"

He changed in that moment. I felt him begin to pull away. When he spoke, his tone was already distant with a poignant note of resignation.

"Isis, sweet and dangerous Isis, you know that our destinies were foretold when we came from the womb."

"My destiny is not all that was told," I answered and then hesitated.

I wasn't sure how River God would react to the news of my father. He must believe, like everyone else, that I was sired by a god.

"If there is something I must know, then you must tell me," he said solemnly. "But if there is something you know but should not tell me, then you must keep silent. Do not reveal what is secret for the sake of my listening."

Time slowed. I could almost see the thoughts turning in his head. Thank the Gods, I'd had the presence of mind not to tell him what might push him yet farther away.

The nightingale sang sweetly, unaware of the change between us. The still air was abuzz with the hum of insects. The cries of night creatures carried from the Nile.

I felt him slip away. I wanted to grab his arm and never let go. Instead, I traced my fingers lightly along his forearm. The hairs rose, and I had hope.

"I feel alone. I do not want to go on this voyage alone," I pleaded without pride. "I fear it. I fear everything about it."

But even I, lost in my pathetic begging, knew he wouldn't go with me. This journey was for me only—and Qeb-ha. It was as Sit-hathor had said, *All that is left is the doing.*

Strangely enough, I took some solace in the certitude. I had no more power in this life than I had in my other, but at least in this one, I had a mission—a purpose. I was somebody. And I had River God.

He stroked my face with the back of his fingers. I was like a cat before him. A purring Pehtes snuggled into his armpit; I wanted to follow her there.

Tracing the mound of my breast with his finger, he whispered gently and regretfully, "I desire you more than any woman I have ever known or seen, Isis. But I must place myself away from you."

He sighed and took his hand away. "The Gods have set us on separate paths. Mine is to serve the Pharaoh. Yours is to serve the Goddess. Our craving for each other has lured us from our rightful paths. The great glory of a wise man is to control himself in his manner of life."

I hated those words. I wanted to put my hands over my ears to keep them from entering. It was my fault. I was too needy. I had gone too far.

He bent and kissed my lips with agonizing tenderness. My heart cracked; a chisel split it as cleanly as a piece of granite. The pain pierced my soul.

"The Fate and Fortune that come, Isis, it is the Gods that send them."

I had been taught a thousand ways to make a man desire me, but there was nothing I could say or do to make him stay. He was gone as quickly and silently as he had come. I had a terrible feeling that I would never see him again.

CHAPTER 8 ENCOUNTER

The bells kept ringing and ringing, louder and louder. Would they never stop? I felt Pehtes purring against me, but when I opened my eyes, it wasn't Pehtes. It was Aisha. I was back.

My spine screamed. My shoulders and hips ached against the cold marble tiles of my living room floor. How many hours—or days—had passed since I fell asleep in front of the Mirror?

The incessant ringing had stopped and then started again.

I found my cell on the coffee table next to my keys—*I really have to change that ringtone*—and checked caller ID before answering. It was Barb.

"Where have you been?" Her tone was frantic and demanding at the same time. "Didn't you get my messages?"

"Barb, I have to tell you something…something big."

"Save it. This is more important. I need you to get over here to the Stirling Club right away."

"Stirling Club? What time is it?" I didn't dare ask what day.

"It doesn't matter. I'm here with clients. Two *very* good-looking men buying drinks and making intelligent—let me repeat—*intelligent* conversation."

"Barb…I bought the Red Mirror."

"What red mirror?"

"The one at the antique mall."

"God, I hope you got a deal."

"Barb, listen. It has some kind of power."

"Power? What are you talking about? How can a mirror have power?"

She paused a moment before asking, "What *kind* of power?"

"I had this...dream. Only it wasn't a dream. I was in Egypt. Ancient Egypt. You know, with Pharaohs. I was myself...but not myself."

It sounded ridiculous, even to me, when I said it out loud.

"You're always dreaming," she snapped, "and you always think they're real." Her voice took on her headmistress tone, stinging and brisk. "Look, you can stay home with a mirror and go on some kind of fantasy trip. Or you can put on your high heels and get over here where a flesh and blood man is waiting for you."

When I didn't answer right away, she threatened, "Don't tell me you have to think about this."

"Okay. Okay. I'll be there in half an hour."

"You're not going to regret it. Who knows? Maybe he's Mr. Right."

I spied Barb right away at the bar. Tall and thin as a model with that silvery helmet of platinum hair, she's easy to spot in a crowd. She smiled and waved discreetly.

Perched on one of the tall leather bar chairs, she faced two men standing with their backs to me. One was blond, the other dark-haired. I already liked the square of their shoulders and the cut of their suits. Money and confidence. I could see it from across the room.

"Hi, Barb! I made it." I kissed her on the cheek before turning around.

My knees went weak, and I gasped out loud. Barb grabbed my arm. I think she kept me on my feet.

"Are you all right? You're white as a sheet." Her voice came to me through a tunnel.

Standing in front of me, dressed in a charcoal silk suit with a blue paisley tie, was River God.

Well, River God with green eyes. Green instead of dark; green like mine. I had the sense to realize I was staring at him with an open mouth and snapped my teeth together. If he knew me, he didn't show it, but he had the same slightly amused expression as the morning I first saw him on the bank of the Nile.

Tailored to fit perfectly over his broad shoulders, his suit narrowed slightly at the waist; it took no effort at all to visualize the triangular torso underneath. His sensuous lips had been carved by the same master sculptor. He had thick black hair cut in an expensive salon style. He was shorter. No, he was the same. I was wearing three-inch heels. My eyes were on level with his lips. I stared at him. The other three stared at me.

"You look exactly like someone I used to know," I said lamely. I couldn't think of anything else.

His clear eyes smiled at me in an inviting way. He might not recognize me, but he was definitely interested.

"You look like you could use a drink." His voice was incredibly, impossibly, the same.

In fact, everything about him was the same as River God, except his suit and hair—and the green eyes. Barb introduced him as Rasheed. His blond friend was Lars.

Yes, I could use a drink. I hoped no one noticed my shaking hands.

"Thank you," I said a bit too gratefully. "I'll have a Plymouth martini."

Rasheed turned away to talk to the bartender and then looked right back at me. I got the impression he was searching for something in my eyes.

He radiated an energy that was both animal and sensual. Just standing next to him rendered me weak, with no will of my own. I sensed that he knew it. That slightly amused, seductive half-smile curved his lips.

We settled in one of the small, semi-private alcoves away from the bar. Traditional oil paintings of hunting scenes in gilt frames covered the walls. A chocolate velvet sofa with plush ochre armchairs, one on each end, formed a U around a low, gleaming mahogany table.

Barb planted herself on the sofa, motioning for Nordic Lars to sit in the chair to her right. It was obvious how the pairing would go. Rasheed kept to my side, close but not too close.

I sank into the down-filled cushions at the other end of the sofa and crossed my black-silky legs; my skirt rode up to mid-thigh. The red patent of my heels shone in the yellow light. Rasheed relaxed into the chair next to me, a man confident and totally at ease.

Wanting to keep a cool head, I barely sipped the martini. A drummer and guitarist joined the pianist, and the noise level rose several decibels. The lounge began to fill up; it was too loud really to talk. But by this time of the evening, most people had other things on their mind.

Rasheed didn't try to make conversation but looked around, observing, seeming to be acutely aware of everything. Toying with the olive on a plastic stick, I studied him from under lowered lashes.

It was not my imagination. Rasheed looked exactly like River God.

But more than that, he *felt* like him. It was the way he moved and his voice—and the way his eyes, even though clear now, instead of dark and mysterious, probed for secrets.

I thought he'd forgotten me, when he suddenly turned and caught me staring at him; the corners of his lips curved up again ever so slightly. He leaned into me; the silk fabric of his suit tightened across his shoulders and thighs. I could smell his cologne, faint but exotic. His look was magnetic. I couldn't have torn my eyes away from his if I wanted to.

He traced his middle finger lightly over my knee. An electric shock ran straight up the inside of my thigh.

"I know," he said in a low, vibrating voice. "I really feel you, too."

When he asked me to dance and offered his hand to help me stand, I was transported at once to the Nile in the early morning sun. I'd never met a man so masculine who moved so gracefully. I folded into his arms, and we flowed as one to classic Sinatra "Strangers in the Night." We didn't feel like strangers at all.

I thanked Carolina Herrera for my favorite scent, 212 Sexy—sweet, animal, ethereal. There were a dozen couples on the dance floor, each lost in their own universe. Rasheed guided us among the other galaxies, never brushing a star.

The music ended, and he lifted my hair with his fingers, putting his lips to the magic spot where my neck curves into my shoulder. The kiss lasted only a second but burned on forever.

Lars and Barb danced, too. They looked like they were getting along fine. Lars laughed a lot. He was low-key, ready for fun, the type who enjoys being alive.

"I think we should go somewhere quiet." Rasheed didn't address me directly but spoke to the group.

"I'm starving." Lars was clear on his needs. "What's your favorite restaurant?"

"Eiffel Tower," I said immediately, and then immediately regretted it. It's pricey.

"You need reservations," I stumbled. "We probably couldn't get a table now."

"I don't think it'll be a problem." Rasheed spoke like a man who rarely encountered problems.

CHAPTER 9 EIFFEL TOWER

S tanding next to the tasting room were two men, both over six feet, well-built and well-dressed in tailored suits. They fell in behind us, following closely down the sweeping marble staircase and out the leaded glass doors to the canopied marquee.

A valet came up immediately for the claim ticket. Neither Lars nor Rasheed turned his attention from Barb and me. Instead, the taller of the two men stepped up to the valet and handed him the parking stub.

My internal warning light flashed red. Were these two guys with us? I hadn't agreed to go anywhere with four men.

Seeing the frown on my face, Rasheed leaned close, touching my elbow. I felt his breath in my ear.

"Marcos and Gamel go everywhere I go. There is no danger. But I need to keep it that way."

I felt broadsided, thrown off balance. Go everywhere he goes? Are we talking about *bodyguards*?

"I have my own car," I stammered in an edgy voice, the pitch a little too high. "It might be late. I-I don't want to come back for it."

I shot a questioning look at Barb. *Did you know about this?*

She looked a little embarrassed but not nervous.

"Come with us. My man Gamel can follow in your car." Rasheed was calm, his voice reasonable. He neither begged nor commanded.

The shorter of the bodyguards looked at me briefly and then away. His silk suit stretched across the bulk of his shoulders, and I imagined I saw the outline of a gun at his armpit. What kind of name was Gamel?

A black limo pulled up, and the second man—Marcos, did Rasheed say?—took the keys from the valet and gave him a tip. Gamel opened the passenger door and stepped aside. No one made a move to get in. Rasheed's tone remained calm, reassuring but not pressuring.

"Gamel is an excellent driver. I trust him with my life."

All eyes were on me. I don't usually get so unnerved, but this had been an unnerving day. Rasheed's face was without guile; I didn't sense he hid anything. I opened my bag and handed him the stub.

His assuring eyes, almost olive in the marquee lights, told me, *Good. You made the right decision. This is going to be fine.*

The tension eased when I moved to get in the limo. Barb followed and was immediately apologetic.

"Bodyguards, Barb?" I hissed. "Yes. You might have mentioned *that*."

Lars climbed in, rummaged in the bar and came up with a bottle of *Moet & Chandon*.

"What about some champagne? Isn't that what you do in a limo in Vegas?"

He popped the cork and looked for flutes.

"*Skål!*"

We drove out of the circular driveway, through the tall wrought iron gates, and turned into heavy traffic going past the Hilton. Little white lights ran all around the edge of the floorboards and along the tops of the tinted windows.

Rasheed's leg pressed against mine. He put his hand at the top of my thigh, so close to the gateway to pleasure. His heat seared through the fabric; I envisioned a brand on my skin in the shape of his palm.

"You don't have to worry about anything happening that you don't want," he said softly in a voice only for me to hear.

I looked directly into his eyes with huge black pupils and then at his lush lips only inches from mine. At that moment, there was only one thing I wanted. Too bad Barb and Lars were in the way.

Rasheed was right about reservations being no problem. I saw a bill discreetly change hands, and we sped up the private elevator. Mahogany doors opened to a gleaming, stainless steel kitchen. The *maitre d'* ushered us to a prime table against tall windows overlooking the Strip.

Bright lights and high-def signs blazed. The colossal Paris balloon glowed against the black sky. The Bellagio fountain show across Las

Vegas Boulevard started with the first tentative sprays and then burst into glory. Orchestrated precisely with the music, the lavish ballet of white lights and sparkling jets ended in thundering crescendos soaring high into the night.

"Great choice!" Lars announced. "If the food is half as good as the view, I'm in heaven."

Course after delicious course arrived, each paired with the best wines served by the *sommelier*. Waiters in tuxedos buzzed around the table. The Bellagio fountains played every fifteen minutes.

Lars told stories about skiing in Norway, and Barb chattered about real estate. Rasheed said almost nothing. His knee pressed against mine; sometimes I felt his hand burning on my thigh. Even when he didn't touch me, every nerve in my body vibrated. I felt electric just sitting next to him.

The *piece de resistance* was the baked chocolate soufflé with warm vanilla sauce. *Courvoisier* filled crystal snifters. Waiters poured dark espresso into tiny porcelain *demitasse* cups with lemon peel twists. Lumps of raw sugar nested in a sterling silver bowl on the white damask tablecloth.

I didn't want to think about the bill. It would cover a month's rent, all my utilities and groceries and still have some left over. The check never came to the table. Rasheed had apparently also arranged that with the *maitre d'*.

Barb and Lars laughed all the way down the elevator. Rasheed was quiet but kept close to me. Neither of us spoke. I was aware of nothing but the heat of his body. When he put his hand on the small of my back, my flesh blistered.

Our entourage passed through the throng in the Paris Casino and made for valet parking with Gamel in the lead. The blood pumped in my ears; I had sampled a lot of wine. I wasn't exactly drunk, but between the furnace of Rasheed's body and the drink, I was light-headed, off balance again.

The six of us were standing in a tight circle, waiting for the limo, when Rasheed took hold of my arm and said, "Please excuse us for a moment."

He guided me around a corner and backed me up to the wall. His body pressed against mine. I felt him grow hard. I could almost feel him throbbing.

"Listen to me. Don't say a word."

I don't know how I could have said anything; the garage around me contained no air.

"I want you to come with me to my hotel. I don't want you to say no."

I felt a twinge of fear. He looked and sounded like River God; he even *felt* like River God, but could I trust Rasheed to *be* like him?

Eons passed. Neither of us said a word. Heat radiated from his body, baking into me. I felt the power of his muscles through his silk suit.

Then suddenly his face relaxed; his whole body relaxed. He put his hands on each side of my face, fingers in my hair, and kissed me. His tongue found mine. He was tender and full of longing.

"I desire you more than any woman I have ever known or seen."

His words riveted me; they were word-for-word the same as they had been 2,500 years ago—or was it only five hours? I couldn't make sense out of this; it made no sense. But he had said those exact words to me before and then walked away. I wasn't going to let that happen again.

"Okay," I whispered and nodded my head. "Okay."

CHAPTER 10 THE WYNN

Rasheed had a suite at the Wynn, in the tower with private entrance and check-in. We rode the elevator in silence to the penthouse. When the doors opened, panoramic windows looked out on Trump Tower and the blazing lights of Vegas Valley.

He spoke quietly to Gamel and Marcos, and they disappeared. Rasheed came up behind me and put his arms around my waist, pulling me back into him, my body melting into his.

"They will stay away. I've given orders to be alone."

Hadn't I said the same words to him in my pink marble pool with white lotus blossoms?

He lifted my hair with one hand and held me tight with the other, kissing each vertebra down the back of my neck and between my shoulder blades to the top of my dress.

I still had on my heels; my pelvis tilted into his. I felt him grow hard as stone against my hips. His hand moved down from my waist, across my belly, to rest on my mound and push hard on the tip of my womb. His palm cupping me burned hot through the knit of my dress.

Heat pulsed through me in rushing waves. Growling low in my throat, I craved him to stroke me like a cat. I would roll onto my back and give him my belly, my legs spread wide.

His hand traveled down the front of my thigh to the knee and then up the back to my buttocks. He still kissed the nape of my neck and my shoulders. He let my hair fall, and his hand found my breast. When he touched my nipple through my bra and dress, I cried out.

We stood like that for an eternity, my back to his front, his hands caressing me all over. We swayed back and forth, something primordial coursing through our veins.

He turned me in his arms and kissed me long and deep. I pressed my thighs against his with all my strength. I felt him huge on my belly, an iron post, and put my hand down to fondle him through his pants. It was his time to moan.

Low lights burned in the room; a mirror covered an entire wall, reflecting our silhouettes against the Vegas night sky. I glimpsed a lush king bed through an open double doorway.

He eased the zipper at the back of my dress, the slider inching past each tooth. I unbuckled his belt and, ever so slowly, matching his pace, unzipped his pants. He slid my dress off my shoulders, and it dropped to my ankles, bundling on top of the shiny red heels. I slipped his trousers down past his hard thighs and let them fall to his polished loafers.

We looked into each other's eyes. We didn't say a word. We didn't even kiss. We wanted no distraction from the unveiling.

I helped him out of his jacket. I loosened his tie and lifted it over his head. His starched shirt was snowy white in the red and black room. I undid every tiny button and unfastened the gold cuff links at his wrists. When the shirt came off, I had my first sight of his bronzed chest and flat belly. No doubt about it—this was River God.

My fingers tugged at the elastic band of his trunks, pulling them down to his knees. Heart pounding and blood rushing all around inside my head, I went to my knees and took him in my mouth. He filled me almost to the throat. I could fell his body shaking, every muscle tense and rock hard.

"Do not move," he whispered with his hands on my face, lifting me to my feet, "or I will come. I want more time. I want it to last."

More words from the past.

His warm fingers slid around my midriff, unfastened my bra and eased the straps off my shoulders. He was slow, deliberate, not in a hurry. My breasts were swollen white mounds with blushing halos, nipples aflame. He took one in each hand. A sound caught in his throat. His eyes, no longer seeing me, filled with a new light.

He moved his thumbs back and forth across my aching nipples, and I arched my back to bring me closer to him, begging him silently to take me into his mouth. I knew that one touch of his moist tongue, and I would explode.

Instead, he slid one hand under my panties and between my legs. He brought back his hand, looked at his dripping fingers and spread my own wet on my breast.

The first rolling wave of an orgasm washed through my womb. I moaned and moaned louder with each successive surge, swaying on my feet, tumbling in a satin sea. I would have lost my way, if he had not held me fast.

Without hurry, he eased my panties down past the slim garters to join my crumpled dress. I lowered my head to his chest. I didn't know a body so limp could still stand. He held me stable, dragging my clothes away with his foot as I shifted balance from one leg to the other.

At last, I stood naked in black and red garters, black silk stockings and my red patent shoes.

Erection probing the air, hands on my hips, he kicked his own clothes away, pulled me forward and slid his iron rod between my clasped legs. I locked my thigh muscles and rocked back and forth, astride him, riding at a slow pace. His hardness pressed on my swollen bud, throbbing again with life.

He walked me backward toward the open doorway, his engorged beast still between my clenched legs. Moving in perfect unison, we glided as one person.

Like dancers in a waltz, our eyes locked in a spinning room.

He lowered me to the lush bed, his eyes fixed unblinking on mine. He kissed my forehead, then each eyelid, the tip of my nose and then full on the mouth, his lips smothering mine, sucking languidly, his tongue penetrating and unhurried. Lingering long with each kiss, he still took his time.

I was wild to feel him inside me, to fill me, to pound me. But I surrendered on the rich covers of the bed and let him do with me what he willed. He knew every sensitive spot to touch and exactly how much pressure to bear. He knew my secret places and claimed them as his own.

His finger hooked under the elastic of my left garter and slipped it slowly down my leg and over my foot. He rolled the stocking carefully past my knee, along my calf, over my ankle and past my toes. One kiss on the arch of my foot, and just as slowly, he removed the right garter and then the stocking, ending with his lips on each toe. He kissed the shallow red marks left by each garter, first high on the left thigh, then on the right.

When I felt his kiss on my clitoris, I relaxed—home again after lifetimes of being lost.

He teased with his teeth and his tongue while shocks jolted my body. An electric current pulsed through the soft under-bottom of my buttocks. When he sensed my need unbearable, he pulled himself up the length of my body, and I felt the tip of him at my gate.

I wrapped my arms around his back, thrusting my hips up, begging him to plunge deep.

And then, at last, he was full inside me. We both exhaled deep at the same moment, a long sigh echoing across eternity.

At first he didn't move. We breathed in and out, together, melting into one person. My vagina pulsed, on fire, swallowing him whole.

Like a starved beast, he began to devour me. He pounded and pounded, his hands grasping my buttocks to better control the rhythm. I raised my legs high into the air, so he could plow deeper.

Lust and desire replaced tenderness. Animal sounds escaped from our throats. A wave crested, and a rapid succession of endless contractions of pure ecstasy rolled through me. His body convulsed, froze, and then shuddered. He collapsed on top of me. I could feel his heart pounding next to mine.

We slept. I slept. The sky was barely light when he woke me. I looked up at him in surprise. Rasheed was dressed in a pressed suit, starched shirt and blue tie. His eyes were shiny bright, glittery like emeralds.

He sat on the bed next to me and stroked my face gently with his fingers, as if memorizing each feature. He spoke even more gently.

"I have to go now. I'm sorry. It is what I must do."

"But—" I started to interrupt him.

"Sh-h-h," he hushed me, his fingertips on my lips. "Listen to me. There are things I can't tell you. Things you must not know. It has to be this way."

I stared at him in disbelief. He wanted secrets? There had been nothing between us last night.

"When will I see you again?" I felt the panic of when he left me in my white villa by the Nile. "I don't know anything about you. I don't have your cell number—or even your email."

For a microsecond, I even thought of Facebook.

"I know how to find you." He smiled his secret half-smile, not with the usual amusement, but sweet with longing.

He could walk away, though; he had the strength for that. He leaned down and kissed me with such tenderness my heart cracked, again with a chisel. The pain this time was also the same.

"We have known each other before, Isis, and we will know each other again."

"No-o-o-o!" I cried out.

But he was gone.

CHAPTER 11   RETURN

Barb called just as I got home to a hungry cat. I almost let it go to voicemail but knew that would be cruel. She shouted in my ear while I put food in Aisha's bowl and turned on the kettle.

"Why haven't you called me? I've been worried sick!" She paused, but not long enough for me to answer.

"Are you okay? TALK to me!"

"I'm fine."

"You don't sound fine. What happened last night?" She paused again.

"He didn't hurt you, did he?" she asked a little fearfully.

Did breaking my heart count? But I knew what Barb meant.

"No, he didn't hurt me. He wouldn't do that."

"How do you know? *Mr. Mystery Man with his bodyguards.* He scares me. I'm sorry I got you mixed up with him."

"I'm not."

Silence.

"Are you home?" Then in a whisper, "Are you with *him?*"

"He's gone, Barb. "

"Gone?" she snorted. "Unlikely! Lars told me Rasheed's Coptic. That's some kind of Middle-Easterner. You know how obsessive they can get."

"Trust me. He's not obsessed. He walked right out the door. And don't be sorry about last night. Calling me was exactly the right thing to do. I'm not sure you had any...choice. I'm not sure any of us had any choice."

"Choice? What are you talking about?"

Then she remembered our conversation before the Stirling Club. "You never told me about the dream. What was that Egypt stuff about?"

"I'll have to tell you later, Barb. I need to go now."

There was no way I could go to work. I called in sick, turned off my cell and sat at my laptop, sipping milk-laced Assam tea from an old X-Files mug. Aisha snuggled into my lap.

I googled 'Copt' and went to the Wikipedia link. The first paragraphs explained that Copts are modern-day Egyptian Christians, and then I read, "Copts are direct descendants of the Ancient Egyptians."

I looked over at the Red Mirror. I had no idea how any of this was possible, but I wasn't crazy. I'd never felt more sober in my life.

Next I googled 'Hathor.' A photo of the statue of the goddess in the inner sanctum popped up. I tried to remember if I'd seen the image before, to explain how it appeared in my dream. But I didn't really believe I'd dreamed about Egypt.

Rasheed had called me 'Isis.' I had heard him clearly. There was no doubt in my mind at all. Rasheed was River God, and he knew it, too.

Vegas bookies wouldn't give odds on the chance of our meeting at the Stirling Club. The Universe had put River God and me together for a reason, and I didn't intend to leave our path to fate—or the gods. I had the Red Mirror. I was going back to find him.

I curled up in my gray leather chair with Aisha and stared at the Mirror, replaying each sight and smell, each change in the room. How did it begin? It all started when I began to polish the strut. Rubbing was the key. The comparison to Aladdin's lamp was obvious. This was some genie I'd summoned.

I put out extra food for Aisha and filled her box and a plastic dishpan with clean litter. I put the toilet lids up in case she needed more water.

The bottle of olive oil and the cloth were still beside the Mirror. I rejected trying another strut; I needed to return to exactly where I had left. I'm not much of a scientist, but I remember from high school chemistry that you have to limit your variables.

Sitting cross-legged on the floor, exactly as before, except dressed now in sweats, I picked up the cloth. Aisha snuggled against one thigh. She was already familiar with this routine. She liked it; she knew it meant I would stay put for a while. At least, that's how it would seem to her.

CHAPTER 12   THE NILE

It was utterly still except for a hum in my ears. I drifted with no birdsong, no sound of hammer on stone, no rustle of wind through the palms. The hum was not constant, but more a repeating rise and crest of subtle sound waves, a kind of *swoosh*, somewhat like the sea trapped in a conch, but without any hint of a roar.

Golden sunshine filtered through sheer saffron drapes. Not even the faintest breath of a breeze relieved the heaviness in the air. A light layer of perspiration welled on my skin.

I sat straight up. Not in my gardens. Not in my chambers. Not at the Temple. I wasn't anywhere I recognized. The river! The swooshing sound was the current of the Nile as it swirled under and all around me. We'd sailed from Thebes; I couldn't guess how many days had passed on this side of the Mirror. How would I find River God now?

The banks of the Nile were distant bands of green against tall dunes bleached white in the sun. The river was quite wide here. The barge moved swiftly and effortlessly in the water; we must be sailing with the current, downstream toward Lower Egypt, toward the Delta. The Mediterranean is there; they call it the Great Green.

Maia appeared from nowhere and knelt at the foot of my lounge on a green and yellow striped carpet covering most of the wood deck. She wore the same braided wig twisted with white and blue cords.

"Is Mistress unwell? Does she have need of something?"

I brushed past her, not answering. Her eyes followed me, but she didn't speak.

I'd been disoriented when I found myself on the river instead of at Thebes and then annoyed, but otherwise I experienced none of the turmoil of my first visit. In fact, I felt remarkably at one with Isis; the barrier between our minds and hearts blurred more with each breath. I was losing myself in her, but not completely. She was also losing herself in me. And we were both vexed to be on the boat.

We were midships on a slightly raised platform, barely concealed by the linen curtains that moved not at all. Below me lay a dozen or more men sleeping under awnings suspended loosely across the deck to shade them from the glare of the sun.

The prow of the boat curved up in a bowsprit carved into a bundle of papyrus reeds reaching for the sky. Long wooden oars with blades at the ends leaned at an angle on the side rails, shipped and unmanned now, but ready for plunging back into the swiftly moving water. A giant winged cobra in vibrant blues and greens covered a square yellow sail hanging lifeless in the afternoon doldrums.

To the rear, I saw the steersman with a massive pole-like rudder. Full awake, he maneuvered the ship down the current. The stern of the boat also curved up and mirrored the bowsprit's bundled reeds. The boat was long and narrow; my cabin divided the barge into fore and aft with barely space to pass on each side.

The enclosure had a low ceiling made of woven reeds, but I could easily stand. Long rolls of the same reeds were mounted like rolled bamboo curtains on the four edges of the roof. When lowered, the shades would afford some privacy. Well, privacy from the outside anyway. I was not alone.

Bodies stirred in the corner. Young women lay close to each other on mats. I counted four from my household, plus Maia and me, all in this small cabin filled with chests. This voyage was going to be even longer than I'd feared.

"Does Isenkhebe require my attention?"

The old priest Qeb-ha stood outside with only the filmy weave of the drapes separating us. The last thing I wanted was his attention. I hoped the sheer fabric and the distance between us would shield my thoughts.

"Qeb-ha, how far do you judge we have sailed?"

I wanted to ask if there were any chance of turning back. But I already knew the answer. *All that is left is the doing.* Our mission had begun. My only recourse was to finish it as quickly as possible.

"We shall be at Abydos by Re's entry into the Underworld, Isenkhebe. The Gods favor our mooring there for the night."

"Would the Goddess not prefer we hasten? Could we not sail through the night to shorten our journey?"

He was clearly startled by my request. He straightened his shoulders to make himself taller but still couldn't pull in his belly; the fat hung over the top of his long skirt. Tiny beads of perspiration dotted the smooth scalp of his glistening brown, shaved head.

"Isenkhebe is aware the Gods do not favor travel on the great river by night. Set the Destroyer sends evil into the world under the cloak of darkness. We must have patience, as does Hathor. All actions are weighed on the Great Balance; the Balance determines the Right Measure for all things."

He paused, but he didn't make me wait long to learn how the Great Balance determined our voyage.

"A wind that is greater than its Right Measure wrecks ships."

As always, the old priest turned every phrase to his advantage. He knew I would not risk a shipwreck.

"I am humbled, Qeb-ha, by your profound knowledge of the will of the Gods."

"All good fortune, Isenkhebe, is from the hand of the Goddess," he mumbled, bowing low from the waist.

Behind him, I saw Goliath rising from the afternoon sleep, his skin glistening like polished ebony in the sunlight. The muscles across his shoulders rippled as he adjusted his white kilt and headdress. His legs, twice as long as Qeb-ha's, were surely powerful enough to break the eunuch's neck with one squeeze.

Tearing my eyes away, I announced, "When we moor for the night, Qeb-ha, I wish to bathe in the Nile. The day has been long and hot."

Unable to hide his alarm, Qeb-ha stepped so close to the sheer curtain that the cloth clung to his damp body.

"Isenkhebe is aware that Set waits in the shadows for the innocent to lose their way."

"I shall take the Nubian for protection," I countered, making no effort to mask my intent. "He looks as if he could battle Set himself and emerge the victor. Please arrange it."

"As Isenkhebe desires," he yielded with a bowed head. But he couldn't resist a parting shot.

"It is in women that good fortune and bad fortune are upon the earth," he complained silently as he moved through the curtains. Of course, he intended for me to hear.

Pehtes purring in my lap, I nibbled dates and pomegranates and drank watered sweet wine. I stayed in the cabin with my ladies and played endless games of *senet*, throwing sticks and moving pieces around the safe and danger squares. The game was tedious and boring. Whether by design or because of their poor skills, I always seemed to win.

The afternoon faded into long shadows.

Scheming of ways that I might block Qeb-ha's probing, I came up with nothing I was certain would work. My head was filled with thoughts I didn't want him to read, but I was at a loss as to how I might block him. Surely I could find one amulet in my chests that could keep him out of my head. For the time being, I would try to avoid him.

The sun god Re was low on the horizon when we pulled into the port of Abydos. As the city lay at the end of a broad canal well away from the Nile, I hadn't expected such a mob at the riverfront.

Boats of all sizes were lashed to the long sandstone wharf. Sweaty stevedores swarmed like a colony of ants. Everywhere I looked, I saw clusters of merchants trading mountains of Egyptian grain for giant, curved ivory tusks from Kush or clay *amphorae* filled with olive oil and wine from Cyprus.

A fleet of small fishing craft made of bundles of papyrus cruised up and down the river hawking tilapia and Nile perch. Qeb-ha was busy dickering over price; he would need several baskets of today's catch to feed the crew.

I had daydreamed all afternoon of the cool of the Nile on my skin—of rising from the water, my body wet. I would order Goliath to follow me into the grasses and lie on his back.

I would make of him a stone post and then straddle him, gradually—so gradually—lowering myself onto his pedestal.

He wouldn't touch me; he would be too afraid. When my aching bud fully flowered in its lust, I would throw back my head and call out to the Goddess, tsunami waves crashing in my surf.

Oh, it would have been divine. But I could see it was not possible this night, in this place.

CHAPTER 13 ABYDOS

The moon was rising when Qeb-ha came to the edge of my pavilion on the boat. The reed curtains were lowered, and I was reading a papyrus scroll by the low light of an oil lamp. We had only just returned from a bathhouse near the docks—not the bath of my daydreams, but the perfumed water soothed my frayed nerves and calmed my fire.

"May I speak with Isenkhebe Nefrusobek?"

Qeb-ha's high-pitched voice pierced my resting ears.

What could I do?

"Alone, if it pleases my mistress."

I nodded to my ladies, and they disappeared into the night.

As was the custom, he asked my permission before settling on a broad cushion at my feet. He was so close, I was sure I could hide nothing from him. I studied his face, looking for any sign of suspicion.

"Isenkhebe is reading. May I inquire what?"

"I am studying the course of the Nile and the cities along its banks."

"Yes, most wise. Sit-hathor would be pleased to see Isenkhebe using her time well."

"Better than at the river with a Nubian?"

If I shocked him, he didn't show it, answering benignly, "I am certain Isenkhebe's mother would advise her to enjoy herself with whom she wishes, as long as no fool joins her."

"Would that be me—or he who joins me—who would be the fool? Or would being with a fool make one of me also?"

He was not the only one who could talk in riddles, but he didn't rise to the bait and only shrugged his stooped shoulders, folding his hands neatly in his lap.

"I am only a priest," he said in a matter-of-fact tone. "The Gods know the impious and the pious by his heart. I must rely on words and actions to know the man—or woman."

The air was milder now, almost pleasantly warm. My skin was cool and dry. A soft, snowy white caftan folded along the slender curves of my body. The silver-tasseled bracelets around my ankles twinkled in the soft light.

Qeb-ha seemed entirely at ease with me. He spoke so fluidly of my mother that he must not suspect anything. I felt more confident in his presence and decided there were limits to the number of layers he could probe.

"We must play *senet*, Qeb-ha; I would enjoy a meeting of minds on that battleground."

"It is in battle that a man finds a brother—or sister. It is on the road that one finds a companion. It is my wish that we were both."

Seated across from me with crossed legs and placid expression, he appeared more a Buddha with *kohl*-lined eyes than Egyptian priest. His face was plump and remarkably unlined for his age. The fat of his belly lay in rolls. His breasts were as generous as a woman's.

I felt an inexplicable revulsion when he spoke of us as companions or brothers.

"I am who I am, not by my own choosing," he said without a sound passing his lips. *"Man, even a godly man, cannot alter the life the Gods assign him."*

My face went hot. Although cooler, the night was still, without a breath of moving air. I busied myself with a sip of wine, avoiding his eyes. I was ashamed of my disdain of him. Of course, Qeb-ha hadn't chosen to be castrated; no one would choose to be mutilated, to have his manhood ripped away.

For the briefest of moments, I thought of asking how he came to be a eunuch, but I had more pressing questions.

"Qeb-ha, tell me why I am here and where we are going."

"We are going to your father."

Was he deliberately trying to irritate me? I think he enjoyed keeping me in the dark.

"Please, Qeb-ha, do not insult me. There is more to this mysterious odyssey than a father."

"It is complicated, Isenkhebe, as are all matters of Gods and politics."

"Explain it to me."

I knew I was too brusque, but I'd had enough of his oblique talk. He had settled back, visibly preparing to tell a long story, while I wanted a quick synopsis.

He looked first at the river and then back at me, smiling almost fondly.

"Isenkhebe is a woman of no patience. She would hurry the moon to rise, so that it might set again. What of savoring the moonbeam that ripples on the black river?"

"There are many things that I savor, Qeb-ha. Long stories are not one."

He sighed. I clearly robbed him of one of his few pleasures.

Small waves from the current lapped against the cedar hull and the stone quays. Night birds called out and were answered. My handmaidens were not far away; their laughter was a medley of tiny bells.

"The Gods are displeased," he confided in that odd, somewhat hissing whisper peculiar to him. "It has been foretold that a time of chaos approaches. *Kemet*, our Black Land, faces great danger."

"*Some believe the Crown Prince is not fit to rule,*" he said to my mind. "*It is said that a God leaves his city during the rule of an evil master.*"

If he meant to shock me, he succeeded. A Pharaoh is without fault, a god, Horus-on-earth. Qeb-ha's silent words, tantamount to treason, could be very dangerous for both of us.

"I prefer not to speak of such things," I told him.

He leaned back again, settling into his spot on the cushion. When he next spoke, he talked out loud, but still in a quiet voice meant only for our ears.

"The Persians have long hungered for the riches of Our Mother Nile, Isenkhebe. They now sniff the scent of discord and weakness." He paused, then said in an ominous tone, "The omens are not favorable."

"I am only a priestess of Hathor, Qeb-ha. Trained for sacred pleasure. What role could I play to stop the Persians? Surely these are matters for the military."

"A role to which Isenkhebe was born. Her destiny now calls. It is her fate."

"If my destiny is so important, then surely I am worthy of knowing to where I am called. Enough of your riddles, Qeb-ha. What is our destination?"

"We sail to the Temple of Neith in Saïs, Isenkhebe."

Of all the places in Egypt, it had to be Neith's Temple. The vision of the rotting carcass of the lioness from my forbidden hunt flashed through my mind. I felt the panic again of being trapped on the barge, not knowing how long the journey might take—Saïs was very far away, almost to the Sea. But more than panic, I suddenly feared that I might never return.

Qeb-ha was full of unsettling news this evening. I almost regretted my insistence on knowing our plans.

"What has my father to do with the Goddess of Hunt?" I asked with dread.

"He is the Master of the Library of Neith, Isenkhebe. The Oracle of Saïs."

I'd heard of stories all my life of the mysterious mystic who was never seen. "Well, at least he is an Oracle. That is some consolation for him not being a god."

"Not a God?" Qeb-ha's eyes widened. "But the Oracle *is* a God, Isenkhebe. How else might Sit-hathor have borne a child?"

A true believer. In a way, I envied his certitude. Life must be so much easier without questions.

I could hear the oarsmen playing *senet* or another game. They gambled as usual, their voices animated and loud. The sounds of laughter and shouting reached us from the decks of other ships as heat-weary crews and tradesmen relaxed in the cool of the night. Their voices carried easily over the water and through the breathless mist.

"Why does he meet me now," I asked, "after all these years?"

"I am told only that the Oracle has a plan," he said with a shrug. "And that Isenkhebe is part of the plan."

"You tell me every day, Qeb-ha, that our fates are in the hands of the Gods, yet now you speak as though we might have influence over events, after all. That *I* could have influence."

"Our destiny is decided when we come from the womb," he stated calmly and without a trace of doubt. "Our duty is to follow the path the Gods set for us."

"And what exactly does my father know of *my* duties, Qeb-ha?"

"He has selected Isenkhebe's tutors and guided her education."

"And my training in the Temple?"

"Isenkhebe is her mother's daughter. The great Sit-hathor recognized early Isenkhebe's exceptional talent and set her on Hathor's path. All is as the Gods ordain."

We were silent for a moment. Qeb-ha watched me with his enigmatic inky eyes. His face was placid with no hint that the world faced chaos.

Swarms of insects buzzed outside the cone of sheer linen encircling us. The cloth hung perfectly straight without a whisper of breeze to move it.

"And so, Qeb-ha," I sighed, "we sail to the Temple of Neith."

Until tonight, I had wanted to get to our destination as quickly as possible; I now dreaded what might happen when we did.

"Face the challenge of every day with fresh eyes, Isenkhebe. Live each day to its fullest. By completing the sunrise and sunset in Right Measure, one arrives safely at his goal."

I stared at him from under half-closed lids. I would get no more information from Qeb-ha tonight.

"Good night, Isenkhebe Nefrusobek. All good fortune is from the hand of the Gods. May the Goddess protect Isenkhebe and bring her sweet dreams."

And then he rose, bowed low and moved clumsily through the break in the reed curtains. I was left alone with my own ideas about sweet dreams.

CHAPTER 14 THE WIZARD

A terrible dry wind tore at my scorched skin. My sweat evaporated into the brittle air before it could form beads. My parched throat burned. I was blinded by the glare of a golden disk with rainbow-colored wings filling the silver sky.

Then the cobra appeared—rising up taller than me, back curved into an S, tail coiled upward, his round unblinking eyes staring into mine. So close his forked tongue almost flicked my cheek, he hissed in my face. Inches away, two fangs glinted in the bright sun. Clear drops of venom oozed from the spiky tips.

I tried to scream, but as wide as I opened my mouth, no sound came. It was a silent world.

With wings of white feathers spread wide, a vulture swooped down from the sky and seized the cobra with razor-edged talons, carrying him off in a cloud of swirling red sand. I squeezed my lids against the fiery dust and felt the wind suddenly fall still. I stood in a sweltering vacuum of crimson light.

I wanted to cry, but there was no moisture for tears. I opened my eyes to a silver-haired wizard, majestic in a sapphire blue gown glittery with shining stars. He raised a silver sword above his head; the rays of the winged sun exploded off the tip in a bright burst of white light. In his other arm, he cradled a rectangular, glassy green tablet, engraved with words I couldn't read, no matter how hard I tried. I knew that I should follow him, but when I took my first steps, he was there— and then he was not.

I was alone again in a vast space. I was alone in the Universe.

The earth cracked; a massive gash yawned and green water rushed forth. A lake began to rise and rise, filling the whole desert until it reached my knees, then my thighs, then my waist.

I struggled to wake up but couldn't. I was trapped. Was I to drown in the High Desert? Could someone drown in a dream? Was this place a dream inside a dream?

My mouth moved; my lips formed the prayer, *Hathor, my Mistress, Gold-of-the-Gods, do not desert me! Every hand stretches out to You, but You accept only the hand of Your beloved. Accept me, Great Goddess, I beseech You.*

But no sound came. It was still a silent world.

A falcon landed on my shoulder, and Hathor spoke in my ear.

"How do you expect to understand what is going on up in the sky, if you do not even see what is at your feet?"

I looked down; a hippo swam by my legs. I grabbed hold of her ears with both hands and pulled my body onto her back.

The hippo turned immense liquid eyes to me and whispered, "I, too, am Hathor, my beloved Isis. Why do you not trust me to carry you to your fate?"

"Isenkhebe Nefrusobek! Isenkhebe Nefrusobek, come back to us!"

The only water was under the boat. There was no hippo, only the frightened face of Maia beside my bed, on her knees next to me. She was in her sleeping gown. Her head was bare; her scalp glowed in the light of the clay lamp she held in her hand. There were no lines of *kohl* around her eyes. She looked panicked; she was frightfully pale. The others sat up on their mats in the corner, staring at me with round, startled eyes.

"Mistress was in the Land of Dreams. I feared she would not return to us. I called and called, but Isenkhebe was too far away to heed my cries."

"Isenkhebe, may I enter?" Qeb-ha's squeaky voice was even more high-pitched than usual.

I nodded numbly to Maia, who opened the slit in the reeds. Qeb-ha rushed to my side. He took my hand and placed his fingers on my pulse. My heart was pounding like a gazelle hunted by Berber dogs. Qeb-ha looked carefully into my eyes as if to reassure himself that I had returned. His concern was so great, I wondered if some people never came back from this Land of Dreams.

"Hathor was with me in the desert—" I started to explain.

"Do not speak of it. Words could summon the dream world to the real world. Do not give it voice."

Qeb-ha's tone said he was sure of the rules. I was sure of nothing.

"The Goddess spoke to me, Qeb-ha, but she spoke in riddles."

"The dream could be a warning. The Gods created the dream to show the dreamer his blindness. A blind man stumbles on any path, even well-paved. How can he hope to navigate a road fraught with danger?"

Once I was fully awake, the dream began fragmenting into vague bits of memory, pieces of a puzzle I hurried to assemble before they disappeared.

I called for papyrus and ink and began frantically describing the images, struggling to recall the right sequence, but the details slipped away faster than I could write. I felt desperate to record the dream before it was lost. I recognized Hathor in both the falcon and the hippo, but who was the Wizard? And what was written on the green stone?

No one spoke. They watched me as I wrote. They seemed frightened by my intensity. I don't think they were convinced I had fully returned. Or perhaps I had come back a different person.

Qeb-ha didn't leave until I finished. Maia brought me a cup of watered wine, and I drank in huge gulps, then lay back exhausted. I felt cold, then hot, then cold again. Pehtes pushed her damp nose onto my cheek and kissed me with her dry, scratchy tongue. If I had been away in the Land of Dreams, she didn't know it. How simple life must be to a cat. How simple life used to be for me.

CHAPTER 15 KHENT-MIN

Screaming baboons in a nearby sycamore grove awakened us before daybreak. Wood smoke blended with the morning mist. The sleeping jetty came alive with workers hurrying to make the most of the day before the heat rose. Before preparing to cast off, our crew drank beer and finished the remainder of last night's broiled fish with fava beans and cone-shaped loaves of bread.

I had seen nothing of the fabled monuments of Abydos with its sacred burial grounds as old as Egypt, older than the first Pharaohs. The head of the god Osiris, King of the Earth and the Underworld, is buried here, beneath the sacred Osireion. There is no place more holy in all Egypt.

"May we not at least see the Wall of Cartouches, Qeb-ha? The Temple of Seti cannot be far."

"We have no time for sightseeing. If Isenkhebe wishes to see the List of Pharaohs, it must be on another visit."

As soon as I saw Qeb-ha occupied, I stepped from the boat to the stone quay. A vendor was setting up his stall a few yards away. My eye went straight to a handsome statue of an ibis, the symbol of Thoth, god of wisdom. The body of the bird was exquisitely carved of rose granite, its head and legs cast in bronze.

I traded my necklace for the piece without haggling; there was no time to bargain. I had a chest brimming with fine jewelry, and this ibis statue was unique. Thoth is the patron of writing and all knowledge. The statue was the perfect gift for my father. Hathor herself had placed the ibis on the wharf for me this morning, of that I had no doubt.

The whole transaction took less time than for Qeb-ha to arrive at my side, panic-stricken that I left the river boat alone.

🐍

A scant hundred feet from the quay, the Royal barge was just getting under weigh. The First Son of Egypt, Psamtik, stood at the rail with his Scribe and the Commander of the Royal Guard.

"Commander," he hissed, pointing his finger to shore. "Do you see that woman? The priestess. Why is she here? Why is she not in Thebes?"

"There are few reasons for a priestess to travel, Your Grace," answered the Commander. "She is most likely on pilgrimage."

"Did you not say, Setne, that she would never leave Thebes? Has my father summoned her? Is she to bear witness to the cleansing ceremony?"

"I cannot say with certainty, my Prince. It could mean nothing. It could mean everything."

As they watched, a priest appeared and hurried her back to the barge.

"Commander," ordered Setne, "I want to know why that priestess has left her Temple."

"Yes, Sir. I shall alert my spies." There was nothing in the Commander's voice or face that hinted at the worry raging in his mind.

O Isis, you do not want the attention of Setne. What foolishness have you been up to now?

River God congratulated himself that he had kept Isis from revealing her secrets their last night in her bed; his allegiance to the Pharaoh would compel him to tell all that he knew. Thank Horus, he knew nothing. Well, nothing his duty required him to report.

🐍

Our winged-cobra sail unfurled against a fiery dawn sky. The barge entered the current of the Nile and was swept downstream. Marshy reeds and high golden dunes lay on the West Bank; low yellow cliffs edged the East. Behind the craggy cliffs stretched the desert in a flat expanse of dun-colored sand to distant mauve hills. Oars rising and falling, the rowers sang a rhyme that kept them in beat as the shore moved swiftly past.

The day suddenly turned breathless. There was no wind at all, unusual for the river at this time of year. The sail hung slack against the mast while the rowers pulled on their oars. Even with the current in our favor, we seemed barely to move. The white light of the sun reflecting off sheer precipices of rugged limestone blinded us.

We had sailed a fair part of the day when Qeb-ha informed me that our next stop was Khent-min.

"Why Khent-min?" I asked.

"The Gods favor it," he replied.

When we arrived at the port, a thick dust cloud hung over the city. The sound of banging and clanging of stone construction carried as far as the docks.

I made one last effort to tempt Qeb-ha to reveal his purpose in this hot and miserable place.

"Have you seen the Serpent of Khent-min, Qeb-ha? They say he gives power to magicians. I read in my scrolls there are more sorcerers here than in any other city."

But Qeb-ha was no fool and would not be led into telling what he did not wish. If we were here for magic, he kept it to himself.

"There are many wondrous sights in the great city of Min. May I suggest Isenkhebe visit the old Temple of Ramses the Great with her ladies? I am told the colossus of Merit-amun, The White Queen, Ramses' daughter and Great Royal Wife, is not to be missed."

"And so now we have time for sightseeing?" I shot back.

My ladies were more than eager to leave the barge. They donned fresh gowns and their best wigs, stained their lips deep purplish red with pomegranate juice and painted thick lines of *kohl* around their eyes.

Accompanied by Goliath and two guards, Ti and Wah, we made our way through the clamor of the docks to Ramses' crumbling temple surrounded by high, thick, never-ending walls. In a terrible state of disrepair, the ancient Pharaoh's fabled complex was undergoing massive restoration.

All around us, scores of workmen in stained loincloths and filthy headdresses hammered and plastered without pause. If we took our hands from our ears and covered our mouths to keep from choking on dust, the banging deafened us.

"Please, Mistress," my ladies begged, "may we not go to the market?

They say Khent-min weaves the finest linen in the world."

But the mammoth market square turned out to be as chaotic and disagreeable as the worksite. Roasting meat and burning incense mingled with the stench of blood and urine.

We were immediately surrounded by small, bird-legged nut-brown boys trying to sell us barley cakes sweetened with honey. Clouds of black, ugly flies swarmed them, and then us.

Canvas-covered stalls selling cloth, spices and beads lined the perimeter. In the center of the square, mountains of snowy white natron used in mummification glittered in the sweltering sun alongside crystal mounds of Sinai salt.

Terrible cries of animals being slaughtered filled the air. Goats, oxen, horses—all screaming at the scent of death. In the southwest corner, a panicked bull dragged four men to their knees.

Only fifty or so feet away, a giant Nubian, nude save for a loin cloth, armed with a curved dagger, slit the throats of one goat after another. With each slash, bright blood sprayed his ebony chest and arms.

When a Bedouin in a bright blue turban and wielding a long whip began to beat at a mob grabbing at Eastern spices newly arrived from the Red Sea, I wanted out. Khent-min market was a vile place, harsh and crude.

But my ladies appeared immune to the horror around us and begged to stay. "Please, Mistress, may we not see the beads? There are so many and so many kinds!"

I gave each a handful of scarab and frog amulets to trade for polished turquoise, carnelian and garnet beads strung on long strands.

"Return to the ship in one hour," I ordered Ti and Wah.

Goliath pushed a path for me through the crowd, and we were almost out of the square when a passing procession of priests forced us to stop next to a stall selling carved figurines of the God Min.

"A blessing for a poor man, priestess?" the vendor asked with a lewd smile of black teeth. "In return, I can offer a souvenir of our city to sweeten the nights."

He was a filthy creature, but his statues were well crafted, and there was something perversely appealing about his daring to tease a High-Priestess.

"I shall bless you with a crocodile charm to make your Min rise," I teased back. "Let us pray one is enough."

He laughed. Even more black teeth showed.

The glossy onyx statue fit neatly in my palm. Jet black and naked, the city's patron god held a flail in his right hand and an erect penis in his left.

"The priestess has her own Min, I see." The vendor cast a sly look in Goliath's direction. "If the Nubian is the lady's taste, she will find more like him at the Temple. It is not far."

It was not difficult to find the Temple of Min. A wide avenue lined with billboard-sized paintings of the god Min and his sacred erection led straight to the pylon.

The Temple was eerily quiet after the din of the city—and dark. Long shafts of dust-filled sunbeams angled to a polished stone floor. Vast murals covered the walls. Most depicted the giant-phallused Min seated at a banquet table piled high with *cos* lettuce oozing white milk from its tall leaves. White bulls and barbed arrows covered a forest of square columns.

No one tried to stop me from entering the inner sanctum. Such a thing would be impossible in a Hathor Temple. Only the highest rank of the cult is allowed inside the *naos*. But if the handful of Min priests busying themselves with offerings objected to the presence of a strange priestess, they didn't signal it.

A ten-foot statue of Min carved from a single block of black basalt towered over us. The Fertility God's phallus was as long as a man's arm and thick as a log.

Kneeling at the white marble altar, I placed a garland of lotus blossoms at Min's colossal feet and sang a hymn of praise memorized in one of many catechism classes for the multitude of gods in the Egyptian pantheon.

Min, Bull of the Great Phallus
You are the Great Male, the owner of all females.
The Bull who is united with those of the sweet love,
of beautiful face and of painted eyes,
The goddesses are glad, seeing Your perfection.

The room was hot and the air thick with frankincense, but not thick enough to mask the smell of sex. Two priests in a trance ejaculated into silver offering bowls. A sea of the silver vessels surrounded Min's gargantuan feet.

Certainly this cult didn't pledge celibacy; the raw sensuality in the air was palpable.

The worship of Min must take many enticing forms, the best hidden in secret sanctuaries behind closed golden doors.

I wandered down a narrow corridor lit by torches in niches populated by mighty basalt statues with monster erect members. Goliath was never more than a step or two behind. If I didn't stumble upon an obliging priest, then perhaps I would find a private corner and measure the Nubian against the new standards set by the God Min.

CHAPTER 16   TEMPLE OF MIN

Pipe music and the sound of chanting drifted through a closed single door. The voices were deep, not at all like the high-pitched chorus in Sit-hathor's temple. I quietly lifted the latch and eased the heavy wood door open just wide enough that I could see inside.

A dozen men or more, all nude, engaged in the worship of the almighty phallus. One bent over, sucking on a second man's penis, while a third penetrated him from behind. Another man penetrated the second and so on, forming an endless Gordian knot of copulating men, who at the same time performed *fellatio*.

At the far end of the small chamber was a low dais with two men seated in ebony chairs. I recognized them at once as the Crown Prince and his Scribe who had shared me in the inner sanctum. Prince Psamtik, his face in a trance, was being serviced by two pubescent boys. A thick wreath of lotus blossoms draped his nude chest.

The Scribe lounged in a chair of carved phalluses with a young child not more than ten between his legs. Their depravity had certainly not been cured by our ritual in Hathor's Inner Sanctum. With the boy's hair gripped in his fist, the Scribe jerked the child's head back and forth, back and forth, in a wild, ruthless rhythm.

Maybe it was my thought of the Goddess that disturbed his psyche. I'm certain I didn't make a sound. Without warning, the Scribe suddenly stared straight at me. His eyes widened. He sat up erect, pushing the boy's head away. The black cloud of evil surrounding him rose in a swarm and rushed at me like a thousand buzzing hornets.

I shoved the door shut with my shoulder, leaning into it for a heartbeat to control my shaking. Heart hammering, palms sweating, I turned to Goliath to motion for us to get out, but it was not the Nubian who stood behind me. The metallic insignia of the Royal Guard flashed in the torchlight.

A hand went over my mouth; another grabbed my upper arm, dragging me around the corner and pushing me through an open doorway. There were no windows and no lighted lamps. It was black as the darkest night. In the hallway outside, the flicker of torches cast dancing shadows.

I struggled to free my arm, but the weight of the soldier's body crushed me to the wall. Terrified, yet resisting with all my strength, I tried to bite the hand on my mouth.

"Stop!" the voice commanded in my ear.

O Hathor, I worship at Your feet for the gift You have brought me!

I looked into the face of River God.

"Say nothing, Isis," he urged. "Nothing at all."

I nodded, and he released his hand from my mouth. My whole body trembled so violently, I'm not sure I could have stood if he hadn't held me up against the wall. In a flood of emotion, I burst into tears of relief.

"Sh-h-h! Listen to me carefully. This is no time for your foolishness. I do not know what madness has brought you here, but the scribe Setne is a dangerous man—capable of any evil. You must leave now. No hesitation. Now!"

I couldn't quite believe it was River God. He felt real enough. His scent was real enough. I touched his jaw and then traced his lips with my fingertip.

"But I thought you were in Thebes," I whispered.

"Prince Psamtik is under my protection. We return to the Pharaoh in Saïs."

I heard the words but was only aware of his heat. I kissed the base of his throat, above his leather chest armor. He tasted of sweat and myrrh. I put my hands on the back of his head and lifted my face to his.

In spite of the tension, I could feel him grow hard against me. Our bodies were so taut that one flick of a finger would shatter us into a million shards. I was fragile as glass.

My life force flowed into him; I couldn't tell where he ended and I began. His hard lips yielded, and he kissed me as tenderly as the night at the Wynn.

Our need for each other bound us so tight, we might have been shackled in chains. But he had the strength to break away.

"Go! You were never here. Do you understand? You were never here."

He released me from the wall, took my arm more gently and steered me down a new corridor, Goliath on our heels. I heard a voice in the distance calling out, "Guard!"

Bright sunlight blinded me when he pulled open a small red door in the rough stone wall. It gave onto a tiny side street, not more than four feet wide.

"Do not speak of what you have seen to anyone, Isis. Do you hear me? Tell no one."

He didn't follow us into the alley but closed the door without a word of goodbye.

O Hathor! River God and I traveled the same river. We both sailed to Saïs. The Universe wanted us together. My feet didn't touch the pavement all the way to the boat.

⮑

The Scribe rose from his chair, draped a loincloth around his hips and entered the hallway as River God made his way back.

"Where have you been?" Setne demanded. "Do you not stand guard?"

"I checked on my men." River God's voice was steady, his face a mask. "Does the Lord Scribe fear for the safety of his Highness?"

"Was there not someone in the corridor? A woman?"

"A woman, Sir? It is forbidden here."

"I saw that Theban priestess. I am certain of it. She has followed us from Abydos to Khent-min."

"Why would she do that, Sir?"

"Perhaps she is here to spy on us."

"I find it unlikely this particular priestess would do her own spying, Sir. I have heard she is too self-indulgent to occupy herself with more than a bath and the hunt."

"You did not mention before that you were acquainted with this woman."

"These are habits of which all Thebans gossip, my Lord Scribe."

Silence. The man was hiding something, of that Setne was certain;

his narrow set, glassy bird-of-prey eyes probed. From the other side of the door came a faint drone of chanting and the muted notes of a lyre. The hiss of the torches roared.

River God surrendered nothing, not a dilation of his pupils, not a glimpse of his contempt.

Finally, Setne turned, pulled on the latch and slithered back into the chamber, dragging the heavy wood door into place after him with a solid *thunk*.

River God allowed his eyes to close and the tension to flow from his body in one long, slow exhale. Isis. He tasted her still, honey-sweet. He had promised himself he would forget her, put her out of his heart. But he knew that wasn't possible the moment he felt her lips on his skin. Isis was not a woman you could forget.

ꟼ

When I returned to the barge, Qeb-ha was frantic with worry. I didn't try to hide my thoughts from him. Two powerful forces had revealed themselves to me in the Temple of Min. I was both terrified and euphoric.

The evil of the Scribe had enveloped him in a black cloud of pestilence visible from across the room, even in the dim light. But my River God loved me. O Hathor! He loved me. I could still smell his desire and need on my skin. His taste, salty-sweet, lingered on my lips.

"I think we should set sail, Qeb-ha. I do believe the Gods would approve."

To my surprise, Qeb-ha didn't reprimand me with a lecture on the dangers of Set in the night but studied for a long moment the banners of the royal barge moored a few hundred yards away.

"Yes, the moon is full, and the river broad," he said at last. "There can be greater dangers than the peril of Set the Destroyer. I shall ask the Gods to forgive our arrogance that we sail tonight."

I finally noticed the young man by his side, dressed in the manner of the Canaanites, heavily robed even in this heat. He had the eyes of a gazelle, soft brown with long lashes; his luxuriant reddish-brown hair fell to his shoulders in tangled waves. He was wide-eyed. I must have looked a sight.

"May I present Eben to Isenkhebe Nefrusobek? He shall travel with us."

I had nothing to say about that. Too much had happened this day for me to question why this stranger would join us now. I knew that with Qeb-ha, there was a reason. I knew that with Qeb-ha, I wouldn't know until he was ready to tell me.

"Be welcome," I said simply, still in a daze. I turned and entered my cabin, ordering the reed curtains lowered, closing out the sights of Khent-min. My heart told me to get away—and get away fast.

℥

Qeb-ha watched the oarsmen maneuver past the royal barge and head out into the current. What had happened today that so frightened Isenkhebe? He perceived shadowy images of men melding into each other, but the details were obscure. He looked around for the Nubian.

The slave could say they had been in the Temple of Min but could not say what his mistress had seen behind the closed door or what the Royal Guard had said to her. Qeb-ha was certain the Nubian told all that he knew. Qeb-ha, who could read the thoughts of men like glyphs on a papyrus, could always tell truth from lie.

He turned to the young man with doe-like eyes.

"Now tell me, Eben, of the magic you bring from Jerusalem. I am fearful we shall soon have need of it."

CHAPTER 17 THE POEM

Time on the river stood still. We flowed past verdant fields more like clusters of gardens than farms. Laborers toiled naked in the fading light, repairing the irrigation canals after the yearly Inundation. The waters had receded, leaving behind rich deposits of nutrients carried thousands of miles from mountains deep in Africa. Freshly planted barley glistened bright green against gold sand encroaching in some places right down to the banks of the Nile.

I kept looking behind us, expecting to see at any moment a yellow sail emblazoned with the Shield and Crossed Arrows of the Saïte Dynasty. But there was no sign of the royal barge.

The youth Eben was reading in the shade of a green and yellow striped canopy. Back straight and legs folded under him, Qeb-ha sat on cushions not far away. A servant waved a palmiform fan to move the still air.

My ladies chattered endlessly about nothing. I was restless, both anxious and bored at the same time.

"May I join you? I have lost interest in the price and beauty of a bead."

They both stood immediately and bowed low from the waist.

I settled on a thick cushion, under a stretch of heavy linen. The unrelenting sun beat down without mercy. Any man not rowing dozed under makeshift awnings. It had been a long, tense night; no one had been happy to be on the river during the hours of Set.

I gave Eben a languid, seductive smile.

"You are from the East, I believe. Yet you speak excellent Egyptian."

"I have family, my Lady, in the Jewish colony at Elephantine."

He was exceedingly shy and reluctant to look into my face; he avoided meeting my eyes. I sensed he had few conversations with women.

When I saw he was not going to speak further, I urged him in a teasing tone, "Please tell me more. Do not be timid. I shall not bite."

"I have lived my life in Babylon, my Lady. My people were expelled from Jerusalem at the time of the destruction of our Temple."

"What other languages do you know?" I asked, switching to Aramaic, the *lingua franca* of the East. Qeb-ha frowned. I don't think he spoke Aramaic, but I assumed he still could read our minds.

"I have studied Elamite and Greek and, of course, Hebrew."

"You speak Elamite? Is it not spoken only among nobles at the Persian court of Cambyses?"

"I trained as a scribe, my Lady."

Perhaps my smile was a trifle too warm. I flirted a little as a way to pass the time. Qeb-ha's eyes bored into me, but I ignored him. Had he not told me that I should live each day to the fullest?

"If you were in Babylon, Eben, you must also have studied the stars."

"My father says that to study the constitution of the sky helps one understand the constitution of the earth. And if one understands the earth, he might learn something of the constitution of men."

The veins on the back of his hand were purplish-blue. His long waves of uncombed hair didn't hide the dark vein throbbing in his temple. Constellations of blemishes dotted his cheeks. A few scraggly hairs tried to form a beard.

"Why do you travel with us, Eben?"

"It is for Qeb-ha to say. I am but a guest."

Qeb-ha and his secrets. He trusted me with almost nothing.

"You have done well, Qeb-ha," I said, switching back to Egyptian, "to include a young man of such education in our group."

Qeb-ha's eyes in his round face widened ever so slightly. The amethyst sparkled in the sunlight as it swayed back and forth. He looked at me, then at Eben, and then back again to me.

I smiled at both of them graciously, but I doubted the Jewish boy sailed with us because of his languages.

The next hours passed quickly. Eben and I bantered back and forth in Greek, Aramaic and even the elusive Elamite-Persian. He sang beautiful psalms in the melodic Hebrew of his tribe. He strummed the four strings of his lyre.

The shadows grew long, and the air cooled. Lone fishermen stood in their shallow papyrus canoes and cast their nets onto the glassy waters of the Nile. Re sank below the cliffs on the West Bank.

We were far downriver from Prince Psamtik and Setne the Scribe. Having rowed through last night, we would stop for this one.

The sound of animals hunting and being hunted carried across the dark water. A herd of hippos growled and thrashed in the reeds; an angry bull could crush a man's bones in its massive jaws with one snap. Instead of sleeping on the shore as was custom, our men would not leave the boat this night.

The crew ate their regular diet of perch broiled on small clay stoves, raw onions and beer. We dined on salted oxen leg and roasted duck with cucumbers, goat cheese, dates and watered wine. Of course, everyone ate bread, always bread.

Qeb-ha sat to one side with Eben and didn't join the idle conversation. He had lost his Buddha aura; lines of worry etched his face.

"What do you fear, Qeb-ha?" I asked. "What do you see?"

"I see Isenkhebe is no stranger to trouble."

"But surely you can read my heart and know that it is pure."

"One cannot know the heart of a woman any more than one can know the sky," he grumbled.

"Do you truly fear what I might do? What of your pledge to be companions on the road and brother and sister in battle?"

"Isenkhebe is a reckless woman of little patience. That gives me much to fear."

The whites of his eyes gleamed in the starlight; his amethyst was only a tiny glint in the dark.

"Can I not convince you, Qeb-ha, that my faults lie only in small things?"

"Small things are also worthy of respect, Isenkhebe. The little bee brings honey. The little locust destroys the grapevine."

"It is a wonder I was chosen by the Goddess, if so unfit," I snapped.

Qeb-ha, for once, had no response. Poor Eben seemed to shrink inside his heavy robe; our words were too personal for a stranger to hear. I'm certain he wanted to melt into the thick river mist surrounding the barge.

There was a long moment of silence. Set's Land of Chaos, the desert, was black, no lights anywhere, on either side of the river.

Above Qeb-ha's head, *Meskhetiu,* the Ox Foreleg constellation, pointed to the unchanging Star of the North.

Suddenly, Eben's pure voice rang out.

As you smile for us you light the Two Lands,
All of Egypt is filled with your presence;
Gods and men look to you,
No evil befalls them when you shine.
The sky with all its stars
is dimmed by your beauty;
Lovely lady floating on the Nile,
when a beggar beholds you,
he forgets his hunger.

As soundless as a shadow, Qeb-ha slipped away without his usual words of benediction. After Eben's psalm of devotion, he must find me more dangerous than ever.

"I am not worthy of your praise, Eben, but I am moved."

I kissed him gently on his cheek; his skin was hot to my cool lips. Hairs from his beard tickled my nose. The rose scent of my oils wafted around us in a heady cloud of sweetness and femininity.

I felt him tremble. Sweet Eben would have to be content with that. He was too young and too delicate for a woman like me.

CHAPTER 18 HERMOPOLIS

Endless green fields of wheat ended abruptly at the fifty-foot thick walls of the bustling port of Hermopolis on the West Bank of the river. Four colossal baboon statues, yet another totem of the city's patron god Thoth, dominated the waterfront. Their huge eyes gazed serenely across the Nile to the barren East Bank.

We moored north of the docks not far from the Gate of the Sphinx at a vast yacht harbor for luxury barges. Hermopolis was known as a center not only for great learning, but also great wealth.

I was glad to be in a city again and anxious to get off the barge. Since the night of the poem, Qeb-ha had avoided me and only frowned from a distance when I talked with Eben.

"The Pylon of Ramses the Great," Eben pointed out. "The twin obelisks were taken from the ancient capital Armana to the south. Do you remember sailing past?"

"I remember that there was nothing to see."

"Yes. It is a tragedy. Armana was once the jewel of the Nile. The Pharaoh Akhenaton built a glorious new city, but it has been robbed of everything over the centuries. Ramses floated over a thousand decorated stones from there to build his temple here."

"You shame me with your knowledge of our history," I teased.

"Akhenaton was a visionary who saw the universe ruled by one god," Eben answered solemnly. "Not the correct god, but he was on the correct path."

Hermopolis was divided by a wide, paved processional avenue running north and south. The noisy Eastside fronted the river; the Nile was clogged with foreign and Egyptian ships carrying raw materials to trade for the city's faience, textiles and grain. The Westside was home to colorful villas, elaborate palaces and splendid temples.

That afternoon, Qeb-ha finally spoke to me.

"We are invited to a banquet at the home of an old friend of mine, Isenkhebe. On the Westside. I believe the Gods favor us to attend."

My ladies emptied the clothing chests to find exactly the right gown. The exquisite gossamer linen clung to my body like film. My skin, oiled and perfumed, had the sheen of a moonstone. Both my shaved mound and my nipples were stained carmine red.

In honor of Thoth, I chose an wide, gold collar necklace with dangling gold baboons and ibises. Hathor in a topless gown, surrounded by graceful nude dancers, decorated my hinged cloisonné armbands. Gleaming from my hand was the lapis lazuli Hathor ring.

Amethysts strung on gold threads twinkled in the glossy black waves of a shoulder-length wig drenched in oil of gardenia. Turquoise stones decorated sandals too fragile for walking. Maia outlined my eyes with thick lines of *kohl* and painted ground mica and malachite on my lids up to my brows. Accented by jet black bangs, my eyes glittered a startling green.

We held nothing back. Even those who saw me every day turned to stare.

I granted Maia permission to attend her first feast. My magnificent beaded collar necklace of semi-precious stones shimmered against her caramel skin. Her face glowed in excitement; she held her head high. Her delicate beauty had not fully bloomed, yet many eyes followed her, hungry for more.

Muscular Nubians, poles lifted to their massive shoulders, carried us on narrow litters hung with silver bells and red tassels.

Old Qeb-ha knew his way around the city. Many recognized him on the avenue and called out greetings as we passed. The townspeople stopped and bowed low along wide avenues lined with shade trees and lavish mansions painted with vivid murals of hunting scenes.

The feast surpassed all expectation. A naked servant girl with cobra tattoos round her brown nipples greeted us with garlands of cornflowers in a fountain courtyard open to stars. Hundreds of small lanterns cast a flattering light, but not bright enough to dim the night sky. The waning moon had just risen. A gentle breeze scattered flurries of myrtle petals like purple snow.

We followed her to the head table flanked by low cedar chairs padded with blue ankh-embroidered yellow linen cushions.

"Sit here, my brother, close by me," our host Ankh-hor shouted with a wide, drunken smile that showed two missing teeth. "It has been too long! You punish me with your absence."

His gold armbands looked too heavy for him to raise his chalice to drink. A broad pectoral of lapis lazuli and turquoise beads woven with filaments of gold covered his mahogany chest.

"You old fox," he boomed. "Traveling with a beauty like this one. What other treasures are you hiding away in that temple of yours?"

Ankh-hor beamed and patted my knee with his jeweled hand, not in a sexual way, but rather like an indulgent father. He really was quite drunk.

Musicians with finger cymbals, harps and wooden pipes played from a trellis dripping in white jasmine. Nude young girls dipped and swayed among the guests. Gold chains hung round their slender hips and ankles; gold serpents twisted round their arms. The tiny silver bells in their waist-length wigs tinkled as seductively as a *sistrum*.

Our host spared no expense. First came ostrich and duck eggs, cucumbers and *cos* lettuce. We nibbled on olives from Cyprus and mounds of fresh goat cheese drizzled with olive oil. Baked swans stuffed with smaller birds dressed with chopped dates, almonds and cracked wheat were followed by fattened cranes roasted in goose fat and garnished with sycamore figs.

The highlight of the evening was roasted wild game seasoned with cumin and garlic. Only the hunt could put ibex, gazelle and aardvark on the table.

"Your taste is exquisite, Sir," I crooned. "I am overwhelmed by your generosity. Surely Hermopolis is the most hospitable of cities and your home the most gracious."

"I am but a small and selfish man, Isenkhebe Nefrusobek. It is said that the Gods give a thousandfold to him who gives to another at a feast. For that, I ask you to partake more, so that we may both be blessed."

"I cannot get my fill of the wild game, Ankh-hor. I love the savage taste of the beast who has fed in the desert. The very air with its raw, heavy scent is captured in the meat."

"Then you shall hunt tomorrow, my priestess. It is my gift to you."

"Is that not exciting, Qeb-ha? I am invited to a hunt!"

Qeb-ha glared at me, shouting silent messages that I chose to ignore.

I felt beautiful and powerful, not the woman Qeb-ha criticized. Ankh-hor admired me—even found me clever. River God loved me. I was Isenkhebe Nefrusobek, on top of the world. Everyone constantly made demands on me; surely sometimes I had the right to enjoy myself.

Admittedly, I had drunk too much wine, but in truth, I was more intoxicated by my own charms than by the grape.

Merciless, I asked Qeb-ha sweetly, "May I tempt you to join us?"

His eyes pierced me like daggers. The monster amethyst dangling from his ear blazed like a purple sun. It didn't take a mind reader to know what he was thinking. I proved more trouble than even he had believed.

"Come, Qeb-ha my friend, do not be such an old man," chided Ankh-hor. "I promise you that I shall send Isenkhebe with my best men. In fact, I shall send her with my second son, a master hunter. There is nothing Hetmus-hor loves more than the chase."

He squeezed my knee and gave me big toothy grin.

"Unless it is a beautiful woman."

"Isenkhebe has duties of her own to which she must attend. This is not a voyage of pleasure, Ankh-hor."

"Nonsense! A beautiful woman deserves to be spoiled. You cannot refuse me. Would you deny me the promise of a thousandfold return on my gift at a feast?"

A guest could no more deny the wishes of his host than a host could say no to a guest. I refused to look Qeb-ha in the eye. I was sick of the boat. I was sick of the river. I was sick of this mystery quest.

I saw myself riding in a fast chariot, bouncing over the desert stones, hooves thundering on the hard ground. A hunt. I would show them what a woman could do.

Qeb-ha, cold and fuming, didn't speak all the way back to the barge. My ladies were undressing me when he slipped inside the curtains. He didn't ask permission to enter.

"Do not go on this hunt, Isenkhebe Nefrusobek."

"But I have accepted the invitation, Qeb-ha. What excuse could I give?"

"Say you are ill. Say anything, but do not go." In his fury, he addressed me directly, as an equal.

"It is you, Qeb-ha, who constantly reminds me of my irresponsible behavior. Am I now to change my mind on a whim and then lie?"

"What of our sacred mission?"

"There is small risk in one hunt, Qeb-ha. I do not ask that we delay our voyage."

"A high-priestess should not hunt; a high-priestess should not kill. It is foolish to take any risk, when there is so much at stake. You disgrace your mother with your selfishness and arrogance!"

I had never seen Qeb-ha angry. His high squeak, almost in panic, pierced my ears. My ladies stood to the side with their eyes cast down.

"The Nubian shall be at my side," I argued. "Ankh-hor's son shall lead the way. There is nothing to fear. The Goddess has chosen me. You said so yourself. She shall protect me as she did in my dream."

Qeb-ha clenched and unclenched his fists. Would he strike me? That seemed impossible, but I had a small doubt. He turned abruptly and pushed through the curtains. The flames in the lamps flickered as his stubby body stormed past.

I knew he was right. I don't know why I wouldn't admit it.

CHAPTER 19   THE AMULET

Maia woke me long before the sun god Re began to light the horizon across the Nile. The last stars disappeared as she dressed me in a linen shift looser than my normal gowns and not sheer at all. Wide sleeves covered my arms to the elbows. My sturdy sandals had only the slightest decoration; the lions tooled on the insoles said I vanquished the untamable forces of the desert.

I chose a simple chain necklace with small gold charms in the shapes of crocodiles, vultures and rabbits. I would be aggressive like the crocodile, abundant as a rabbit and protected by the vulture. The image of the vulture in my dream flashed into my mind, but I pushed it aside.

Gold wires with single amethyst teardrops went in my earlobes. The brilliant purple would ward off evil spirits. The stones reminded me of Qeb-ha, but I resisted all allusion to him and his disapproval. Maia insisted I hang her *tiet* charm from my golden chain girdle; the protective amulet with the cow-eared Hathor dangled on my thigh.

I slipped the Hathor lapis ring with golden horns on my middle finger. The ring was too precious to wear on a hunt, but Qeb-ha had unnerved me more than I admitted. I wanted protection from all sides.

"Bring me my custom bow and quiver of arrows, Maia, and my hunting knife."

Ankh signs and colored glass mixed with semi-precious stones encrusted the dagger's hilt. The edge of the steel blade was razor-sharp.

Eben spoke softly on the other side of the reed curtain, and Maia opened the slit for him to enter. He handed me a tiny leather pouch with a slim leather thong.

"There is a scroll inside."

His eyes begged me to accept it.

"It is a talisman, Isenkhebe, made especially for this hunt."

I unrolled the miniature papyrus and saw it covered in Hebrew letters.

"And what does it say?" I asked, raising my eyebrows in surprise.

"They are words from Kabbalah, the power revealed to Abraham, my people's first prophet. Every Hebrew letter represents a number with secret powers."

"Are you a Kabbalist, Eben? Then you are a magician, as well."

So our visit to Khent-min had involved magic, after all. I looked at Eben with a new respect; I hadn't given him credit for a magician's strength.

"Please wear the amulet, Isenkhebe. Please do not remove it. It offers protection and guarantees a safe return."

"Why would Hebrew magic protect an Egyptian priestess?"

"Our God is the god of all beings, whether they recognize Him or not."

Eben's eyes were deep pools of still water. For a fleeting moment, I thought I might read the future there. Not wanting to see, I looked away and held my arm out to Maia to tie the scroll to my wrist with the leather cord.

"Thank you, Eben. We Egyptians have a saying that an amulet that does no harm protects its owner from it. With the blessings of Hathor and Neith, I shall return with antelope for our late meal."

I shined my brightest smile on him, but my mention of Neith evoked the feeling of dread I had steadfastly ignored. The gnawing in my stomach returned.

"Our paths shall cross again, Isenkhebe."

His eyes glazed over; I'm not sure he saw me at all.

"Our meeting has been of the river,
something stolen from another dream world.
But this is not the beginning of the river.
The water has been living for a long time,
under the ground,
in the mountains,
and among the songs of the desert."

I saw the water in my dream, the underground river spewing onto the sand to form a vast lake. Was this indecipherable murmuring more Kabbalah? I didn't want to think about what Eben meant. Why must everyone talk in riddles all the time?

"Of course, our paths shall cross again, Eben. I shall return with fresh meat for us to savor under the stars tonight. And you shall sing your sweet poetry."

Ankh-hor's ferry pulled alongside our barge. I was lowered in a canvas sling; Goliath and the guards Ti and Wah crawled down a rope ladder.

Qeb-ha was nowhere in sight. He hadn't said goodbye to me. He hadn't given me his usual benediction. He hadn't spoken to me at all since last night.

I waved to Eben and Maia, and Maia waved back. Even from that distance, I could make out the worry in her face. The fragile pair grew ever smaller and smaller as the oarsmen ferried us across the river to the hunting grounds that Ankh-hor boasted were the best in all Upper Egypt.

ᒲ

I didn't see that Qeb-ha watched me lowered over the side, his eyes never leaving my black wig with gold trinkets sparkling in the predawn.

His gaze followed our landing on the other shore and our climbing the embankment to reach the desert plateau stretching forever to the east.

Re had once again conquered the serpent *Apep* of the Underworld and begun to light the sky above the mauve mountains.

The hunting party was silhouetted against Re's golden glow, when Eben came to stand next to him.

"She shall return, Qeb-ha, I know it. I have seen it. The planets and the numbers assure me that she shall."

"Yes, Eben, that is all well and good. The question is when and in what state."

ᒲ

On the western bank of the river, a soldier tied a miniature scroll to the leg of a pigeon and send the bird flying into the air, toward the south. Hours later, another soldier in Khent-min removed the band from the bird's leg and carried the message to his commander.

In Hermopolis. No word of purpose. Priestess (glyph Isenkhebe Nefrusobek) on hunt with son (glyph Hetmus-hor).

A hunt? What foolishness was Isis up to now? He had heard tales of this Hetmus-hor and his useless life of hunting parties and ladies.

The Crown Prince, hoping to catch a breeze from the river, reclined on the royal barge under a canopy of palmiform sunshades. A dozen slaves in white kilts and yellow and white striped headdresses moved the stagnant air with feather fans.

"Your Highness, the Commander has a message from his spies."

"Good! Tell me something exciting, Commander. I do believe I am bored."

"The old priest and the priestess have arrived in Hermopolis."

"Yes? Is that all? Is there nothing more?"

"The priestess is on a hunt with Hetmus-hor, Ankh-hor's second son."

"You see, Setne!" gloated the Prince. "I told you the woman has nothing to do with us. You worry excessively. She is dallying with a man as charming as a courtesan. I venture she has her own pleasures to fill her time.

And well done, Commander. You have proved worthy of our confidence. Now send word to my father the Pharaoh that our voyage has been delayed by pressing business."

PART TWO
HATHOR POWER

CHAPTER 20 THE HUNT

A t the top of the first rise, in the midst of a grove of shady sycamore trees, stood a small hunting lodge of mud brick with a palm thatch roof. More than a dozen chariots with restless horses stirred up clouds of golden dust. The first rays of Re rising glittered off gold-studded vests, the brass trim of carts and the bronze points of spears.

Built for speed, the chariots were so light that a single man could lift one easily onto a boat. Imported birch and elm formed the frames, wheels and axles. The chassis had leather fronts, embellished with paintings of date palm branches or rearing horses facing each other. The cart was mounted forward of the metal-covered axle with the driver and hunter standing close on it. The two wheels had six spokes each. A leather harness attached a pair of thoroughbred horses to the yoke and wooden shaft. Only the wealthiest could dream of owning a hunting chariot.

Packs of tall dogs with long legs ran in circles with tongues hanging out. They snapped and growled at each other but didn't fight. I recognized Berber breeds, the best hunting dogs in the world.

Groups of laughing men in short white kilts and leather vests drank beer and ate barley bread. They no doubt exchanged bawdy tales from last night. I recognized some from the feast. When they noticed me, they grew quiet, bowing from the waist.

My heart pumped in excitement. Hot blood rushed through my veins. I left all my doubts behind. At this moment on the Low Desert, Re a glorious glow at the eastern hills, nothing existed save the stench

of the horse sweat and the baying of hounds. The wildness went straight
to my head.

"Welcome and Blessings, Isenkhebe Nefrusobek! I am Hetmus-hor, son
of Ankh-hor, and honored to lead you in hunt on this most magnificent
of days."

Hetmus-hor stood a head taller than the other men and was covered
in gold. Handsome as Tutankhamun, his smile flashed perfect white
teeth, rare among Egyptians. A white triangular headdress framed a
bronzed face dominated by a high-bridged, straight nose. His shining
red-flecked brown eyes outlined in *kohl* took me in, without an ounce
of shame, from head to toe.

He bent low and kissed the lapis Hathor ring on my hand. When
he straightened, my eyes were on level with his wide chest clad in an
elaborate leather vest patterned in gold sunbursts. Re rising over the
mountains was not brighter than Hetmus-hor.

"My father tells me that you have hunted before. Does that mean
we may run with the dogs and see where they take us?"

"I hunted many times in the desert near Thebes. I have my own bow
with arrows that hunger to fly."

"You shall have my best charioteer," he announced grandly. "My
chariot shall be in the lead. You shall follow directly behind with your
Nubian in third position."

He still held my ringed hand when he lowered his voice and leaned
so close that his speckled eyes were only inches away.

"If that is agreeable to you, Isis?" he asked with a hint of tease. He
dared use my private name, and he knew me not at all. This Hetmus-
hor was indeed a confident man.

"You advance as swiftly as your chariot, sir. Do not spend all your
strength at the beginning of the hunt."

He threw back his head and laughed in delight. It was all a game
to him. He had been born to the hunt. There would be other moves.

"By Horus, I love a woman with wit. If you hunt as well as you speak,
we shall come home with enough trophies for another feast."

I couldn't help but find him appealing. He acknowledged I had a
brain and that I might also be able to hunt. Never dimming his smile,
he took my hand again to lead me to the shade of the sycamore grove.

"Bring wine," he shouted. "Let us toast our honored guest, Isenkhebe

Nefrusobek, who graces us with her beauty and intelligence."

He certainly knew how to flatter and adapted his game quickly when he saw that his compliment to my wit pleased me. It was hard not to be taken in by his charm and confidence. I had the feeling he had never struggled for anything in his life.

Servants appeared with tin goblets of heavily watered Delta wine and passed them to the nobles who gathered around us. Charioteers and servants stayed with the horses and took clay cups filled with beer. The morning air was splendid in the early sunshine, with no trace yet of the heat that would rise as the day swelled.

Hetmus raised his goblet to me.

"May thou spend millions of years,
thou lover of Thebes,
Sitting with thy face to the north wind,
thy green eyes beholding felicity."

He had taken the words from the inscription on an ancient royal wishing cup, but added 'green eyes.' He was charming, no doubt about that.

One of the nobles called out, "A toast to the kill!"

Everyone, including the slaves and servants, cheered. I'd never felt more alive.

We flew across the sand and stone. I balanced on the rawhide flooring woven like strings on a tennis racket. Hares and wild dogs fled when we passed. Gazelle and oryx grazed until we thundered toward them, Berber dogs in the lead. Legs leaping through the air, horns high, the wild herds scattered to the winds.

I raised my prized bow, a composite made from layers of wood, sinew and horn. Its draw weight had been specially engineered for a woman's strength. I bent the bow to full shaft length and let fly an arrow with a barbed bronze head designed to kill. The arrow arched in the blue sky, then dropped with precision into the flank of a doe. She stumbled and fell. The dogs were on her at once.

"Behkai! Abaqer!" Hetmus barked the names of the pack leaders, commanding them in Berber to back off.

They circled the fallen animal, snarling, tongues panting, saliva dripping in long strings. The other chariots gathered around, horses snorting and pawing the ground, anxious to run again. Dust welled up in swirling clouds.

Hetmus pulled up beside us, dismounted and extended his hand.

"It is your kill, Isis. The first kill of the day."

His red-flecked eyes glowed with pride.

I stepped down from the chariot and walked with shaking knees toward the wounded doe thrashing on the ground. Hetmus parted the snarling dogs with kicks and Berber barks, and I followed the path he blazed through the pack and the blood.

The female lay helpless, dark crimson flowing from her wound onto the golden sand. She turned her eyes toward me, big, brown and liquid. I saw Eben's eyes and stopped, not wanting to go farther.

"Come, Isis, give thanks to Neith and then put the animal out of her misery," Hetmus said gently.

His tender tone surprised me. There was more to this nobleman than charm. He nodded his head and smiled to reassure me, his eyes saying, *You can do it.* Then he handed me a knife, but not my knife. I shook my head and drew my jeweled dagger from its tooled leather sheath hanging on my hips.

After offering a silent prayer to Neith, goddess of the hunt, and another to Hathor, asking her forgiveness, I went to my knees, took the doe's muzzle in one hand and drew the steel blade deep across her throat, from ear to ear. Hot blood gushed onto my white gown. I felt both ill and elated. My hands trembled.

"Isenkhebe, Isenkhebe, Queen of the Hunt!" the men cheered.

The dogs howled at the scent of fresh blood, and Hetmus smacked one with his spear to keep him away.

My charioteer hauled the carcass onto our cart and draped her over the railing, the head flopping down toward the ground, blood still pouring from the wide gash. Her eyes were open but sightless. They were already drying in the heat. Flies swarmed in an instant; they must hatch in the very air.

Blood oozed from the flank wound and fell in droplets. Spots splashed on the tops of my feet and the hem of my caftan. The doe's heart no longer beat; the drops fell from the pull of gravity. By the time we returned to camp this afternoon, the animal would be bled.

The wind shifted suddenly and blew from the south with vengeance.

Horses spooked and pulled at their reins; charioteers used all their strength to hold them in check. The hounds, lapping up blood-soaked sand, stopped and raised their noses, sniffing the charged air.

My gown whipped around my legs. I clutched the chariot rail for fear of being blown off, looking around frantically for something—anything—to protect my face from the biting sand. Holding on with my left hand, I bit the sleeve of my gown and used my bloodied, jeweled dagger to saw off a strip of cloth. In spite of the wind and the jolt of the chariot, I managed to wrap the linen around my nose and mouth.

I would have crouched down in the chariot, but there was only room for two to stand. My driver struggled with the horses; they reared up on their hind legs and pawed the air.

A brown wall approached, sweeping across the plateau as we stared. Hetmus shouted vainly into a wind that roared like ten thousand lions. I couldn't hear what he yelled but assumed he ordered us to head back to the camp.

The charioteer pulled on the reins with all his might. At last our white steeds put their hooves to the ground, but when they did, they refused to turn toward the west. Instead, the horses bolted north in a desperate attempt to outrun the storm.

I hung on with both hands. Shouts faded behind us. The dead doe's head flopped wildly as we rolled over rocks and bounced high in the air. The wheels of our chariot scarcely touched the earth. The driver never took his eyes from the backs of the horses and the treacherous ground ahead.

A wrathful wind became impossibly more vicious, and sand quickly enveloped us in a dense fog. I could no longer see the tails of the horses. Soon, I couldn't see the charioteer, who stood so close beside me that I felt his body movements in the thick dust.

He battled the horses and drove blind. We were thrown from side to side with such force that I would have flown from the cart if not hanging on with both hands. I don't know how he could stand. The reins, taut in the pull between man and beasts, were his only anchor.

There was no time or space in the thick haze. I felt a terrific jolt when the chariot collided with something I couldn't see. Then we were flying, the wind swirling all around us. Had we been taken up into the sky?

We crashed in soft powder, and I was thrown from the chariot. I rolled, tumbling through a storm of sand, caught in swells as wild as any tempest at sea. I tried to stand up, but the force of the wind and sand kept me on my knees. The more I struggled, the deeper I sank.

I stretched out on my stomach, my head pointing away from the wind, my arms up to shield my head, the remaining sleeve of my dress for cover. The blowing sand cut my skin like a thousand shards of glass.

I could barely swallow through the dust in my throat. Pursing my lips, I forced myself to inhale through my nose and not take sand into my lungs. A person could drown in sand. It had happened many times in such a storm. I could be buried and never seen again.

Where was the driver? He must have been thrown, too. I thought him on the other side of the chariot, although he could have been thrown forward over the horses.

The horses! Where were the horses? I could hear nothing but the howling wind. It seemed to go on for hours. Drowsiness overcame me. A hippo in soothing water swam by but didn't offer me a ride.

Why hadn't I listened to Qeb-ha? Why hadn't I listened to my own heart? Even a fool acts wisely if he follows his heart.

"O Qeb-ha! Forgive me. I am a fool!"

My thoughts crawled through sand, and my mind ground to a standstill. Silence engulfed me; I could no longer hear the wind. I was grateful. They say that silence conceals foolishness. I would hide and pray that my fate might pass me by.

CHAPTER 21 LION

I coughed once. Nasty brown phlegm came up. My eyes were dry and filled with grit. The weight of the sand lay heavy on my back and legs, but there was an air pocket around my head that allowed me to breathe shallowly without gulping dust into my lungs.

There was barely enough space for me to move; the muscles in my arms cramped from being so long in the same position. I managed to use my hands to clear a tunnel to the surface. I could see daylight. Was it the same day, or had I slept through the night?

The sand wouldn't budge when I tried to rise, so I pulled myself forward, like a snake slithering out of a hole. At last I crawled free, sand streaming from my face, and rose numbly to my knees. There was nothing around me except a river of hot sand ending at the high sides of a *wadi*, the dry river bed now choked with fine, gritty powder blown in from the storm.

My raw skin, chafed red from the blasting sand, was on fire. But I lived.

My caftan, once snowy white, was filthy. Brown dust had settled in the fibers of the weave; a dark splotch covered the bodice. Blood. It seemed a lifetime ago since I slit the helpless doe's throat.

The chariot had to be close by. Had the driver survived? I saw no sign of the horses. Could creatures so large be buried out of sight? Nothing in the sand indicated a horse or chariot entombed beneath the surface.

I couldn't walk in the deep sand on my shaking legs so crawled on my knees in what I hoped was the direction of the chariot. I was unbearably thirsty; my tongue swelled and filled my whole mouth. My lips were cracked. When I tried to moisten them, no saliva came. The desert had tried to suck the life from me, but still I breathed.

My knee banged against something hard, and I touched the shaft of the chariot in the sand. It must be standing on its end. The horses had simply disappeared. I clawed at the sand in a state of near hysteria; I couldn't bear the thought of being alone—alone in a silent Universe.

The hunting dagger with jeweled hilt was still tied around my hips. My bow and arrow must be buried with the chariot. Water! We carried goatskins of water for a day of hunt. I dug and dug and never looked up.

I didn't see the horsemen on the top of the rise. I didn't see the sun glinting on their metal trappings. I didn't see the leader signal the three men to dismount and climb down the steep sides. If I had seen, what could I have done?

They were on me without warning. One came up from behind and grabbed me by the waist, just as I saw his shadow on the ground. I screamed. My fear echoed off the rock walls of the dry river bed. Surely if I screamed loud enough, I could wake myself up back in Las Vegas.

We struggled in the sand; my attacker kept sinking deeper. I fought with all my might but was no match at all. They were so strong that one man could easily carry me, but I made it difficult. One grabbed my feet, another my shoulders, and they dragged me between them as they stumbled for footing.

At the top of the ridge, they dropped me onto the rocky ground. The men were angry, hot from exertion and humiliated that a woman could have caused them so much trouble. The brute who had grabbed my shoulders kicked me in the side with a foot encased in a heavy sandal lacing up to his knee.

"Stop! She's no good to us dead or broken."

A harsh voice. I recognized the guttural words of Aramaic.

I was pulled to my feet to stare straight at a golden lion with massive legs and curled mane glinting in the sun. The Lion of Persia! They were Persians! How could they be here, so close to the Nile?

I had been too busy fighting to look at their faces. They had full beards decorated with colored ribbons and real hair, not wigs, to their shoulders. They were all of the same build, stocky and powerful, with the muscles of oxen. Their calves looked as big around as my waist.

They were on horseback; Egyptians prefer the chariot. The horses looked like their masters—massive chests, long manes braided with ribbons and ferocious eyes. They constantly snorted and pawed at the ground. What did the Persians feed them to make them so wild?

A man threw a filthy, coarse wool cape over my head and tossed me onto a horse. I hung upside down, belly across the felted pads used as saddle. In my mind's eye, I saw the doe draped across my chariot rail, her head bouncing as we rolled. This was swift justice from the gods. Neith would have her vengeance, after all.

The rider mounted behind me, and the horses thundered off. I could not tell in which direction but felt certain they would not head west toward the Nile.

What of Hetmus-hor? Had he made it out alive? And Goliath? Had he lost his life to follow me on this folly? Or did they search for me? Would they come, but too late?

☙

Hetmus-hor hadn't shouted to return to the hunting lodge but to form a circle with the flipped over chariots. With the unhitched horses in the middle, the men crouched in their shelters and lasted out the storm. When they had dug their way out and calmed the animals, a somber Hetmus faced the grim reality.

Isis had been under his protection. He couldn't return to his father and say he had lost her in the desert. His family's honor would not survive this shame. *He* might not survive it. But it was not fear of the consequences of her loss that brought him to despair.

He remembered her shining emerald eyes when she made the first kill and how her eyes clouded over when she saw the animal's suffering. Yet she had the courage to draw the blade in one movement, without hesitation, deep into the doe's throat.

There was much to admire in her. This priestess awakened new feelings. He had known and forgotten a thousand beautiful women, but no one like Isis.

Hetmus allowed the hunting party some of the water and refreshed the horses. Most of the dogs had perished in the storm. He ordered the hitching of a chariot and called for Goliath.

"Return to Hermopolis for help. Go to my father Ankh-hor."

But instead of mounting the chariot, Goliath stood with his feet apart, massive shoulders slumped and head down.

"Why do you stand here? Go, I tell you. We have no time to waste."

Goliath shook his head, his eyes still lowered.

"Nubian! We have survived the storm together! Do not force me to use the whip."

Goliath raised his eyes and looked straight at Hetmus.

"The whip is nothing. I have lost her. If I cannot find her, I wish for death."

It was the anguish in the Nubian's eyes that moved him—and the terror, not of the whip, but of the loss of Isis.

"Stay, man," Hetmus said, putting his hand on Goliath's shoulder. "Stay and find your mistress."

A chariot raced back toward the Nile; the others spread out in pairs to canvass the wide plain.

They explored the desert in quadrants, returning at regular intervals to organize a new grid. There was no sign of the chariot or Isis. The desert had simply swallowed them up. The sun god Re began his descent for the night; the last rays of heat cast long shadows on the rocks.

Hetmus himself came upon the tracks in the sand. Horses. There were several and with riders. The trail headed northeast. He backtracked to the edge of the *wadi* and saw the riders had dismounted. Their prints made a riotous, chaotic pattern in the dirt. It was impossible to be certain how many had been there, but he guessed five or six.

From the edge of the ridge, he saw the indentation of sand around a large object. A chariot?

He climbed quickly down the side. There were signs of digging and struggle. Then, in the last rays of sunshine reaching the depths of the ravine, he caught a tiny glint of gold. Lying on the brown sand was the delicate *tiet*, the amulet of Hathor he had seen dangling on her thigh.

Isis was alive. She had tried to dig out the chariot. He had at least that to rejoice, but the report to his father could hardly be worse. The priestess Isenkhebe Nefrusobek, daughter of Sit-hathor, the highest priestess in the land, had survived the sandstorm but been carried into the desert by unknown men on horseback. They could not be Egyptians; she would never have struggled.

Who knew what wrath would fall on his father's house? It was said that even the Pharaoh feared Sit-hathor's power.

Returning to the others with the gold *tiet* in his hand, Hetmus sent another chariot back to the Nile, this time for armed reinforcements. His party of rich nobles was equipped to hunt antelope not men, but he would not return without Isis or at least knowing where to find her. The horsemen couldn't be far ahead; he turned to follow the trail northeast.

He told himself over and over that no one would harm an Egyptian priestess. The price was beyond thinking.

He prayed he was not too late to gods he didn't believe in—Horus, Thoth, Hathor and any other that came to mind. He prayed last to Set for mercy and to set aside his evil for just this night.

CHAPTER 22   THE GENERAL

I lost track of time but don't think we rode that far before stopping. Feet, belonging to man and horse, were all I could see. I was so thirsty. I had never imagined such a thirst, the pain beyond bearing. I would sell my soul for a sip of water.

We were in a camp. I could tell by the clanging sounds and the many voices, but I couldn't see much beyond the dusty, hard ground. The earth had been churned up in a mad pattern of footprints and horse hooves.

Rough hands dragged me from the horse and threw me over a shoulder. I had no strength or will left to struggle. Helpless, exhausted and near despair, I blamed only myself.

We swept through wool panels into a tent, and I was tossed down on thick carpets like a sack of old rags. The room quieted. My captor prostrated himself beside me. He didn't speak.

"What is this?" The voice was more growl of a beast than man, but I guessed an educated beast from his accent.

I silently blessed my father for my language tutors; I felt paralyzed with fear, but at least I understood the Aramaic, understood what was being said.

"We found her in the desert, General, after the Great Storm. She was alone, her chariot and horses buried in the sand."

"Idiots!" the General roared. "Why did you not leave her there to die?"

The prostrate man beside me kept his face buried in the carpet. Out of the corner of my eye, I saw his trembling hands.

"Show her to me," commanded the General.

A rough hand grabbed my arm and dragged me to my feet. The foul-smelling cape was pulled away, and I stood as straight as I could, considering the beating my body had taken. Every muscle screamed from bruise and dehydration. My caftan, one sleeve jagged from the cut of my blade, was filthy with the dust of the storm and the stain of blood.

I faced six standing men around a wooden table covered with scrolls. They wore their hair in the same shoulder-length plaits entwined with colorful ribbons. No one shaved his facial hair; every beard was carefully groomed into long curls.

Leather military waistcoats, armored with small metal plates and emblazoned with the golden lion of Persia, covered their massive chests. A double-edged *akinaka* thrusting sword hung from each belt. I could tell by their bearing these men were high-born. This was no small raiding party.

An ogre with bulging eyes and thick lips moved so close to me, I could smell his foul breath and the sweat under his perfume. He appraised me from head to foot, like a man in a brothel before making his choice.

"She is no ordinary Egyptian, my General. Look at her jewelry. There could be a fine ransom here."

The lion roared louder.

"Imbeciles! If she is a woman of importance, do you not think they will be searching for her? Do you suppose she was in the desert by herself, driving her own chariot?"

He moved slowly toward me, a great bulk of a man with the soul of a beast. When he fingered the necklace of gold charms at my throat and lifted a tiny crocodile, his hand grazed my chest, and my skin crawled.

But I knew his character by that choice. This was a man who lusted, and not only for power.

I forced myself not to flinch but to stand perfectly straight, head high, concentrating on breathing slowly, ignoring my racing heart.

"Well, she is here now. There is no changing that."

His face turned thoughtful; he studied me from under half-closed lids. I sensed he formulated a plan, but he never took his eyes off my face.

"They are looking for her. Place extra guards. Follow the tracks backwards and erase them. Post men five miles down the ravine toward the southwest."

Three men left the tent immediately.

He put his heavy sandal on the back of the neck of my prostrated captor and bore down. The man didn't move, but now his arms as well as his hands shook. I think his whole body quaked.

"You made an unwise choice," the General chided, not looking at the soldier, never taking his eyes off me.

I met his look without blinking, determined not to show fear.

"But perhaps these emerald eyes bewitched you. I shall decide your fate when I decide hers."

The soldier slithered forward on his stomach and kissed the General's other foot. My green eyes had saved his life for the moment—and mine.

"Get her cleaned up. Get her out of those rags. Feed her."

He turned his back and went again to the scrolls.

They were not going to kill me, at least not right away. He wouldn't have ordered me to be fed. I had no idea how much time had passed since I had eaten, but I couldn't feel hunger when my need for water was so desperate. A person can live weeks without food, but without water, the desert sun can suck the life from you in one day.

Three women came to me when I entered the tent. The guard grunted orders about bathing and food, and then turned and exited without a glance back.

They touched the soft linen of my spoiled gown and rubbed it between their fingers to appreciate the delicate weave. They removed my wig and passed it around, fingering each golden trinket. One put a small piece between her teeth and bit down. Her eyes grew wide when she recognized gold. They toyed with the amethysts hanging from my ears, shrieking when they realized the stones weren't glass.

Exhausted, I couldn't stand. I hurt everywhere. Purple bruises from the struggle at the chariot already marked my raw skin. It would take days to heal, but I didn't know if I had days. I didn't know if I had hours.

When they removed my ruined caftan, I saw that the *tiet* amulet Maia had given me was gone. I took it as a sign that I would never see her again. Hathor had deserted me. Neith had her revenge. I had no protection. The small charms of my necklace were but mere trinkets of beauty. The chest of magical amulets was on the barge, a universe away.

I sobbed and sobbed, rocking back and forth like Eben in one of his trances.

The women ignored my anguish; misery must fill every moment of their lives. They tried to untie the leather thong that held the Kabbalah amulet on my wrist, but I slapped their hands away. My eyes blazed. That shocked them. They stepped back. They were afraid of angry green eyes.

A servant brought water at last, and I gulped it down so quickly that it came right up again. The next time I sipped slowly, small swallows with time in between to settle. I began to feel human again. I told myself that I would survive even this.

Hot water flowed from brass jugs into deep copper basins. The women sponged me from the crown of my shaved head down to my henna-tipped toes. They wore their own hair. How did they keep clean and free from vermin in these stuffy tents with no bathhouses?

A young girl, scarcely more than a child really, with a perfect oval face like Maia's, smeared balm on my cracked lips. Her touch was soft, almost timid, as Maia touched me. I was certain that her smile would also be Maia's. I despaired once more of ever seeing that smile again.

O Hathor! If You grant me another chance, I shall forsake my selfish path and follow only Your will.

But more than Maia's smile, I despaired of never seeing Barb's.

O Barb! Call me! Wake me up! Bring me home!

The women massaged my bruised body; my skin soaked up the warm oils like a sponge. They polished my nails with a pumice stone, smoothing the broken edges. My beautiful hands! Cut and blistered raw. Gold gleamed from the horns in the ring that matched my mother's. It gave me strength to see it on my middle finger, a reminder that I was Isenkhebe Nefrusobek, High-Priestess of Hathor.

Finally, I was clean, oiled and perfumed. They brought me a splendid robe of floral-patterned yellow silk, spun from the worms that live only in the East. But even it rubbed painfully against my skin; I grimaced when they slipped it around my shoulders.

A long, sapphire blue sash with golden tassels and tinkling bells went around my waist. The girl with slanted eyes and high cheekbones put delicate slippers on my feet, curled-up toes in front, open in the back. They had been woven from thousands of red silk threads.

The hot tisane was syrupy sweet, overgenerous with honey. A platter appeared with rice and mutton stewed with figs and raisins. I choked down the meat. Isis had never eaten sheep. No Egyptian of status ever ate the flesh of a goat—or pig or fish.

They brought me a small pipe and bade me to smoke. The scent was sweet. I drew one deep breath, coughed and pushed the pipe away.

My eyes drooped. I floated above the rich carpets and drifted between the poles of the tent.

A rough, guttural voice broke through the trance, and two men in leather vests with curved daggers in their belts stood over me.

"Come," they growled in a crude Aramaic and hauled me to my feet.

CHAPTER 23 ISHTAR

Only heartbeats later I was back in the tent with the table of scrolls, thick carpets, rich pillows and glowing lamps. *How did they transport such luxury to this wasteland?*

The guards pushed me first to my knees and then my face into the dusty rug.

"On your face, Egyptian whore, before the great General Sher, Lion of the Desert and Beloved of Cambyses, King of the World."

The General reclined on cushions, his uniform replaced with a robe, silk like mine, but deep green.

"Bring her up to her knees. Let us see her face washed of desert filth and tears."

They pulled me to rest on my haunches, the saffron gown flowing around me, shimmering like gold in the yellow of the oil lamps. The women had cleaned my wig and covered it with a long scarf of emerald silk, woven with gold thread in an intricate arabesque pattern. It cascaded around my shoulders in stark contrast to the yellow of the robe. My amethyst earrings glittered in the lamplight.

The same officers were there and still in uniform. They stood while the General lounged. Unlike Egyptians, the *kohl* was drawn around their eyes to make them appear perfectly round. They stared at me. I didn't need a mirror to tell me how I looked. I saw it clearly by the lust in their eyes. But I saw hatred, too.

They talked to each other without looking away from my face. They spoke Elamite-Persian, not the Aramaic of the soldiers. I understood it well enough to hear them discuss if I should be killed now and taken down to the plain and dumped. They reasoned that a search party would find me and take my body home. Any Egyptians looking for me would leave.

The officers fell silent when the General rose from his seat. He loomed over me, a great bull with a massive chest and legs like the thick columns of a temple. I looked up into his eyes and saw a slight spark of something human.

I refused to look away but willed my eyes to be unreadable, forcing myself to show no fear. No one spoke or moved. The wicks in the lamps spluttered, making small hissing sounds like a thousand serpents.

"Leave us."

He never took his eyes away from mine. We had locked into battle, and I didn't imagine him a man accustomed to defeat. I steeled myself not to waver.

The tent emptied in seconds, and we were alone. When the last man had exited, his face relaxed a fraction; an ironic smile curved his lips. He still stared at me but with less intensity.

It was he who turned away first. He reached for a goblet on a brass tray set on a short wooden tripod and sank again onto his cushions, contemplating me from across the carpets.

"I shall call you *Ishtar*," he said idly in Elamite. "You are the glittering evening star in a lavender desert sky."

I had heard that all Persians are poets. I thought of Eben and his poem on the river under the stars. Would I ever again hear his sweet song?

"I am worth much to my people," I said in Aramaic. "They will pay well for my safe return."

My voice rang out strong and clear, reflecting none of the terror I felt.

The General sputtered into the wine cup he held to his lips, no doubt stunned that I had spoken without his permission and in flawless Aramaic. I would not let him know I also understood Elamite, his private language of noblemen.

"You speak Aramaic? But are you not Egyptian?"

"I am Theban but speak several tongues, Your Excellency."

I thought it wise to use a title of respect. The man held my life in his thick fingers.

He studied me for a few long moments, first watching my expression, then savoring the curves of my body in the silk gown. His hooded eyes settled on my hand with the Hathor ring on the middle finger.

"The ring you wear. Is it not the symbol of Hathor?"

"Your Honor is well-schooled in Egyptian theocracy that he recognizes the horns of our Cow Goddess."

He ignored the compliment. His world is populated with sycophants.

"What does it mean that you wear the ring of the Goddess of Love?" he repeated impatiently.

"Hathor is more than the Goddess of Love, esteemed General. She is the Solar Goddess, the Gold-of-the-Gods."

"Do not presume to instruct me in the inferior gods of Egyptian dogs," he snapped. "Why do you wear the ring?"

His face had gone hard—I couldn't afford to anger him. I counted to ten silently, and when I answered, I was careful to modulate my voice, keeping it low and respectful.

"I am a High-Priestess in the cult of Hathor, Your Eminence. There are only two rings such as this in all Egypt; I am one of two who may wear them. I assure you the Temple will pay whatever you demand for my return, safe and untouched."

"And if you are *touched*? What then, High-Priestess of Hathor?"

He smirked and almost—but not quite—smiled. One eyebrow arched. I thought I saw the hint of a twinkle in his eye. He was amused.

There was no amusement on my side. I stared back at him, not quite defiantly, but still unflinching and unyielding, clearly signaling I would not fold under his intimidation.

Morphing before me again, his eyes went cold and soulless with the beady stare of a predator. Only moments before, I had felt a connection. The General was a chameleon, a hybrid of bull and lion, with only occasional glimpses of man.

"I am not in need of a ransom from effeminate Nile priests," he dismissed my offer in a voice as frigid as a winter wind.

He sipped his wine, watching me over the rim of the goblet. I could tell he waited for my response. Everything depended on the next moment—my future and my life.

"Is it possible for a lion of Persia to have needs not met?" I asked boldly, meeting his look with more than a hint of promise in my eyes.

I saw his pupils dilate, even surrounded by the coal black orbs. His eyelids jerked slightly; I had touched a nerve. He tried to keep his face stone, but revealed all in the blink of his eye. No matter his words, he was a man of many needs, some never met.

◝

The hunting party chariots raced at full speed across the flat plain and into the low hills, Hetmus-hor at the lead. Up steeper and steeper paths he forced the horses, following a rough trail winding through ravines between sheer cliffs. He would have kept going, but his friends at last convinced him to stop. The horses and men needed rest. Night was falling. The terrain was too treacherous to risk in the dark. The moon would not rise for an hour.

◝

Yet another soldier bound a tiny scroll to a carrier pigeon's leg and let him loose to wing south. It was with panic and rage that River God read the note.

Sandstorm. (glyph Isenkhebe Nefrusobek) lost. Struggle. Taken by unknown horsemen. (glyph Hetmus-hor) in pursuit.

The fool Hetmus-hor! This would never have happened if she had not been with that worthless idler. What kind of man loses a woman on a hunt? Especially a woman like Isis.

River God had regained his control when he reported to Prince Psamtik. His face a mask, his voice level, he appeared calm and detached; his stony eyes gave no hint of the fury raging inside.

"The priestess was caught in a sandstorm on the hunt, my liege, and then taken by men on horseback. We know not who they are, but it is highly unlikely they are Egyptians. There were signs of a struggle. The son Hetmus-hor, a civilian unequipped to handle the task, is in pursuit."

"Kidnapped? Great Gods! Did you hear that, Setne? The priestess has been kidnapped. How is that possible?"

"Were they not hunting close to the Nile, Commander?" demanded Setne. "What is the meaning? You know so much about this woman." He turned to the Crown Prince. "This could be a ruse, Your Grace."

"Whatever can you mean, Setne? Ruse? What wild imaginings do you now entertain?"

"A trick of our enemies at Court, Sire. A way of sequestering the woman, of bringing her to your father without our knowledge."

"Let us ask the Commander. He is the military man. Tell us, Commander. What are *your* thoughts? Horsemen? Near the Nile? Is that not most unlikely?"

"It is most unusual, Your Grace."

"But who would dare to take an Egyptian priestess? It is madness. It...it is a supreme insult to my father's house! To *my* house."

"May I speak freely, Your Grace?"

"Speak! I command you to tell us your true mind."

"I propose to leave immediately for the north and personally investigate the disappearance of the priestess. It is my belief the Pharaoh would desire it so."

"Yes!" the Prince shouted. "An excellent idea! Who better than you, Commander, to discover the truth about this priestess? My father praises you as his most capable captain—and he is a harsh judge, indeed."

"Well, Setne, is it not a superb solution? What think you on this?"

Setne didn't like the idea at all, but he had only vague suspicions about the Commander, nothing concrete. As hard as he tried to pierce his armor, the man revealed nothing. Whatever he was up to, he was discreet. But the Commander was hiding something. Setne had known it since the day in the Temple of Min when he had seen the priestess. His eyes hadn't fooled him. He was certain the woman had been spying on them. And certain the Commander knew it.

But as Psamtik had just declared that his father held the Commander in the highest regard, he had no choice but to keep silent. No man, not even one under the protection of the Crown Prince, could question the infallible judgment of the Pharaoh.

CHAPTER 24   THE TEST

The General sipped from his goblet and drew smoke from his pipe. I smelled the same sweet scent as I had in the women's tent. Only a narrow slit beneath thick lids showed the hard glint of his eyes.

"I have a proposal for you, Ishtar. I sense you like a challenge. I hear that certain priestesses of Hathor have—what shall we say?—exceptional talents. Your reputation reaches as far as Persia."

He hesitated only long enough for his words to sink in.

"If you please me, you shall belong to me and me alone, but only for as long as I am pleased. When you no longer please me, I shall return you to the women's tent, where you can please the other men. And when you please them no more, I shall have you killed."

I watched his lips move in his impassive face. How easily he talked about my inevitable death. It had been decided; it was only a question of when.

"But because you are a High-Priestess, I shall return your body to your temple, so that the priests can mummify you, and you can live forever in your Egyptian dream of eternity."

Silence.

"What do you say to that, Ishtar?"

Not more than one minute passed. Instead of answering, I rose from my knees to my feet in one movement. I no longer felt the pain in my body. I glided slowly toward him. The emerald scarf slipped from my head to the carpet; the gold in my black wig glittered. The silver bells on my sash jingled seductively, like the tinkle of the *sistrum*.

I fixed my eyes on his and knelt at his feet. I took the goblet from his hand and placed it on the brass tray beside his cushions.

They teach in the Temple that there is a sexual power inside us that, when summoned, oozes from our pores. It is an animal energy that conjures up base desire. But the magic of Hathor is special; it transforms raw lust into a promise of pleasure and satisfaction known only to the Gods.

I turned on the Power. My body radiated animal sex mingled with the potent allure of intense sensuality—and deep mystery.

"I have secrets," my aura teased. "Wonderful secrets that only I can share."

Electricity sparked in the air. Great sensuous waves rolled over the General. Mesmerized, he barely breathed, his eyes fixed on my every movement.

I slowly untied the purple silk sash of his robe. I pulled it free in one long, smooth motion. He felt its slick slide across the small of his back.

I opened the front of his gown, folding back the rich cloth without hurry. I never took my eyes from his. His breathing came shallow and fast.

He was nude under the robe. I let my eyes wander. I caressed him with only my gaze, appreciating the muscles of his broad chest with its mass of thick, curly hair like a beast. His nipples were already erect. I looked long at them but did not touch him.

The line of hair down his hard belly crossed his navel and descended into a great black bush. His thighs were thick tree trunks.

I leaned back on my heels to study him. My eyes lingered on his manhood, erect and hard, thick as my fist, an obelisk to the sky with huge swollen sacks at its base. The man was truly a bull.

I started with the sacks. I took one in my mouth while I gripped the other in my hand—hard. The General gave an involuntary cry. I sucked harder and gripped harder. The rougher my touch, the more he moaned.

When I felt him near the edge, I stopped and traced my tongue up the throbbing vein, massaging his balls gently, a new caress, light and ethereal.

When I arrived at the head, I eased his foreskin down with my fingers, pulling harder and harder, the skin stretching almost to breaking point.

Squeezing his shaft in my fist, I pumped him up and down, up and down, in a steady rhythm. He thrust his hips for me to go faster, but I stayed in control. I took my time, tormenting him with his own urgency.

I slowed and put my tongue to the head, exploring the surface, licking its smoothness, biting with my sharp teeth. One hand held the shaft; the other was back on his balls, first rough, then gentle, then rough again.

The General twisted and panted. Each time he came close to exploding, I stopped. How many times could I bring him to the edge before I let him go over?

Putting my knees between his thighs, I forced them apart. I lowered my open mouth onto his manhood and took him in as far as I could, deep into my throat, rocking him hard with my hands gripping his hips.

And then, when I sensed he was just there, I pinched his erect nipple hard and put my finger at the lip of his anus and plunged in.

He erupted with a powerful shaking and bolting like a wild horse. I held onto him, my finger in his anus, twisting his nipple without mercy, his manhood filling my mouth until he collapsed and sucked air in great gulps.

He had never touched me. I had never opened my robe. He lay spent, his massive chest rising high and falling. I rolled back on my haunches and to my feet, standing over him. I said nothing.

The General opened his eyes, looking up at me. There was something new there. Only a flicker, but it was a start.

Reaching down slowly, I folded his robe across his bare chest and loins. I handed him his goblet of wine and stepped backwards, folding to my knees again on the carpet, in front of him. Not one word had been spoken since his life-or-death challenge to me.

I waited. I looked straight at him, unblinking. I believe my face was expressionless. I tried hard that it was. Inside I quaked. I had given it everything I had.

Shouting outside of the tent broke the spell. A guard called out, begging permission to enter. The General jumped to his feet and tied the sash around his waist.

"Enter," he snarled. "This had better be good!"

A captain prostrated himself at the General's bare feet.

"Speak, damn you! Why do you keep me waiting?"

"The outward sentries have spotted Egyptian chariots, Excellency. They camp for the night."

The General was instantly alert.

"How many? How far away?"

"Eight, Sir. They are not military. They have not entered the canyon area."

"A search party. It is as I said."

He paced back and forth.

"Have we covered our tracks?"

"Yes, Excellency. The trail is wiped out."

"Keep watching them. Do not let them see you. If they do not find our spoor, they will turn back. If they discover the trail, kill them all and bury the chariots. They must not see us and live to tell." His eyes flashed with cold fire.

"But hear this," he threatened. "I do not desire more Egyptians disappearing into the desert. We cannot have their army join the search. Our work here is not finished."

As furious as he was, his thinking was clear. I saw why he was so respected and feared.

"Call my staff and have them here at once."

"Yes, General. At once."

"All this for a woman! Damn the Gods."

He fumed; his aura was black and evil. I despaired that all my efforts were for naught.

Then he turned on me. I stared back, praying I hid my terror. Would he kill me right here, right now? The flush on his angry face faded slightly, and when he spoke, his voice was almost human.

"You have gained yourself a night, Ishtar. The reputation of Hathor is well deserved. Maybe even more than could be imagined."

I caught the twinkle of a tiny spark of delight in his eyes.

"Go to the harem and sleep. No one will approach you."

I was dismissed. He started to dress. A soldier appeared to take me to the women's tent, but not before I saw something glint on the table. It was the jewel-encrusted hilt of my hunting dagger.

CHAPTER 25 SEARCH

H etmus-hor and his men slept fitfully. They were not trained cavalry, but mere nobles and servants equipped for a day of sport. Their bellies rumbled; they were just this side of thirst. The goatskins of water were emptying fast. They'd eaten all the food. The horses managed to forage the rocky ground for coarse grass that grew among the stones.

Restless on the cold ground under the stars, Hetmus planned his strategy for first light. He realized they couldn't go much farther without water. And the chariots held them back. They would have to continue the search on horseback, without proper pads or bridles.

They would split up into pairs to explore the dozens of trails leading into deep ravines and long canyons. Most ended blind at sheer cliffs.

All trace of the horsemen had disappeared about a mile back. The ground had been swept of hoof prints, and the wind had done the rest. Whoever the kidnappers were, they were smart. They had brushed the coarse sand and gravel on several paths, making it impossible to tell the actual trail from others. Even now, Hetmus-hor realized, he could be far off track.

But if he waited for reinforcements from Hermopolis and the kidnappers were on the move, he might never catch up to Isis. She could be in the Sinai, or anywhere, before they took up the search again. They could not stop now; they would continue with the little resources they had until help arrived.

Hetmus-hor was a realist and aware of his limitations. He had trained as a military officer since boyhood; all Egyptian noblemen prepared for war. But his skills were honed in war games with other nobles. None of his hunting party had been in battle. His men were armed with bows and arrows for hunting; they weren't equipped to rescue Isis from armed marauders. His thoughts never went to the Persians, never imagining they penetrated this deep into the Kingdom.

ꙮ

River God commissioned the fastest boat in Khent-min. He chose twenty of the best oarsmen he could find, ten to a shift, rowing round the clock. It took nerves of steel to travel the river by night, but the promise of double pay helped allay their qualms. If the Gods sent a strong southerly wind, the river could carry them downstream to Hermopolis by late tomorrow.

He sent word by carrier pigeon to the Governor—a good man, a man to be trusted—to have a company of mounted soldiers ready to leave immediately upon his arrival at the hunting lodge. He calculated he should be in the desert where Isis went missing in less than two days. He prayed to the patron gods of his regiment and to Hathor that it would be soon enough.

It made no sense to him that desert nomads had taken her. The price for kidnapping an Egyptian woman of high rank, much less a priestess, was dear. Their tribe would be decimated, their animals confiscated, their women and children sold into slavery.

He spent the long hours on the river thinking about what horsemen could be so foolish and so brazen. He planned the search and, from time to time, allowed himself to curse Hetmus-hor. He never once thought of the Persians.

ꙮ

Qeb-ha had been desolate when Ti and Wah returned with the news of the sandstorm and Isenkhebe's separation from the hunting party. When the messenger arrived with the account of her capture by unknown horsemen, he struggled desperately to hang onto hope.

Isenkhebe was alive. At least she had been alive when taken. His mind tumbled from one awful peril to another. What horrors might she have endured? Was she yet of this world, or had she passed into eternal darkness, no incantations from the Book of the Dead to guide her spirit, no mummified body to give her *Ka* form in the afterlife?

She had been given into his care by Sit-hathor herself. He had failed utterly. He was her guardian. He should have gone to Ankh-hor and called off the hunt. And even though he knew there was no way he could have stopped her, he should have forbidden Isenkhebe to go.

He despaired of ever seeing her again. In spite of her willfulness, in spite of her behavior unbecoming a priestess, he had grown fond of her spirit and, yes, had begun to succumb to her charms.

He tried hard to think positive and trust in the Goddess, spending hours in her Temple reciting incantations. But no matter the sacrifices he offered or the length of his chants, Qeb-ha saw only blackness and doom.

◡

Eben fell into a Kabbalah trance when he heard the news. He fingered without pause the amulet with magical symbols hanging on a leather thong around his neck. He sat in the stern of the barge and rocked wildly back and forth, his head almost hitting the deck.

When the shock wore off, he dragged out his scrolls and recalculated the position of the planets and compared them to Isenkhebe's birth chart. He worked the mystical numbers of her name, of Hermopolis and of the month. He compared numbers to passages from the sacred Book of Formation as revealed to Abraham more than a thousand years before.

Finally, he went to Qeb-ha with his findings.

"I do not see death. I mean, I see death, but not that of Isenkhebe. It is not her destiny at this time. The signs do not lie."

Qeb-ha only shook his head and muttered something about the womb and fate. The death of Isenkhebe would be unbearable, but it would also signal the failure of their sacred mission. Who knew what punishment the Gods had in store?

"Do not give up hope, Qeb-ha. The story has not come to an end. Forces are at work in the cosmos, forces greater than us."

"We are but pawns, Eben, in the hands of the Gods."

Qeb-ha the fatalist wondered that he had ever been so arrogant to imagine that a mortal man could influence events.

"No, Qeb-ha, listen. Kabbalah teaches that the spiritual plane and physical reality are interwoven. By meditating on the Light, we harness the power of good against evil."

"I do not know, Eben, I do not know. The Fate and the Fortune that come, it is the Gods that send them."

"Qeb-ha, you said yourself that Hathor chose Isenkhebe. Would the Goddess choose her and then desert her?"

"Who can understand the heart of a Goddess?" Qeb-ha would not be consoled.

☙

No one was more frantic at the disastrous news than Lord Ankh-hor. The High-Priestess had disappeared into the desert, and his son was responsible. Ankh-hor himself had invited Isenkhebe on the hunt and made all the arrangements. Over Qeb-ha's adamant objections, he'd insisted she'd be safe with Hetmus-hor.

She was the daughter of Sit-hathor, for Set's sake! Of all the mothers in Egypt, it had to be Sit-hathor. The dreaded woman controlled more resources than the First Queen herself. And everyone knew of her fits of rage.

Rumor was that even the Crown Prince was interested in the daughter. He didn't know why; it was not for him to ask. What might this all mean for his family? If they fell into disfavor with the Pharaoh—or Sit-hathor—they could lose everything.

Damn these stomach cramps. The pain was a hot poker in his bowels.

He gave instructions that his son was to have whatever he needed to find the priestess. No expense was too great. He shouted orders, then countermanded them, and then issued them again. The cramps worsened with each change of plan.

Ankh-hor was an aristocrat. He managed his estates, paid his taxes to the priesthood and had more left over than his family could ever use. His daughters married well; his sons were healthy and strong. But he was not a military man, not a tactician. In truth, he had no idea what his son needed.

Never having thirsted, he couldn't imagine the need for water. Always traveling by litter or chariot, he couldn't envision the need to ride horseback. Never venturing more than one hour from the Nile, he couldn't conceive of the true perils of Set's desert. He knew nothing of armed men who would kill a man with no more thought than Ankh-hor gave to killing a gazelle.

The more he dithered, the more his stomach hurt, until finally, his head slave suggested seeing the Governor.

Yes! The Governor would know what to do. He would go to him and explain the situation. *That* is what he would do. Speak to the Governor.

So instead of sending horses, men, weapons, water and food, Ankh-hor sent for his litter to carry him to the provincial palace.

Ti and Wah waited impatiently on the barge for word from the Lord Ankh-hor. They sharpened the broad blades of their iron swords and the bronze tips of their spears. They gathered quivers of arrows, filled goatskins with water and prepared hemp sacks with dates, bread and salted meats. But still they had no word from the nobleman. When would they head back into the desert? They had no horses themselves.

"Master, we must buy fresh horses in the city. The son Hetmus-hor has need of them. We cannot rejoin him on foot."

"Of course. Of course." Qeb-ha awakened from his stupor and called for the treasure chest. "Get whatever you require."

Relieved to be able to take some kind of action, he poured a thick stream of precious amulets that overflowed the guards' palms and spilled to the ground at their feet.

"Qeb-ha, I am going with them," announced Eben solemnly.

"Yes, you should go to the market with them."

"I shall do that, Qeb-ha. But I mean that I am going with them to search." He had thought this carefully through. He had meditated on it. He had made up his mind.

"You, Eben? But you know nothing of these things. We are men of learning. You might slow them down. Can you even handle a chariot or ride a horse?"

Eben took more amulets from Qeb-ha's hand, gathered the ones on the ground and from Ti and Wah and placed them all in a leather pouch that disappeared into his heavy robe.

He saw nothing before him save Isenkhebe's brilliant smile.

⸱

River God's ship sped down the Nile. With oars moving as quickly as the men could sustain, he changed shift every four hours. The Gods favored them with a steady wind. He could rely on the Governor in Hermopolis to have supplies waiting for him, men ready to ride.

He blocked any worries of what could be happening to Isis. She might be foolish at times and a slave to her senses, but Isis was strong-willed, a survivor. He couldn't afford negative thoughts. He must keep focused on the mission. If properly prepared and in the correct state of mind, he would be ready when the time came—ready for anything. Anything except what he feared most. He would never be ready for that.

⸱

Hetmus-hor watched the stars disappear and the night sky turn pale. There would soon be enough light to move into the hills again.

He came to terms with the desperate reality that they didn't have enough water for both the men and the horses, assuring himself that it was only a temporary setback. His father's reinforcements must be on their way. They could arrive at any moment.

"We shall search on foot in the cool of the early morning," he declared. "Supplies and more men from my father should arrive before the heat of the day."

He would not waste one hour. He would not give up. Nothing would stand in the way of his promise to Isis.

CHAPTER 26 THE SASH

Would today be the last dawn of my life in this world? A soldier shook my shoulder and barked to get up. I still had on the yellow gown, my wig on my head. Sleep had taken me the moment I lay down, and if I'd journeyed to the Land of Dreams, I had been too exhausted to notice.

He took me to a place to relieve myself, and finally I could see the camp. Tents formed regular rows in a narrow canyon with steep walls. The only approach was from the north. The horses were tethered outside the camp perimeter at the mouth of the ravine. I saw only one guard posted there.

The General's tent stood apart from the others with its back up to the canyon wall. Deep grooves carved by erosion etched the cliff surface. When I looked more closely, I spotted small trails at a much shallower slope. They could be the paths of mountain goats or maybe shepherds. Bedouins lived in these rocky hills.

When we came to the General's tent, the guard pushed me roughly through the flap, and I immediately prostrated myself. I didn't want my face shoved into the filthy carpet again.

"Up!"

I came to my knees and faced the General.

He was drinking hot liquid from a ceramic cup, his big feet clad in heavy sandals propped on a red silk cushion. He had on his leather tunic with a short dingy kilt. Did the man ever sleep?

More of the rice and a pile of dates filled a platter in front of him. I couldn't help my eyes glancing at it; I was ravenous and thirsty.

"Come, eat, drink." He motioned me over with a dismissive wave of his hand.

With the practiced grace of a dancer, I rose from my knees to my feet and then settled again on the opposite side of the dish. He handed me a cup filled with a honey-sweetened herbal tea. I smelled mint. The tea was too hot to swallow more than small sips, and I fought to control my urge to down it all at once.

Scooping up rice with my right hand, I used my fingers and palm to craft a small ball. Slowly putting it in my mouth, on my craving tongue, I willed myself to chew. My hunger was like that of a dog; I could have swallowed each chunk whole.

He watched me, detached, as if observing a prized mare feeding in the stable.

"Persians never eat with women. Did you know that, Ishtar? But you are Egyptian. I am curious to see if you are different."

I had no comment. What could I say? How many ways are there to eat?

"Women must chatter while they chew. They cannot be silent. It is distasteful to see."

I was silent.

"Perhaps you are different, after all. I sense your mind working, but your lips are still. Would I dread your words, Ishtar, if I could hear them?"

I had no idea where he was going with his idle, one-sided conversation. I continued to eat and looked at him only when he spoke. I took a black date and nibbled around the pit, then drank deep of my tea, which had cooled.

"My officers want me to kill you, Ishtar. They say you are endangering the mission. What do you say to that?"

His tone was lazy, as if he casually mused over the fate of a pig.

Still I did not speak. Did he want me to beg for my life? Would that elicit pleasure—or scorn? They say that one should not give way to the tongue when not asked. I would not give way to my tongue, until I knew *why* I had been asked.

He continued in the same languid tone.

"I told them that it would be a pity to destroy such a creature as you. But then, they do not know you as I do."

He waited. It was obvious he expected a response. I had to gamble.

I had no choice. I modulated my voice carefully, choosing a confident tone with a hint of challenge.

"You told me that I would be yours as long as I pleased you. Have I not pleased you? Or are you not a man of your word?"

He actually laughed. He threw back his head and gave a mighty roar of a laugh. He smiled at me, exposing square, slightly yellowed teeth, big and strong enough to grind flesh. His *kohl*-lined eyes crinkled in the corners.

"I am certain, Ishtar, that there are few men you would not please."

Appearing utterly at ease, he refilled his cup and mine and settled back.

"I value beauty, and I value brains, but I value talent most of all. And you, beautiful and clever Ishtar, have been given an extraordinary talent. It would be a crime to waste it."

For the first time, I thanked my mother for developing my special talent with all the skills of her cult. And my father for the tutors, who taught me languages so I could understand and spar. Most of all, I thanked Hathor for giving me the Power. I owed my life today to all three.

I waited for a signal, a sign what he wanted next. He wouldn't tell me, of course. He played the cat to my mouse. He wanted me to squirm, and then he would pounce with his deadly paw when he was ready.

Neither of us spoke, each waiting to see what the other would do. Leaning back on a pile of cushions, his face revealing nothing, the General watched me, never taking his eyes away. I looked all around the tent and saw a whip, the kind Persians use on horses, on top of a pile with saddle pads and a bridle.

When I moved the tray of food between us to one side, his pupils dilated. He stopped smiling.

I stood up before him and untied the blue sash of my yellow robe. The gown fell open in front, not all the way, but enough that he could see the curve of my belly, my shaven mound, and a hint of my breast.

Taking the sash in my hand, I doubled it, forming a loop.

As fast as a striking cobra, I slipped the loop around his neck and yanked hard. I caught him totally off guard. The little bells tinkled; the silver tassels swung back and forth. He went wide-eyed with shock. I released the pressure, so he could breathe.

"You go too far!" he bellowed.

My voice cut through the air. "I have not begun."

Holding onto the end of the noose with one hand, I reached for the whip with the other. My robe fell open when I stretched, revealing my firm breasts, crowned with dusky roses and tightened nipples.

He didn't try to remove the sash from around his throat.

Gripping the whip in my fist, I lashed him across his biceps; the leather thongs stung his flesh. I jerked hard at the noose at the same time.

A deep, rumbling moan heaved from his Titan chest. His manhood rose under the kilt. I lashed him again, on the other arm, harder this time. Angry red welts came up on his skin. His erection grew larger still.

All the time tightening and releasing the noose with each stroke, I whipped his thighs. He snorted like the wild bull in the market in Khent-min. I expected him to rise up and paw the ground.

I only struck a half dozen times, but each blow was more forceful than the one before. He grabbed the whip with one hand and seized my hand holding the noose with his other. He pulled me on top of him, crushing my breasts into the stiff leather of his vest, the metal lions and mesh imprinting a pattern on my skin.

He flipped me forward on my knees like I was no more than a loaf of bread and dragged me backward. I felt his massive rod ram deep into me. Thank Horus, he had chosen the canal of my womanhood and not the other. I feared I would split apart. Could I survive such a weapon?

But he exploded the moment he entered me. He lost control. Gripping my hips flush against his groin, he breathed hard and fast like a runner after a race. Then he released me, shoving me face down on my stomach when he fell back onto the cushions.

I saw through a crack at the base of the tent that Re had vanquished the serpent of the Underworld and begun his journey across the day sky. I wondered once again if this would be my last sunrise.

CHAPTER 27 A PLAN

Hetmus-hor gathered the men at first light. A charioteer stayed behind to await the arrival of his father's men. The rest would search the maze of valleys and rifts on foot, regrouping at regular intervals to report. They agreed it was too dangerous to signal each other with whistles, horns or calls that could echo for miles among the rocks.

Thirsty and hungry, nobles and servants listened silently to his plan. Only the Gods knew if the priestess was still in these hills. The captors could have ridden all day and all night.

Their day of pleasure and thrills, of wine and horses had gone all wrong. What would they do if they found the horsemen? They were not equipped to confront armed men.

In truth, they longed for nothing more than to go home and leave the fate of the priestess to her Goddess. But there was much more at stake than the life of one woman. Clans rise and fall in such times. Fully aware that the future of Hetmus-hor's entire family was in peril—a family they had known all their lives and married into—they would stand by him as they knew he would have stood by them.

Bound to follow their masters, the servants and slaves had no voice at all in the course of their lives.

Except the Nubian. Everyone knew he would die before he gave up the search for his mistress.

ꆍ

Eben grew more impatient as each hour passed with no sign of Ankh-hor's men. Qeb-ha sent Ti, who returned to report that Lord Ankh-hor had consulted with the Governor. A company of cavalry was massing on the East Bank, ready to ride as soon as a great commander arrived from the South.

"I am leaving now," declared Eben. "We have eight horses—four to ride and four to tow. Hetmus-hor needs supplies. Isenkhebe cannot wait."

"Take much water and grain for the horses," advised a Qeb-ha much more himself this morning. "They are weaker than men."

Re had risen, and the docks along the Nile buzzed with the new day. Eben hired ferries to carry his party of Ti, Wah and a third guard, Pasi, with the horses across the river to the East Bank.

The Governor's men were staging the expedition from the hunting lodge. Scores of small boats were anchored in the marsh grasses at the river's edge. More than two hundred horses stirred up dust, snorting, pulling at their tethers, restless to run. Servants bound food and weapons in hemp bags. Cavalrymen practiced swordplay, the clash of their sharpened iron blades splitting the morning air.

Six men, brothers of noblemen in the hunting party, chose to join Eben and his party of four. Eben purchased more arrows, a handful of deadly, curved sickle swords and extra horses. They placed pads and bridles on the animals and loaded them with sacks of food and goatskin bags of water. The new group headed east within an hour of Eben coming ashore.

ꝥ

The women bathed me and dressed me in new gowns. The first layer was a blue-green caftan, the color of Sinai turquoise, with elaborate embroidery in gold around the neck, cuffs and hemline. Over that they placed a delicate open robe in a rich lapis blue.

Persian women always cover their heads. They chose for me pale lavender silk with thousands of shimmering silver threads. When they brought the red slippers with turned-up toes, I asked for my sandals.

They looked at each other and shrugged. The child-woman with the oval face came back with heavy-soled leather sandals that laced up the leg. I took them into the folds of my gown and put the slippers on my feet.

They watched me but said nothing. I hated looking into their empty eyes; I could not see their souls.

A guard came for me, and I returned to the General's tent. The officers were all there, very animated, gesturing wildly with their hands. It is said that Persians drink copious amounts of wine when making decisions but wait until sober to act. I couldn't tell if they were sober or drunk.

The men fell silent when I entered and prostrated myself. Their hatred for me sucked the air from the tent. I sensed they waited only for one word from the General to slit my throat right there on the rug.

"Go to the bed," the General commanded, not even looking in my direction.

I rose and went to the mattress with silk pillows and settled myself on my knees. Conscious of each movement in my body, I did everything to suppress the Power. This was not the time. My eyes avoided the group of staring men as I tried to fade into the patterns and shadows of the tent.

They soon forgot me and spoke rapidly, some of it military jargon, using words I didn't know. But I understood 'supply lines' and 'direction of attack.' I understood 'invasion.' They talked freely in Elamite-Persian, unaware I could follow. They outlined the weakness of Egyptian defenses and mocked the Pharaoh and the Crown Prince. I didn't dare look to see who was speaking but recognized one voice.

"It is a gift from the Gods," said the man with ogre eyes, the one they call Zavan the merciless, "for such a weakling as Psamtik to face Cambyses, the Master of All Lands. What a battle we shall give them. They shall taste our steel and feel the crush of our feet."

"Our Gods spit on the weak gods of the Nile," snarled someone. "Their power is at an end. The glory of Egypt is finished."

"Long live the new Pharaoh, King of Persia," they shouted as one. "May the dynasty of Cambyses rule forever!"

My fear grew with each moment, but I feigned a look of boredom as I picked at the threads of my dress and touched Eben's leather amulet, hidden by the long sleeves of my gown.

Images of the peaceful Temple grounds with green fields and colorful gardens by the Nile played in my mind. I saw them invaded and trampled by these beast-men with their perfumed beards and savage hearts.

Worry and fear overwhelmed my desire to remain strong. I began to think of dying as preferable to this unknowing. When worry such as mine arises, the heart seeks death itself as escape. Still I was jolted when I heard them switch to talk of killing me.

I felt their eyes piercing me like twelve deadly daggers. The hatred was palpable in the heat of the stuffy tent. Couldn't they open one flap? Did these people never need fresh air?

I forced myself to stare at the golden threads frayed by my nervous picking, pretending not to understand their calls for my death.

"Enough talk of this," growled the General. "When the time is right, I shall act."

The language switched to Aramaic when a captain appeared with a report.

"The Egyptians are on foot, Your Excellency, exploring the canyons. There is no sign of reinforcements."

"They do not take their horses? Then they are low on water. But reinforcements are coming, of that I am certain. They do not leave. They expect more men and supplies."

No one spoke. It was dead quiet inside the tent. Outside, the wind howled; flapping wool panels strained at the wooden stakes.

I ventured a look in the General's direction from under my lashes. He stared at me, but I couldn't read his face.

"I want to see for myself," he said abruptly. "Bring my horse."

It wasn't until he left that I realized I had been holding my breath.

"Bring her food and water and whatever else she needs," I heard him command on the other side of the tent flap. "I want her here when I return."

I was alone. I waited a few moments, then rose to my feet and went to the table. Some of the papyri were maps, but I also saw long lists and official-looking documents. I moved two scrolls and uncovered the jeweled hilt of my hunting knife.

After putting the dagger in the folds of my robe, I replaced the scrolls exactly where they had been. The table looked undisturbed. I hurried back to the bed and hid the knife with the Persian sandals.

I was on my way to the back of the tent when the guard entered with a platter of rice, some meat and a water jug.

"Do you have any bread?" My voice showed no fear.

He looked surprised; he wasn't used to women or prisoners asking for anything. But he returned with a flat, round loaf of dark bread, the kind Bedouins bake in the sand under a campfire.

The bread went with my knife and sandals. I spied the green scarf from last night lodged between two pillows and added it to the hidden pile.

I had no real plan. I moved on automatic. The only way out of the camp was past the horses, through the narrow canyon mouth. Soldiers were everywhere.

One of the flaps in the back toward the cliff was not staked to the ground; the wind must have loosened it. I went to my knees and cautiously lifted a corner at the bottom edge. Bright light poured into the dim interior. I saw the cliff wall about six feet away. There were no guards; they must keep around front.

I forced myself to eat the food, choking down the foul mutton, swallowing gulps of the water. A small stack of goatskin water bags was neatly arranged not far from the table of scrolls. I took one from the middle of the stack and filled it with the remaining water from the jug. I put that with my secret stash and settled onto the bed to await the General's return.

CHAPTER 28 DECISION

The Egyptians on foot posed no threat to the General. They were few and essentially unarmed. From his vantage point on the high ridge, he immediately assessed that his men could make short work of them. There would hardly be a fight. The giant Nubian might be worth saving, but the others could be thrown into a box canyon for the vultures to pick their bones.

Reinforcements were on the way, though. They would not be using the last of their supplies out here in the searing desert if they did not expect help to arrive soon. He sent a scout farther west to look for the men he knew were coming. The question was how many—and how well-armed.

The situation called for damage control, but he had to act with extreme caution. If he killed these men, there would be more tracks to cover, their chariots to dispose of, all closer to camp. Others would start a new search, and they would be fresh, perhaps military.

A viable option might be to decamp and move on before reinforcements arrived. Let these pathetic civilians wander in the hills. His troops could be gone by nightfall.

He weighed his alternatives, not happy with this unexpected turn of events. All because of a woman!

But what a woman. A hint of a smile curved his lips at the thought of Ishtar waiting for him in his tent. *What tricks would she next invent?* If he abandoned camp, could he allow himself to take her with him?

Without a body, the search for her would continue. It might expand into areas Egyptians had not reconnoitered in months. He sighed. His officers were right. It was clear what he needed to do. He must have her strangled and plant evidence of Bedouins. A lone woman, even a High-Priestess, might easily encounter cutthroat desert outlaws too foolish or reckless to fear reprisal.

And the captain who had brought her back had to be executed at once as a lesson to the men that poor judgment would not be tolerated.

"And my own poor judgment?" he chuckled to himself. He should have killed her as soon as she arrived in camp. Any fool could see that.

But even with the risks, he didn't regret this priestess. He had never met another like her. In truth, he desired her more than any woman he had ever known or seen.

I shall have one more taste, but this time, I shall be in charge.

Stones from his horse's hooves flew into the air as he bolted, racing back to the camp.

ᘄ

Re rose high in the sky with no sign of his father's men or of Isis. They needed to get out of the sun or risk dehydration. Left with no choice, Hetmus called off the search.

He sent another chariot west with the best horses.

"Find the reinforcements and tell them to hurry."

He watched until the thin plume of dust disappeared over the horizon. The sun was a white orb in a white sky. Exhausted, settling into shade cast by rocks or chariot, the search party slept immediately.

Re was not far above the horizon when Hetmus woke and spotted the cloud of dust silhouetted against the reddening ball. Help at last.

ᘄ

When River God's ship was spotted by the lookout, the men waiting impatiently at the hunting lodge rose as one, stamping their feet in unison, pounding the shafts of their spears on the hard ground.

"Avenge Hathor! Avenge Hathor!"

Their cheers reached River God's ears, and he was off the ship and wading to the shore before the rowers pulled up the oars. The East Bank of the Nile had no quays; the barge would run aground in deep mud if they moored too near the shore.

The cavalry greeted him with a mighty roar when he crested the top of the bank.

"Hail Commander! Loved by the Pharaoh! Loved by a God! Live long! Live long!"

Men waved short killing swords in circles above their heads, singing the Commander's praises. Sunlight flashed on the metal studs of the round crocodile shields slung across their backs.

A groom rushed forward with a glossy black stallion, its long mane and tail brushed smooth and braided with silver twine.

It took River God less than ten minutes to assess the troops and confer with his captains. He mounted and whipped his horse to a gallop at the head of the cavalry, one of Hetmus-hor's men at his side. Two hundred armed horsemen raised a great cloud of dust that could be seen across the broad river in Hermopolis.

ᘭ

Qeb-ha saw the dust cloud from the barge. Near choking with tears, he thanked Hathor for her goodness and patience with mere mortals. His eyes pleaded with Maia to assure him that he might dare hope.

"Oh Maia! I never dreamed I could have such deep feelings for Isenkhebe. I miss even her foolishness. May the Gods give strength and power to Eben's Hebrew magic."

"We are taught that we should put our affairs in the hands of the Gods," Maia explained gently. "But Eben believes that his god helps those who help themselves. He says we must always look to the Light."

ᘭ

Watching the great cloud of dust rise high into the clear desert sky, Lord Ankh-hor stood on the rooftop terrace of his Westside mansion and prayed to every God in the vast Egyptian pantheon that the priestess would be rescued. He was terrified of Sit-hathor and her fearful vengeance; an envoy from her might arrive at any moment demanding a report. The woman herself might show up. If this Isenkhebe wasn't located soon and brought back unharmed, his family would pay and pay dearly. Sit-hathor would never forgive the loss of her daughter.

He gave no thought that he should also pray for his son, Hetmus-hor.

☜

As quickly as he arrived in the makeshift camp, Eben brought food and drink to Hetmus-hor, who downed it like a jackal. The son showed no reaction when informed that his father had given the task of raising reinforcements to the Governor. That was a family affair he would not discuss with a Hebrew.

"There is no sign of her, no sign at all. There is simply no trace," he told Eben.

He was exhausted and struggling not to admit defeat. Never in his life had Hetmus failed to charm. But here in these hills, his charm was worth nothing. He was worth nothing. He could never forgive himself the loss of Isis.

"The signs tell me, Hetmus-hor, that Isenkhebe survives; it is her destiny to live. I have awakened the power of Kabbalah. The Light shall give her strength and show her the way."

"Your Hebrew magic had better be stronger than our Egyptian witchcraft. We have so many gods, I do not know whom to beseech. I see only the hand of Set, the Destroyer. He, and he alone, rules here in the land of chaos."

"Let us start the search again at first light. We shall find a sign," Eben assured him. "Isenkhebe shall return to us. It has been promised."

☜

The General thundered into camp, his horse in full lather. He was at the flap of his tent and about to enter, when a rider rode through the mouth of the canyon and galloped directly to him.

"We have word, Your Excellency. Egyptian reinforcements have arrived. Fewer than a dozen men on horseback with more horses and supplies. They are not military."

"Amateurs? They send more amateurs? Perhaps this woman is not so important after all."

He allowed himself to envision tasting Ishtar each night in a fresh camp in a new ravine. There might yet be a way out. Perhaps the magical Egyptian temptress could live to pleasure him still.

CHAPTER 29 THE BITE

C overed in dust and stinking like a stable, the General stomped into the tent, his hungry eyes searching for me. I sat up and looked for my death sentence in his face, but if he had decided I must die now, I couldn't see it there. He hurried towards me, shedding his armor with each step.

"You smell like a horse," I said calmly. My strength came from somewhere outside me. Inside, I quaked from anxiety and fear.

He stopped short—speechless, his leather vest half on, half off.

I reclined on one elbow, slightly on my side, accentuating the seductive curve from my shoulder to narrow waist that rose again along my hip. My legs stretched out, ankle resting gracefully one on the other, knee slightly bent, toes pointed. The blue silk folded on every inviting contour of my body. I stared at him boldly from under half-closed lids and dialed up the Power.

"Water!" he bellowed. "Bring me water for a bath. And food."

He pulled off his thick sandals and tossed them aside, standing in his loose shirt and kilt with monster feet spread wide. Sweat made rivulets in the pale powder on his skin. Stripes from my whip flamed bright red on his arms and legs. I wondered what his men thought when they saw those.

Pots clanged and voices rose as the camp prepared for the evening meal. The wind had died. Re had retreated under the western horizon. Other night sounds echoed through the canyon, subtle but different vibrations that went with the changes of texture in the late evening air.

I felt it slightly cooler in the stifling tent.

The General grabbed a jug of water and poured a stream down his throat, the water spilling into his beard caked with dust. Why don't Persians shave like civilized people? All that hair is so unclean.

The food arrived first. He sat on cushions in his foul shirt and kilt, stuffing slabs of fatty meat into his mouth. Bits of it clung to his beard. And he tells me that it's distasteful to eat with women who chatter while they chew.

I saw him as raw animal. I envisioned him returning from battle, covered in human blood and ravenous for the taste of rare meat.

Twilight had settled when they brought the stacks of coarse cloth, large copper bowls and steaming water in brass jugs. Vine-embossed silver flasks of perfumed oil stood on a round brass tray.

"Do you wish me to bathe you?" I asked politely.

"Do you see anyone else here?" His voice was gruff but not threatening.

I took several lengths of the cloth and spread them over cushions.

"Lie here," I told him.

He called the guard.

"Do not disturb me. Do not enter unless there is news of the Egyptians."

The guard fixed on the General when he spoke, but I could tell he looked at me out of the corner of his eye. I wondered what gossip spread through the camp. There must be wild speculation about the power of the Egyptian sorceress who had bewitched their General Sher, Lion of the Desert.

The General settled on the cushions, his massive frame bending with a grace I wouldn't have thought possible in a man his size.

I removed his shirt and put it carefully aside. Then I removed his kilt and placed it on top. He was already erect, but I ignored it.

Beginning with his arms, I wiped the layers of dust away. I moved to his thighs and stroked downward to his calves and ankles, dipping the cloth from time to time in water. When the cloth became too brown, I took a clean one. When the water became brown, I poured fresh.

"What is that leather strap around your wrist?" His deep voice was almost soft, idly curious but not demanding.

"It is an amulet, Your Excellency. I never take it off. It protects me from harm and gives me strength."

"I hope that is true, Ishtar. I truly do."

I rinsed his hair and long beard and wiped the grime from his face. I washed his feet and between his toes. I bathed him as I would a small child. I did not summon the Power.

His body relaxed; the erection melted. He closed his eyes, and I thought him asleep. But when I started to move away, he opened them and asked, "Where are you going?"

"To get more towels and the oil, Excellency."

I dribbled scented oil into fresh water and swabbed his whole body, now clean of dust and sweat. Only when I gently washed his testicles and penis did the erection come back.

It had to be dark now. The lamps in the tent gave off a mellow glow. I could hear the camp laughing around the cooking fires, eating the evening meal, enjoying the soft night after a fierce day.

When finished, I set the water basins and dirty cloths aside and put the remaining clean fabric by the bed.

The General relaxed, lying on his back with his eyes closed. I brought him his pipe with the sweet smelling smoke and lit it for him. He leaned up against the pillows and drew deep drafts, the muscles in his face calming even more. He was quite handsome really, in a brutish way.

I slid out of my robe and pulled the caftan over my head; both tumbled to a lush pile. Deliberately, slowly, I straddled him, unhurriedly stretching forward, slithering from the black bush, past his thick waist, to his gorilla chest.

I kissed him deep and caring, my tongue probing the inside of his mouth. No urgency, just languid, very tranquil. The last hint of tension in his massive bulk evaporated into me and then flowed through me into the thick, hazy air.

My nude body lay fully on top of him. The warmth of his skin burned into mine. The beat of his heart reverberated into my chest. My lips pressed softly on his. We floated up from the cushions.

I kissed him on his broad chest, everywhere, in a language that said, "I adore you." I kissed the red welts on his arms. I kissed his hands and put them to my breasts. He squeezed me, but gently. Expecting pain, I got tenderness.

His hands moved up and down my body, stroking me with his rough and calloused palms. My skin, chafed from the blasting sand, was velvet compared to his battle-worn flesh.

"Let us go to the bed," I breathed in his ear.

He picked me up while still reclining and then stood. My legs draped across his massive arms; my feet dangled in the air. He kissed me as he lay me down. The power and sensibility of it surprised me. I was breathless.

He began to make love to me, not animal sex, but a kind of raw passion with tender emotion that moved me. I felt myself stirring; I couldn't help it. He was overwhelming me.

I stretched my neck so that he would find the trigger points that ignite my fire. He found them. He found them all, and he tasted them all with his wet lips, thick tongue and sometimes his teeth.

It was building in me from deep, secret places I hadn't known existed. I didn't want to believe it, but my wet was thick on the inside of my thighs. The low growls of a lioness rumbled in my throat.

No more touching. My hand found his manhood, so thick I could scarcely close my fingers around it. I guided him to me and placed him at the gate. He moved his hips slowly, probing a little deeper with each thrust.

My juices flowed so that even he, in his great size, was gliding with ease. He filled me and stretched me, and still I wanted more. I couldn't get enough of him. When he lunged into me, my hips rose to meet him. I hung onto his broad neck while he pounded me amid cries of pleasure, his and mine.

"Deeper," I pleaded. "Deeper!"

My words electrified him. He came to his knees, lifting me as he rose with the strength of ten bulls. He stretched his legs out and held me in his lap with his Min manhood so deep in me that it crushed against the tip of my womb.

My legs locked around his hips. My own weight pushed my swollen bud into his iron shaft.

He rocked me back and forth, and I could only hang my head backwards and plead for mercy. But when he slowed, I begged for more.

When I could bear it no longer, a comet erupted up through my cervix and out the crown of my head. I soared to the heavens. Contraction after contraction pulsed in my womb. It went on forever; I wanted it to go on forever. I held onto his massive arms, my nails digging in his flesh. I would not let go.

He lay me down and still moved inside me, slowly, all the way in, and then almost out, before sliding deep again. I stopped swirling and came back to earth. Reaching between his legs, I took his sacks in my hand and squeezed with each thrust. I stretched for his neck with my lips, and he lowered himself.

I bit him in that place that is my own trigger point and tasted a drop of blood.

It was the bite that brought him over. His body convulsed; a long, protracted howl escaped his throat. I feared the guards would come, but they didn't. They knew now was no time to enter.

He collapsed on top of me, struggling to catch his breath, his crushing weight pressing my lungs.

"You are too heavy. I cannot breathe," I whispered into his chest.

He rolled off me and lay spread-eagle on the bed. His eyes closed. His massive chest rose and fell like the panting of a winded stallion. His manhood lay limp against his thigh.

The jeweled hilt of my dagger was cold to my hand. I didn't think; I didn't hesitate. I grabbed his beard and plunged the blade deep into the soft tissue under his jaw, drawing the razor sharp steel across his throat from ear to ear. It took all my strength.

My hand found the green silk scarf, the one that matched my eyes, and I stuffed it in the gaping hole. He choked. His eyes were immense and bewildered. He stared at me in utter disbelief.

"I'm sorry," I whispered to his lips quivering in death throe. "I'm so sorry, but you would never have let me go."

I covered his nude dying body with a blanket. I wanted to dress him but didn't dare take the time.

Grabbing the sandals, I hurriedly tied them up my shin. After pulling the caftan over my head, I stuffed a scroll, the first one my hand touched, into a cloth with the bread and goatskin water bag.

At the last moment, I threw the General's dark hooded cape around me; it would blend into the night. Running to the back of the tent, I opened the flap and crawled through. I was out.

Stars filled the night sky. The moon would soon rise and turn the rocky hills white. I found one of the trails in the cliff face that ascended more slowly and began picking my way through the rocks, as silent as I could be. The crunch of my sandals on loose gravel exploded in my ears. I hardly dared breathe.

I could hear the sounds of the camp, the laughter and talking of men. They might even be joking, making lewd suggestions about the Egyptian who pleasured their General. Of course, they never imagined in their wildest fantasies that he lay dead in a pool of his own blood.

I clutched the bloody dagger in my right hand. If captured, I had to drive the blade deep into my own throat. My own fantasy was not vivid enough to imagine what the Persians would do to me now.

CHAPTER 30 DISCOVERY

I didn't allow myself to look back until reaching the top of the cliff where I could see for miles in all directions. The campfires still burned bright in the Persian camp below, but there was no unusual activity. They hadn't yet discovered the General's body.

His wild, bewildered eyes stared at me from the dark. The haunting image of his face as he bled out burned in my mind. Trembling all over, I leaned against a rock and clenched my shaking hands. They were caked with blood.

Only then would I allow tears to come—sweet tears of relief mingled with bitter tears of sorrow. I don't know how long I cried, but I don't think it was long.

Far to the west, I saw a massive cloud of dust heading in this direction. Then closer, maybe only a few miles away, a lone rider galloped at full speed toward the camp. Only urgent news would merit a night ride like that, urgent enough to disturb the General.

The moon was rising; rocks and sand shimmered like snow. It would be easiest to travel the paths in the moonlight, but also easy to be seen. In the dark of the desert, moonlight casts shadows. I would stay in those shadows where possible.

As best I could, I wiped the blood from my hands on the hem of the wool cape and then picked up the dagger and sack. I didn't have time for sorrow, worry or doubt. I had to get away fast.

⌇

River God stopped at the edge of the ravine and studied the tracks of the horsemen. He climbed down the ridge to the buried chariot. The *wadi* walls protected the site from the wind; footprints and the signs of digging still showed in the sand.

Isis had been here. He imagined her attack and struggle. Why had she been alone, without protection? The fool! Ankh-hor's son Hetmus-hor, a worthless parasite who lived off his father, enraged him as much as the attackers.

But River God's anger was cold, not hot. He had no time for emotion. Emotion led to mistakes. There could be no mistakes.

At the top of the ridge, he bent low to the prints of bulky sandals and tracks of horses.

"Bring me a torch," he commanded, an uneasy feeling gnawing at his gut.

An aide struck a flint and lighted a small baton wrapped with a head of linen soaked in oil.

"Impossible," he murmured under his breath, examining the weight of the horses and the telltale pattern of hooves bound in leather.

But the tracks of the horses, supported by the size and shape of the sandal imprints pointed to only one conclusion. Persian military. Persians this close to the Nile! He must alert the Pharaoh at once.

His swiftest rider turned back with the message.

Persians in region. Number unknown. Alert Pharaoh (glyph Amasis II).

He remounted and veered northeast, the two hundred horsemen raising another cloud of dust visible for miles in the moonlit sky.

ᘔ

The messenger went immediately to the General's tent where the sentry begged for permission to enter.

"Your Excellency, a vast cloud of dust is moving toward us."

There was only silence from within.

"General Sher, Your Excellency. We fear it is Egyptian cavalry, Sir."

No response. The two looked at each other in alarm. They were terrified to enter without permission, but the General's order had been clear. Do not enter unless there was news of the Egyptians.

Taking a deep breath, the sentry opened the flap and stepped into the silent tent.

The General lay alone in his bed. His open eyes loomed large and glassy. The sentry pulled the blanket back. A green silk scarf at the General's slashed throat was black with blood. Blood was everywhere.

Panic set in at once. Shouts rang through the camp and bounced off the canyon walls. Men stumbled from their drunken sleep to their feet.

At first the officers could only stare in disbelief.

"The whore! The Egyptian whore has killed him," wailed Zavan the merciless. "I shall tear her to pieces with my own hands."

"Where were you when this happened?" screamed Araxa, the General's second-in-command.

The sentry fell at Araxa's feet, face down into the carpet.

"The General gave instructions not to be disturbed," he blubbered. "I but followed his orders, Excellency."

Araxa responded by grabbing a pointed *akinaka* from the belt of a soldier next to him and bringing the iron sword down full force across the back of the sentry's neck, severing his head from the spine. A bright red fountain sprayed their legs.

The head rolled to a stop against the messenger's foot. He would have jumped back in horror, maybe kicked the head away, but too many eyes were on him. He didn't want to end with his own life force flowing into the carpet. Only minutes had passed since he stood next to the sentry outside the General's tent, begging to enter. Now the man's blood was hot on the skin of his ankles and legs. The man's sightless eyes stared up at him.

"She cannot have gone far," snarled Zavan. "We must find the witch now—before she has a chance to get away."

Araxa grabbed the beard of the soldier whose sword he had taken, dragging him to him, spitting words into his terrified face. "Have any of you fools checked the horses? Is the bitch on foot?"

"Your Excellencies," pleaded the messenger, "may I report?" If he didn't speak up now, his own death might not be as merciful as the sentry's.

"What is it, man? Make it quick."

"Men and horses are moving toward us and moving fast."

"The whore!" howled Zavan. "All of this because of that slut of Hathor."

The officers yelled at each other in their secret Elamite; each had a different plan. Araxa tried to assume control, but wild ranting drowned him out. The soldiers didn't understand a word, but it was clear that no one was in charge.

The General never doubted what to do. He never allowed shouting and arguing like this, at least not in front of the men.

The circle of confusion widened. Outside the tent, men gathered in small groups; the buzz grew louder and louder. The General was dead. The Egyptians were coming. Would they fight or flee?

ꟷ

Eben woke Hetmus from the deep sleep of exhaustion. The nobleman had traveled to the Land of Dreams where he saw Isis on the back of a falcon. She beamed her dazzling smile at him as she flew past his ear.

"Hetmus-hor, wake up! Many horses are approaching. It must be the Governor's men."

Hetmus jumped to his feet and followed Eben to a high piece of ground where they watched the soaring dust cloud move toward them.

"The power of Kabbalah is at work."

"You can keep your superstition and omens, Hebrew. My faith is with those men. We make the future ourselves, and I intend to see Isis there."

ꟷ

It was with a satisfied smile that Psamtik received word of the Pharaoh's illness; the old man's *Ka* would soon be on its long journey to the afterlife. No longer would he be the Crown Prince, subject to his father's demands and at risk of his displeasure, but Horus-on-earth himself. He could do whatever he pleased, whenever he pleased and with whomever pleased him.

"I regret sending the Commander to the north, Setne. Who cares now about some whore priestess and what tales she might tell? We could use him to speed our return. Should we not recall him from this desert odyssey?"

"I do not trust him. I am certain he has secrets. And his loyalty is not to you."

"All men have secrets. Even you, Setne. And loyalty can be bought. We shall need capable men. Is the pious Commander not without hope?"

"We perhaps could find a use for him, but I advise only if he proves more adaptable than I have known him to be. Let us sail tomorrow for Hermopolis. We shall send word for him to join us there. If your father still lives when we arrive in Saïs, it shall please him to see his precious Commander. If your father has begun his journey to the afterlife—well—you can decide then what to do with him."

"Always working the angles. That is what I admire most about you. Well, nearly the most. You have other talents I perhaps value more." He leaned back, settling onto the furs of the divan, waving to a slave to bring him wine. "Enlighten me as to this evening's entertainment. If this is to be our last night in the delightful city of Min, I imagine that you have devised something special. Something with the twins? Or have you found a new treat?"

CHAPTER 31 TRANSFER OF POWER

Every minute counted. My water and food wouldn't last long. I stumbled over stones and tripped in small holes but stayed on my feet and kept going. I had to get as far away as possible before daybreak. But once I climbed over the hill and out of sight of the camp, I wasn't sure which direction to take.

Hundreds of trails wound through the sharp rocks and narrow gullies. Was I going in circles? I was terrified that after hours of trekking, I could end up near where I started.

I remembered from the maps in my scrolls that the desert and rugged mountains of the east ended at the Red Sea. To the south lay more desert and mountains with miles and miles of wilderness to cross before meeting a caravan trail.

The Persians had arrived from the north. There could be more Persians; there could be a whole army of Persians. I needed to go west, toward the Nile. But west was the direction they would look for me.

In any event, I had no idea where west lay. I was lost without the sun.

Battling despair, I collapsed against a large, smooth boulder and tried to calm my breathing. The stone still held traces of today's scorching sun; my hip and shoulder warmed. Could I allow myself a few moments of rest?

It was when I removed the hood and adjusted my wig that I noticed the missing amethyst earring. What did the loss mean? Did it have meaning? Qeb-ha wore one amethyst drop. Now I did, too. Perhaps it was a good omen. I felt desperate for a sign.

I gripped the leather strap with the scroll, closed my eyes and tried to summon Eben. The General's eyes, wild with disbelief, stared at me from inside my lids. I kept pushing him away. Finally, Eben came to me.

Long hair falling in tangled waves, he sat not far away, singing his sweet Hebrew psalms, strumming the four strings of his lyre.

"Study the constitution of the sky to learn the constitution of the earth," he crooned. "Look to the Light."

Even with a moon, the canopy of stars blazed overhead. I spotted *Meskhetiu*, the Ox Foreleg, pointing the way to the Star of the North. I could use the polar star as a bearing. But it looked so small in the vast sky.

The moon was bright; it lit the dark desert. It must light all of Egypt. Did River God look up now and think of me? River God. I came back through the Red Mirror for you. Where are you now?

Alone. I was so alone. And it was all my own doing.

"O Hathor! Do not desert me! I have been foolish, but I have learned."

The shadows and ridges on the surface of the moon seemed to mirror the barren landscape around me. At first the black dot was barely visible in the white glow. But as I watched, the spot grew larger and larger and came closer and closer, until I could make out the silhouette of wings.

As if gliding on a moonbeam, the falcon drifted toward me. Hathor's voice was barely a whisper as she flew past my ear.

"Follow me, Isis. Trust me to lead you to your fate."

Perhaps I hallucinated, but I didn't care if the falcon existed in this world or another. I would follow wherever she led.

⌇

The exhausted noblemen and servants had cheered with relief when they spotted the cavalry approaching. After days of searching first on horseback and then on foot, with no food and little water, help had arrived at last.

River God leapt off his black stallion and covered the ground in ten strides, his feet raising billows of dust that blew ahead of him toward the cluster of men. Instead of gathering around him in welcome, they pulled back. Coming out of the dark desert, burning with fury, eyes fiery as black opals, he might have been Set himself.

"Who of you is the son of Ankh-hor?" he roared. "Show yourself!" After days of battling his anger and frustration, resolving always to control his emotions, he gave in to his rage.

The hunting party melted to the side, and Hetmus-hor stood alone in a ring of flickering light close to the campfire.

"I am Hetmus-hor."

"So! You are the coward who lost her!"

"Bide your tongue, soldier! No man speaks to me in such a manner."

"I give respect only to those worthy of it. What kind of man would let her out of his sight?"

"One overcome by a storm. The horses bolted. We came for her—but too late."

"Too late? May Set curse you! She was taken by Persians, you fool. Do you have any idea what those animals are capable of? We may wish her dead rather than face what they do."

"Persians? This close to the Nile? Impossible!"

"All the signs point to them. Did you not see the tracks?"

Yes, Hetmus had seen the sandal footprints and the tracks of horses, but how could he recognize them to be Persian? Ibex or wild boar. That was the spoor he knew.

Images of Isis among butchers, scenes more horrible than any nightmare, flooded his mind. He went numb; he felt nothing. For a moment, the desert around him morphed into a gray vacuum. Would death be like this? A vast void free from pain—free from shame?

Overhead burned a billion stars in an inky sky. The desert was pitch black all around. Silently, on feet barely crunching the dry rock, the cavalry coalesced into a wide circle with the two men facing off in the center.

From the arc of the circle nearest the fire, the nobles who rode from Hermopolis watched in silence with the hunting party. No one dared intervene. The mood of the cavalry was grim. To a man, they would follow the Commander anywhere, and to see him seethe, on the edge of losing control, sobered them. If he wanted satisfaction, he would have it.

"Hetmus cannot charm his way out of this," a cousin whispered. "If it is knife against sword, he is finished."

A piece of dry wood exploded in a shower of sparks. It was a dead still night with absolutely no wind; smoke from the fire rose high into the air. The desert was eerily quiet save the snorting and labored breathing of winded horses.

"Speak!" River God screamed. "Has the *great hunter* nothing to say for his failure?"

"What words can I offer? I am responsible for Isenkhebe's fate. I bear that heavy burden with no rest. But nothing I say now can change what has happened."

The utter logicality of his admission that nothing could be changed snapped whatever control River God had left. He plunged into a black fury that exploded in bright crimson. He was at Hetmus in an instant, grabbing his throat with both hands, digging thumbs into his windpipe.

Hetmus-hor wasn't a trained soldier, but he was strong. In sheer survival mode, his big hands with long fingers were around River God's neck, shoving him backward a step.

River God dropped his right hand to the hilt of the thrusting sword in his belt. Hetmus countered by drawing his hunting dagger.

"Stop!" shouted Eben, trying to force himself between the two Egyptians towering over him. "You do not help Isenkhebe. She needs both of you! It has been revealed to me. It is together that we shall save her!"

Half their size and slight as a gazelle, he grabbed Hetmus' knife arm at the wrist with his left hand and River God's hand on the sword hilt with his right.

"Hear me! Isenkhebe lives! Her destiny is to survive. *Your* destinies are to find her—*together*. It is written. Trust in the Light, Hetmus-hor!"

The Jew was right. Hetmus dropped his hands. He was no good to Isis dead. Neither of them was any good to Isis dead.

"Put your anger aside, Commander," urged Eben. Then he repeated what he had so often heard Qeb-ha say. "The Gods set you on this path. Your duty is to follow."

River God held on just long enough that it looked like he might not back down.

With River God's fingers still at his throat, Hetmus said, "It is over. Let us find Isis."

A moment passed. And another. The crackle of the fire was deafening. On the third heartbeat, River God released his grip from Hetmus' throat and took his hand from his sword. He turned then on fragile Eben swallowed by his heavy desert robe.

"And *who* are you, Hebrew, to dare counsel *me*?"

"I am one who cherishes Isenkhebe and is willing to do anything to get her back. Are we not brothers?"

ʔ

Last night's drink was washed from their blood and the officers dead sober when they gathered before dawn. The initial shock of the General's murder had worn off; Araxa was in full command with training and discipline restored.

"Do we stand and fight, Araxa? Our scouts tell us that the Egyptians number about two hundred. We would have the advantage of surprise."

"My heart urges me to massacre these dogs, but General Sher would not act until the plan was fully ripe. We shall return with the army of Cambyses and lay waste to more than one company of Egyptian curs."

"And the witch? Are we not to search for her?"

"I desire nothing more than to chop this woman into pieces and take my time about it. But we cannot risk discovery. We must wait for our revenge. Egypt shall soon be ours. I, Araxa of Susa, give you my word that I shall hunt her down personally. There is no place she can hide."

"And I, Zavan of Ecbatana, pledge to dream every night of a lesson worthy of the General. When the whore begs me for death, I shall see that she suffers more."

"Break camp immediately," Araxa ordered. "Leave men behind to sweep the area of tracks. We do not want the Egyptians to know our number. And kill the women. Strip them and dump their bodies into a ravine for the vultures and jackals. The Egyptians shall find only bones, if they find them at all."

CHAPTER 32 BROTHERS

R iver God organized the men into small parties. Searching without rest through the heat of the day and into the twilight, they found no trail. The Persians and Isis had vanished into the hills.

They started again at first light. The message from the Governor didn't arrive at base camp until River God roamed deep among the craggy cliffs; he didn't receive it until he returned to camp at nightfall. When his aide handed him the scroll with the glyphs, he looked at the words and crushed the papyrus in his fist.

Return. Crown Prince (glyph Psamtik) arrive Hermopolis. Sail Saïs. Pharaoh (glyph Amasis II) gravely ill.

Insubordination. An unholy thought. Without question, disobeying a direct order would be the end of his career, perhaps with the new Pharaoh, his life. He had brothers to consider, and their children. One does not cross the Crown Prince—or the lowlife Scribe Setne—without the entire family paying the price.

The evening star burned so bright and so near, it seemed he could reach out and touch it with his fingertip. Isis. He tasted her, honey sweet. The Hebrew was right. She was alive. He couldn't allow himself to believe otherwise. He sensed she waited for him—prayed for him—to find her. He couldn't give up the search now.

So many unfamiliar conflicts raged in his mind. Until Isis, his path had always been clear, uncluttered with distractions, never plagued by doubt.

When he weighed his options, he came up short—there was no easy way out.

"I did not receive this, Corporal. You could not give me the message because I did not return to camp. Is that understood?"

His aide didn't hesitate a heartbeat.

"Yes, Sir. It is clear, Sir. You did not return. I did not see you. You did not receive the message, Sir."

Remounting his black stallion, River God rode back into the night.

↜

On the third day, his men found the canyon where the Persians had camped. Faint spoors told them that many men and horses had been here, but it proved impossible to assess the exact number. They fell silent when they stumbled upon remnants of women's clothing tossed among the rocks.

Goliath brought them the amethyst teardrop earring found at the bottom of the steep cliff. Eben and Hetmus recognized it at once; they had last seen it sparkling in the sunshine, dangling from her earlobe. Isis had been here. The knowledge brought both relief and sorrow.

Not long after, a soldier discovered the deep ravine with the corpses of the women, mangled and half-eaten. They counted five broken and naked bodies among the sharp rocks. The three men stood a long time on the side of the chasm, looking down, not speaking.

Finally, River God gave the command to descend. He and two cavalrymen rappelled as far as they could on lengths of sedge rope knotted together. The sides of the ravine were a sheer drop to the bottom, and there were few footholds.

Hetmus and Eben stood together on the edge, watching the descent, measuring the distance to the bodies of the women.

"I had a dream, Eben. I saw Isis on the back of a falcon and she smiled at me. I do not believe the future is seen in dreams, but still I believed she was safe and coming back to me. I woke with hope. That hope is now gone."

"The Kabbalah is the Light, Hetmus-hor. Trust."

"We make the future ourselves," declared Hetmus. "I have created this future. It is borne of my error."

When the ropes proved too short to reach the bottom of the ravine, River God and the two cavalrymen climbed up again.

He sat back on his haunches and stared out at the barren landscape, seeing nothing before him but the images of the shattered women. This is what he had feared since he first received word of Isis missing. But no matter what it took to get her body up, he would return her to the Temple to prepare for her *Ka's* journey to the afterlife.

It took him a few moments to focus on the Hebrew when he came to kneel beside him. If it had been Hetmus-hor, he would have thrown him from the edge.

"Commander, think hard. When you were closest, could you see if any of the women had a shaved head? From here it appears they all have long hair."

River God thought back, visualizing the carnage, recreating each torn body in his mind.

"By Horus, you are right! They all have hair. Isis is not among them!"

He grabbed Eben, crushing his slender shoulders in the vise of his fists.

"Why did I not think of that? O blessed Hathor, it is so simple!"

"Your heart is ruling your head, Commander. I told you that Isenkhebe needs you to be in control."

Even a rebuke from a Hebrew wanderer couldn't lessen his joy. He didn't know if Isis still breathed, but at least she wasn't lying at the bottom of this gully for the animals to feed upon.

There was still hope.

❧

I only had a few drops of water left. To keep my body temperature from spiking, I walked in the cool of the morning and rested in the shade during the heat of the day. I was sheltering in a small cave high up a rough hillside when I saw the dust of many horsemen headed northeast at full gallop.

The Persians were leaving! Had they left behind a search party? I thought not. They rode at top speed. Battle-hardened soldiers wouldn't respond with such urgency to a handful of Egyptians. There must be a greater threat.

But whatever caused their retreat, I could now head directly west toward the Nile. I could go home.

Thank you, Eben! Thank you, Hathor!

I even thanked Set the Destroyer. If I kept my wits about me, I would yet make it out of this hell.

↜

When the search party with River God, Hetmus-hor and Eben hurried back to base camp to rally the men in pursuit of the Persians, a messenger in Royal Guard uniform waited.

"The Crown Prince is in Hermopolis, Commander. He is anxious to sail, Sir. Your orders are to return at once, Sir."

The Gods damn Psamtik! This was no time for his whims. The Persians were on the run; there was not an hour to lose. That imbecile Prince will cost them their initiative. He allowed himself a deep breath and exhaled slowly. *The man's folly would cost him Isis.*

Rapidly his mind ran through a dozen scenarios and found none viable. He was trapped. If he refused to return, he would be placed under arrest. He would do the same to any soldier who disobeyed a direct order. And there was no advantage to his arrest. His best strategy was to send his Captain in pursuit and get word immediately to the Pharaoh. Amasis the old warrior would grasp at once the necessity of committing all resources to the interception of the Persians.

What must be done, must be done quickly. Without emotion or doubt. He glanced around him at the men readying to set off into the desert. *Would he ever wash from his mouth the bitterness of the words he must say?*

"It would seem the Hebrew was wrong about my destiny. I shall not find Isenkhebe, after all."

Incredulous, Hetmus challenged, "You would abandon the search *now*? When we have reason to hope she still lives?"

"You *dare* call it abandon? I send my men; I put all matériel to the task."

"Do not send, man. Lead!"

"I gave my sacred oath to the Pharaoh! Do you imagine I have a choice?"

"You would choose the Pharaoh over *her*?"

"Watch your tongue! You know nothing of duty. What would a *sportsman* understand of promise?"

"I understand well enough my promise to Isenkhebe."

"You have the freedom to choose," River God shot back. Then he whispered grudgingly, "I envy you that."

"I shall never be free," Hetmus declared, "until Isenkhebe is home."

Men shouted, and weapons clanged. Horses pawed at the parched earth, raising clouds of dust. Overhead a white sun burned in a sky bleached of all color. A day's ride to the West lay the green Nile; to the East stretched the vast brown wasteland of Set and the Persians.

"You are good with words, nobleman. That is something, I suppose, to admire. And fool that you are, I believe your heart is pure. Perhaps the Gods chose this path so that you might redeem your honor."

"Gods do not choose my path, Commander. We are masters of our own fates and suffer or prevail because of our choices. Ride with me now! Let us find her together."

"Do you not know that I desire nothing more? To ride to the East? Now! At this moment! But it cannot be."

"Then *you* are the fool to live in this torment of inflexible rules." Grasping River God's right forearm and left shoulder, he swore, "Hear *my* sacred oath, Commander. I shall find Isenkhebe and bring her back."

"If it is her lifeless body you return, then *I* swear you will pay the price."

In a replay of that night of their first charged encounter, the night around the desert campfire, Eben joined them. This day, he put his right hand as well on River God's arm.

"Do not despair, Commander. We have a destiny. Our destiny is with Isenkhebe. It has been written. I have seen it. Trust. Trust in the Gods."

"I trust no one, Hebrew, except the Gods." He reached out and clasped Hetmus-hor's right arm. "Know that I make this pact, not because I desire it, but because the Gods have spoken."

And so, the three bound themselves as brothers in battle—one man with hope, one faith, and one in seething resentment.

ᘝ

Far to the north in his Delta palace, the Pharaoh Amasis labored to breathe. The heat was stifling. Thick clouds of *kapet* incense ordered by the royal physicians choked the darkened chamber.

To purify the spirit and ease passage from this dream world to the next, an army of priests with shaved heads and leopard skin-draped shoulders droned never-ending incantations.

"Where is that good-for-nothing son of mine?" rattled Amasis.

"The Crown Prince," soothed his old scribe Harwa, "the honored First Son, is in Hermopolis, Your Majesty. He sails when the Commander rejoins him."

"Rejoins him? Why is the Commander not with him now? I gave orders for him to protect the Prince."

"Psamtik sent the Commander to the desert to rescue a kidnapped priestess, Your Grace. Her capture involves Persians, but I have no details."

"Persians!" Amasis struggled up to lean on his elbows. "Shall I never be free of those monsters?" he growled. "Why was I not told?"

"Your Highness has not been in this world for many days."

"Is the Commander in pursuit? He must be in pursuit. He is my best man."

"Psamtik has recalled him, so that he might escort the Prince to Your Grace's presence."

"That pathetic excuse for a man that is my son! Any fool can sail on a barge down the Nile. I need the Commander to bring me hard facts, not the soft buttocks of my worthless heir."

He collapsed back on the divan, turning his head to the side to hack up bloody sputum.

"Damn him," Amasis choked. "Damn the Gods."

"Your Majesty must not exert himself," Harwa murmured, dabbing the Pharaoh's lips with honeyed water. *Not long now, my old friend. The Gods await you.*

"Send word. At once. The Commander is to go after the Persians and report directly to me."

"As Your Majesty commands."

"Why, Harwa, why, did the Gods choose such a wretched successor? Why does Psamtik survive when more worthy have perished?"

"Only the Gods know Their Plan, O Holy One."

"Am I not a god myself—the son of Horus? Why can I not see Their Purpose? Must I die to be privy to the Mystery?" He sighed. "I welcome death, old friend, rather than see Egypt fall."

"The Fate and the Fortune that come, Sire, it is the Gods that send them." *And unless the Gods have plans not yet revealed, the Fate and the Fortune of Egypt shall soon be in the hands of Your Grace's worthless son.*

The last, of course, were thoughts that Harwa the Scribe kept to himself.

CHAPTER 33 ECHO

The men on horseback were far below me and far away. I thought they might be Egyptian, but I resisted shouting and letting the echo carry my voice to them. I dared not risk giving away my position.

The falcon circled overhead. She seemed distant, too. I felt alone in the universe. The goatskin water bag was empty. I had long ago eaten the bread. My feet were cut and bruised; pains shot up my legs with each step.

The words of Qeb-ha became my mantra. *By completing the sunrise and sunset in Right Measure, one arrives safely at his goal.*

Repeating the phrase over and over kept the possibility of survival alive.

I could hardly remember the time before my misery. Everywhere I looked, I saw the General's eyes and the bright red of his blood against the green scarf.

I fingered the amulet and spoke to Eben as if he were seated in front of me.

Lying back on the rocks, in a tiny shaded crevice, I drifted back to the Nile. It brought me peace to summon the warm, damp air of the river and the sound of the water rushing past the hull.

When I dreamed, two giants lifted me with four hands and lowered me gently onto the East Bank, under the sycamore trees by the hunting lodge. The baboons made a great racket, and flocks of white herons rose into the sky. It seemed that my life had begun there on the edge of the river, that everything before that morning was a dream. When I woke, I recognized the faces of the giants as River God and Hetmus-hor.

ꙮ

Hetmus left at the head of the troops pursuing the Persians, riding beside River God's most trusted officer. With the hunting party following in their chariots, River God returned to meet the Crown Prince in Hermopolis. The guard Pasi hurried to carry word to Qeb-ha on the barge. Goliath, Ti and Wah stayed with Eben, who refused to give up the search in the hills.

The Light had revealed to him that Isis was still here.

He first had the idea of the echo while in a Kabbalah trance. He climbed to the summit of one of the deep gorges honeycombing the mountains. Standing at the edge, he tested the wind. With his hands cupped around his mouth, he shouted, "Isis!"

The echo repeated a dozen times as it faded into the east.

"Isis! Isis! Isis!"

He paused between each set to let the echo reverberate on the rocks. His voice became hoarse. He drank water and called out again. Then he moved to another ravine and started all over.

ꙮ

"Isis!" The echo ricocheted around and around, filling the vast space. I couldn't tell from which direction, but understood that someone who knew me well called out my private name.

I stumbled down a steep incline to a *wadi* that wound through the hills toward the west. The ground was flat and less rocky, not nearly so punishing to my stone-bruised feet and exhausted legs. The falcon circled overhead in wide arcs. I was afraid to answer the echo. Who knew what evil lurked?

The sun burned down without mercy. At least there was no dry wind to suck the last of the moisture from my battered body. The General's heavy cape around my shoulders protected my skin from the sun and kept my perspiration from evaporating. It covered the silk caftan which would have flashed bright turquoise for miles. As much as I wanted to be found, my survival depended on it being by the right person.

More in a stupor than awake, I forced my feet to keep moving forward. I was alone in the stillness of the canyon; I saw no other life than the falcon circling in a white sky.

I came around a deep bend in the river bed and instantly flattened myself against the cliff.

A group of men rested three or four hundred feet ahead; they wore the heavy robes of desert people, no matter the heat. Their heads were wrapped in turbans fashioned of cloth as blue as the sky. One man's turban was red.

They took shelter from the heat of the day in the shadows of large boulders and strange-looking brown bushes. They were a ragtag lot, too few for a proper caravan—and caravans don't roam the desolate mountains. Traders follow ages-old routes that lead from oasis to oasis. These men looked to be on foot.

My instincts told me that they must be hiding, like me. If they talked, I couldn't hear them. The stillness hummed in my ears.

I eased backward, body glued to the canyon wall, until hidden by a sharp turn in the cliff wall. It took several deep breaths to calm my pounding heart.

I couldn't go forward and couldn't go back. Behind me stretched miles of *wadi* leading away from the Nile. The cliffs were too steep to climb out.

"Isis! Isis! Isis!"

It had been quiet for a while. I wondered what the men thought of my name cascading down the *wadi* walls, reverberating against the rocks.

The guttural sounds of a Semitic tongue carried through the stillness. I caught a few words and decided they must be from the Island of the Arabs, the land between the Red and Persian Seas.

I didn't know if they were moving toward me or away. I panicked and looked around for tracks. The sand in the center of the *wadi* had been churned up; the prints were deep, made by heavy animals, not men. Whose tracks were these? I'd been too dazed to notice the trail.

"*Be more alert!*" I chastised myself.

Beastly sounds joined the men's voices—nothing like the high whinny of a horse or the complaining of a donkey. In the brief moment I had glimpsed the men, I saw no sign of animals.

Inching slowly forward, I stretched to peer around the corner. The brown bushes were not bushes at all, but camels, monstrous beasts with humps on their backs, lying with bellies on the ground, legs folded at the knees, one foreleg tethered with rope.

The prints must be those of their camels; the trail I saw meant we were going in the same direction. I could follow them out of here.

Deep throaty complaints rumbled from foaming mouths as the men beat the animals with slender rods and pulled them to their feet. Enormous hooves like padded boulders supported painfully thin legs; their knobby knees looked like ghastly skin tumors. One camel bared his teeth and spat saliva. Another spread his legs and urinated, the thick stream blasting backwards in a yellow torrent through his hind legs.

Seven or eight had a chair-like saddle on top of their hump, secured by straps tied around the belly. Each man climbed into a seat and whipped the camel's rump with a baton. First the back legs extended; the men tipped at a sharp angle toward the ground. Then the front legs straightened, and the men sat perched high in the air.

Led by the red turban, the caravan of blue turbans waddled down the riverbed away from me, high seats swaying as if they rode the swells of the sea.

I waited until they turned the next bend in the *wadi* and then started after them, always hugging the edge of the sheer cliffs.

CHAPTER 34 COBRA

When news of the kidnapping reached Thebes, Sit-hathor refused to believe it and threatened to have the messenger flogged.

"Impossible!" she raged. "No one would dare take my daughter. Do they not fear the wrath of Hathor herself?"

But after she accepted that the impossible had indeed happened and that the Persians had no fear of the Goddess, she closed herself in the inner sanctum for two days.

When she emerged, she ordered a barge readied and called for the nursemaid Kiya, who had wept without pause since hearing of the nightmare. The two women fell into each other's arms and spilled yet more tears.

"Our Isis, our beautiful and perfect Isis, Kiya! She has been defiled by Persian beasts!"

They wailed and rocked back and forth. This wasn't the powerful Sit-hathor whose anger, the only emotion she ever allowed, made grown men quiver. Her eyes never shed tears, but tears flowed as though they would never stop.

"We shall travel to Hermopolis, Kiya. We shall be there for Isis. Hathor has revealed to me that She comes as a falcon in the desert and guides our Isenkhebe from the land of Set. The Goddess shall return Isis to us. I have Her word."

ꝏ

It took some time for the cavalry to find the Persian trail. But once found, they rode as fast as the horses could travel, stopping only when the animals needed rest and water. The Persians could reach Pelusium on the Great Green and be over the border before the Egyptians caught up.

Hetmus, unaccustomed to riding horseback, struggled not to show his fatigue. The Captain came to him when they next rested the horses.

The sun overhead was bright white. Heat rose off the sand. The Captain barely sweated. He looked at the horses for a brief moment and then directly at Hetmus.

"Hetmus-hor is as fine a horseman as I have seen in the nobility."

Hetmus understood immediately that he held the cavalry back.

"This is our life, Hetmus-hor. My men ride without sleep. They sleep when they ride. We shall find the Persians, and if she is with them, we shall find Isenkhebe Nefrusobek. You have my oath."

"I can spare a few men to travel with you," he continued. "The Commander would expect me to ensure your safe return."

Heartsick, Hetmus acknowledged reality. He was useless outside of his privileged life. Hunting parties and flirtations were his talents. Had he ever done anything of value before Isis?

ᘰ

The shadows grew long; I could no longer see Re from the bottom of the canyon. The sky was the deeper blue of late afternoon, but the air was still brutally hot. The falcon glided in giant circles above my head, not flapping her wings for long periods of time.

Vultures also circled the ravine. Could they smell my hunger and thirst? If I allowed myself to think of the pain in my feet and legs, I would give up and lie down to die. Barely conscious from fatigue and thirst, I stumbled on the loose stones of a landslide.

A cobra curled not three feet from my bloodied sandals. He reared his head, rising up so that only his tail remained curled on the rock. His hood fanned out around his gaping mouth. Sharp fangs framed a flicking, forked tongue. I didn't move; I didn't blink.

Mesmerized by the swaying fanned head, hypnotized by the teardrop mark below his eye, I heard the wind as the minor key of a snake charmer's flute echoing down the *wadi*.

Tall as me, his cold eyes with round pupils stared straight into mine.

Tiny droplets of clear liquid glistened at the tips of his fangs.

If I flinched, he would strike. How long could I stand perfectly still? My breath was shallow, my chest barely moving. My dry, fat tongue filled my mouth.

The venom of the cobra brings death quickly. Paralyzing my lungs, I would be dead in less than an hour, maybe faster.

A shadow fell across the rocks, and the movement distracted the snake. I jumped to the side, throwing the General's thick cape over my face and arms. The cobra should have struck, but the vulture seized his hooded head in her talons and flew high into the sky.

My feet carried me blindly over the rocky sand; I saw only the snake's forked tongue and the sharp tips of fangs. When my sandal sank into a hole, I slipped into terrible images of eyes—the cobra, the gazelle and finally the General.

It was dark when I woke. Small animals scurried around in the rocks, coming out in the cool of the night to feed. I went forward, but not far.

The men gathered around a fire, eating their evening meal. They had to have water. My tongue was as swollen as when I dug my way out of the sand at the chariot. I tasted blood when I tried to moisten my cracked lips.

If I didn't get water soon, I would die. I might not last another day in this heat. I touched the dagger under my caftan.

Wait until they sleep, then sneak into their camp. It was a wild plan, but I was desperate. Help was near. I had heard the echoes calling my name. I refused to die of thirst in this burned-out ditch.

The fire burned to embers. There was no moon. The men posted no guard. All was quiet except for snoring and occasional low grumbles from the animals.

I arranged the General's cape around me to make my form as tight and controlled as possible. Edging cautiously along the rock wall, I blended into the shadows. When opposite the dying fire, I stepped away from the side. Impossibly quiet, my feet walked on a cushion of air.

A goatskin water bag lay on the ground close to a camel; I couldn't believe my luck. Wanting no swift movements, I lifted the bag an inch at a time. A camel snorted and grumbled. A sleeping man, not more than six feet away, stirred. I stood perfectly still, watching him. He rolled over and farted but didn't wake.

My stomach growled with hunger, but I had to be content with water. One shouldn't tempt fortune. I backtracked to the edge of the *wadi* and then thought of my footprints. Retracing my steps, I bent from the waist and dragged the hem of the cape on the loose earth, spreading gritty sand over the imprint of my sandals.

I would have made it away but for the jackal stepping too close to the edge of the ridge above. Pebbles cascaded down, loosening more and more rocks the farther they tumbled. A shower of stones fell all around me. A half dozen or so bounced off my shoulders and back.

The racket of the falling rocks wakened the camels. The men might have slept through the rockslide, but not the animals; they pulled at their tethers, trying to stand, making hellish noises.

In an instant, the men were awake and on their feet, daggers in their hands.

I froze, hoping the dark cloak blended into the black contours of the cliff. But they saw me almost at once.

The air exploded in wild shouting. Four men rushed me with raised knives. Starlight flashed off the blades. I threw my hood back, so they might see my pale face and lush wig and recognize an Egyptian woman even in the dim light.

They moved to encircle me, as natural as a wolf pack, no word spoken between them. The man with the red turban stood in front of me, so close I could stretch out and touch him. He had the yellow eyes of a jackal.

"*Anna* Isis!" I shouted in the little Arabic I knew. "I am goddess woman!"

They stopped in their tracks, visibly shaken by this shadowy woman speaking their tongue, shouting out the name they had heard echoing through the hills.

The tribes of the desert are said to be a superstitious lot, believing in a beautiful witch who lives in the mountains and steals men's souls while they sleep. They were frightened of me. I took advantage of it.

"I go home. I have gold, very big."

I could see them relax slightly. They clearly liked the mention of gold.

"Egypt big happy. Give big gold."

I stepped forward one step, and the yellow-eyed man in the red turban stepped back.

Summoning a whisper of the Power, I started toward the embers of the campfire. The men moved silently aside to let me pass.

I held my shoulders straight and my head high. My feet felt as large and heavy as those of the camels.

Folding my legs, I eased to the ground beside the campfire and took a careful drink from the goatskin bag. The brackish water, drawn from a desert well, tasted sweeter than honeyed tea to my parched mouth. I sipped small amounts, giving each time to settle.

They stood around the embers and stared at me; some dared whisper to each other.

"Give me food," I commanded.

Bread and roast goat appeared, and I ate.

"Tomorrow ride camel."

So far they seemed awed by me. I wanted to keep it that way. I would show them no fear. Wrapping my cloak tight around me, I lay down beside the coals and pretended to sleep.

No one came near. I heard hurried whispers and the slight crunch of footsteps in gravelly sand. They must have agreed on something, because soon it was silent. Then I heard soft snoring again and allowed myself to sleep.

CHAPTER 35   RESCUE

River God reached the hunting lodge on the East Bank to find an envoy from the Governor waiting with an urgent message from Saïs.

Commander to pursue Persian incursion Eastern Desert. By decree of Pharaoh (glyph Amasis II)

When his silent outrage was sufficiently under control, he inquired in a steady voice if Psamtik was still in port.

"The Crown Prince sailed this morning, Sir, with a captain chosen by the Governor."

River God couldn't decide if he was relieved or disappointed. The worthless ass Psamtik was not yet Horus-on-earth. He wanted nothing more than to plunge his double-edged sword into the Prince's soft belly and tear out his entrails before the horrified eyes of the depraved Setne.

If the Prince proved to be the loss of Isis, he might do it yet.

The cavalry led by his best man would be far to the northeast by now. There were not horses fast enough in all Egypt to catch up with them.

Night was coming. The hunting lodge had food and fresh water. His handful of men merited a rest. They would sleep here tonight.

He sent Pasi across the Nile to Qeb-ha with the devastating news. The Persians had escaped. No one knew if Isenkhebe still lived.

River God, who seldom dreamed, tossed and turned, his sleep disturbed by the strange vision of a caravan of camels led by Isis. A lion's skin covered her shoulders, its head with gaping mouth and glassy eyes perched on her black wig.

He roused the men with first light. They would ride back into the desert and find Eben. He didn't trust in Hebrews or their Kabbalah magic, but where else could he turn?

☙

"The safest route to Hermopolis, my Lord Hetmus-hor, is to head west to the Nile and follow the river south."

"I do not intend to return to Hermopolis, Sergeant, but to rejoin the Hebrew in his search for Isenkhebe Nefrusobek."

Hetmus didn't believe in magical visions—not those of Hebrews—or Egyptians—but to return now to Hermopolis was to surrender and admit defeat. Eben was a long shot, but it was all he had. He wasn't giving up on Isis.

The small band of horsemen turned southwest and retraced their tracks across the barren wasteland of sand and rocks.

☙

The sound of "Isis" echoed off every hill. Eben continued, not because he thought Isenkhebe would find them by the echo, but because she would draw strength from the knowledge that she was not alone.

He didn't know if it were the best thing to do. He didn't allow himself to doubt. It was the only thing he could think to do, and so he did it. He would trust in the Light.

☙

My little caravan of twenty camels and a handful of desert men wound its way down the *wadi*. Riding atop the hump was much more difficult than it looked. My saddle chair swayed back and forth as if on a rolling sea. Heat shimmered off rocks and sand.

Tiny particles of gritty dust coated the inside of my nose and mouth and scratched my eyes. White light blinded me. If I closed my lids, I was overcome with nausea. But I would have endured anything to be off my bleeding feet and avoid putting my weight on the hard ground.

When the echoes of "Isis" began again, the men spooked. They stared at me when they thought I wasn't looking but turned away quickly to avoid meeting my eye. They no doubt still feared I was a sorceress who could steal their souls.

After midday, the caravan left the bleak mountains and began the long, dusty trek across the flat desert plateau. We stopped as usual for the heat of the day, and I napped in the shade of the camel's hump. The falcon overhead was the last thing I saw before I closed my eyes.

In the Land of the Dreams, I visited my garden with the birdsong, the scent of sweet blossoms and the sculpted face of River God. But the face kept changing from River God to Hetmus-hor and back again.

⇗

It was Goliath who first spotted the cloud of dust approaching from the southwest and then the other cloud from the northeast. Whoever they were, they were not many, not the cavalry or the Persians.

He studied a thin black line moving away from the hills, watching the specks inching across the flat plain until he made out a train of camels.

Nodding his head, he pointed to a tiny dot circling in the white sky over the caravan. Like any animal with good sense, a falcon avoids the heat of the day.

"Ride toward the camel train," ordered Eben. "You, Ti, ride to the group coming from the northeast. And you, Wah, head to those coming from the Nile. Rendezvous with Goliath under the falcon."

The three had barely ridden off before Eben settled with his amulet, rocking back and forth from the waist in time with the wild rhythm of a Kabbalah chant.

⇗

Wah galloped at full speed to River God and turned him toward the falcon circling in the sky.

"Where are you directing us, man? What do you know?"

"We are following the falcon, Sir. It is Eben who orders it."

Ti reached Hetmus-hor and turned him toward the falcon. Hetmus didn't ask why. He followed without question.

⌇

I woke to excited shouting. A horse approached; I felt the vibration of hooves reverberating in the hard earth. As I watched, my eyes straining to see in the white glare, a lone rider drew closer and closer. Waves of heat shimmered above the sand; the distorted figure, tall as a giant, bore rapidly down on me. Was it a mirage?

Dust blew into my eyes, and I turned my head. The pounding of hooves stopped, and I could hear the heavy breathing of a winded horse. When I looked again, Goliath was leaping to the ground.

Rocking back and forth in the delirious swaying of one of Eben's trances, I called out to the heavens, "O Hathor! Thank you! Thank you!"

Goliath rushed to me and then abruptly stopped. He had never touched me; he had never even brushed against my skin. I went to my knees and grabbed his ankles, my lips on his feet. I would have cried a river on those big, beautiful feet, but the desert had sucked away my last tear.

The turbaned men kept their distance. I was vaguely aware of awed voices in the background. The sight of the mountain witch kissing the feet of a Nubian slave must have spooked them more than anything they had seen or heard on the trail.

I tried to stand but collapsed at once from the stab of pain in my feet. Goliath lifted me into his arms but was careful only to glance at my face before looking away. He stood, eyes straight ahead, like a giant basalt statue of a Pharaoh carved for a temple in Aswan. I held him so tight, I don't know where I got the strength.

More horses approached and then suddenly, as if they rode straight from my dreams, River God and Hetmus-hor thundered up and dismounted together. The two men stood side by side, Hetmus half a head taller than River God. Goliath, holding me in his arms, towered over them both. For what seemed like an eternity, no one moved. The shadow of the falcon circled us.

It was Hetmus who shouted, "Isis! You are alive!"

Rushing forward, he pulled me from Goliath into his own arms and crushed me to his chest.

I wasn't especially conscious that it was Hetmus who held me. My only thought was that the nightmare was over. I clutched his neck as if I would never let go. I didn't even try to control my sobs of relief.

When I raised my face, he kissed me full on the mouth. I forgot my blistered lips and drank in his strength. He had saved me. Hetmus had saved me. I kissed him with the passion of gratitude.

Then over his shoulder, I met River God's wounded, angry eyes.

CHAPTER 36 CONFESSION

Music and laughter carried in the desert air long before we could see the hunting lodge and the flotilla of pleasure boats moored in the rushes of the Nile. Every nobleman and priest from Hermopolis must have been on the East Bank to greet us.

A thunderous roar erupted when Hetmus rode up with me seated in front of him on his white stallion. The ecstatic chant of the crowd rang in my ears.

"Hetmus long life! Hetmus long life! Hetmus long life!"

Ankh-hor, flanked by six slaves in shimmering white kilts and blue and yellow striped headdresses, stepped into our path. Ankh-hor himself wore so much gold, I was nearly blinded looking at him.

"Welcome home, my son, Savior of Priestesses! Welcome to your victory feast!"

All around was the smell of meat roasting, but it only made me nauseous. Whole oxen, oryx and hippopotamuses turned on spits. Low wooden tables piled high with breads, cheeses and fruits were arranged in long rows. Judging by the shouts and swaggers, the party had long ago started on the *amphorae*-mountain of wine.

After the silence of the desert, the clamor deafened me. There were too many people. So much noise. My head pounded.

"Let me pass! No one shall see my Isenkhebe Nefrusobek in such a condition."

The crush of bodies parted for my mother Sit-hathor dressed for a temple ritual in the solar disk headdress with twin horns and fluttering white ostrich feathers. She even wore the sacred beaded *menit* around her neck. A cadre of priests trailed after her. Four slaves carried an empty litter trimmed with blue and white tassels.

The esteemed Lord Ankh-hor stepped aside and bowed low.

"Out of my way," she menaced. "You are responsible."

"Yes, Your Highest-of-High, but we have brought her back." He looked terrified, as well he should.

Over the heads of the crowd, I saw River God still mounted on his black stallion with silver-braided mane and tail. He hadn't spoken to me during the long trek to the Nile but rode at the head of the convoy of horsemen, leaving me to ride with Hetmus, never looking back to see me looking at him.

His men gathered around him, sunlight flashing on their swords, singing their Commander's praises, competing with the cheers of 'Savior of Priestesses' intended for Hetmus-hor.

Clearly Hetmus was the hero of the day; everyone seemed to have forgotten that it was he who lost me in the first place. Except Sit-hathor. She hadn't forgotten. She cast a withering glare at the father Ankh-hor as we passed.

Waiting inside the splendid tent Sit-hathor had set up for my arrival was Qeb-ha. I kissed his old hand and begged his forgiveness.

"I am only a priest," he said kindly. "The Gods know the impious and the pious man by his heart. The Goddess has judged Isenkhebe to be pious. Why else would Hathor appear as a falcon to lead her out of the desert?"

The heat, the thirst, the pain, the fear, the desolation, the panic, everything crashed on me at once. I'd never known such exhaustion.

I lay on the bed and wept for what seemed like hours. My mother and Kiya both held me and would not let anyone near. Maia brought herbed water to soak my swollen and lacerated feet, but Kiya grabbed the bowl and slapped her hands away. My mother, the great Sit-hathor herself, shaved my head tenderly with a new copper razor.

"Burn this foul wig," she commanded. "And burn this wretched cape and those sandals as well."

But she fingered the smooth silk of my turquoise caftan in the same way the women in the camp had touched my linen hunting gown. She studied the delicate embroidery and the superior quality of the fabric—the turquoise color still sublime, even stained by the dirt of the desert.

"This smells like an animal! But perhaps it could be cleaned? I should like to learn more of the weaving and the thread," she admitted, touching it longingly.

Beauty has the power to surmount impossible barriers.

"Keep it, but get it out of the tent now! I want nothing of those Persian beasts near my Isenkhebe."

They shaved me and bathed me and then massaged the best fragrant oils into my skin burned by the sun and chafed by sand. A gown of the finest weave in all Egypt was pulled down over my shoulders, raw from the General's coarse wool cape.

Kiya fretted over my bony hips, urging a warm duck broth down my parched throat but not letting me taste solid food until she saw the soup settled.

When she started to take off the leather amulet, I wouldn't let her touch it. I would never take it off.

The celebration was loud with singing and the sudden shouts of gamblers. I wondered if River God was still here. He hadn't tried to see me. Hetmus had come to the tent but been turned away. Sit-hathor let him know that she held his father and him responsible for everything that had happened—for the desert, for the Persians. She gave orders to the priests that no member of Ankh-hor's family be allowed near me.

She didn't ask me about the Persians or what had happened to me in the camp. No one asked me about how I got away—not Hetmus, not Eben, not Qeb-ha. They didn't want to know. I wanted to forget but couldn't.

Bathed, oiled and dressed, a full and glorious new wig on my head and my eyes painted with mica and *kohl*, I lay on the low bed unable to see anything but the shock on the General's face. My lips, too cracked to stain with pomegranate juice, made it painful to talk, but I was compelled to unload the weight of my guilt.

"Mother, I must tell you."

"Yes, you must tell all, but later. Forget the desert and be joyful you are safe with us. Hold only happy thoughts in your head and beautiful visions before your eyes."

"But, Mother, I have visions that do not go away. They are before my eyes when open, and they are there when my lids close."

"Let her speak," interceded Kiya. "I can see she shall have no rest until she does."

"Yes, Kiya. I see, as well," sighed Sit-hathor. Her face was sad with a trace of dread in her eyes. "Speak of the horrors, my beauty, if you must. But scabs must not be picked too soon. Wounds need time to heal. And remember that this evil happened to your body, not to your soul."

"My wounds *are* to my soul, Mother."

Her eyes widened; she looked sharply at Kiya. When she took my hand in hers, our twin Hathor rings flashed in the light.

"Then we shall call upon the Goddess, my precious one," she crooned in her voice of liquid gold. "Hathor delivered you from the desert. She shall deliver you from this. Once the words are spoken, purge them from your mind. What happened is no longer part of your life."

As she spoke, the Hathor energy flowed through me. I felt the General again—the pain and the ecstasy—and then finally the ride on a comet. I shuddered and exhaled all the air in my lungs, feeling my breath vibrate in my throat. To my ears, the sound was a wail.

"I killed the General, Mother," I whispered. "I made love to him—and then I cut his throat."

Her black eyes were wide with horror before her lids nearly closed, and she exhaled a long hiss, not unlike that of a serpent.

"He bled to death, Mother. I watched his *Ka* leave his body."

My voice took on a flat quality devoid of emotion. I heard myself speak yet was detached from the meaning of the words.

"His blood spilled down his chest and onto my hands. It was everywhere. I tried to staunch the bleeding with a green scarf."

"Listen to me!" she commanded. "Do not *ever* again speak of love with this animal. You owe him nothing, do you hear? Nothing."

"He had to die, Mother," I sobbed, "but I did not want him to. Can you understand? I did not *want* him to die!"

Sit-hathor leaned forward until I saw nothing but her face. I'd never seen her eyes so glittery, like black glass. Her fingers dug into my shoulders.

"Stop, Isenkhebe! I forbid you to have feelings for that monster!"

I closed my eyes. I felt dead myself.

"I had no choice," I said flatly. "It was him or me."

She relaxed her fingers and kissed me lightly on the forehead. When she spoke again, her tone was matter-of-fact, as if she commented on a household chore.

"Of course you killed him, my daughter. And I hope you cut off his filthy balls and stuffed them in his vile mouth."

I felt safe. Everyone thought I was safe. I assumed the desert renegade band to be satisfied with the generous chunks of roasted meat and the heavy sack of gold amulets. I didn't know the man in the red turban understood a few words of Egyptian—*priestess, Persian, escape.* He roamed the banquet to catch small phrases from tales that grew more fantastic with each telling. I didn't know that he already plotted how this Isis of the desert might bring yet more gold.

CHAPTER 37 BARB

I could hear the pounding of hammer on stone, never ceasing. The Saïte Dynasty was rebuilding Egypt all around me. They must be carving a column outside my bedchamber.

A door opened; I heard voices and opened my eyes to the Red Mirror. Barb rushed in with the property manager beside her, a ring of keys in his hand.

"Are you okay?" she yelled at me from the end of a long tunnel.

My ears rang. Awakened abruptly as if from a coma, I felt drugged and disoriented. Was I dreaming inside of a dream, or was I truly back?

"Are you okay?" she repeated, her voice filled with alarm. "Do you need a doctor? Should we call 911?"

The manager had his cell phone out, ready to hit send.

"No! Don't call! I'm fine. I was just…sleeping. I didn't hear you knock."

"Sleeping? What is *wrong* with you?"

I'd never seen Barb so grave. She collapsed on the floor beside me, put her palm on my forehead and then placed her fingers on my pulse.

"I've been calling you for *two* days. Your office has been calling you. Why haven't you answered your cell? We thought you'd been kidnapped—or were dead."

I looked at her and wondered how she knew.

"I'm okay…really I am. I'm sorry I worried everyone." Then I asked the manager politely. "Would you bring me a glass of water, please?"

He walked over to the kitchen, and I heard him open a cabinet door.

"Get him out of here," I whispered urgently to Barb. "I'll tell you everything."

"Thank you," I said gratefully and emptied the glass in one go.

"Do you mind if I have a look around? Make sure everything is okay?"

He didn't wait for my answer but tested the sliding glass doors. They were locked. He stepped into my bedroom. I heard him check the glass doors to the terrace and go into the walk-in closet and my bathroom. He checked the second bedroom and bath and then came back and stood looking down at me.

I still sat on the floor, the empty glass in my hand.

"Everything seems like it should be." His tone said he didn't believe it.

"Thank you so much for your help." I tried to sound cheerful and normal. "I'm so sorry to be such a bother."

The manager closed the door behind him, and I got up off the floor and headed straight for the toilet. Barb followed me to the door.

"What the hell is going on? You check out for more than two days and then act like you are high on some drug. Have you been taking something? That's not like you."

Barb sounded exactly like my mother when she caught a boy in my room in junior high.

I had no idea where to begin, so I started with the beginning.

"Barb, remember I told you about the Red Mirror?"

When I finished, Barb sat motionless on my Bauhaus-inspired red suede sofa she hated because she said it hurt her back. She clutched a polka dot throw pillow in her long, thin arms. I saw her flaxen hair as a gleaming electrum helmet molded to her small, oval-shaped skull. She would look great with a shaved head.

Because she didn't say anything—unusual for her—I doubted briefly that she had heard me. In fact, I had doubts that she—we—actually sat here. That is until Aisha crawled up into my lap, purring. Yes, I truly was sitting in my gray leather chair.

Barb looked over at the Red Mirror and then back at me.

"You know," she said quietly, "if I hadn't seen you and Rasheed—*River God*, you say—at the Stirling Club and the connection between you—right from the first moment—I'd think you were out of your mind."

Barb believed me! I never expected anyone to believe me. I could hardly believe myself.

"Thank you, Barb. I know it sounds insane and impossible. But I don't think I'm capable of dreaming something like this."

"No, not even you could dream this up."

Barb, down-to-earth Barb, seemed willing to fly a little.

Encouraged, I dared tell her, "I'm not as happy to be back as I thought I would be."

"How can you say that? It sounded perfectly terrifying."

"It was. I came so close to dying. I think Isis might have died if not for me."

"Listen to yourself. This woman *did* die. Thousands of years ago. You are you. You are here, and she is long dead."

"Maybe it's impossible to understand if you haven't experienced it. But I don't look at Isis as someone separate from myself. I see her as me."

Barb took my hand, gripping it a little too tight. Her blue eyes, usually sharp and a bit critical, had a trace of panic in them.

"It's going to be fine," she assured me in a voice that trembled ever so slightly.

She was trying to convince herself as much as me. Stiff upper lip in the Scotch-Canadian way, Barb wasn't one for displays of emotion, even sympathy. She was definitely upset, unnerved even.

"You'll see," she said a little more forcefully. "Now you're back, and everything will be just as it was."

That was exactly what I feared. Life being normal. Boring job. No River God. No Hetmus-hor. A nobody with a nothing life.

"Are you okay to be alone? Do you want me to stay with you?"

I shook my head. "I need some time to…process everything."

"We'll get together later," she ordered. Barb was back to her bossy self. "Keep your cell on and don't go near the mirror."

I nodded my head.

"Promise me. Say it out loud."

She stood at the open door, looking at me, waiting for my answer.

"Yes, I promise. Cell on—and no Red Mirror."

I checked my missed calls. Besides Barb, there were a string from my boss. I couldn't deal with that, at least not yet, so I continued to scroll. Carla had called yesterday—twice. She answered right away.

"I'm having a party!" She sounded excited; her voice was high with happiness. "I want you to meet my new boyfriend. He's a doll. I'm in love."

Carla fell in love easily and out again just as fast. Beautiful and rich, she had the kind of money you work for—not a trust fund, not easy. She owned a penthouse at the exclusive Turnberry Towers with a heart-stopping view of the Strip. She was spoiled, but she spoiled herself.

At the top of her game, she was mature enough to be taken seriously but young enough to have muscle tone. Jewish, with shiny black hair cut short like a pixie, she came from Rio and spoke English with the same rapid-fire speed as Portuguese. Her mind, too, moved at the speed of light. I wished I could be more like her. Carla always knew exactly what she wanted and got it.

"Tonight, darling. Come by after nine. It's intimate, only a few friends."

I knew what that meant. Carla had a lot of friends.

"May I bring someone?"

"Of course! Is he good-looking?"

I laughed. Carla always made me laugh.

"It's my friend Barb. I promised to see her tonight."

"Of course, bring her along. It's dressy; be sure and tell her that."

Carla didn't need to remind me. I don't think she ever threw a casual party.

CHAPTER 38 THE BOYFRIEND

When I finally got up my courage to make the call, Ed answered on the first ring, blasting my eardrum with "Where the hell have you been?"

"I called in, Ed. I told Cynthia I was sick. Didn't you get the message?"

"Hell, yes, I got the message, but does being sick mean you can't answer the phone? I hope you were in the hospital."

Thanks, Ed.

"Well, I'm on the phone now, Ed. What's up?"

I heard him catch his breath at my confident tone. Ed always tries to bully people. But after the General, he didn't seem that tough anymore.

"Huh? Well...well, the deadline's been postponed until the end of next week," he stammered. "But the client wants changes, *big* changes."

I could tell he was blowing it out of proportion, as he usually did.

"I can't come into the office today, Ed. I just can't. Why don't you email me the changes you need? I've got Photoshop. I can work at home."

Ed was quiet for a couple of seconds. I waited.

"Sure. That'll work, I guess."

Then after a silence so long I thought he had hung up on me, he asked, "Are you okay? You don't sound like yourself."

"I'm fine, Ed. It's been a rough couple of days, that's all. Don't worry about the project. I always come through for you, don't I?"

"Yeah," he begrudgingly agreed. "You do come through, but it can be touch-and-go right to the end."

"Thanks, Ed. Email me the info. I'll take a look at it."

"See you Monday?" he asked a little uncertainly.

"Sure, Ed. See you Monday."

The others on my missed calls list got text messages; I didn't feel like talking to anyone else. I took a long shower and hung the towels on the balcony to dry in the sun. The sky was as blue as Egypt. I grabbed a rice bowl from the freezer, stuck it in the microwave and thought of my breakfast with the General.

They were all dead now. Everyone was dead—Qeb-ha, Maia, River God, Hetmus—all dead. The Persians were dead. Even the camels were dead. All the drama of life seemed so pointless.

If you look back from 2,500 years later, it doesn't actually matter when you die. Or how. But I felt inexplicably sad. I missed them all. Well, not the Persians. But the General still haunted me.

When I looked into the Red Mirror, I saw Isis in my face. I took out the scissors, wet my hair again and cut bangs straight across my forehead. It surprised me how much I looked like Isis then—Isis in her wig, of course.

On an impulse, I called Elaine back in Pennsylvania. We'd been roommates in college and friends ever since. She was married with two kids and lived in a wonderful two-story colonial on the edge of Amish country.

"Elaine, it's me."

"Hi, how have you been?"

Elaine was always so calm. She reminded me of the nurturing side of Hathor, the benevolent aspects of motherhood and fecundity.

"I'm okay, but I've had some strange experiences. It'd take too long to explain. Is the timing bad?"

"What kind of experiences?"

"Elaine, you believe in reincarnation, don't you?"

"Well, yes, I have my own ideas about it. Why do you ask?"

"You believe that we've lived before, right? That you, Elaine, lived another life in another time?"

"I think we live many lives—that our souls are progressing through experiences on the path to higher consciousness."

"Do you believe you can meet the same people in other lives, but they're different and yet the same?"

"I think we keep encountering the same souls over and over until we learn the lessons we need to teach each other."

"Do you think you have known me before, Elaine? In another lifetime?"

"Absolutely. We have known each other before, and we will know each other again."

Rasheed said exactly the same thing the morning he left me in the Wynn.

"You haven't told me why you're asking me all this. What's happened?"

"I'm sorting some things out. You've really helped me. I'll tell you all about it someday, but there's too much to explain right now."

"I'll take the time, if you need me." That's Elaine. Always my rock.

"No, that's all right. I think I'm starting to understand. Thank you. Thank you, so much, Elaine. Say hi to Steve and the kids."

It took me a while to decide what to wear to Carla's party. I dug out a snug, low-cut white silk tunic and a white, long clingy skirt. At the bottom of my closet, I found gold sandals with turquoise-looking stones embedded across the straps. My feet looked so bare. No henna patterns. I'd seen lots of girls with tiny tattoos on their toes and ankles and always thought it silly. I wasn't so sure anymore.

I fastened a heavy gold chain low on my hips and then remembered a necklace my aunt had given me years ago, something she bought on a tour to Israel. Three golden chains fell across my collarbone with strings of turquoise beads in between. Not quite Egyptian, but close enough.

The valet whisked away my car, and the doorman opened the glass doors into the white marble foyer. Barb was waiting for me in the sleek, ultra-modern lobby dotted with lush orchid bouquets in Chinese vases.

She looked hard at me but didn't say a word until we got into the stainless steel elevator.

"Well, you certainly are playing the part. Did you cut your bangs?"

It was a silly question, and she knew it.

"You look great, Barb."

She did, too. Her flaxen hair glistened. She wore hot pink and yellow. I wondered when we had known each other before.

When we rang the bell, a slim young woman in a black dress, white apron and giant gold hoop earrings greeted us and took our coats. Barb followed me down the walnut parquet hallway into the living room plastered with bold, abstract paintings in primary colors. A broad terrace, furnished with white outdoor sofas and heat lamps, stretched outside the living room glass doors. The lights of the Strip blazed beyond.

Brazilian jazz played through hidden speakers. The kitchen was crowded with handsome young men in black suits and T-shirts, their hair short and spiky. Most of them were speaking Portuguese. This was Carla's group of Brazilian friends. Their dates, gorgeous girls in the shortest of skirts, balanced on the highest of heels.

Carla had a rule. You have to be beautiful to attend her parties—or rich.

Two cooks were busy at the gleaming Viking range. The aroma of *empanadas* and other South American delicacies wafted through the air. There was anything you wanted at the bar; a bartender in a white jacket mixed drinks. I saw my choice right away—*Moet & Chandon*.

Barb and I took flutes with champagne and wandered out onto the terrace, looking for Carla. I spotted her at the edge of the balcony, laughing with a small group. The top of her head barely reached the shoulder of the man she leaned into.

Maneuvering my way through the sofas, I eased up beside her.

"Oh, my God! I didn't even know it was you! You look like Cleopatra!" she squealed, kissing me on both cheeks. She beamed.

Yes, Carla was definitely in love.

The new boyfriend looked out over the city when we came up. Carla squeezed his arm, and he turned.

"Meet Hector," she said triumphantly. Her black eyes glowed.

"*Encantada*," he said with a wide smile of brilliant white teeth.

I was perfectly calm. I wasn't even that surprised. I took his hand and smiled back.

"Hello, Hector."

He had the natural confidence that comes with being tall, handsome and privileged. What had Carla said about him? Something about Argentina and polo?

He held onto my hand a little too long, and Carla looked from my face to his and back again.

"Do you two know each other?"

"*Si*," Hector said, "but from a very long time ago."

Then Barb was there with a look on her face that shouted, "Oh no, not again!"

I took my hand away.

"Carla, this is my friend, Barb. Barb, this is Hector, Carla's boyfriend."

Carla liked the boyfriend bit. She put her arm through Hector's and snuggled against his biceps. Whatever had gone on before, he was hers now.

"Now tell me how you know each other," she insisted. "No secrets allowed!"

She beamed up at Hector and actually batted her lashes. Hector smiled at me a little too warmly.

"It was long ago, Carlita, in another life," he said, kissing her lightly on the cheek. "Please, excuse me while I get another *cerveza. Más champaña*, ladies?"

With another gracious smile and slight bow of his head, he excused himself, "*Con permiso.*"

I don't think anyone noticed his sideways glance into my eyes as he squeezed by me, his dinner jacket brushing my arm. Carla's starry eyes followed him.

"Isn't he gorgeous? He's a perfect gentleman, but not too much, if you know what I mean."

Her eyes twinkled, and her dimples deepened. I knew precisely what she meant.

A handsome couple joined us. They knew Barb and started to talk real estate. I slipped away.

I went into the living room and then into the kitchen. No Hector.

The hallway to Carla's bedroom was empty. When the door to her bathroom opened with a blaze of bright light, a man with white hair and a tuxedo came out and smiled.

"It's all yours," he said gallantly.

Hector waited by the picture window across the room from Carla's bed buried in guests' fur coats. The Stratosphere behind him looked close enough to reach out and touch.

"Hello, Isis."

I walked right up to him, put my hands on his chest and leaned my head back to look into his eyes. Those eyes that I'd know anywhere.

"Hello, Hetmus. I never expected to see you here."

CHAPTER 39 FORTUNE-TELLER

He was like a man who had thirsted in the desert for days. Taking me by the shoulders, he pulled me tight to him, my hands still on his chest, my elbows crushed between us. He kissed me with such force that I had to use the muscles in my neck to keep my head from bending all the way back.

He wrapped his long arms around me, nearly lifting me off my feet, kissing my lips, my neck, my shoulders, my throat, everywhere he could find flesh. He buried his face in my hair and breathed in. His whole body sighed. If he held me tight enough, I wouldn't disappear. An image of him devouring me flashed in my mind; he could have swallowed me whole.

"Hector, my arms. Please, you're breaking my elbows."

He released me then, not all the way, but relaxed his arms enough that I could move mine. I slid my hands under his dinner jacket, burying my face in his broad chest. I smelled starch and the faintest scent of soap. He tightened his grip again. He was rock hard against my waist.

With no effort at all, he lifted me into his arms, my feet dangling down, the same as he had held me in the desert under the shadow of the circling falcon.

"I've waited a few thousand years for this," he breathed in my ear as he carried me to the bed.

"Hector! Stop! Are you crazy? You can't do this! We can't do this. This is Carla's bedroom. Stop!"

He lay me among the silk pillows and pile of guests' furs, running his fingers down the length of my body from my face to my ankles, his eyes soaking up every curve.

"You are perfect, Isis. I could never tire of touching you."

He kissed me again, long and hungry.

"Leave with me," he breathed into my ear.

"I can't do that to Carla. She's my friend."

I could see by his face that meant nothing to him. I sat up to the edge of the bed. Hector put his feet on the floor beside mine. The bed was low; his knees poked up at an angle, but he still easily and gracefully pulled me onto his lap. He held me as if I were a child.

"She is nothing to me. I like her—I liked her. But I will not lose you again."

Suddenly Barb was in the doorway, looking so much like an angry headmistress, I expected her to put her hands on her hips or shake her finger at us. Waves of rage rolled through the room.

"I, uh, hate to break this up, but Carla is looking for you, Hector."

She spoke to Hector but glared at me, her eyes shooting daggers. *What are you doing? Have you lost your mind?*

"Go to her," I told him. "We don't want a scene."

Thank Hathor, it was Barb who had come in and not Carla. There's no telling what hot-blooded Brazilian Carla might have done.

I got up from his lap, straightened his jacket and smoothed his wavy chestnut hair.

"Go to her, *please*," I pleaded with my palms on his cheeks.

He kissed me lightly, a brush on the lips. His eyes were warm brown with red specks.

"Don't leave without me," he said.

As soon as Hector's back disappeared through the doorway, Barb snorted with disgust. "Bloody hell, could you be more obvious? Both of you disappearing like that. And in Carla's *bed*?"

"I need a drink."

It was the only answer I had for her.

I ordered single malt, straight with a splash, no ice. The bartender, knowing the code of those words, filled my short glass three quarters full. My hands trembled.

Barb glared at me. I could read her thoughts. *Show some control, girl. Get yourself under control.*

I think she might have lectured me right there at the bar, but I was saved by a buxom redhead in a sapphire blue knit sheath.

"Have you been to the fortune-teller yet? You have to try it. He'll blow your mind."

Barb went in first. I admit to being a little scared. My mind still dwelled in the past, the distant past; I didn't know if I could handle the future. When she came out, it was with a dazed expression.

"It's really, *really* strange. He told me things that nobody could possibly know."

I didn't think Barb had any secrets.

"Were they good things?" I couldn't bear any doom and gloom. I was far too emotionally fragile for anything but good news.

The fortune-teller sat in a darkened room at a small table. A low lamp with a red shade burned nearby. He didn't look directly at me but motioned for me to sit in the straight-backed chair on the opposite side of the table. The bare surface of the wooden top gleamed.

His suit was all wrong; it didn't fit him at all. Even his body language was awkward. The way he moved and the way he spoke made me think he wasn't all there—not crazy or retarded, but autistic maybe.

Taking my hands in his, he closed his eyes. His body swayed from side to side; the rocking reminded me of Eben when he went into a Kabbalah trance. I looked hard to see if the Hebrew mystic was buried somewhere inside this strange, lost creature, but I got no feel that Eben was here.

He mumbled. I couldn't make out anything he said. Should I ask him to speak up? Then he stopped rocking with a jerk and sucked in a short breath. His hot and sweaty hands gripped my cold fingers in an iron vise.

"You are in great danger," he intoned.

His voice came from some distant place, the sound hollow, like a soft echo. I had the sense he wasn't here in this room, but far away.

"You think you are safe. Everyone thinks you are safe. But they are wrong."

I hated this. I didn't like it one bit. This wasn't what you'd expect at a party. He should be telling me that I would meet a tall, dark stranger and didn't need to worry about money.

"You must get out. To stay is more horrible than you can imagine. If they find you, they will do terrible things to you. They will find you, if you stay."

I pulled my hands away and actually put them over my ears in a vain attempt not to hear more.

He jerked again and opened his eyes, looking straight at me for the first time.

"You have to go back, Isis. Or you will suffer. You can't imagine the suffering."

I stood up so abruptly, the chair tipped over and hit the parquet floor with a smack. I don't know what terrified me the most—the words he spoke—or his eyes.

Eben sat before me, trapped in this pathetic shell of a man. Eben's eyes pleaded with me.

"Go back, Isis," he begged. "Go back and save yourself."

My heart exploded in my chest. I couldn't get out of the room fast enough. Flying through the door, I collapsed against the wall in the hallway, bending from the waist, gulping air.

A freaked Barb held me tight.

"My god, what did he say to you? It's a party game. The guy's not real. Nothing he says is real."

She had conveniently forgotten her own awe when she exited the room.

People looked at me, trying to decide if I'd had too much to drink or overdosed. I heard '911' for the second time today. I imagined how ridiculous I looked, dressed up like it was Halloween.

Barb maneuvered me into a third bedroom and closed the door.

"Sit down," she commanded. "Put your head between your knees. Don't move. I'm getting you some water. "

I felt dizzy and sick and hoped I wouldn't vomit on Carla's Marimekko rug.

Voices conferred outside the door, but no one came in. Barb reappeared with a glass of water and made me take sips. Then Carla was there.

"What happened? Did you drink too much? Why don't you lie down? You can sleep here tonight." She was distraught and caring at the same time.

I had difficulty understanding; voices sounded thick and syrupy, as if played on too slow a speed on a tape recorder. Hector stood behind Carla, distress all over his face. He came forward and bent on his knee, taking my hands in his and leaning so close that only inches separated us.

I lifted my head and sat up straight on the edge of the bed.

"I am here for you," he whispered softly. "Whatever it is, I am here."

Carla looked at us in bewilderment. Barb was so apprehensive, I could almost see her wring her hands. There was no sign of Eben, the fortune-teller.

CHAPTER 40 HECTOR

More than fear, it was terror of everything. I didn't want to be alone, but I didn't want anyone around. I couldn't stay at Carla's; I had to get away from the crowd. Dread numbed me; I couldn't think.

Then I took a deep breath—inhale, exhale—and pulled myself together. Isis wouldn't sit paralyzed on the edge of a bed.

"I think I'm okay now. In fact, I know I'm okay." I started out shaky but sounded stronger with the second okay. I almost convinced myself that I was fine.

"I had a silly shock," I blabbered. "I feel like an idiot. I can't believe I caused such a scene. I hope you'll forgive me, Carla."

I seemed to be apologizing all the time. I felt so awkward, with no social grace. Isis always knew what to say, what to do.

"Don't be silly." She dismissed my words with a impatient flick of her pink-lacquered nails. "Everyone drinks too much sometime. But I don't think you should drive."

"She is not going home by herself, and that is final," declared Hector. "I will drive her and take a cab back."

Carla didn't look too happy about that option. She stared hard at Hector and then at me. Something was going on; she'd have to be an idiot not to notice. But she could never imagine the truth.

Once clear the excitement was over, everyone else went back to the bar.

Carla walked us to the elevator. The last I saw of her before the stainless doors slid shut was the rage and jealousy seething in her eyes.

Well, there goes that friend. I didn't think it was my fault. Blame Isis. Blame Isis for everything.

Hector started in as soon as the valet shut the car door.

"I will explain to Carla. I will tell her that you are someone from my past, that we left things unfinished years ago and I realize it's not over."

"Tell me, Hector, how did you recognize me?"

I didn't recognize Eben in the sad body of the fortune-teller until I looked into his eyes.

"*No puedo explicarlo.* I cannot explain it. I never thought of you before tonight, not even once. But when I saw you on the terrace, my mind flooded with memories. Strange visions rushed in front of my eyes *como*—"

He snapped his fingers to show how rapidly the images came. The sound was incredibly loud in the small space of my little car.

His eyes flashed in the dark when he turned to me. His intensity was ferocious.

"I feel the most powerful of emotions. I sense I have known you forever, *pero* each time I find you, I lose you."

"Do you believe in reincarnation?"

"*Yo?*" he laughed. "I don't believe in magic things." But then he sobered. "Maybe that's not true anymore."

The light at Koval turned red. His face turned red. Even his eyes flashed red.

"But *no importa* how we know each other. I have never wanted a woman—no!—*needed* a woman—like I need you. I care nothing for the reasons why. I will do whatever it takes to have you. *Cualquier cosa.*"

He squeezed my hand when he said he would do whatever he must. I believed him. I remembered when he took me from Goliath's arms. He had held me tonight like he held me then; no force of nature could tear him away.

When he opened the door to my condo, Aisha was there immediately, rubbing against his legs. He picked her up, stroking her black fur. She didn't struggle at all but relaxed into his arms and purred louder.

I started to tell him about the Red Mirror, but I didn't. I started to tell him about Eben the fortune-teller and the danger to Isis but didn't. I knew if I did, he would never let me do what I needed to do.

"Don't say anything to Carla. Please, Hector. Not yet. It's too soon."

I understood her completely. I'd be furious, too. It wasn't fair, but it was nothing any of us could have foreseen. I never intended for it to happen. I never imagined it could happen.

"It is not too soon for me, Isis."

Hector looked at me with complete openness. He hid nothing from me. I could see to every corner of his soul. His heart was on fire.

He kissed me again. This time he held me without crushing. His lips lingered on mine, his tongue gentle, penetrating, but not devouring. He didn't stroke me; he didn't explore me. He didn't use his hands at all except to hold me.

But I could feel the need all through his body. My body responded with a will of its own; the heat of a sudden flush warmed my skin. I pressed up against him and felt him rock-hard again. I wanted to please him; I wanted him to please me. But not now.

"Hector, I'm not ready."

He was gentleman enough to stop, but I could see he was confused and frustrated. And why wouldn't he be?

"Give me time, Hector. Please. So much has happened." I felt helpless to explain without telling him too much—or just out and out lying to him. "It's too...soon," I finished lamely.

He took my face in his hands and raised my chin so I looked straight into his eyes. The little red specks sparkled in the warm brown.

"It could never be too soon for us, Isis."

He stroked the side of my cheek, then stroked once across my forehead as if to wipe the tension away.

"Put every worry out of your mind. Nothing will happen to you when you are with me."

He kissed me again, very lightly, another brush on the lips, and then whispered in my ear, "*Hasta mañana.*"

He closed the door, and I went straight to my laptop. I googled 'Egypt Pharaohs.' The list covered more than three thousand years with dozens of dynasties. I started at the beginning and scrolled through almost to the end. I saw it then.

'Saïte Dynasty. Psamtik III. 526-525 BC.' *The idiot Psamtik actually became Pharaoh, but not for long.*

The next dynasty was called the 'First Persian Period. 525-404 BC.' Cambyses II was listed as the first Pharaoh of the Persian era.

I googled 'Cambyses' next. It's all history now. The Persians routed the Egyptians at Pelusium, and Psamtik fled to Memphis where he lost everything, almost 2,500 years of Egypt, to the Persians.

It hit me hard when I read it. I shuddered to think of River God, Hetmus, Qeb-ha and Sit-hathor. What had been their fates?

What had been *my* fate?

Everyone thinks you are safe. But they are wrong.

If I didn't get Isis out of Egypt, the Persians would get me in the end. *Go back, Isis. Go back and save yourself.*

CHAPTER 41 TRUTH

My story was that I was going out of town on an emergency. I wasn't sure how long I would be gone. Sonny next door was thrilled to keep Aisha; his cat was lonely.

"Oscar adores Aisha. Have a safe trip. Don't worry about a thing."

I worked almost through the night on the project for Ed and attached it to an email with my excuses for not being at work on Monday. He'd be a maniac, but I'd deal with him later.

Barb would be the only one who would know. I couldn't fool her. Besides, I needed her help with Hector. Hector would try to stop me. He wouldn't let me go back.

I finally went to bed when dawn was breaking. I dreamed of a party on the roof of Carla's high-rise, the blaze of Las Vegas Valley stretching for miles all around, ending in purple mountains at the edges. The car lights on I-15 were an endless strand of sparkling diamonds coming toward us and fiery rubies moving away.

I danced with Hector, my head on his chest; he towered over me. Carla danced with someone I knew. When he turned his head, I saw it was Rasheed. She flashed me a triumphant smile.

"You have my man, but I have yours."

Her eyes glittered as bright as the sea of lights stretching into the horizon behind her.

Barb was there too, dressed all in black. Her hair looked like moonlight. She was on the arm of a bull; the man's silhouette was broad and powerful like a linebacker. When his face came out of shadow, I saw he was the General.

I wanted to warn Barb of the danger, that she had to get away, but a sudden sandstorm swallowed up all forty stories of the building. I closed my eyes to keep out the grit. When I opened them, I was alone, buried in golden dust to my waist.

"Barb, I need you to keep everyone away for a couple of days." The gravity in my voice said everything.

"You can't possibly be taking that fortune-teller seriously."

"I was meant to meet him, Barb. It wasn't an accident. None of what's happening is coincidence. Surely you see that."

"What I see is that you've lost touch with reality."

"It's real, Barb. I keep telling you. It's just as real as this moment."

"Listen to me!" she almost shouted into the phone. Then she said slowly, enunciating each word, "Isis—is—dead."

I heard her like a broken record.

"She's been dead for thousands of years," she nagged on. "Does it honestly matter when or how?"

"It matters to me," I answered in a quiet voice.

I heard Barb make her soft snort of impatience. Maybe in this case, it was frustration.

"But we don't know anything about this," she argued. "Maybe you're only allowed so many trips."

I'd already thought of that myself.

The cell was quiet until she uttered the forbidden words, "What if you can't come back?"

"I'll come back," I stated firmly. I really think I believed it. I had to believe it.

"How can you be so sure?"

"I can't explain how I know. I just do."

Silence.

"All I'm asking is for you to keep everyone away for a few days."

A moment or two more passed before Barb sighed. I recognized her tired surrender in that sound. Relief washed over me.

"Thank you, Barb. And thank you for being my friend," I said quietly.

"Don't say it like that!" she snapped in a voice tinged with panic. "It's like you're saying goodbye forever."

Hector called for the second time, and I picked up. If I didn't, he might come over.

"Hi." I couldn't say anything else. I dreaded lying to him. I was afraid he could see right through me to the truth, that I was transparent, like an X-ray.

"Did you sleep well?"

It hurt to hear his voice. He put so much affection into mundane words.

"I stayed up all night to finish a project for my boss."

"When can I see you?"

"I need to take care of some things. It's going to take me awhile. Can I call you when I'm done?"

So far everything was the truth.

"Are you sure you are okay?" he asked, obviously doubting that I was.

What if he could read my mind, like Qeb-ha? But not even Qeb-ha could do that on a cell phone. Well, I had no way of knowing that, did I?

"I'll call you, I promise." I almost pleaded with him.

Silence. I waited, holding my breath.

"*Bueno*," he said finally. "I am here. I am here when you want me. I am not going anywhere."

"Hector, did you tell Carla?"

He sounded surprised at my question. "Do you believe I could go back to her and say nothing?"

No, he couldn't do that. He was as open and honest as a child. How did he survive in the real world? Is there a real world?

"Thank you for last night, Hector." I wanted to get off the phone before I had to lie to him.

"Isis," he spoke clearly, without any hesitation. "*Te amo*. I love you."

I hung up and leaned against the kitchen counter, closing my eyes. He had said the words I had waited for all my life. I just didn't know if I wanted to hear them from Hector—at least not now.

I recorded a vague new message on my phone about maybe being out of cell range for a while, put the ringer on silent and plugged in the charger. I made my bed and checked that all the doors and windows were locked. The red lamp, on a timer, would be the only light at night.

I showered, changed into a running suit and got a glass of water from the kitchen. The rags and the oil were by the mirror; the metal strut that took me to Egypt was half polished.

Everything depended on time moving forward, even as I traveled backwards. I didn't want to end up in the desert—or, even worse, in the General's tent. That possibility broke through my defenses, but I pushed it away. Those thoughts would keep me from going.

The Red Mirror still leaned against the white wall. I considered hanging it but decided there would be time for that later. I hoped so, anyway.

PART THREE
THE GREAT GREEN

CHAPTER 42 SAÏS

We sailed a different part of the Nile. The river was narrow and clogged with boats; the land on both sides lush with fruit trees and neat rows of vegetables and grains. No dun-colored cliffs rising from the banks, and no great golden sand dunes creeping down to the water's edge. Endless green fields flowed into a far horizon. The Delta.

My gardens in Thebes were a barren desert compared to the lavish color of these low, humid lands. The cloying scent of flowering trees mingled with the earthy perfume of black loam and lush grasses. Papyrus reeds by the millions flowered in the shallow muddy water along the banks.

The morning was unbearably hot. Moist, heavy air pressed on my flesh. I reclined lazily on the yellow divan, sipping watered wine, watching naked farmers in the fields slide past.

Kiya dozed on a mat in the corner of the pavilion.

"I have been with you all your life, Isis," I remembered her saying in Sit-hathor's tent. *"I almost lost you. I shall not leave you again."*

River traffic was dense; a grain-laden barge passed within feet of us, almost brushing our bow.

"Watch out!" our steersman bawled. "Yield!"

Our oarsmen relaxed against the wooden benches, laughing, telling jokes and singing bawdy songs. The winged cobra sail filled with a stiff breeze from the south speeding us north with the current.

According to my map, the Nile had divided into seven narrower branches north of the ancient pyramids of Giza. Saïs lay about 50 miles from the sea on the Rosetta Branch.

Not long after midday, an industrial zone with endless factories replaced the fields of waving grain. Thick black smoke rose from massive forges smelting copper, tin and iron for weapons. Workshop after workshop hammered and pressed papyrus reeds into the long sheets used in scrolls from Iberia to Persia. Stacks of precious imported woods waited to be carved into gilt chairs, ivory-inlaid beds and elaborate painted chests.

The closer we came to the port, the heavier the traffic. By the time we arrived at the wharfs of Saïs, I could have walked across the Nile on boats.

Towering obelisks with gleaming electrum or gold tips pierced the azure sky. Everywhere the sun sparkled on sapphire, emerald, ruby and citrine. Above the jeweled city rose the majestic Temple of Neith, goddess of the hunt and patroness of the city; immense cobalt blue flags waved from her twin pylons.

I smiled at Qeb-ha, and he nodded; the calm swing of his amethyst earring told me that he was more than satisfied. I read relief on his face. Saïs. At last.

Amidst a great deal of shouting back and forth, the pilot jockeyed for a mooring spot next to a round-hulled Phoenician cargo ship carrying cedar and hump-backed cattle from Lebanon. Our crewmen tossed thick ropes of braided sedge to Nubian dockworkers drenched in sweat, muscles rippling under glistening obsidian skin. Alert for danger, Goliath scrutinized every movement.

"You there!" Qeb-ha screeched in his high, eunuch voice. "Lash the stern cable to the bollard."

All along the wharf stretched a double row of neon-bright, painted carved columns supporting the stone roof of a bustling marketplace. Merchants traded ivory, ebony and exotic skins from deep in Nubia, spices from India and olives from Cyprus. The clamor of voices in dozens of languages rang in my ears. Metal clanged against wood and stone.

Maia and Eben stood close together at the stern. Eben pointed to one thing or another, undoubtedly explaining some wonder to her. From time to time, she laughed softly in her gentle way. There was a glow about her I hadn't seen before.

No sooner had we docked than a party of priests in long white skirts accompanied by armed guards in short snowy kilts and sky blue headdresses arrived to escort us to the Temple of Neith. Thank Hathor, we wouldn't spend our days on this crowded barge in the clamorous harbor.

I was at peace with Neith. Surely my ordeal in the desert atoned for the death of one lioness on a forbidden hunt so very long ago. I sensed no imminent danger. I had time. Isis still had time.

We formed a quasi-military formation with the entourage of priests at the rear. I think we might have been crushed without the Temple Guards and their shields. The crowds parted for us like a ship plowing through clogged waters.

Neith Temple Avenue, a wide promenade shaded on both sides by rows of stately sycamores and flowering *persea* trees, shimmered in a dizzying kaleidoscope of color and pattern. Near-naked Nubians with scarred faces. Phoenicians wrapped in patterned cloth to the ankles. Libyans in feathers and gazelle skins. Syrians and Hebrews in heavy, woolen robes. Lydians in turbans, belted tunics and tall suede boots. I saw very few women and no foreign women, at all.

Greeks were everywhere, almost as many as Egyptians. The older men wore long *peplos* with the right shoulder bare; the younger Greeks' *chitons* exposed muscular thighs. Most were clean-shaven with curly, short-cropped hair shaped by hot irons in Greek barbershops.

A thousand red granite stelae topped by winged disks framed the entire length of the avenue. Every hundred feet or so, gentle fountains spilled into rectangular pools sprinkled with multicolored rose petals. White almond blossoms fell like snow on green grass.

With a thunderous creaking, a pair of massive cedar gates opened, and the madness of the street gave way to the serenity of Neith's Temple grounds. High-pitched mating calls of peacocks welcomed us as rumbling wood and iron clanged shut behind.

So many obelisks and sphinxes. So many species of trees and flowers. Rainbow hollyhocks, blue delphiniums and red roses bloomed along arrow-straight, paved paths.

The Temple turned out to be not one building but a mammoth complex spreading over acres of botanical gardens, more vast even than Karnak in Thebes.

At the heart of the gardens was the great sacred lake reflecting the façade of the main temple with its emerald and sapphire painted columns topped by rich floral capitals. White swans and black swans glided on glassy waters. Iridescent dragonflies swarmed.

There was no shortage of water in the Delta. Dozens of papyrus-choked ponds and lotus-covered pools sparkled in the sun. The pink lotus of Persia—ethereal beauty from the beast—clogged a circular water basin in the center of a vast labyrinth of immaculately trimmed white oleander bushes in full flower.

And of course, birds. Always the birds. Songbirds by the thousands. Drab peahens roosting in the willows. Flocks of long-legged snowy ibis feeding on grassy lawns.

At our backs, on both sides of the pylon gate, armed with long spears and rectangular painted leather shields as tall as their torsos, stood the erect and silent Temple Guards in their cerulean triangular headdresses.

Only the invited may enter this world; I prayed to Neith that She would keep us safe.

⌇

Not even Goliath had noticed the two men in the marketplace by the docks. No one had heard the man whisper and point in my direction.

"Yes, it is she. That is Isis of the desert."

No one had seen the man in the red turban follow us to the Temple and then hurry off in the direction of the city.

CHAPTER 43 QEB-HA

Qeb-ha came to me after my bath. We shared our meal on a marble balcony overlooking a pond surrounded by sunny chrysanthemums and fiery celosia. The branches of a flowering white myrtle brushed the edges of the balustrade; a fresh breeze moved the palm fronds. From a hidden spot under the arbors, musicians softly played harps and flutes. The Nile, noisy and crammed with boats, lay in the distance. All was peaceful here.

We dined on pigeon pie, cucumbers, lettuce, grapes, melon and bread. The Temple had its own vineyards; the wine was dark and sweet, the grapes ripened in strong sunshine, black soil and intense heat. Delta vintage is a luxury reserved to the few.

"Qeb-ha, I am sorry I have not listened to you well. I pray you can forgive me."

"I have said that there is nothing to forgive. The plans of Gods are one thing; the actions of men are another. Isenkhebe has done foolish deeds, but also brave ones. The Gods lay the heart on the Great Scales to measure its final worth."

"Where are the Commander and Hetmus-hor?" I asked with no attempt at guile. I didn't even try to hide my thoughts.

He took a grape the color of his amethyst into his mouth and spat out the seeds before answering.

"The Commander is at the Royal Palace, Isenkhebe. His duty to the Pharaoh is sacred and comes above all else. Hetmus-hor is in Hermopolis."

"Hermopolis?" My surprise was obvious to Qeb-ha who looked

back at me with amusement. I imagined him thinking, *This woman will never learn.*

"Isenkhebe perhaps thought that he might be here?"

"Yes. As a matter of fact, I did."

"Do I need to remind Isenkhebe Nefrusobek that she is a High-Priestess bound to Hathor? It would be most inappropriate to entertain the attentions of a man outside of the Temple."

"I should not think that would hinder Hetmus-hor. Rather I believe the challenge might inspire him."

"Indeed. The Governor himself attempted to convince Hetmus-hor that his presence here would be ill-advised. But such were his vehement objections that he was commanded to remain at the home of his father—under guard."

"Guard?"

Qeb-ha shrugged his shoulders and raised his eyebrows as if to say the follies of ordinary men were quite beyond his understanding.

"Hetmus-hor has difficulty accepting limitation," he stated in a manner that made it clear he had little regard for the nobleman. "He is a strong-minded man, spoiled by his father and unaccustomed to conforming to rules."

So that's how it was to be. River God had his duty that seemed always to come before me, and Hetmus was days to the south under house arrest. Was I to save Isis on my own?

"And what of my father, Qeb-ha? When shall I meet him?"

"When the time is ripe, Isenkhebe. All things happen when the Gods ordain."

He rose and bowed.

"Eben requests an audience, if Isenkhebe is not too fatigued."

I had the sense this was not a message he wished to deliver.

"He is such a tender soul," he added. "So innocent in both spirit and mind."

"Do not fear for the innocence of Eben, Qeb-ha. My taste runs to men, not boys."

"May the Goddess continue to favor Isenkhebe with wisdom."

"Thank you, Qeb-ha, for everything. You have proven a dear friend."

"Did I not say that it is on the road that one finds a companion? I wished for that from the beginning."

"You also told me that it is in battle that a man finds a brother. Are we brothers now, Qeb-ha?"

"The battle is not yet begun, Isenkhebe. But it soon shall."

Eben came to me shortly after. Just above the western horizon glowed a brilliant white Venus, the evening star. Ishtar.

He brought his lyre and sang Hebrew psalms. We sat together on the balcony, stars over our heads, the night fragrant with sweet jasmine blooming on tall trellises just outside my rooms.

Nightingales sang in these gardens, too, like at home in Thebes. Home. Thebes. Las Vegas seemed at the end of a very long tether that stretched yet longer and longer with every moment I was here.

"Thank you for teaching me about the constitution of the sky, Eben. The Star of the North kept me going in the right direction. But most of all, it kept me from panic. You kept me from panic. Thinking of you calmed me."

I told him about my time in the camp, but not everything. I couldn't tell him exactly how I pleased the General to stay alive or exactly how I escaped. I was sensitive to his innocence.

"I drew strength from your amulet's powers, Eben. I am convinced of that. Thank you."

"It was the Light, Isenkhebe, that gave you strength."

He sat as close to me as he ever had, but not close enough to touch. I was a goddess to him; he worshipped me but knew it could only be from afar. I believe it pleased him that I was an ideal. It suited his poetic spirit. A real woman is messy, with too many imperfections.

"You Egyptians," he said solemnly, "have a saying that one does not discover the heart of a friend, if one has not consulted him in anxiety. You have discovered my heart, Isenkhebe. Now it is yours."

Sometime in the night, warm hands moved across my breasts and over my belly. They caressed my hips and the slope of my thighs. They explored all of me, leaving no place untouched. There was a faint scent of myrrh. I moaned in my sleep; Pehtes purred in my ear.

"Isis," a low voice exhaled my name in a heavy breath. "Isis. Isis."

I didn't open my eyes. I wanted it to go on. I didn't want it to be a dream.

CHAPTER 44   RED DOOR

Bright sunshine flooded the balcony when Maia came with my breakfast of grapes, dates, pomegranates and *seremt*, the wheat porridge liquid enough to drink.

"Why did you let me sleep so long?"

I stretched among the cushions and pushed Pehtes off my feet. How delicious to be off that wretched boat. Today, I would explore the grounds and take lunch in the garden.

Maia put the brass tray on the balcony next to the low stools where Eben and I had sat last night. A sudden vision of Maia and Eben on the barge, their heads close together, Maia laughing shyly, played before my eyes.

"Maia, do you not find Eben pleasing? His voice, his music, his presence. They are such blessings."

She blushed and averted her eyes.

"He seems lonely, so far from his people. I owe him much, even my life. It would please me greatly if you would befriend him, make him more welcome."

She blushed deeper.

"Look at me, Maia."

Her eyes were huge and round. How terrified she looked.

"Come, Maia. You know my meaning. You have my blessing. You are young and beginning to bloom. The future is uncertain. It is a pity to waste this time. You were born to please and be pleased."

I kissed her palm and then, holding her tiny hand, recited a verse favored by our harpist in Thebes.

"Revel in pleasure while your life endures,
never weary grow
In eager quest of what your heart desires,
do as it prompts you."

The color drained from her face as I sang. She had a heart-tugging look about her, maybe more wistful than sad. I believe she sensed that a way of life she had always known was coming to an end.

"It is your nature, Maia. Do not deprive its fruition. Savor it."

Silver serpents with green glass eyes hung from my earlobes and coiled around my ankles and upper arms. Kiya was finishing the final adjustments to my short plaited wig trimmed with silver when the message came.

The small papyrus scroll with Greek letters said nothing except that I should go with the guard.

Kiya and I looked at each other. Fear flashed in her eyes.

"Did you know about this?" I asked.

She shook her head and gripped my hand so tightly, her aged, twisted knuckles went white.

A lone Temple Guard in the reception room carried a spear but no shield. A short iron sword with a broad, double-edged blade hung in his leather belt. He stood fearfully straight and avoided looking directly at me.

"Get me the heart amulet, Kiya, the one my mother gave me at her Temple."

I followed the guard, and Goliath followed me. The Nubian would not stay behind, and the guard did not object. We passed through two lush courtyards with porticos of papyriform columns overgrown with grapevines before entering a green granite chapel. The guard turned at the first vestibule and went briskly along a deserted stone corridor ending in tall double wooden doors. He knocked.

We waited only a few moments before a priest with a shaven head, long white linen kilt and bare chest with a broad golden collar opened the door but didn't speak. A leopard skin cloaked his stooped shoulders.

A heavy ankh-shaped key as large as his hand hung from a gold cord tied around his hips.

He was old, older than Qeb-ha. He smiled to reassure me.

Half of his teeth were missing; the remaining ones were dark as aged ivory. Enormous gold ankhs stretched his earlobes and grazed his shoulders at the bottom of a stubby neck.

He motioned for me to enter, and the guard stepped aside. Apparently, he wasn't going any farther. When Goliath moved to follow me, the guard held the spear in his path and shook his head.

"He goes everywhere with me," I protested.

"Only the priesthood may pass through these doors. All others are forbidden. Your man can wait for you here." The guard was firm. He didn't move the spear.

"The penalty for entering is death." He looked for the first time straight at me.

I nodded to Goliath, and he reluctantly stayed behind. The priest closed the heavy wooden door and bolted it from the inside.

Beyond the door lay a shadowy silence. The narrow hallway with vaulted ceilings had no windows or doors. Long walls of limestone blocks fitted so tightly, I could scarcely make out the hairline joints where they met.

I had the impression no one had passed here in eons. The sound of our footsteps in leather sandals raised the faintest of echoes.

The passage widened into a small chapel area with a false door carved in the stone of the end wall. It was through the illusory door that the *Ka* spirit may pass back and forth to visit this life from the afterlife.

Torches flamed in niches on both sides. The priest handed me the closest torch and then bent to the floor. His fingers went straight to an unseen lever on the bottom edge of the false door jamb.

Stone ground on stone. I felt a draft of musty air on my cheek. The torch sputtered for a moment and burned straight again.

I stepped closer, lighting the shadows to make out a tiny fissure along the seam in the corner where the short wall met the long. Next to the crack, embedded in the end wall, was a square basalt plaque. Alien symbols, not Greek or Egyptian, covered the polished stone. The engraved glyphs weren't any alphabet that I recognized.

The old man never spoke, and I was careful not to make the slightest of sounds, unable to imagine even a whisper breaking the silence of eternity.

He pushed hard on the plaque; his hand disappeared. He pushed again. The crack widened to a gap large enough for one person to squeeze by. The priest took the torch from me and slid through. I followed.

Narrow travertine stairs disappeared into black. The torch lighted a small circle around us as we went down. I counted thirty steps; we were deep in the earth beneath Neith's Temple.

The stairway cut through a domed ceiling painted midnight blue; more of the strange symbols glowed white amid hundreds of tiny yellow stars. The steps ended in a perfectly round room, walls plastered and painted the same deep blue as the dome. There was no light except for our one torch; I wished we had two.

Polished ebony doors encircled us. Each was carved with the same strange glyphs in gold and silver, seemingly arranged in coherent patterns. I decided they were a language, maybe incantations, not unlike the phrases from the Book of the Dead that cover tomb walls to guide the spirit to the afterlife.

The old priest inserted the ankh-shaped key hanging at his hips into the latch of a door with a seven-pointed silver star above the lintel. Beyond the door loomed a tunnel leading to a black hole. I followed the old priest into the void.

The flame of our fire burned in utter darkness. Moisture seeped through the sandstone walls and ceiling; I smelled mildew or mold, maybe both. The only sound was our footsteps on stone and the hissing of the torch. The tunnel turned and twisted until the priest finally stopped at a single wooden door.

That door, too, opened with the ankh key, and our torch lit a spiral staircase twisting into the bowels of the earth.

The steps were steep with no railing. The priest moved quickly for an old man; his feet knew the way. I followed him cautiously, never taking my hand from the wet, slimy stone encasing us, careful not to slip and tumble to the bottom. There was darkness above and blackness below. Again I wished we had a second torch.

We stepped from the bottom of the stairwell into a black cube, high enough to the ceiling that a man could stand on another's shoulders. Directly across glowed a massive electrum septagram mounted on a glossy red door with a curved top.

The priest knocked hard and soft—a code. The door opened wide, and I squinted my eyes against a light as blinding as the noon glare when exiting a temple.

A burning hand took my icy one and led me inside. When the door shut firmly behind me, the hand dropped. I resisted the wave of claustrophobia that washed over me. I resisted the feeling of being entombed.

Dozens of lanterns hung from stone arches, their golden light illuminating thousands of rolled papyri crammed into wall niches carved from floor to ceiling. I had a vision of catacombs lined with bodies wrapped in white linen. If interred here alive, the reading on these shelves would fill the days of a long life.

A tall man with shining silver hair stood just in front of me. Behind him was a heavy wooden table buried in rolled and unrolled papyri. I thought for a moment of the scroll I had carried through the desert. I had never read what was written there. It might have been nothing. It might have been everything.

The blue of the man's robe was woven with seven-pointed stars; the silver threads shimmered when they caught the light. He was the wizard from my dream but held nothing in his hands—no tablet and no sword.

His eyes were so pale, almost without color, that I didn't think it possible for him ever to go in the sun.

With a smile that dimmed the lamps, he announced gaily in lilting Greek, "I am Hermes *Trismegistus*. Welcome my daughter, Isenkhebe Nefrusobek, to the Library of Neith, the greatest Mystery School of all time."

CHAPTER 45 HERMES TRISMEGISTUS

M y father's palms were large, square and remarkable in their smoothness. I placed the gleaming heart amulet that said 'one-who-has-entered-the-heart' in his right hand.

Some believe you can divine a person's character and destiny in the lines and shape of their hands. Hermes had only three lines in his palm; his path must be exceptionally clear.

His eyes gazed with fondness at Sit-hathor's golden heart talisman, ghosts of sweet memories passing liked wispy clouds across his face. A small, secret smile softened his mouth. After a few moments in the pleasures of the past, he returned to me.

"I see the beauty and strength of your mother carved into every curve and plane of your features."

He smiled warmly, took my hands in his again and kissed me on the cheek. He smelled like lamp oil, and even a little musty.

"They call me Hermes *Thrice-greatest*, but I find that pretentious. I am not great—much less three times—and certainly not the incarnation of the god Hermes these superstitious Egyptians believe."

"I am pleased to meet you, my Esteemed Father."

I spoke also in Greek and, thanks to my tutors, without a trace of accent. All music and poetry with no guttural sounds or hiccups, Greek is a lyrical tongue that tickles the ears with vowels.

"Come sit beside me," he said, patting the seat of an unadorned ebony chair with straight arms and a high back. "There is no need for formality."

Hermes touched my shoulder gently. His hand was hot and dry. He left it there a moment, not hurrying to take it away.

"You have been through a terrible ordeal, my daughter. I am sorry for that, but it has made you stronger."

I didn't want to talk about the desert.

"I was shocked to learn that I have a father. Why have you never before asked to see me?" My tone was more accusatory than I'd planned.

"Yes, I regret that. I truly do. A father and daughter should not be apart." Not in the least abashed, he chuckled and patted my hand. His pale eyes twinkled. "Ours is no ordinary family. Indeed, your mother is not ordinary, at all. Yes. An extraordinary woman."

For a moment, he looked to be far away, perhaps back in time with a youthful and tender Sit-hathor I had never known. Then he moved a pile of scrolls aside and replaced them with three silver chalices embossed with seven-pointed stars around the rims.

"I hope you can forgive me. But it is as it had to be." He squeezed my hand in a loving way before passing me a chalice. The wine was deep red, near black in the yellow light. "How is Sit-hathor? Is she as beautiful as ever?"

"My mother is well, strong and beautiful. She has the ear and blessings of Hathor, Supreme Goddess, Gold-of-the-Gods."

"Yes, of course. Hathor. The powerful and demanding Hathor who is responsible for all things." His tone said he didn't believe it.

"Is it the custom of all Greeks to mock the Gods? Or only the gods of other peoples?" I regretted my words immediately.

Hermes might be my father, but I didn't know him. One never bantered with Sit-hathor.

But his reaction was to laugh out loud with delight.

"Your mother's sharp tongue. And I am told, her sharp wit. I admire a woman with intelligence as much as I admire a woman with beauty. You, my dear, are blessed with both."

"Do you not agree, Antinous?" he asked, turning his head to speak behind him. "Is my daughter not both beautiful and quick?"

I was thrown a bit off balance that Hermes hadn't mentioned we were not alone. I should have questioned the third chalice on the table and felt that I'd failed some kind of test.

"I do indeed, Hermes. Your daughter is much more than you described." The voice was one of an educated Greek—deep, musical, trained for oratory and theatre.

Antinous leaned casually against a nearby wall; a soft blue wool *chiton*, belted at the waist, ended at mid-thigh. Fabric draped in soft folds from the left shoulder across his chest. The right shoulder was bare, as were his arms. The contour of his muscles ended in strong wrists and graceful hands.

His beauty was so perfect, he might have been sculpted from marble. A mane of waves with streaks of gold crowned his head; ringlets fell on his brow and around his ears. He had hair you wanted to run your fingers through and watch the curls spring back. He had a body you wanted to run your fingers over and watch the gooseflesh rise. I averted my eyes and hoped neither had noticed my too obvious appraisal.

Antinous joined us at the table and took the seat to my right. Hermes sat to my left. I faced the red door.

He was even more beautiful up close. I didn't think it was possible for eyes to be so blue. His demeanor was reserved with an air of detachment—very hard to read.

Once Antinous settled, Hermes' tone shifted to more somber; he seemed eager to move on to the purpose of our meeting.

"Antinous is my trusted assistant. Everything I know, he knows. He has been here two years, helping me prepare for your arrival."

"Two years?"

"A blink in the cosmos. Less than a blink." Hermes smiled and took a sip of wine as if to ready himself. "I know you have a thousand questions, my daughter, but first I shall tell you what you must know."

I glanced at Antinous. He had a most earnest expression on his face, intense yet impersonal. There wasn't the slightest hint of flirtation. I sensed he was deliberately distant, as if he had put up a wall.

Everything I know, he knows. I felt exposed, vulnerable—uncomfortable that they knew so much about me and I knew so little about them. And that they knew things that I knew nothing about.

There was a casual superiority in their bearing, an air of supremacy peculiar to Greeks that makes others feel inferior, inadequate and out-of-date. Logic and reason, beauty and harmony. The Greek world is a perfect natural state marred by imperfect people.

Glowing lanterns above the table bathed us in amber light. The niches with the thousands of scrolls hovered on the edges of shadow.

Hermes glanced around the cavern with pride. "You are in the heart of the greatest library of the ages. All knowledge is contained in these scrolls. The most esteemed scholars and magicians have studied here. Pythagoras, the eminent mathematician, is here now. Pity there is not time for you to meet him. Such a superior mind."

All knowledge. Was there a blueprint among the thousands of scrolls for the Red Mirror? I sorely needed it to get home.

Throwing me off balance again, Hermes asked abruptly, "What do you know of Atlantis?"

I hadn't expected him to start out with a fable. Rather like a dummy, I repeated, "Atlantis?"

There was nothing in his face to indicate he wasn't serious. Another test? I glanced at Antinous; he stared enigmatically back. Both waited for my answer.

"Some say it is a myth," I went on cautiously. "Some believe Atlantis was an ancient kingdom that sank into the sea." I searched their faces for a clue as to the satisfaction of my answer. Seeing none, I finished lamely, "Other than that, I know nothing."

"Let me assure you that Atlantis is no myth." Hermes reflected for a moment before he spoke again, perhaps reaching for words that a simpleton like me could understand.

"In the beginning, it was a mighty civilization. Far more advanced than ours. They could harness the power of the cosmos to manifest matter from pure energy. Or to change one form of matter into another."

"Like alchemists?" I asked hopefully. I so wanted to impress him.

"Indeed, the Atlanteans did invent alchemy—or more accurately, they discovered the natural law upon which alchemy is based."

"The strange symbols I saw in the blue chamber. They are like no language I have ever seen. Are they Atlantean?"

Hermes glanced at Antinous and nodded. They both looked pleased, and I felt a wave of relief. At last, I had passed a test.

"Yes, very astute of you, my daughter, to make that connection. Those are spells taken from Atlantean scrolls, put there long ago in an effort to prevent us from making the same mistakes."

He paused. I was on the verge of asking which mistakes when he continued.

"Like men today, Atlanteans proved to be arrogant and greedy. They could have lived any life of their choosing without labor, yet they pursued odious and dangerous misuses of power. To no useful purpose, they cross-bred humans with animals to create half-man and half-beast monsters—poor, lost souls belonging nowhere."

Truly, I looked hard at him, wondering if he were testing me yet again— or a little crazy.

"But the worst of all their follies was the abuse of cosmic energy. A runaway chain reaction destroyed their world. The few who survived came here, bringing their knowledge—as well as the monsters that the simple men in this land saw as gods."

Hathor with cow ears? Thoth with the head of an ibis?

The catacomb-like chamber was tomb silent. I couldn't help but think of the silence of the grave. I wanted to get back to the surface, out of the stale air—to feel a fresh breeze on my skin.

"Please do not think me impertinent, Father, but what has all this to do with me?"

"It has everything to do with you, Isenkhebe. You are the one I trust."

"Trust with what?"

"With the Tablet, of course."

"Tablet?"

Riddles. Always riddles. Hermes was proving as maddening as Qeb-ha.

"I have broken their Cosmic Code, my daughter. *Macrocosm* and *microcosm*. Above and below. Spiritual and physical. Each is a reflection of the other, a mirror."

He took my hand and spoke to me again in the patient voice of one leading a child through a difficult mathematical proof.

"The power of the cosmos, Isenkhebe. The power to manifest. Think of it as an equation. Thought equals matter. Matter reflects thought."

It took me a moment to grasp the import of his words. "Do you mean to say that by merely *thinking of something*, you can make it happen?"

"In the most simple terms, yes. Ultimate power. Exceedingly dangerous. You see, the world is not ready for this. We are evolving—but not fast enough; our consciousness is still too low. Our task, Isenkhebe, is to ensure that the knowledge does not fall into the wrong hands. Especially not the Persians."

"But you say you have the key to harness the cosmos. Why not simply manifest a way out of whatever danger you foresee?"

"Oh, my child, but I *have* manifested," he answered in a quiet voice not much above a whisper. "I have manifested the Emerald Tablet, and I have manifested *you*."

CHAPTER 46 CHOSEN ONE

A sweet and spicy cloud of *kapet,* incense of transition from this life to the next, fogged the chamber. The air was hot, humid and utterly still. All windows and doorways were hung with heavy drapes to trap the magic and allow no fresh air to pollute the sacred perfume of Royal Death.

Around the edges of the room, against the colorful paintings of marshes and gardens, circled chanting, leopardskin-draped priests swinging clay braziers belching thick trails of cloying smoke.

The sound of the Pharaoh's breathing was a labored wheeze—shallow in and shallow out. He lay on a narrow divan, weakened by fever, the back of his neck resting on a polished cedar block. Amasis, Horus-on-earth soon to be Horus the God.

To his right knelt Egyptian advisors and generals with a dozen Greek dignitaries perched on low, three-legged stools behind them. His wives and concubines prostrated themselves at the foot of the bed; his dozens of children spread out on the left. Except his eldest son, the Crown Prince, the heir chosen by the Gods by virtue that he still lived. Psamtik knelt just next to the old man's limp right hand, the one bearing the Regent's signet ring, the ring that would pass to him upon the Pharaoh's death.

But the father wasn't dead yet.

"Help Us sit up," he demanded, and two of his personal slaves, each taking a shoulder, lifted him. A third sat on the bed behind him to support his back.

"Persian jackals!" he snarled. "They shall not rest until they piss on the world! The father Cyrus dared to threaten Us. Now the dog son Cambyses comes sniffing. But Egypt does not surrender so easily. Where is my most trusted Commander? Let him come forward."

Commander! What in Set's name did his father want with him? The man was his personal bodyguard. Why hadn't Harwa informed him? Psamtik shot an angry glare at the scribe who steadfastly avoided his eyes.

The Prince wasn't the only one taken by surprise at the summons. There was a sudden hush in a chamber already silent. One second. Two seconds. And then three passed before the low, monotonous drone of the priests started again. A handful of Egyptians dared to cast sidelong glances at each other. The Greeks shifted their weights on the stools, turning their heads to look directly at each other. *Had the old man at last come to his senses to name a new successor? Egypt might yet be saved.*

River God made his way to the royal divan and prostrated himself, arms stretched, palms and forehead on the mosaic tiles, beside Psamtik. Amasis reached out his right hand, the one with the Regent ring.

"Rise to your knees, Commander. Let us look upon the face of true devotion and loyalty."

"I am but a humble servant of Egypt, my Pharaoh. My life is at Your Majesty's command."

"We should like to meet this priestess of yours who felled a mighty general and brought us the list of traitors. But not now," he sighed. "Not now. We have so little time."

He motioned then to Harwa who came forward with a plum silk cushion in his hands. The Greeks craned their necks to see what was on the pillow. A transfer of power would most likely involve the ring. Psamtik couldn't tear his eyes away from the fist-sized disk attached to a gold chain thick as a man's thumb. The medallion of the Chancellor of the Armies! *His* chain of office by birthright!

"Approach, O devoted son of Egypt," Amasis commanded. "We call you to your Destiny."

Inching forward on his knees, River God closed the distance between them and, with head bowed, murmured, "The Gods choose our Destiny, my Pharaoh, when we come from the womb."

"Let it be as the Gods ordain," Amasis intoned.

"Let it be as the Gods ordain," repeated the priests.

The Gods answered with a tremor convulsing Amasis at the moment he reached out for the necklace. His whole arm shook violently; he struggled to grip his fingers around the chain, but the hand wouldn't still.

Harwa was immediately there to grasp the sacred fist and guide the chain of office over River God's striped headdress.

Only inches away from Psamtik, the golden medallion, engraved with bold hieroglyphs, gleamed against River God's bronzed chest. The chain of office of the highest post in the land, the office that belonged to *him*. *He* was Crown Prince. *He* should be Guardian of the Nile. Until he was Pharaoh, of course.

Through a fog, he heard his father saying, "We name you Chancellor of Our Armies, Commander. Our Trusted-of-Trusted, Our Guardian of *Kemet*, Our Black Land."

"But Father, my Pharaoh, should it not be me who—"

"Silence! We have spoken. It is the will of the Gods."

A bold step, the Greeks signalled each other. A wise step. But not enough. It would seem the old man still intended for the fool son to succeed him. *Damn these superstitious Egyptians and their paths from the womb.* They were hellbent on losing everything.

᠍

Every port has a tavern where foreigners gather. Along with regional Greek dishes and wine, the Cypriot owners of the Golden Falcon in Saïs served up pleasure and intrigue. A man might get anything he wanted for a price.

When a sailor tired of gambling, he could choose among the exotic women and young boys waiting in the curtained alcoves at the back of the room.

The inn buzzed with news of the failing Pharaoh. Gamblers were busy placing bets on when the Persians would invade and how long it would take Cambyses to crush the effete Psamtik.

Two men talking in low voices huddled over a small table in a dark corner. The larger had the chest of a bull and round, *kohl*-lined eyes. Colored ribbons tied the ends of the long curls of his beard. The man in the red turban spoke rough but understandable Aramaic.

"She is here; I have seen her with my own eyes. She is the priestess from the desert, the one who escaped Sher's camp. There is no doubt."

"Priestess!" the Persian barked. "You mean the whore of Hathor who slaughtered him in his bed! I spit on the day the devil spawned her."

"I have heard rumors," admitted the Arab, shrugging his shoulders. "But who I am, a simple man of the desert, to understand the ways of the world?"

"You must seize the witch and bring her to me. The Great Cambyses himself desires to oversee her death."

The Persian placed a leather drawstring pouch of Lydian electrum coins on the tabletop.

"A down payment, shall we call it?"

The bag quickly disappeared into the folds of the desert robe.

"Count on me, Sire. It may be difficult to take her from the Temple, but she must leave someday. I assure you that we shall be waiting when she does."

The man in the red turban went directly from the tavern to the Royal Palace and passed through a hidden green gate at the bottom of the garden. A waiting guard led him through back hallways to the private quarters of Setne the Scribe.

When he entered the chamber, the Egyptian was amusing himself with twin boys, about ten years old, curled on a blood red carpet at the foot of his gilt chair. The twins looked to be Eastern Greek, maybe even Persian; they wore their own curls, unusual in Egypt. They stared back with the large, frightened eyes of pets abused by their master and unsure of what might come next.

Setne motioned for the Arab to approach, but raised his hand to stop him before he came too close. These dirty desert people never bathed, and their filthy turbans crawled with lice.

"What is the Persian interest in this priestess?" he demanded.

The boy at his left knee repeated the Egyptian's question in fluent Aramaic.

"They say the woman slit the General Sher's throat in his own bed, Sire."

The same twin relayed the news in Egyptian.

"She killed him! That part of the story I had not heard." Setne considered this new information for a few moments, caressing the shoulders and neck of the boy on his right, the one who kept silent, in the offhand way one might stroke a cat.

The changes to Setne's expression were subtle, but the slight dilation of pupils and nearly imperceptible sly curving of the lips didn't go unnoticed by the Arab.

This Egyptian is as poor at hiding his thoughts as his lust. He, too, wants the woman. If he worked things right, he might get both the Persians *and* the Egyptians to pay.

"The Persians are offering a handsome purse for her," he volunteered.

"Are they indeed?" That piece of information came as no surprise. It did mean that the Arab would not come cheap. But he hadn't expected a bargain. Still, whatever the cost, the woman was worth it. This priestess just might be his ticket out of here when the Persians arrived. Her life for his safe passage.

"The problem, Sire," the Arab suggested, "is getting her to leave the Temple."

"Leave that for me to arrange."

Setne reached down, pulled the boy-interpreter's face up and licked once across his lips. Without taking his eyes from the boy, he dismissed the stinking desert man with a wave of his hand.

"Report back to me. I shall double any sum the Persians offer."

℞

Antinous set a rectangular package about the size of a very thick atlas on the table and folded the soft antelope skin back to reveal a smooth tablet of polished green faience exquisitely carved with precise Greek letters. The glassy surface glowed in the lamplight.

I read quickly.

And the following to be the truth.
That which is below is like that which is above,
and that which is above is like that which is below,
in the accomplishment of the miracle of one thing.
And as all things came from the One,
through the meditation of the One,
so all things were born from one thing by adaptation.

"It speaks of a cosmic mirror," I said. "Above and Below reflect each other. *Macrocosm* and *microcosm*. But what is the One?"

"Everything comes from the One Energy," Hermes answered, again using that soothing, patient tone of instructing a child in the mysteries of the Cosmos. "Both what you see around you, and what you cannot see. We may seem separate, but we all come from the One. We are all one."

Reading the future, reliving the past. Was time also One?

"Have we known each other before?" I asked. "Shall we know each other again?"

"Time is a continuum that loops back on itself. Have known and shall know exist at the same moment. There is only here and now."

Was that a yes or a no?

He swallowed my hand in his vibrating palm; his energy flowed into me and filled me with calm. How unlike his touch was from that of my mother, Sit-hathor.

"I know you feel loss at our separation, my daughter. But all is according to plan. All has transpired for you to be who you are. Strong. You must be, for it is your destiny to protect the Tablet."

Hermes squeezed my fingers harder. A slight buzz in my ears grew louder and louder still. The room was suddenly hot, and I no longer felt the chair under me. Neither did I see Hermes or Antinous, although I was vaguely aware of the oil lamps casting shadows on the rows and rows of scrolls.

Just as I had in my living room the first night with the Red Mirror, I drifted outside of time in a warm velvet sea.

"Surely you recognize your power, Isenkhebe." Hermes' voice swam through deep water to my ear. "You are the Chosen One."

I'd never thought myself powerful, but I was here; I had passed through eternity to this life. That must be significant. It certainly couldn't be common. I had another power, too. The Hathor Power.

The room came sharply back into focus. Antinous looked intently concentrated; a crease furrowed between his perfect eyes above his perfect nose.

I had no idea how long I had been in the Library. The silence of the earth swallowed up time.

Hermes smiled at me, still holding my hand, patiently waiting for me to ask what he knew I must.

I took a deep breath.

"So, what am I supposed to do with the Emerald Tablet?"

CHAPTER 47   ISIDORA

Pleasure would have to wait. An opportunity had presented itself, and Setne intended to seize it. He sent the twins away and waited impatiently for the Crown Prince to return from Amasis' deathbed.

"The old man lingers on and on," complained Psamtik. "But at last I have an hour or so free from his ghastly stench."

"I have news of the priestess, my liege."

"Forget her! When I am Pharaoh, I shall have her silenced forever. I am more concerned about the Commander. Chancellor of the Armies! For a terrible moment, I thought my father might name him his heir. You were correct, Setne, not to trust him. He has been plotting all this time to seize power from me."

"The Commander is not a poor choice to defend us against the Persians, my Prince. And he turned out, as I predicted, to have a strong connection to the priestess. He may yet prove useful to get to her."

"*Isenkhebe this. Isenkhebe that.* I am sick of this cow."

"The Persians, my spies tell me, are offering an impressive reward for her capture."

"I have no need for more gold. Not when I am Pharaoh."

"Not gold, Sire. Leverage."

"Leverage? Surely you do not mean with the Persians? Do you fear for us, Setne? Do you fear for Egypt?"

"I fear the Army's allegiance—most of all those Greeks. Who can trust them? These are perilous times. Consider how close the Persians are to invasion."

"You *are* full of negative thoughts, Setne. The Gods created this land for Egyptians, not those uncouth barbarians with their curled beards and foul breaths stinking of mutton. Can you imagine them *here*? Impossible!"

"Of course, Your Grace. But would it not be prudent to think of the woman as—shall we call it?—insurance. If she has value to Cambyses, she has value to us. He will give anything to have her. Her ultimate worth shall be revealed in time."

"Intrigue. Intrigue. All this talk fatigues me. You understand these things, Setne. Do with the priestess as you see fit and inform me of the outcome."

"I shall arrange everything."

"Good! Are we finished then? I need a bath to wash the stink of my father's dying flesh from my hands. And I need a visit from the twins. The Babylonian ambassador has been most instructive today. I want to try some new toys and see what games the boys might play for me."

ᖗ

"Everything you say is based on a scroll delivered by a woman," shouted the Count of Tanis. "Who knows what treachery lies behind that list? It might have been planted where the priestess would find it."

"Yes! Perhaps it is a ruse," yelled a noble from Aswan. "A trick to confuse and divide us."

"We can afford no risks." River God held up the Persian scroll taken by Isis from the General's tent. "I have ordered the arrest of every man whose name is written here."

At his signal, the tall double doors of the war chamber opened to a platoon of Royal Guards in blue and white striped headdresses. Three Egyptian generals from the South, men known to harbor ages-old ambition left over from ancient days when Thebes ruled Egypt, were led away. And then two Greeks with polished bronze helmets and flowing red capes.

He held them in the most contempt, these arrogant general-kings of minor Greek states who were nothing more than mercenaries selling allegiance to the highest bidder. They'd been at it for centuries.

Looking for deceit in each man's face—Egyptian or foreign, he cautioned, "The others are being taken into custody as we speak. If there are yet traitors among us, your names shall soon be revealed."

He couldn't read the Greeks. They stared back with unwavering, steely eyes set in expressionless faces. It seemed unlikely they would stand by Psamtik. No one wanted to align themselves with a loser.

More than one Egyptian couldn't mask his alarm. Fear of exposure as traitors—or of what lay ahead? They all dreaded Psamtik's reign. *It is said that a God leaves his city during the rule of an evil master.*

"I have given my oath to the Pharaoh," he challenged the room. "I have pledged to defend Mother Egypt with my life. Are we brothers?"

No one moved. The silence was deafening. Was all lost before he even began? Then a general from Memphis jumped to his feet.

"Long live the Pharaoh!" he cried out, thrusting his sword into the air.

And with his pledge, the fervor ignited. Another and yet another joined him, all brandishing drawn swords.

"Curse on the dog Cambyses!" they roared.

"May Set eat their souls! May Set eat their souls!"

In the end, even the cool Greeks stood to swear their allegiance. Thank the Gods! He needed their legions desperately; it had been generations since Egyptians faced a foreign invader on their own.

"Prepare an analysis of your troops, their number, strength and mobility," ordered River God. "Do not glorify yourselves. Now is not the time for arrogance or rivalry."

Strategy was his goal, but he knew that tactics are the building blocks of success. With proper preparation and correct state of mind, Egypt would be ready when the time came. Ready for anything, that is, except treachery and incompetence.

ᴥ

Qeb-ha paced the marble floors. When he heard about the message Isenkhebe had received, he could only pray it was from Hermes. Eben sat before his scrolls, reading his numbers and stars. From time to time, he stopped to rock back and forth and recite hurried incantations.

"Well?" Qeb-ha demanded impatiently. "What do you see?"

He had taken on the boy in Khent-min because his spies told him that Eben was a talented Kabbalist. The Jew had not disappointed; Qeb-ha couldn't argue with the results of the Hebrew magic.

Eben had seen from the beginning that Isenkhebe would return, and although Hathor had come to her rescue as a falcon in the desert, Qeb-ha was certain that it was the Kabbalah amulet that delivered Isenkhebe from Set the Destroyer.

"I see danger, great danger." Eben's sunken eyes were huge and round in a face at the same time both painfully youthful and desperately old. "But there is a tiny door through which she may escape. Everything depends upon our actions. The outcome is not yet written."

"Is it an actual door, Eben? Or is it an allegory? What signs do we look for?"

He wanted reassurance from the boy, not unknowns. He saw nothing but unknowns ahead.

ᘒ

"You must take the Emerald Tablet out of Egypt. There is very little time, Isenkhebe."

Hermes squeezed my hand. His energy streamed through my body, igniting each nerve ending. We were one in urgency.

"Negative energies amass at an alarming rate. They come from within, and they come from without. The risk to the Tablet is great. Everything depends upon you."

He was so earnest. So convinced. How could he count on *me* to save the Emerald Tablet? I'd come back to save Isis, not the world. This was way above my pay grade. I felt barely able to take care of myself.

"Antinous will take you from here to Greece, beyond the reach of the Persians."

Were they crazy? Greece was in the wrong direction. I envisioned mighty armies of perfumed and bearded monsters expanding out from Susa and certainly into Greece, practically Persia's neighbor.

"But, Antinous," I protested, "is that wise? The Persians are conquering everything. Should we not go farther to the west, away from them?"

"We shall be safe in Greece," he said firmly. "At least for some years to come."

We. Years to come. This plan involved much more than my immediate escape.

"You must be Greek now, my daughter." Hermes smiled in a way to assure me that I was capable of everything required.

"Greek?" I said it in a rather dazed tone, trying to imagine what that would entail. And then I thought of my tutors and the years of language training. For the first time, it truly began to sink in that Hermes might have, indeed, planned this extraordinary intrigue long ago.

"We have chosen a new name for you. *Isidora.* Gift of Isis." Hermes hesitated, looked over at Antinous and then back at me. His hand squeezed mine a little harder. His tone was soft and soothing, like a doctor giving a patient startling news and trying to deliver it in the gentlest way possible.

"You shall be the wife of Antinous; he shall bring you home from his travels. All has been arranged."

I would have pulled my hand away if Hermes hadn't held it so tightly in his grasp. He must have known the shockwave his words would send through me.

I stared in disbelief at Antinous. Wife? He was handsome, even beautiful, but what life would I have with this cold stranger? Would he expect me to be faithful to him? I met his eyes; I couldn't hide what was in mine. I couldn't read what was in his.

"A woman cannot travel alone," Hermes was saying in the most earnest of tones. "A woman cannot live alone. This you know to be true."

He touched the leather amulet on my wrist and abruptly changed the subject.

"The Kabbalist is devising a new amulet."

I didn't bother to ask how he knew about Eben. Hermes knew things far greater than that.

"Remember, Isenkhebe, time is a continuum that loops back on itself. Because something appears to end now, in this moment, it does not preclude yesterday and tomorrow."

Was he talking about River God?

I dared to look again at Antinous, this time in a more guarded way. What and how much did he know? His face had no expression; his eyes gave nothing away. It couldn't be easy for him to commit to a woman he didn't know, a woman with a reputation—and not one for constancy.

But Eben the fortune-teller at Carla's party had been clear. If I were to save Isis, I must leave Egypt at once. I accepted everything as Hermes offered.

"When do we sail?"

CHAPTER 48 ANTINOUS

Each with our own torch, thank Hathor, we climbed the damp, narrow spiral staircase in silence. I supposed Antinous to be as lost in his thoughts of our future together as I was in mine. The tension between us was electric.

He was familiar with the way and led us quickly down the long, echoing tunnel until we arrived at the bottom of the steps that led up to the little chapel with the false door carved in stone. Without warning, he stopped and turned to face me, standing so close I had only to lift my hand to touch his chest. There was a heady scent of lamp oil about him and a slight hint of male sweat without a trace of perfume or myrrh.

Our torches cast dancing shadows around us, lighting his face, accenting his bones. A muscle in his left jaw knotted and unknotted. Behind his head with a halo of shimmering golden curls, the exotic white symbols glowed in the midnight blue dome.

His lower lip was slightly fuller than the upper, which was shaped into a bow; his mouth almost formed a pout. An Aphrodite's cleft, made deeper by shadows, split his chin. Unlike Egyptians who outline their eyes in *kohl* and drape themselves in beads and gold, his only adornment was a matching pair of thick leather bands around his wrists.

I couldn't read anything in his mask expression; where was the hunger I always saw in men's eyes? Did he wait for a sign from me?

Not a whisper of air moved; there wasn't a sound in the still, silent chamber except our breathing. I reached up and ran my fingers through the short curls on his neck. The emerald glass eyes of the serpent coiling around my arm glinted in the torchlight as my fingertips traced around his ear. My eyes invited him.

He put his free hand on the nape of my neck, his grip firm but not forceful. He leaned his head toward me and into me but didn't close his eyes until his mouth was on mine. I opened my lips and took him in, sucking his tongue in a gentle, tempting way, urging him on.

In spite of his hardening, he pulled away in the middle of the kiss. His eyes locked with mine again, and again I could read nothing; it was as if he were separate from his body and had no connection to the changes there.

Why did he fight me? He was my husband and my future.

With the tip of my index finger, the one that traced his ear, I eased aside the strap of my dress, each slow, seductive, deliberate inch exposing bare flesh pulsing with promise. My breast was a pale mound in the yellow light.

Antinous looked at my blatant invitation and then back into my eyes. He took his hand away from the nape of my neck and slid the sheer fabric in place, covering me, never looking from my face.

I blinked and jerked my head back.

He took my torch, put it into my right hand and took my left hand in his right.

"Come." It was all he said. Then he led me up the stairs, gripping my hand as firmly as he had gripped the back of my neck.

Goliath must have heard us approach, because he stood at attention when we opened the double wooden doors. He looked sharply at Antinous and then, for only the second time I could recall—the other being in the desert—he looked directly at me. A slight widening in his eyes told me that he saw my discomfort, but not perceiving danger or fear, he looked quickly away.

Shame washed over me that I ever entertained thoughts of abusing him, he who was wholly devoted to me and entirely at my mercy. I would have made him miserable for my own pleasure, the first man to hold me in his arms after my escape, after the desert—after the General.

"I shall return with the Nubian," I told Antinous with as much dignity as I could summon.

"I shall see you to your quarters." His voice and face were utterly devoid of expression.

The awkwardness between us was palpable. Goliath shifted his weight slightly; I sensed a heightened tension in his stance. As for Antinous, I was no closer to understanding what thoughts swirled behind the wall he now fortified. He had kissed me. I had responded. Had I violated some Greek taboo at the foot of the stairs? Were we not to live as husband and wife? Or was that precisely what he resisted, my woman to his man. Greeks. Everyone knew of their preference for their comrades-in-arms.

Antinous led the way; I followed him with Goliath following me. We returned to my chambers in uncomfortable silence to find Qeb-ha standing watch on my balcony with Eben. Maia and Kiya hovered just inside the bedchamber door.

Of course, they hadn't expected for Antinous to be with me and were taken aback, although they concealed it well. I introduced him as Hermes' assistant. Nothing more. Maia and Kiya took in every detail of his tall frame and golden curls. They saw his beauty and bearing, and they knew me only too well. Their eyes moved from me to Antinous and back again. I could see them thinking, *Who is this new lover?* I kept my face a mask.

Qeb-ha could scarcely restrain himself in his desire to hear of my meeting with Hermes. It occurred to me that, even with his special powers, he knew very little about the inner workings of the Library and almost nothing about the Hermes *Trismegistus* he worshipped as a God.

"Hermes shall send word very soon," Antinous said in the flat tone of a messenger with no personal interest in the message.

He nodded to the two men and started to leave.

"Antinous! Do not go. I wish to speak with you."

He turned back to me, casting an uneasy glance at Qeb-ha and Eben.

"Please, leave us," I said.

They looked quickly at each other, hesitated only a moment, bowed low and left the room with Maia and Kiya. Goliath went no farther than a step outside the open doorway; his giant frame cast a shadow across the threshold.

I moved to the balcony, and Antinous followed to lean against the railing, his elbow on the edge. His stance appeared relaxed, but not his face; the muscle knotted in his jaw.

"I do not consider it safe to talk here," he said in a tight voice.

"You would leave me with too many unanswered questions, Antinous."

I slid closer to him so that we could speak softly. It was obvious he was painfully ill at ease. He shifted his weight; he avoided looking into my face. I had no time for his discomfort; more pressing for me at this moment was a plan, not only to get myself out, but also my household.

"Tell me more about the doors in the blue chamber. Where do they lead?"

Instead of answering, he turned his face in the direction of my bedchamber door and then surveyed the terrace, searching for I don't know what. Spies? We were obviously alone.

"Please, Antinous." When he didn't respond, I repressed an irrresistible urge to slap him and forced myself to plead, "Look at me."

At last, he faced me. In reluctant surrender, he exhaled once sharply, and then spoke in the quietest of voices, measuring each word to ration out his secret knowledge.

"The doors open into a vast underground tunnel system. All tunnels save one connect to other buildings in the Temple complex. One sole passageway leads directly to the river harbor."

"So our escape is via the Temple. We can avoid the streets." I felt suddenly hopeful that it was indeed possible for everyone to get away.

"Hermes and I have a plan, Isenkhebe," he cautioned. "All has been carefully arranged." The knotted muscle in his jaw looked the size of a quail's egg. A deep furrow above his nose gave his face a look of intense concentration.

"Am I not to know the plan, Antinous?" I insisted, moving right next to him.

I brushed his forearm with my fingertips, only the lightest of touches. His male scent mixed with burnt oil filled my nose.

"My life and those of my household are at stake," I whispered.

He bit his lower lip and ran his fingers through his curls. How he struggled before he acquiesced. When he finally spoke, the words poured out in a flood.

"A Phoenician ship waits at Rosetta, where the Nile meets the sea. We must get from Saïs to the ship without detection. But only you and I."

When he saw my alarm that I had to leave behind the others, he said earnestly, "It is as it must be. Trust the plan. Trust Hermes."

He stood very erect now, his whole body tense.

"You must speak of this to no one, Isenkhebe. No matter how tempted you are. Absolutely no one must know."

How bitter was this destiny Hermes had bequeathed me that I must leave everything and everyone dear to me behind. For a heartbeat, I despised Hermes' great plan; I had no want to be the Chosen One.

Antinous started again to leave, and again I stopped him, this time by gripping his forearm. He must have been months underground with Hermes, his skin was so pale next to my hand. He felt warm but not damp.

"Antinous, please tell me. Did I offend you—in the tunnel?" I looked at him directly, holding his gaze, confronting that which we both avoided. "Is ours to be a marriage in name only?" I paused before daring to ask, "Do you not desire me?"

It took some courage for me to voice my fears; I still felt the unfamiliar sting of rejection and humiliation. But we were to be married; I was to spend my life with him. Not River God. Did Antinous, too, love another? Did he desire a man over a woman? If that were the case, I wanted to know now.

He looked away to stare out at the Temple grounds for such a long moment that I began to doubt he would answer. Birds flocked around the myrtle tree; a peacock trilled his mating call. The tinkle of women's laughter carried across the garden like the musical notes from a glass wind chime.

My breath caught when he turned his eyes back to me. They were exactly the same blue as the sky behind him, the bright clear shade of a Theban spring morning. And at last I saw in them the kind of wistful yearning that I commonly see in men's eyes. But I also saw doubt.

"I know you can satisfy me, Isis. But can I satisfy you?"

CHAPTER 49 INVITATION

Qeb-ha begged permission to enter and made straight for Antinous and me with Kiya following on his heels. His eyes were panicked; the amethyst earring swung wildly back and forth in erratic arcs. Sweat glistened on his scalp and face. In his clenched fist, he carried an elaborate papyrus scroll bound with golden ropes ending in tassels of silver threads. Not typical Egyptian design, this exuberance of style had a flavor of the East.

"The Royal Guard has just now delivered it!" he squeaked in panic.

I read quickly and paraphrased the text, "It is an invitation to a banquet at the palace of the Crown Prince Psamtik."

"There would not be a feast when the Pharaoh is ill," Qeb-ha whispered.

"It says the feast is in my honor, to thank me for alerting the Pharaoh to the Persians."

I felt my own panic tighten my throat in a vise.

"This is a trap," Antinous said immediately. "You cannot attend."

That much was obvious to me.

Antinous quickly scanned the scroll; he appeared to have no trouble reading Demotic, the handwriting style of hieroglyphs favored at Court.

"A guard will accompany you to the Palace." He looked up at me. "I doubt you shall be free to leave again."

"I do not intend to go."

A desolate Kiya fell to her knees, rocking back and forth, sobbing in a voice almost as high as Qeb-ha's. "How can you not attend a banquet given by the Crown Prince in your honor?"

The stress of the last weeks had been hard on her. She looked so terribly old—and frail. Her cheeks were so hollow. This was not the same spunky woman who shouted at everyone in my villa the day we packed for my voyage from Thebes with Qeb-ha. She suffered; they all suffered. Because of me.

Antinous gripped my shoulders with his wrestler's strength and turned me to face him. "We must act quickly. Stay in your quarters until you have word from us. I shall request extra guards."

He hurried through the door without looking back.

No sooner had Antinous left than Qeb-ha came up with his standard excuse. "We must send word at once that Isenkhebe is ill."

Too bad I hadn't listened to him the morning of the hunt. How different everything might be if I had.

My mind raced through various plans and strategies, discarding one after another. I settled on the simplest, at least for the moment.

"We do not respond. Nothing is required. The Prince cannot imagine anything other than my attendance. We have time to think this through."

Eyes round as solar disks, Qeb-ha and Kiya nodded their heads. Qeb-ha's amethyst twirled and banged against his neck.

I couldn't travel as a Greek in my priestess gowns and Egyptian wigs. My shaved head had to be covered. What did Hermes know of a woman's needs? Why hadn't I asked Antinous if they had thought of these details?

I called for Maia.

"I need you to help me."

Taking her by the shoulders, I forced her to look into my eyes. "This is extremely important, Maia. Do you understand?"

She nodded her head so hard the tiny bells in her wig jingled like an erratic *sistrum*.

"Go with Eben to the market," I told her. "Buy the *peplos*, sandals and head covering of a Greek woman. Complete from head to toe."

A look of sheer panic came over her face.

"Eben knows these things," I assured her. "He has seen these woman many times."

I don't know how she kept from bursting into sobs; one tear after another rolled down white cheeks washed of all color. Her eyes were wide with terror, and there was little I could do to calm her. It took all my strength of will to keep my voice level and confident.

"Do not buy more than one item from any vendor. Gossip spreads faster in the marketplace than anywhere. Do you understand?"

I grabbed her arm as she turned to leave. She was so delicate, her arm so thin.

"Look for a wig arranged in the hairdo of a Greek noblewoman. And Maia, do not speak of this to any of the servants, not one."

I had to trust her. She would never betray me willfully, but one slip of her tongue, and I was doomed.

I ate lightly and sat with Pehtes purring on my lap. The night birds began to sing. Venus glowed like a brilliant white coal in a tangerine sky. The evening had grown dark and the first stars come out when Eben and Maia finally returned.

They had everything I'd requested, including a wig that parted in the middle with dozens of braids twisting backwards into an elaborate knot at the nape of the neck. Small curls framed the face. The color was dark blond and, like Antinous, streaked with gold.

The Greek *peplos* gown involved confusing wide lengths of dark green wool with yellow geometric embroidery on some edges and purple braid on others. They brought me an outer cloak dyed deep violet, also in a fine quality lightweight wool that was still rough on my skin, not soft like our gossamer linen.

I tried to make sense of the complicated array of cloth managed with cords and pins but soon gave up, hoping that Antinous had sisters—or lovers—who had instructed him.

Qeb-ha and Eben came to me, grave-faced and united.

"Isenkhebe must leave at once for the South. It is too dangerous here. We shall all travel to Elephantine, to the Jewish community. Eben can find shelter. Isenkhebe can disappear there."

When I didn't immediately agree, Qeb-ha went on, almost in tears; his voice was impossibly high with angst.

"War is coming. The Crown Prince will think only of the Persians. The Persians think only of the Delta. They would not go as far south as Elephantine; that is almost Nubia. The Persians want nothing from the Nubians."

"Thank you," I said solemnly. "I shall consider it and tell you my decision tomorrow."

"Isenkhebe must leave tonight!" Qeb-ha screeched. "We should all leave now." He seemed to have forgotten about Hermes and our sacred mission—and even the dangers of Set in the night.

Fearing the response, I nonetheless asked, "What do you see in your stars and numbers, Eben?"

"I cannot get a clear picture. I have never experienced the dark mists obscuring my vision."

With every minute that passed, I grew more anxious. The Crown Prince had changed everything with his invitation. In my mind's eye, one door after another slammed shut. I no longer had time.

What if I didn't escape? What if I went through a horrible torture that only a Persian could devise?

What if Barb was right and I got stuck here? I stopped the panic of what ifs before fear ran away with me, but the effort exhausted me.

Then I remembered what Hermes had said.

"Do you have another amulet for me, Eben?"

I think it startled him that I knew, but no sooner did I mention it, than he pulled a tiny leather amulet out of his robe; the pouch and strap were identical to the one on my wrist. I wondered what these words said. Did they grant me safe passage to Nubia? I didn't need that.

He removed the first amulet and tied on the second. His hands shook; he had trouble tying the knot. I fought the feeling of dread.

My nerves felt like the frayed ends of electrical wires with live current sparking out.

A warm bath did nothing. The nightingales did nothing. The breeze rustling through the palm fronds did nothing. Not the sweet scents of jasmine, not the heady waft of myrrh—there was nothing that could soothe me.

Kiya brought me a draught of potent herbs to help me sleep.

New guards stood in the shadows below the balcony. New guards stood in the atrium in front of our rooms. The priests ran their own fiefdom on the Temple grounds; I felt safe as long as I was within these walls. Well, almost safe.

CHAPTER 50 NIGHT VISIT

A hand pressed down on my mouth. I tried to sit up but couldn't move my head. There was no moon. I could see nothing in the darkness except the form of a man directly over me. I kicked and thrashed, but I couldn't dislodge him. Bile came up into my mouth.

"Sh-h-h, Isis," River God breathed in my ear.

I clutched him to me, digging my fingertips into his muscled back, hoping to draw strength from his power. He took his hand away, replacing it with his lips. He tried to kiss me, but I sobbed too hard.

His arms wrapped around my back; I felt his muscles tighten over the full length of my body. I wanted to melt into him, to become one with him. I could walk out of here, and no one would see me.

With his warm lips and hot tongue, he kissed down my neck, across the hollow of my throat and up to my ear. He took the lobe between his teeth, gently, and then sucked, long languid pulls that I felt right down to my womb.

Tongue at my ear, he breathed warmth and life into me. His touch caressed me as tenderly as a breeze. He took his time, unhurried, savoring my need. My breath was so shallow, I scarcely took in air.

His fingers went in my mouth, across my tongue, wetting them, and then his fingertips, moist with my saliva, went to my breast.

"I have thought of you every moment, Isis. I have tasted your sweetness with each sip of wine."

"Why have you waited so long to come to me?" My voice was deep, husky, betraying my hunger. "I needed you. I needed you so."

My hand found his hardness. I felt him swell and grow even harder, hard as iron, as I squeezed the first droplets of wet from the tip. With my saliva, I made him wetter still, rubbing his smooth bulb in gentle circles, then grasping his shaft, pumping up and down slowly.

The muscles in his thighs and butt tightened; the nipples on his bare chest rose to sharp points. He grew thick as a stone phallus of Min.

He kissed me finally, his tongue embracing mine, his lips smothering me, devouring me. He was almost—but not quite—brutal. His warm palm pressed along my ribs, across my belly and over my mound. I moaned, spreading my loins, shifting my hips to open wider to welcome his touch, to give him everything.

No one had a touch like River God.

When his lips left mine and began their trail of kisses to my breast, my back arched, begging him for his tongue. My hips rose and fell, his fingers possessing me. I rocked on the palm of his hand.

My cries must have wakened the household, but Maia didn't come. She knew those sounds well. Pehtes curled at the top of my bare scalp, purring a lion's roar, wallowing in the animal scent.

My mind was light, but my head heavy from the potent drug that induced my sleep. It still fogged my senses. The night stars disappeared; the open balcony faded. Las Vegas sparkled through the tall windows of the Wynn.

In one breath, he was River God, in the next, Rasheed. Our souls glided back and forth between two worlds.

"Why did you not come back to me?" I whispered. "I came back for you."

Of course, he thought I meant I came back from the desert and not through the Red Mirror. River God knew nothing about the future.

He stopped his caress and let his hot hand rest on my damp thigh for a moment until he rolled onto his back.

"I came for you in the desert," he said in a flat, cold voice.

He put his hands behind his head and looked up, not at me. The spell was broken, like the night of the bath in Thebes. Words are always the spoiler with River God.

The seconds ticked by like hours. Two tomcats came together under the balcony, their howls piercing the night.

"But you allowed Hetmus-hor to take me from Goliath," I pleaded. "It could have been you. It *should* have been you."

His response was to get up from the bed. His silhouette moved quietly in the room to find his sandals and his sword.

"You must leave Saïs," he said. "It is not safe for you, even here in the Temple."

I listened to his voice in the dark, telling me the reason he had come.

"I have heard rumors the Persians are offering any price for your capture. Cambyses wants revenge for General Sher's death."

I closed my eyes and saw the General's startled face, eyes huge with disbelief, blood gushing from his slit throat and spilling onto my hands.

River God sat down again, this time on the edge of the bed. He took my hand and kissed the palm. My eyes had adjusted enough to the starlight to make out the angles of his cheekbones and the worry in his eyes.

"I fear the Crown Prince and his vile Scribe are scheming to trade you when Cambyses invades."

You have to go back, Isis, or you will suffer. You can't imagine the suffering.

"That explains the invitation to the feast tomorrow at the Palace," I said in a voice surprisingly steady given the invisible vise crushing my throat.

"Invitation? There is no feast. You must leave at once for the South, maybe as far as Kush."

"I cannot go south."

He leaned over me, his hands gripping my upper arms, pulling me up to him. I winced from his fingers digging into my flesh.

"You shall do exactly as I say. Do you hear me? This is no time for your foolishness. The Persians are masters of torture, Isenkhebe. It takes days for their victims to die."

Foolish. That's how River God still thought of me, his Maia, weak and malleable, even after all I had been through. But I was not the same woman. I had survived the desert. I had survived the General.

He didn't know what I knew. He didn't know the Persians would drive deep into Egypt, that not even Kush would be safe, but I did. I had seen it from the future.

I had to tell him. It might save his life; it might save him from the Persians.

"Cambyses will invade in the month of Payni."

"So soon!" he exclaimed, jumping to his feet. "How do you know this? Has the priest Qeb-ha seen it in the Temple?"

River God certainly had great belief in his Gods.

"Eben the Kabbalist has divined it. He says everything is written in the stars and his numbers." I amazed myself with how easily the lie came.

He sat down abruptly again on the edge of bed and said grudgingly, "The Jew was right about you in the desert. What else does he say?"

"Do not trust the Greeks."

"Yes, I know about the false Greek allies. I have gauged their worth. They shall run away from Psamtik to the winning side. They do not believe in him."

He paused and then whispered, "*I* do not believe. How shall I worship him?"

Not to worship the Pharaoh, Horus-the-God-on-earth, would be sacrilege and high treason, the negation of a life devoted to duty and honor. I took his hand, trying to imagine his torment. He raised my hand to his lips.

The tip of his tongue wet my fingertips; his breath was hot and moist. *Would this be the last time in this life I would feel his sculptured mouth on me?*

"Make ready to leave at sunset tomorrow. Look for a ship under my banner—Chancellor of the Armies. Disguise yourself."

I thought of the pile of Greek clothing in the chest by the wall. Our minds worked the same, but our paths went in different directions. Is that forever to be our destiny?

I had said nothing at all to him about Antinous and Greece; I couldn't. It was too dangerous. One couldn't tell—even under torture—what one didn't know.

So I lied to him with my silence.

"Be ready," and not "I love you," were his last words as he headed toward the balcony.

"Why do you always leave me?" I cried out as he slipped over the side into the night.

CHAPTER 51 THE SEED

Kiya came to me while I still slept. Re had barely risen, and the trees were full of morning birdsong. She was kneeling on the yellow and blue striped wool carpet beside my bed when I opened my eyes into her grave face. What news now?

She took my hand when she saw I was awake. Hers was smaller than mine and bony with paper-thin skin. She wore no rings.

Dread crushed my chest.

"What is it, Kiya? You are frightening me. Tell me at once!"

"You have not had your monthly bleeding, Isis."

I looked at her, stupefied. Of course, she would know that about me. She was responsible for everything that I ate, everything I put on my body. She was responsible for my laundry.

"Who is the father, Isis? Do you know?"

I closed my eyes and unraveled the crazy quilt of time and events as they had been woven on this side of the mirror. I counted backwards the number of weeks since the hunt. Since the desert. Since the General.

"Is it the Persian, Isis?"

I didn't answer. I kept my eyes closed. My whole body was still.

"You cannot carry this child, Isis. You are a High-Priestess. You are forbidden to bear children."

"What of me, Kiya? Am I not the daughter of Sit-hathor?"

"That is different, Isis. Your father is a God. This father is a monster. The child is an abomination."

What of the man-beast abominations that are Egyptian Gods?

"Let me do something now, Isis, this morning. It can be over in a few hours."

"Kiya, I cannot be weakened in any way today. I must be strong. You must be strong. We all must be strong."

After the initial shock, my first thought was of Antinous. First the scene in the tunnel, and now a child by another man. A fine start to a marriage already in peril.

My mind sped through my options. If I seduced Antinous as soon as possible, I could easily pass the child off as his. But could I look into his eyes every day of a lifetime and lie? And if the child looked like his father, would Antinous even believe me?

Kiya sighed and dropped my hand. She looked so incredibly sad. She stood and bowed before leaving.

"I cannot tell your mother, Isis. That is your task."

The plan was for Antinous to come for me right before sunset. The gardens would be empty; priests and priestesses would be in the temples, and everyone else occupied with their evening meal. I thought we cut it too close. The Royal Guard escort was expected when the first stars came out.

What would happen to my household, to old Kiya and gentle Maia? I couldn't tell them that I would go north while they went south.

The day passed in sadness and goodbyes to sweet memories. I could take almost nothing with me. I clutched Pehtes, arguing with myself that she could come. A Greek woman raised in Cyrene on the Libyan coast might have a cat with a Berber name meaning 'the black one.' But in my heart, I knew Pehtes would stay behind.

Greek scrolls with the writings of the great thinkers could come, but not my precious Egyptian papyri with their exquisite hieroglyphs in black and red ink. I opened a medical papyrus to the section on women and read its useless advice.

Prescription to make a woman cease to become pregnant for one, two or three years: Grind together finely a measure of acacia dates with honey. Moisten seed-wool with the mixture and insert into the vagina.

Too late for that.

The steel blade of my dagger was razor-sharp. Again I saw dark red blood flowing from the General's throat and shocked betrayal in his eyes. His death haunted me. The desert haunted me. Were my bow and arrow still buried in the sand with the charioteer and the horse? Would their mummified bodies be discovered in the arid riverbed thousands of years from now?

I lovingly touched each piece of my jewelry, so beautifully crafted in gold, silver and electrum. I put the Hathor ring with the lapis lazuli as large as a plump grape in its box and then divided my jewelry, placing it in small leather purses with handfuls of amulets.

The ibis from Abydos was at the bottom of the chest. I sighed. I would never have a chance to give it to my father. At least not in this lifetime.

In the end, I couldn't part with my necklace from the hunt—the one from the General's tent. I held it in the sunlight and watched tiny golden rays reflect off the delicate charms.

The vulture had saved me from the cobra in the desert. The General gave me the first clue to his black heart when he took the crocodile between his thick fingers. I smiled at the fertile rabbits and thought of the General's seed growing inside me.

Would I allow his child to live? Would I claim Antinous as the father—or I would tell him the truth? My options were all painful. The General managed to hold me prisoner even after his death.

The heat of the day passed, and Re slid toward nightfall. The fading light fell on the high walls of the old Pharaoh Amasis' rose granite naos at the end of the garden; the sanctuary glowed golden red. Birds feeding on evening insects raised a deafening chorus.

River God waited for me at the wharf to sail south, not knowing about Antinous and Greece, not knowing I would never come.

I gathered Qeb-ha, Eben, Kiya and Maia in my bedchamber and gave each a pouch with amulets and jewelry.

"We must not travel together," I explained in the calmest voice I could muster. "You shall need these for bribes."

"Take five drops each morning, three days in a row." A haggard Kiya pressed a small vial into my hand. Sorrow deepened the lines in her face. "It is slower but safer."

"Please, Kiya, give this into my mother's keeping."

Kiya's eyes widened in terror when she saw the small box with my lapis lazuli ring, the one of two in all Egypt.

"It is too dangerous for me to have it on my person. You understand that, do you not?"

Kiya nodded her head, but the tears kept flowing.

"Please, return the menit to the Temple in Thebes, Qeb-ha. It belongs to the cult."

The sacred menit necklace had been given to me at my naming ceremony, three days outside of my mother's womb. To surrender it was to give up myself. Qeb-ha kept his head bowed to avoid looking in my eyes.

"We shall all meet in Thebes, and then I shall go south to Elephantine and farther to Kush, if I still sense danger."

They knew I didn't speak the truth but chose to say nothing. They had resigned themselves to destiny. The Fate and the Fortune that come, it is the Gods that send them.

We stood in a small circle, each of us lost in our own worries and dreads. Eben took my forearm with the leather strap in his soft hand. He'd never touched me before, except with the tips of his fingers when he replaced the amulet of the desert.

"Isenkhebe, the amulet you wear has no scroll."

"What? What do you mean no scroll?"

I had visualized magical spells with tiny Hebrew letters that would save my life again.

"It holds a vial instead of a scroll."

Eben's eyes were so full of anguish that I almost couldn't look there. I saw the large brown eyes of the gazelle as the life force left her the morning of the hunt.

"It is over in seconds," he said in the flattest of tones.

Although none of us needed an explanation, he added, "If you are captured."

So I carried two vials, both filled with potions designed to end life.

⌐

We did not see the Royal Guard approach the Temple gates and demand entrance. We did not see the two renegade men from the desert hiding in the shadows outside the pylon gate.

"The Scribe means to cheat us out of our reward. He thinks to take the woman himself," grumbled the man in the red turban.

"Hurry! I know a way in, but we must be fast."

The two scurried along the towering wall of the stone palisade and found the postern, a hidden green-painted door servants used to exit and enter. They had only moments to act; Temple Guards lock the small, rounded-top gate every sunset and allow no person entrance until morning.

They slipped through the postern, and the man in the red turban handed the guard a small pouch with Lydian coins. The guard grunted, stuck it into his waistband and turned his head away from them.

They were on the Temple grounds. Now to find the priestess.

CHAPTER 52 RED TURBAN

Goliath rushed breathless into my bedchamber. His eyes were enormous; the whites showed all around the black. Beads of sweat glistened on his forehead.

"The Royal Guard is at the pylon gate! Our guards have disappeared."

Grabbing my bundles of cloth and scrolls, I kissed each of my inner circle on the cheek, trying to reassure them with words.

"It is in battle that one finds a brother. We are family. We shall be together again, I promise you." I spoke from my heart and believed it to be true, although not necessarily in this lifetime.

"Take Maia to Elephantine," I whispered in Eben's ear. "Thebes will be safe neither from Psamtik nor the Persians. Please do it for me."

"Tell the Guard when they come, Qeb-ha, that I am praying in the inner sanctum. They dare not come for me there. Tell Antinous to meet me at the double doors in the Green Granite Chapel."

He gripped my hand in his. I remembered that first day in my mother's temple when he had waited for me in the shade among columns with heads of Hathor carved at their tops. I had despised his high voice then. Now I yearned for the sound of it, never to stop hearing it.

"Thank you, Qeb-ha. We have surpassed both companion and brother, have we not?"

"Happiness will come to Isis out of misfortune, after what she has undergone," Qeb-ha said for my mind only.

His final benediction, a prophecy from his Gods, was our last intimacy.

Goliath and I had entered the second courtyard when a heavy weight hit the ground behind me, like the falling of a tree. The Nubian lay dead still, blood flowing down his face from under his white linen headdress.

I fell to my knees beside him. A hand came from behind and stuffed a cloth into my mouth. I tried to lash out, but iron arms held me in place, and then a rough sack went over my head, but not before I saw the flash of red turban.

The sack had held grain. I breathed chaff up my nose, and the cloth in my mouth gagged me. Vomit came into my throat, then into my lungs. It would be a strange end to this affair, if I choked to death in a filthy bag.

Hands lifted up the sack and threw me over a shoulder. I hung upside down and jostled wildly as my captor ran. The bag held me as tight as a swaddled infant. Unable to kick or punch, I rolled my body back and forth, trying to throw him off balance. But I was helpless—helpless to move, helpless to reach Eben's vial.

We fell. I hit the ground with a smack. I could see nothing but willed my body to roll sideways, over and over. I could feel soft grass now instead of stone. I heard scuffling but no voices. My hands were not bound, and I ripped wildly at the sack to free myself.

But I was picked up again, higher in the air, by a taller man who ran with long strides. I struggled even harder but had no impact on him. I jostled and bounced against his back. He entered a building, and I sensed he was alone; his footsteps and movements were the only sound.

I felt hard stone when he set me down, and then the filthy sack was pulled off and the cloth came out of my mouth. My vomit stained it. I gulped in air. By some miracle, I still held the bundles. When I no longer felt sick, I dared look up.

It was Hetmus-hor crouching over me! I threw my arms around his neck, sobbing with relief. He held me so tight I thought my ribs would break, but never have I so enjoyed pain.

"Qeb-ha said you were in Hermopolis. That you were forbidden to come to me."

"I told you that I'd do whatever it takes to have you, Isis. *Cualquier cosa.*"

I stared into his red-flecked eyes.

"Hector? Is it *you*, Hector?"

"*Sí*, Isis, it is me. Barb told me everything. When I crossed through the Red Mirror, I—or am I Hetmus now?—was under house arrest. I came as fast as I could."

Hector had come through the Red Mirror! I struggled to process first that he was able to pass through—that I wasn't the only one who could—and then that he did it for me.

"Did you think I would let you face this alone, Isis? You do not know me at all."

He kissed me lightly. His brilliant white smile flashed again.

"But you will."

Shouts rang out. I couldn't tell if they were outside or in. The thunder of feet pounding stone paths reached us even through the thick walls. I thought I felt the earth quake under the weight of an army invading the Temple grounds.

"Royal Guards are searching everywhere for you; they were at your chambers."

Vomit came up in my mouth again. Gentle Maia. Old Qeb-ha and dear Kiya. Sweet Eben. They would be forced to tell everything. But the Prince and his evil Scribe would never believe they didn't know my plans.

I rocked against Hector, squeezing my eyelids shut, trying to push the nightmare visions of their agony from my mind. How right Antinous had been that I must tell no one.

"There is nothing you can do for them, Isis." Hector shook me gently to bring me back. "We must get out of here now. Now!"

Just knowing me was a death sentence. What would they do to *me* if captured?

"I must meet Antinous!" I could barely speak from panic. "Only he knows the way to the port through the tunnels."

"Antinous?" Hector's smile dimmed. "Who is Antinous?"

I put my hand on his bronzed forearm, above the gold armband; his skin was warm and moist. Closing my eyes, forcing myself to breathe slowly, I focused on the Light.

Suddenly and inexplicably, I was calmer. The Universe had sent Hector to me. I was going to make it.

"There is too much to explain now, Hector, but Antinous is to take me out of Egypt. It is the only way."

He rolled back onto his haunches; the sparkle in his eyes was gone. I don't think saving me for someone else is what he envisioned when he went through the Red Mirror. But after only a moment's hesitation, he stood up, took my hand and pulled me with no effort to my feet.

"Then let us find Antinous."

The tall double doors at the end of the corridor were closed and locked. No Antinous. The empty hallway had no place to hide. We waited, exposed and vulnerable. What if Antinous didn't come? There were no windows in the corridor, but I was certain Re had descended to the Underworld by now. I felt the panic again and tried to focus on the Light, but no matter how hard I tried, I couldn't push the fear away.

Hector leaned against the stone wall next to the doors. I finally noticed the dried blood on the iron thrusting sword at his waist.

"Goliath? Is he dead? Please, tell me that he is not dead."

I saw him lying in a pool of his own blood, his headdress bright white against the dark red. I had kissed with sheer joy his dusty black feet in the desert; they were the most glorious sight I had ever seen.

"The Nubian is a giant; he lives. The two men who grabbed you are dead. I recognized them. They were with you in the desert."

"Two, there were only two?" Their boldness amazed me.

So River God was right about the price on my head. They could have been working for the Persians. They could have been working for the Crown Prince and Setne. There might be more of them, right at this moment, looking for me. I could wait no longer.

I pounded on the wooden door. Nothing. I pounded even harder. Still no response. But when I raised my fist for the third time, the door opened. The same old priest stood with a torch in his hand. He still didn't speak.

He looked up at Hector, appraised him quickly and stepped aside. The door shut behind us, and he bolted it.

"Where is Antinous?" I asked, trying to keep my voice low and calm, to believe that the Universe was on my side. But I was losing the battle with panic.

His eyes pleading, the old priest shook his head and placed a gnarled finger on his tongue to tell me that he couldn't speak. Was he deaf as well as mute? He must be able to read lips.

"Where is Antinous?" I formed each word clearly. "Has he been here?"

His shiny head nodded up and down; the ankhs in his earlobes swung wildly. He handed Hector the torch and began waving his hands and holding up fingers. Sign language! My Greek tutors had overlooked that.

"He says Antinous left to go to your quarters."

I looked up at Hector in amazement. "You know sign language?"

"*Sí*, although I am not sure how. I am not quite used to being Hetmus-hor," he answered, the twinkle back in his eye, the charm in his smile. We might have been on the Nile the morning of the hunt.

Footsteps rang in the corridor on the other side of the doors. Not a few men, but many. Then came pounding on wood with metal shields or the hilts of swords.

"Open up! Open in the name of the Pharaoh. Psamtik orders that you open these doors."

Psamtik! The old Pharaoh Amasis must be dead. We stared at the bolt rocking back and forth and ran. We no longer cared if they could hear our footsteps. It was a race to get through the secret door before they burst through the others.

The priest pulled on the hidden lever and then pushed on the basalt plaque with Atlantean symbols. The wall moved an inch at a time. I thought my pounding heart would burst from my chest. The palms of my hands left damp patches where I gripped the bundles.

We slid through the crack. Hector leaned his weight against the stone slab, and the door slid into place with the faintest of sucking sounds, like the seal of an airlock. There was no trace of the opening, at least not from our side.

"Someone must wait for Antinous to tell him to meet us at the river," I whispered in terror. "I know nothing except that a boat waits there to take us to the sea."

Why had Antinous told me so little? There were thousands of boats on the Nile. I envisioned myself trapped beneath the Temple, passing the rest of my days in the maze of secret tunnels.

Hector and the priest spoke with their hands waving in the air. I looked from one to the other and then at the wall, expecting it to move at any second.

The priest's face was solemn but held no fear. He took off the gold cord with the ankh key and handed it to Hector.

"Thank you! Thank you!" I cried, kissing the mottled skin of his ancient hand.

The muffled sounds of shouting and pounding came from the other side of the wall. The Royal Guard had reached the little chapel with the false door.

Hector grabbed my hand and bounded down the dim stairs, taking three steps at a time. I couldn't keep up. He scooped me into his arms and, within seconds, was at an ebony door, but not the door that led to Hermes *Trismegistus*.

The priest nodded his head from the halo of the torch at the top of the steps. His giant ankh earrings swung erratically about his short neck in staccato bursts of light.

Standing me to my feet, Hector looked quickly around the blue room and grabbed the only burning torch. He inserted the key into the lock, turned the latch and shoved on the door. It swung open into absolute blackness. We stepped through, and the door slammed behind us.

On the other side was silence and unending black. We ran down the tunnel toward nothingness, our lone torch spluttering wildly.

CHAPTER 53   THE SHIP

I struggled to keep up with Hector's long stride and was soon out of breath. The bundles in my arms slowed me down. My sandals flopped and slid on my feet. I stumbled on a loose stone and almost fell.

"Hector!" I gasped. "I can't keep up! Where are we going? What did the priest say?"

He stopped, not winded at all.

"The tunnel leads to the far end of the harbor. The priest says a small boat is waiting there for you."

He seemed to have gotten a lot of information from a few hand signs. I had no choice but to trust him.

Handing me the torch, he quickly tied the bundles around my waist and picked me up. My knees bent over his forearms; I wrapped my free arm around the back of his neck.

Hector moved extremely fast now. We sped through the tunnel; his paces were long and steady. He may have been the spoiled son of a rich man, but he kept himself in shape.

The tunnel took a sharp turn and sloped upward, the incline not steep but certainly heading to the surface. We ended abruptly at a small wooden door, rounded at the top, bolted on our side. Hector put me down, signaled for me to move backwards with the torch and slowly slid the bolt open with only the slightest squeak.

Fresh air poured into the tunnel. The wind had come up since sunset; the flame of the torch bent sideways. It was dark outside but not as black as the tunnel. The sky over the harbor lingered between twilight and night.

Hector showed me a special knock, a pattern of hard and soft. I was to bolt the door and stay inside. An eternity passed while I waited.

At last the knocks came, and I opened the bolt. Hector slipped in, quickly shutting the door behind him.

"We are in the wall of a barricade, across from the wharf. Soldiers are everywhere, mainly Egyptian, but Greek and Lydian mercenaries, too."

"How shall we find the boat? I do not know what to look for!"

My panic bounced off the rock walls. I could smell my own sweat. Hector gripped my shoulders and pulled me close, his eyes boring into mine.

"We shall find a way, Isis. I am here for you. I shall do whatever it takes."

I almost believed him. If only it were that simple. I leaned against the damp wall, closed my eyelids and envisioned the tiny vial in the leather pouch at my wrist. Surely it would not end with the poison, not after all this. Then I straightened my back and opened my eyes again.

I couldn't give up. Isis doesn't give up.

"Did you see a warship?" I asked.

"Yes, moored at the far end of the quay. It flies the banner of the Chancellor of the Armies. No soldiers approach it, but they swarm over all other boats."

"The ship is for me to escape to the south," I said, gripping his forearm with all my strength. "But my only hope is north to the sea, to Rosetta."

I took off my black waves with gold ankhs and pulled the Greek wig with dark blonde plaits and curls over my shaved head.

"You are transformed!" His smile blinded me.

Lifting the long skirt of my linen gown, Hector gently wiped the *kohl* and mica from my eyelids. He erased the heavy line of my eyebrow.

"Promise me that Aphrodite shall be your new name," he demanded with a smile.

Then I tried to unfold the Greek *peplos*. Yards of fabric as tangled as a ball of yarn tumbled to my feet. My hands trembled as I picked up one end and then another. I could make no sense of what went where.

"Give it to me," Hector ordered impatiently.

He gathered the length of green wool, some cords and two round brass pins and set them aside. Then he grabbed the purple cape, wrapped it around my small packet of medicines with Kiya's vial and the charm necklace, reformed the bundle and bound it around my middle. In the dim torchlight, I looked ready to give birth.

"No room for the scrolls," he declared without apology.

Hector took the green *peplos* cloth and draped it around me expertly, fastening it in place with the cords and pins. When he saw my look of surprise, he gave me another of his blinding smiles.

"Hetmus-hor knew a few Greek ladies in his day." Then he kissed me lightly and said, *"Vámos!"*

This time we stepped through the door together. Even with Hector's warning, I wasn't prepared for the numbers of men in uniform. One deadly act in a faraway tent propelled my destiny.

We stood in the shelter of the doorway for a few moments. Soldiers, soldiers everywhere, but not close by. My whole body shook; I breathed deep and concentrated on the Light.

Hector stepped outside the alcove but kept his back to the wall. I watched his tall figure move away from me before I dared step out myself.

A hand came out of the night and closed over my mouth. I started to scream but stopped. I wanted no attention drawn to me. An arm pushed me back into the dark recess around the door. I struggled, but the man held me fast. Who now? I seemed to be forever shoved against walls.

A halo of pale curls glowed in the lights of the harbor. I bobbed my head up and down rapidly, relaxing my body to let him know I recognized him, and his hand dropped from my mouth.

"Antinous!" My voice was a breathless whisper. "How did you find me?"

"Hermes. He has always said that we would meet here."

Hector didn't make a sound when he came up behind Antinous, but his long shadow fell across the door behind me. Antinous pivoted to face the Egyptian, drawing his sword as he turned. I grabbed his wrist to keep him from striking.

"No, Antinous! He saved my life. But for him, I would not be here."

There was a long moment of tension, no one speaking, the two men staring at each other, my right hand on Antinous' arm and my left on Hector. The heat of their flesh seared my palms.

I sensed that Antinous sized up one of my lovers with whom he must compete. Hector judged the man who would take me from him.

Finally, Hector said begrudgingly, "Greek, you are the luckiest man alive."

Then he smiled at me in the most sweet and tender way and put his palm on my cheek. His love flowed into me, giving me strength. I allowed myself to believe again.

"Let us get you on that ship."

Antinous disappeared for a few moments and returned with a hemp cloth sack not much cleaner, but bigger than the one the man in the red turban had thrown over my head. I went in a sack again, but not upside down.

I should not make a sound. No one must suspect anything about the heavy load thrown over Hector's shoulder.

We hurried along the barricade wall, keeping to the shadows. I bounced in the sack and held my body in a tight fetal position, clutching my knees. The night grew quieter. The wind had died again. The sounds of shouting soldiers and pounding feet grew distant as we left the search behind.

Hector laid me gently on the ground. I heard only one set of footsteps crunching on the loose rock as he walked away. Antinous stayed with me. Neither of us spoke. I breathed so quietly, my breasts didn't move.

Gentle waves lapped against the stone wharf. Humming insects swarmed in the cool of the night. Night birds called from the trees. It was so still, I could hear Antinous' shallow and fast breathing.

He had lived up to his commitment. He had come, had waited for me, and he was still here. But I felt his doubt more than ever. And he didn't even know about the General's child.

Footsteps approached. Hector heaved me up high again, over his shoulder. We left the gravel walkway and crossed hard pavement, moving silently except for the rhythmic slap of leather soles. The river hummed to our right, and then I heard the ponderous creak of a wooden ship rubbing against the stone quay.

Antinous walked beside Hector, matching his stride. Then Hector went ahead of Antinous, and the sound was leather soles on wood planks. The footfalls on the deck of the ship sounded hollow; there must be a space below.

Quiet words were exchanged. I heard River God's voice, low, giving orders. Then we descended a short, steep flight of steps. The river current rushed past the cedar boards. There were more hushed whispers and the shuffle of footsteps. Someone untied the sack, and the coarse hemp fell to my ankles.

River God jerked backwards in shock. I had forgotten my belly of Greek wool so skillfully wrapped by Hector. I had forgotten my Greek curls and naked eyes. In the low glow of the lamp, I must have been pale as white sand in moonlight.

"Do not speak. Do not utter one word," River God hissed. "The sound of a woman's voice on this ship will carry all the way to the new Pharaoh's ear."

His tone chilled me. I thought I heard hatred. How could I beg him to take me to the sea, if I couldn't speak?

River God's mouth was hard; every angle in his face was hard. There was no affection at all in his eyes. Was it only last night that he held me with such tenderness?

His aura tonight was black with jealousy and rage, but I saw longing under his anger. This time I was leaving him.

Hector held out his right arm.

"We are agreed then, Commander? You will take Isis and the Greek north to meet the Phoenician ship."

A remnant of his fury toward the man who lost Isis on the hunt flared up in River God's eyes, flickered for a moment and then died.

Hector gripped River God's shoulder; his fingers dug into the hard muscle. I thought Hector might shake him, as if to bring him to his senses.

"I know exactly what I ask of you, man," Hector insisted. "But there is no other way."

I begged River God with my eyes to accept what had to be. My whole being cried out to him, but he stubbornly looked away from me, trying to make of me a non-person, to have me no longer exist.

I had a sinking feeling that he was going to refuse to help me. His left eye twitched as if he had developed a tic.

"Do you think I would give her up," Hector reasoned, "if I thought there was any chance I could have her?"

River God glared at Hector with eyes hard and glittery as obsidian. I had thought him so handsome, but his face was harsh. Cruel lines etched his cheeks. His mouth, with lips so lush when he kissed me, was now tight with rage.

"You must act now, Commander!" pressed Hector. "Psamtik could turn on you at any moment. His men could come any time."

I didn't take a breath waiting for River God's response. I think we all held our breaths.

At last, he gripped Hector's forearm below the elbow. When he put his hand on Hector's shoulder, I sobbed out loud. A man of his word, he made a pact that would not be broken.

The air in the narrow space below deck was as charged as before a sandstorm. My heart raced, and blood pounded in my head.

All the while, Antinous stood silently to one side, almost out of the ring of light. He was no fool. He understood the drama he witnessed and the role he played. One wrong word from him and this scene could end in tragedy.

Hector stroked my cheek longingly with the back of his fingers.

"This is goodbye for now, but not forever," he whispered in a voice both loving and full of regret.

He took my chin in his hand and pulled my face up to his. The red specks in his eyes were iridescent.

"I shall never find another woman like you, Isis."

He kissed me, long and deep. He didn't hurry. He didn't care if Antinous and River God stood next to us. When he pulled away, he leaned down and whispered in my ear.

"You owe me one. *Hasta Las Vegas.*"

Then he kissed me one last time, lightly, only a fleeting touch of his lips, and disappeared up the steps.

CHAPTER 54 THE GREAT GREEN

River God stood absolutely frozen, like a quartzite statue in a tomb. Raw pain sharpened the planes of his face. Finally, he looked at me. His smoldering eyes were accusing and angry. So angry. I also saw betrayal and wounded pride. I hadn't said anything to him about Greece—or leaving with another man.

He ignored Antinous; he wouldn't even look in his direction.

I wanted to reach out and tell him this was not goodbye. I wanted to say the words he had said to me in at the Wynn. *We have known each other before, and we will know each other again.* But River God knew nothing of our other life; he knew nothing of himself as Rasheed.

This was the last time I would see him in this lifetime. I edged close into him, my body yielding, his more rigid than ever. I was desperate to reach him, so I did what I'd never before done with a lover. I summoned the Power.

My skin flushed with heat. A hot aura pulsed from my body. I believe my flesh glowed in the dim light.

"You told me in Thebes that the Gods set us on our separate paths," I crooned in the softest of honey whispers. "This is not the path I would have chosen; this is not the path I want."

Still he didn't respond, not to me, not to the Power.

"I would have lain in your arms until you left me," I breathed. "I would have been there waiting for your return."

Balancing on my tiptoes, my breasts pressing into his chest, I put my lips to his. Chiseled from stone by a master sculptor, they did not yield. My desire burned so bright, I would have lain with him right there on the rough planks, even with Antinous standing over us.

His pride wouldn't let him hold me. He resisted. He stared straight ahead, refusing again to look at me. He would show no weakness. Only the twitch in his eyelid gave him away. I felt him cut me out of his heart at the same time he cut my heart out of me.

He moved past me and up the steps, not looking back at me, never looking at Antinous. *I* couldn't bring myself to look at Antinous.

I leaned my head back against a square beam and watched my heart, ripped from my chest, pumping on the wood planks, spewing blood, the dark red stain spreading in a wide pool around my feet. Not even the Persians could invent such torture.

Then with a great clanking and creaking, the warship pulled away from the wharf with oars moving crisply, in and out, through the water. I heard the sail, filled instantly by a brisk wind, unfurl with a sharp snap. We entered the swift current flowing north toward the Great Green.

Antinous and I didn't look at each other or speak. I was shattered and shamed. There was nothing to say. I curled up on two bales and resigned myself to sleep, even more exhausted than I'd been in Sithathor's tent. How could living flesh endure such tension and pain?

Seagulls woke me. The scent of salt saturated even the stale, close air below deck.

Antinous rose and went up the stairs without a glance in my direction. I sighed the heaviest of sighs and stifled an urge to sob. He should never have seen me with River God. Those images would burn forever in his mind. They would burn forever in mine.

He came back after a short while, curls tousled by the sea breeze. His cheeks glowed rosy pink, not the pale ash from months buried in the Library among scrolls. He didn't speak but motioned for me to get into the sack, tied the end and hoisted me with no effort onto his shoulder. It surprised me that he was as strong as Hector, although I don't know why I thought of Antinous as weak.

Once on deck, bright sunlight filtered through the dusty weave of the hemp bag. The sharp cries of the gulls pierced my ears. Not far away, the waves of the Mediterranean crashed on rocks. Antinous dropped me on the hard cedar planks like a bundle of no value, not in a particularly rough way, but certainly not gently. Did he intend to show that the bundle meant nothing, or did he demonstrate what he thought of me?

Rough hands hoisted me over the side. Someone caught the sack and dropped me against hard boards. The small boat pitched back and forth, banging up against the hull. I was leaving Egypt in a sack.

We rocked on the swells and rowed away from the ship. I heard the oars of another boat approaching. Ropes were tossed amid shouting, and I made out a few words of Phoenician. I was picked up again—I think by Antinous—and handed over to unseen arms.

When we had sailed a short distance, fingers unloosened the knot, and the sack fell away from my head. Antinous pulled me from the bottom of the boat to a seat beside him.

The sailors barely registered surprise to see that the sack contained a woman. Paid to mind their own business, they looked briefly at my false belly of bundled wool and then quickly away. But if stories were told, they would be of a pregnant Greek noblewoman, not an Egyptian priestess.

We headed in the direction of a massive galley with the face of a giant green and yellow sea monster painted on the broad bow. A voluminous red sail flapped in the easterly wind.

Bobbing like a cork in the rolling waves, we floated in a vast expanse of blue sea and blue sky. Why do they call it the Great Green? The water was the rich lapis blue of my Hathor ring.

I dared glance at Antinous. He stared at the military ship rocking near the surf at the mouth of the Nile. His face was devoid of emotion, but I knew his mind whirled. I followed his line of sight and saw the small figure of River God in the prow, watching us row away. River God never raised his hand. I don't think he moved. He grew smaller and smaller, and then the ship was too far away for us to see him.

When I turned back to Antinous, he was staring at me. For a brief second, I wanted to crawl inside his head and read his thoughts, but in truth, I didn't really want to know. I met his eyes with complete frankness. He had seen me stripped naked of all pride and then cast aside. Completely exposed, I had nothing left to hide, and then I remembered the General's seed growing inside me.

They lifted us aboard the ship in a kind of sling, like the morning of the hunt being lowered to Ankh-hor's ferry—the day everything changed.

I balanced on the listing deck, slippery with salt spray. Twenty rows of oarsmen, three to a bench, lined each side. Shackles, secured by chains into large rings embedded in the deck, bound their ankles. The captain barked orders, and the red square sail billowed against the azure sky.

Antinous and I leaned against the wood railing, a wide space between us. I was grateful in the brisk air for the Grecian wool. The shoreline slipped farther and farther away until it disappeared over the horizon. Goodbye, Egypt.

Antinous left and came back.

"Please follow me."

He met my eyes for a moment. Of course, I could read nothing there. Perhaps there was nothing to read. At least, I saw no anger.

I followed him aft to where the captain's cabin filled the deck. An ordinary wooden table and two unadorned chairs stood in the middle of a cedar-paneled room; finely-woven carpets covered much of the plank floor. Several brightly painted chests lined a wall.

There was one bed built into a narrow box hung with heavy rust-colored drapes. A row of small windows near the ceiling let in light and fresh air. The cabin smelled of tangy cedar and salty sea.

"I think it best you restrict yourself to the cabin during the voyage to Cyrene. We want nothing to arouse suspicion. From there we book passage on a ship bound for Kos."

I looked around. My new home. I looked at Antinous. My new husband. He avoided eye contact. What kind of honeymoon voyage would this be?

"If you concur, of course," he added, finally looking at me. "It is only a few days."

At least he considered my opinion.

He placed a clay jar of wine, a loaf of brown bread and a hunk of white cheese on the crude table.

"I think we both need food." His voice had that flat, detached tone that said everything happening had nothing to do with him.

"Do you have the Emerald Tablet?" I asked.

He set the package on the table beside the food. I pulled the soft suede wrapping aside and fingered the bright green faience. It truly was a splendid work of art.

Antinous nodded toward a rectangular cedar box painted with the geometric patterns found on Greek vases.

"I have packed some articles of clothing for you."

The chest was filled with brightly-colored gowns and several blond wigs in Greek style. A leather pouch lay on top. I opened it—a glint of gold—Greek jewelry.

He *had* thought of a woman's needs. I hadn't imagined him capable. Such superficial ornaments seemed too mundane to merit his lofty attention.

"Thank you," I told him, and I meant it. Sincerely.

The corners of his mouth turned up—not a real smile, but still progress. I took hope. The tension in the cabin eased ever so slightly.

"The chest beside it is also for you."

I opened the red lid to dozens of scrolls. For a moment, I forgot the awkwardness between us and gave him a dazzling smile.

He took a swallow of wine and looked back at me over the rim of the cup. The ice in his eyes melted a degree.

"Hermes sent you a gift."

A large rectangle leaned against the cabin wall. I lifted the drape of blue cloth with silver stars. The heavy wood frame was painted a deep red, but there were no flowers; they must have come later. The mirror itself was polished bronze.

A pregnant woman, a little distorted and blurry, looked back. I still had the bundle tied under my gown. I stroked the frame and fingered each silver strut. Brand new.

"Hermes made it for you. He said to tell you that it is a 'cosmic mirror.' He said you would understand."

Above and below, past and future, reflecting back on each other. The Red Mirror. Hermes *Trismegistus*, Hermes Thrice-Greatest, my father, had given me the way home.

CHAPTER 55 THRICE-GREATEST

Antinous spent the rest of the day on deck, leaving me alone in the cabin. I took off the bundle from around my middle, folded the wool, and put it on top of the other clothing in the chest. I tucked my medicines and Kiya's vial along the side, at the bottom. My fingers caressed Eben's amulet on my wrist; the poison vial was hard, like a small bead. Was I safe now?

Yards of fabric, twisted and wrapped in complicated pleats and ruffles, weighed down my body. Surely Greek women sometimes wear gowns less cumbersome and not wool. I rummaged through the chest until I found a simple sleeveless caftan of soft, pale yellow linen. The cloth was so finely woven it had to be Egyptian.

A large clay *amphora* contained fresh water, on the cold side, but it would do for a sponge bath. I looked in the chest for cleansing oils and found a new copper razor. I would let the hair grow on my head; Greek women don't usually wear wigs. But what body hair did they shave? I'd have to ask Antinous. My tutors hadn't included Greek hygiene in their curriculum.

The leather pouch held three short necklaces exquisitely crafted in gold, with no beads or precious stones. One had tiny owl charms; one was made of links shaped into oak leaves. The third was a heavy thick chain trimmed with scores of delicate gold tassels.

But I chose my piece with golden vultures, crocodiles and rabbits. A string of lucky charms, it represented overcoming all obstacles. I wasn't supposed to wear anything Egyptian, but any Greek woman could easily have bought this necklace in the market as a souvenir of her travels.

I dozed. When I woke, night had fallen. Antinous sat at the wooden table, concentrating on an open scroll in the light of a single oil lamp.

"What are you reading?" I asked idly from the shadows of the bed.

"It is the treatise on mathematics by Thales introducing geometry to Greece. He spent years with Hermes in Saïs."

His eyes had a shine I hadn't seen before. I heard enthusiasm in his voice and felt more hopeful at this first crack in his wall.

Careful to modulate my voice to speak in low, mental tones, I said, "Egyptian geometry is merely unit fractions and rules of thumb. Thales went far beyond."

I paused for a breath and then asked, "What is your opinion of Pythagoras and his new theories on proof by deductive reasoning?"

"Pythagoras learned much from Thales but has taken that knowledge to ever more complex levels. I admire him immensely. He has even coined a new term for his broad system of analysis, calling himself a *philosopher*."

Antinous was clearly animated. In fact, I'd say he was eager when he looked in the direction of my voice. I felt the first contact. His eyes certainly weren't detached when he talked about mathematics. We might yet find common ground. I might not need the Power, after all.

Your father has chosen your tutors since you were a child. How long ago did Hermes make his plans? Since my birth? Since before?

"Pythagoras hypothesizes that mathematics is the key to the cosmos," Antinous continued. "He writes that Nature is based on formula and geometric harmony."

He leaned forward in the chair, turning his torso to face in my direction. I don't think he could see me; the only light was on the table.

"Pythagoras sees numbers in everything," he insisted with an intensity that, although far from Eben's feverish calculations, matched his passion.

"Divine numbers, I understand, are the core belief of Kabbalah. Is there evidence, Antinous, that Pythagoras has been influenced by the Hebrew mystics?"

"It is possible. All knowledge is contained in the Library, including that of the Jews. But logic dictates that, with or without contact, theorems based on valid principles lead to similar conclusions."

The night was silent except for the sea washing against the hull, carrying us west along the coast of Africa to Cyrene in Greek Libya. Even the seagulls slept.

"I regret I did not meet Pythagoras while in Saïs," I said a bit wistfully, lowering the vibration of my tone. In the stillness, my voice resonated like the low notes of a lyre.

His eyelids flickered. The glow of the oil lamp lighted his face, casting delicate shadows on perfect bones.

"Pythagoras would enjoy your intellect, Isidora. He teaches that men and women are equal."

Isidora. My new name. He said it easily and naturally. I took his use of it as a sign that we could start anew.

Antinous took a sharp intake of air when I came into the ring of light. His pupils were large and black; only a thin band of blue surrounded them.

The cut of my gown was loose but designed to fall on the curves of the body, along the rise of my breasts and the slope of my hips. The hormones of early pregnancy were rounding out angles, and I was fast becoming a curvaceous Greek.

Antinous sat sideways to the table. His strong legs with tight loins and rounded calves were stretched out and crossed at the ankles. The fabric of his *chiton* draped on his muscled thighs. His body was indeed perfect, exactly proportional, every muscle toned. He must have wrestled all his life.

I glided smoothly and silently toward him. When I leaned over him to ease the scroll from his hands, my swollen breasts pulled at the yellow linen. My nipples rose.

Ever so slowly, never taking my eyes from his, I pulled my gown past my knees and straddled him. My soft loins squeezed his hard thighs.

Antinous was so still, he might have been a statue. He didn't blink; he didn't breathe. I placed my palms on his chest. His muscles were so tense, his skin so smooth, he even felt like marble.

But heat rose off him; I could feel the warmth of the sun in his flesh. The tang of salt mixed with his strong scent of male.

In one day at sea, his skin had turned golden in the way of fair Greeks who reflect back the sun rather than absorb it like Egyptians. His eyes were transfixed on my face. Would he reject me tonight as he did in the tunnel?

"Husband," I whispered and leaned to brush my lips against his.

I had no warning. He was on his feet in one movement, his hands gripping my buttocks, my legs straddling his thighs. The chair crashed to the floor. The table rocked. The lamp teetered, so close to the edge, ready to fall and splatter oil and fire on the carpets.

Antinous drove me straight to the wall. It happened so fast, I could only throw my arms around his neck not to fall. His mouth was on mine and his tongue down my throat. My head slammed against the cedar paneling. He held me with one hand and dragged my caftan up past my waist with the other. Then he jerked his loincloth off and flung it across the room.

He plunged into me and pounded me, both hands back on my buttocks. The rough edges of the wood paneling scraped my back. Banging me and banging me against the wall, he must have rocked the whole ship.

When he stopped kissing me long enough for us to breathe, I used my cheek to force him to turn his head, and then one hand to hold him there. I put my wet tongue in his ear and blew and sucked gently, enough to torment, but not enough to damage.

He went wild and climaxed with a jolt that wracked his whole body. He collapsed against me, pressing me into the wall, his forehead on the cedar panel close to my ear, his breath coming in gulps. He never loosened his grip. I was sure the flesh of my buttocks would forever show an imprint of his fingers.

His biceps bulged when he walked us to the bed, my thighs squeezing around his. He tossed me down and flipped me over in one swift movement, dragging me up on my hands and knees. He ripped the Greek wig away and yanked the linen gown over my head. I heard seams tear.

Not possible, but he was iron-hard again. He thrust into me, holding my hips in both hands and lifting me up and into him. My face buried in the blankets, I reached to grab the back of his thighs and hold on. The two of us rocked with such force, the joint where the bed met the wall creaked with strain.

He rolled me to my back, his tongue deep in my mouth at the moment he entered me again. I wrapped my legs around his waist, locked my ankles, and lay back, eyes closed, surrendering to pleasure.

He was tireless. I let him ravage me, my arms over my head, stretched out on the bed, palms up. We were both drenched in sweat.

With the smooth movement of a wrestler, he turned us on our side and pulled my hips into the curve of his belly, sliding again into my wet. I lay limp and helpless as a rag doll.

His hands massaged my breasts tender from new hormones. I cried out in pain, but put his hands back when he stopped. I'd never felt such raw sensitivity. Agony and ecstasy in the same moment.

He placed his palm on the base of my womb and palpated. A wave began to build. I gasped when he slid his finger onto my engorged bud and rotated hard. Moans reverberated through my chest and vibrated in my throat. My muscles contracted and contracted around his hardness.

Antinous cried out and went rigid, shuddering twice, then a third time.

We lay panting, completely spent, sweat glistening on our bare skin, my full breast filling his warm palm, his arms wrapped around my body. I nestled my hips against his flat stomach and felt his lips cool on my bare scalp, his breath moist on my skin.

When he rolled over to his back, he took me with him, holding tightly, never letting go. I burrowed into his side, my shoulder in his armpit, my cheek on his chest. We lay without speaking, the sound of our breathing louder than the swells of the sea.

I remembered the doubt in his eyes on my balcony. I never wanted to see that again. I rolled over on top of him and began kissing his lips, just small nibbles that teased around their fullness. I felt him harden again.

Three times! Oh, this Greek, indeed, had many talents.

I pushed myself up on bent knees, one on each side of his waist. My hand found his swollen manhood and guided him inside me.

The flicker of twinkling sparkles flashed in the dark; the lamp light reflected off the fragile golden charms of my necklace. Antinous reached up and touched a tiny rabbit with his fingertip.

Fecundity. I knew his character by that choice.

He caught my tender breasts in his hands, gently squeezing their fullness. There was no doubt in his eyes now.

I laughed lightly, a sound like small golden bells, and rocked gently back and forth, milking him. I leaned down, a smile on my lips and in my eyes.

"O Antinous Thrice-Greatest, my husband! We are going to have a wonderful life."

I didn't need to summon the Power at all.

CHAPTER 56 PHONE CALL

I heard no ringing bells or pounding this time. I opened my eyes, and I was back in my condo. With the Red Mirror in the ship's cabin, I simply decided to come back to Las Vegas and was here.

I left Isis in her new life with Antinous. Surely she could be happy with him. The decision about the child was hers; she had a choice.

Aisha didn't cuddle in my armpit or purr into my ear, and I remembered she was next door with Sonny. How many hours had passed? How many days?

"Welcome back."

Hector relaxed in my gray leather chair, the footrest up, a green bottle of Heineken in his hand. He had on straight-legged jeans, a white T-shirt, tight across his broad shoulders, and loafers with no socks. He must have taken a shower. His hair was damp, combed back in chestnut waves.

"I regret I couldn't see you all the way, but it was part of the deal with the Commander." He flashed that brilliant smile. "I trust he was an *hombre* of his word."

I felt a little disoriented. A second ago, I had been on the Phoenician ship. Last I had seen Hector, he wore a white linen loincloth and headdress below deck of a warship on the Nile.

"*Cerveza?*" he offered with another smile. "You must be thirsty."

I hopped in the shower, washed my hair and pulled on a pair of jeans and a black V-neck sweater. Hector still reclined in the chair, but two frosty green bottles now stood on the coffee table.

"How long have you been back?" I asked.

"Long enough to get hungry. I fried some eggs. You could use more food in your fridge."

"I have to watch my weight."

"You do an excellent job." He smiled while his eyes assessed my sweater and jeans.

I sat Indian-style on the zebra carpet, towel-dried my hair and combed it out, taking sips of icy Heineken in between. Hector watched me, not saying anything. When I leaned back against the red sofa, he smiled again, showing those dazzling teeth.

"Is this something that you do all the time—these little *aventuras* through the mirror? Is life on this side not exciting enough for you?"

I didn't have an answer.

He took a swig from the bottle and looked straight into my eyes. There was only a hint of tease in his.

"So what now, Isis?"

"What do you mean 'what now?' I just got back."

"Don't play games," he said a little sharply. "I mean what about us?"

I got the feeling Hector the polo player seldom played these kinds of games. He seemed totally honest about everything. Well, if he wanted honesty, then that's what he'd get.

"I don't know, Hector. I wish things were as straightforward as I used to think they were. I could use some simplicity in my life."

"That usually means there's another man."

He put his feet flat on the floor and leaned forward; his jeans stretched tight over his thighs. He was very fit, with long, lean muscles, not the kind you get from pumping iron in the gym.

I met his eyes, although I didn't want to look there. He made me feel so guilty. The red flecks matched exactly the highlights in his hair. He studied me for a quite long moment, no doubt deciding where to go from here. His face was as serious as I'd ever seen it.

"You could use me in your life, Isis," he said flatly, "but apparently I am not enough."

I felt terrible, like such a bad person. He had just saved my life.

He stared into my eyes and, not finding what he was looking for, smiled the smallest of smiles and said, "Why not get your cat, cuddle her *un poco*, and then we can go for a steak?"

I made it halfway to the front door when he called after me. I knew he was going to say something to make me feel even worse, but Hector proved, as always, full of surprises.

"I will not make your life difficult, Isis. I am patient. I will be here when you are ready. You will be one day."

Barb was over the top with relief when I called. I filled her in with some quick details and promised more over drinks later at the Stirling Club.

"Barb, it's okay that you told Hector. He saved the day."

"I had to tell him. He was positive you wouldn't make it without him. I believed him."

"He's very convincing."

"He's very committed," she corrected, "and you're very lucky." There was a trace of envy in her voice. "It doesn't get better than Hector, you know."

"I know." I didn't sound terribly convinced.

"Is it Rasheed? Is that what's going on? What's *he* ever done to help you? I see only pain."

"He got me to the Phoenician ship."

But I didn't tell Barb how cruel he'd been, how he ripped my heart from my chest and humiliated me in front of Antinous.

I could tell she wasn't ready to hang up, and thinking she was going to nag me more about Rasheed, I braced myself.

But instead, she asked, "What's it like when you're on the other side? I can't imagine having my head in two worlds."

"What's it like? It's...well...hard to explain. I almost never think of Las Vegas. Sometimes I even forget I'm me. I'm myself, yet I'm also Isis. We influence each other. I feel her needs—and her prejudices—like they're my own. I guess they *are* my own...in a way."

I paused. I really wasn't explaining it very well.

"I know it doesn't make much sense when I say it. I think you have to experience it to understand."

"And when you're here?"

"I can't stop thinking about Egypt."

Without calling first, I drove over to the office and walked into Ed's office. His face went beet red when he saw me. Smoke poured out of his ears. He puffed up, eyes bulging, a candidate for a stroke.

"Where the hell have you been? What's this shit about a sick friend? What kind of excuse is that? Whoever it is, they better be dead already."

Pushing the door shut with a small, almost silent click, I closed my eyes and summoned the Power. I slinked over to his desk and slithered onto the leather armrest of the chair opposite him. Ed's eyes followed every movement.

His red color paled to white. His mouth hung slightly open, lips slack. I could almost see his tongue. Smoke still steamed from his ears, but not from anger.

I dialed it up a notch and leaned rather far forward, arching my back and twisting my shoulders just enough that the generous cleavage of my tight red sweater was front and center.

"Ed, I was thinking that I should work more from home," I oozed. "I get a lot more done."

I wet my lips with my tongue and put on the modulated, husky tone that Isis does so well.

"You wouldn't have a problem with that—would you, Ed? We could meet a couple of times a week. Maybe over drinks. You know, to touch base."

Easing down into the chair, I crossed one long leg slowly over the other. Black boots hugged my calves to the knees. From there to the hem of my black leather skirt was smooth skin—lots of it.

I had drawn thick lines along my lashes; emerald eyeshadow highlighted the deep jade of my eyes. My brazen gaze was direct and full of promise.

"Well, what do you think, Ed? Don't you think we can work something out?"

To celebrate my victory over Ed, I stopped by my favorite vintage shop with racks of gorgeous stuff for dirt cheap. Skimming through the hangers, I found a red-hot, sleeveless, scarlet satin number that hugged all the right places.

A tall bleached blonde with thick bangs and white Prada sunglasses grinned and gave me a thumbs-up when I came out from behind the curtain. Her teeth, a little too perfect and white, blazed against her coppery tan. She was trying on a wide-brimmed black hat with a giant pink rose in the band.

"That dress is *bad*, girl. Buy it. Don't bother to think."

"Thanks." I pivoted in front of the mirror, standing on tiptoe to get the effect of high heels. Yes, I'd definitely take the dress.

"Hey, I've seen you at the Stirling Club. You're the Dancer."

"The dancer?" I asked.

"Yeah, I call you the Dancer. You make all those old guys look good, even the *choros* with club feet."

Did I dance with so many men? Maybe Barb was right about the party girl.

"Call me sometime," she said, handing me her business card. "I know a little shop in North Vegas you're gonna love."

The thick, glossy card had a glamour shot in color and said "*Esperanza por la manana.*" The flip side, also with her photo, was in English, "Esperanza in the Morning."

"My TV show. That's why the girl's gotta look good—and I can't afford all those high prices on the Strip." She went on cheerfully, "You should come on my show. I like to mix it up—boxers, politicians, singers—anybody with a story. Don't worry about the Spanish. I take care of that."

Maybe I'd tell her about the Red Mirror one day. Wonder what she'd think of *that* story?

I put the $40 on my Starwood Points card and walked out into the scent of desert spring. The sky was cloudless, the sun warm on my back, but not hot. There was not a trace of wind.

I felt powerful. On top of the world—like I'd lost ten pounds. Great things were coming. I could feel it.

I'd only been home a few minutes and was sipping a glass of chilled Chardonnay when my cell buzzed. I didn't recognize the number but broke my own rule and answered anyway.

"Hello."

"Isis, this is Rasheed."

CHAPTER 57   CLEOPATRA'S BARGE

Just the sound of his voice, exactly like River God, paralyzed me. The air in the room crushed in and then sucked outward. My brain felt like a down pillow.

"Isis, are you there?"

"Yes, I'm here. I'm a little stunned, that's all."

"Why?"

Could he really be that unaware of the effect he had on me?

"I didn't think I would hear from you again."

"Why would you think that?" He sounded genuinely surprised. He saw no problem with coming and going in my life as he pleased.

"You left, remember?" I accused him. "No forwarding address."

"I told you how it has to be," he said quietly. "There are things you can't know. It's safer this way."

Safe from what? But I didn't ask. Maybe I didn't want to know.

"I'm here now, Isis. I want to see you."

Of course, I knew from the moment I first heard his voice that I'd do anything to feel his touch again. But I had *some* pride. He'd torn my heart out on that ship. I'd make him work a little.

"Isis?"

"Yes?"

"Meet me. Please."

Please. That was a start. What I really wanted was for him to beg—like I'd begged below deck. I waited. Wherever he was, it was quiet. The silence on the phone was deafening.

"Isis, what's going on? I want you, and I know you want me. Why are you playing games?"

Games again. Well, my game was to see how far I could push, but I lost my nerve when he turned Commander.

"Why are doing this?" he demanded. "Are you coming to me, or do I have to come to you?"

I was afraid his next words might be goodbye. Besides, it was ridiculous to blame Rasheed for something River God did 2,500 years ago.

"I'll come to you, Rasheed." I didn't want him to sit in the same leather chair that Hector had sat in this morning. They had morphed into each other once, in a dream.

"Good."

I heard relief in his voice. He'd been worried. A small victory, but I'd take it.

"I've got a business meeting at Caesars Palace. I'll get a suite. We can meet there."

I'd felt powerful before I heard his voice. He didn't get to call all the shots.

"I'm not going to wait in your room like some kind of call girl."

I heard him take a deep breath and slowly exhale, summoning patience. I sensed he found me unreasonable but that it was part of a package deal he had to put up with.

"Okay, Isis. You tell me. Where do you want to meet? In a restaurant? In a bar?"

"What about Cleopatra's Barge?"

Rasheed laughed, the first time I ever heard him—or River God— laugh. I thought I was pretty clever myself.

"Cleopatra's Barge. That's perfect! About nine?" His tone was light, almost playful before reverting to his normal intensity.

"I may be late," he warned. "You know how these things are."

"Sure, Rasheed, I know how these things are. I'll be at the bar."

"And Isis, I only have tonight."

"It's okay. I'll wait for you."

I'd wait for him forever. I was pretty sure he knew it.

I wore the red dress. I didn't hold anything back. I put on sheer stockings with the black and red Wynn garters and sexy Vera Wang heels with ankle straps. Even my hair cooperated; I might keep the bangs. I slipped into a full-length, white mink coat that cost me $600 in my favorite vintage shop. Esperanza would approve.

Bring it on, Rasheed.

The traffic on the Strip at this hour was a nightmare. I took Koval and turned left onto Sands, driving past the Wynn with its bittersweet memories of the penthouse suite with stunning views. I used the back entrance to Caesars, the one only cab drivers know.

A blond valet, about thirty with nice shoulders, took my keys, and I stepped out—long legs, red satin, white BMW convertible. The look in his eyes was priceless. The dress had already paid for itself.

It was early for Vegas. No one else sat at the bar. I eased onto a padded barstool and ordered a Plymouth martini, up with an olive. I finished half of it, and no sign of Rasheed. I checked my cell again. The only message was from Barb at the Stirling Club.

"I'm at Cleopatra's Barge—waiting for Rasheed." I said it nonchalantly, as if meeting him was a common occurrence.

"Rasheed! Why didn't you tell me?"

"I was afraid I would jinx it. Besides, I know you don't like him."

"Don't let him jerk you around," she ordered.

Actually, Barb, I'm looking forward to him doing whatever he wants.

"And it's not that I can't see that Rasheed's hot," she chided. "He's a little too unavailable for my taste."

"I'll call you tomorrow, Barb, and tell you all about it."

I put my phone down beside my martini glass. A man took the barstool next to me, but I ignored him.

"It looks like you're expecting someone," he said politely. "May I buy you a drink while you wait?"

I nearly knocked over my glass when I heard his voice. Antinous had traded his Greek *chiton* for a powder-blue oxford cloth shirt, starched and ironed. He had the clean-cut, preppy look of a Brooks Brothers ad. His face was golden tan except for the white around his eyes, like a pair of goggles. He must be a skier. His hair was a mass of shiny curls. Antinous the Greek's deep cleft split his chin. Gorgeous as ever, he outshone any of the statues at Caesars.

"My name's Anthony—Tony—Callis."

He held out his hand for me to shake.

I looked at his outstretched hand and remembered how it gripped my butt so hard on the Phoenician ship that I bruised. For an awkward moment, his hand hung suspended in the space between us, and then he put it on the bar.

"Excuse me, if I was out of line," he apologized, shifting his weight to move away from me. He didn't recognize me at all.

"I'd love another martini," I said with a warm smile. "I just wanted to make sure you weren't a salesman."

"You can tell I'm not a salesman?"

"I can tell."

I didn't embarrass him by saying I also knew he was from out-of-town; he had that expectant look, *This is Vegas. Anything can happen.*

The bartender put two icy Plymouth martinis with plump green olives in front of us.

Tony was so beautiful, it was criminal he was male. I knew a lot of women who paid a fortune to have blond-streaked curls like his.

"I'm from New Jersey," he offered without my asking.

"New Jersey?" The thought of Antinous ending up in New Jersey saddened me a little.

"Well, from Princeton to be exact."

That was more like it. He had to be the best-looking professor in the Ivy League. His preppy clothes didn't hide his muscles at all. He had the same wrestler thighs and powerful arms that had crushed me on the ship.

"What about you?"

"I live here."

"You *live* in Las Vegas?"

I don't know why people are always so surprised when I say that; there are 2 million others like me.

"Living here is like living anywhere, except there's more to do when you go out. And I get to dress up. I like wearing my high heels."

I probably shouldn't have added the last part; the male in Antinous—Tony—couldn't resist looking down the length of my red satin dress all the way to those heels.

"So what brings you to Vegas, Tony?"

"I'm lecturing at a conference at UNLV. Origin of the universe kind of stuff."

I wanted to ask him about the Emerald Tablet's One energy and how it compared to Einstein's Unified Field Theory, but I spotted Rasheed coming down the concourse. Like a lioness in heat, I sniffed his pheromones from afar.

He walked with his two bodyguards, Marcos and Gamel, in a group of tough-looking men in pricey business suits. Some scanned the room while others exchanged jokes or engaged in deep conversation. Rasheed was alone. I saw him looking in this direction.

"It was great talking to you, Tony, but I see my date."

"Sure, I understand. Here's my card. If you're ever in Princeton, look me up. It's quiet there, but I know a couple of places to get a good martini."

He paused as if waiting for me to say something.

"You never told me your name."

I hardly hesitated a heartbeat before answering, "It's…uh…Isis."

Why not? It's what almost everyone who matters calls me.

"Isis? Isn't that the name of an Egyptian goddess?" Something sparked in his eyes. "It seems like I knew an Isis once, but I can't remember where."

Rasheed walked up behind me, put one hand on my shoulder and moved my hair away with the other. He touched his lips to the trigger point on my neck, not a real kiss, but a searing burn that lingered on. He breathed in the scent of my Carolina Herrera perfume. The heat from his hand seared my skin through the satin.

He took the empty stool on my other side, facing me. His legs were open; his left knee pressed against my calf.

"You look good enough to eat," he breathed in my ear.

His chiseled lips wouldn't reject me tonight. I wondered if there existed a Hathor Power for men. I wanted to jump him right there at the bar.

"I approve," he said, touching my new bangs with his magic fingertip. "Let's have dinner in the room."

He was cheerful for Rasheed, almost buoyant. His eyes, warm with affection, glowed like polished jade.

But then his face froze, hardening into those harsh lines that make him ugly. His skin and eyes actually darkened.

"Rasheed, what is it? What's wrong?" *What did I do now?*

He had seen Tony. There could be no doubt about him recognizing the Greek; Rasheed's face took on the black rage of the night below deck on River God's ship.

I put my hand on the inside of his thigh. High up—to get his attention.

"Rasheed, he doesn't know. *Trust* me. He has no idea."

Rasheed scared me, really scared me. He had a look about him I'd never seen, a look that said he was capable of dark deeds I'd never imagined. I slid down from the stool and took his hands into mine.

Leaning into him, my hips between his open legs, my breasts pressing against his chest, I breathed in his ear, "Let's go up to the suite."

It was like I wasn't there. Rasheed glared at Tony with cold hatred in his eyes, the warm jade frozen to green ice. I looked around for Marcos and Gamel. Gamel stared at Tony, too. Marcos was coming across the room. Surely they could see the unsuspecting Tony wasn't a threat.

Marcos spoke in Rasheed's ear, but as close as I was, I couldn't hear what he said. Rasheed nodded, but didn't take his eyes off Tony, who was walking away. For one wild, crazy instant, I thought that Rasheed might be ordering a hit on him.

Then Rasheed took my elbow to guide me across the empty dance floor, saying, "Why don't you take a seat in a booth over here? I'll only be a few minutes."

We passed a group of hard-looking men seated around a table, and I flashed on mafia bosses deciding who will live and who will die. They stopped talking. I felt their eyes following us.

Rasheed helped me into a red leather booth and leaned down and kissed me on the lips in a way that said, *This woman belongs to me.*

Everything with Rasheed has to be mysterious and high drama.

Bodyguards milled around with no attempt to be inconspicuous. This was Caesars Palace; the mob had been coming here since the days of the Rat Pack.

I took Tony's card out of my red patent clutch and read, "Anthony Callis, Ph.D., Director of Cosmological Research, Institute for Advanced Study, Princeton."

He was legit. Princeton was perfect for him, as close to the Library of Neith as you could find in the modern world. I wondered if he were married, had kids. I wondered about his marriage to Isis—Isidora—in Greece. I wondered about the General's child.

At the same time a waiter set a flute of champagne in front of me, a large man slid into the booth on the opposite bench. He moved fast and sat there before I looked up.

He had a salon haircut, styled back on the sides with neck hair too long for an American. He was clean-shaven, but I would have known him anywhere. His massive chest and biceps stretched the expensive Italian-looking suit. I visualized the thickness of his thighs, pulling at the cashmere of his pant legs.

My eyes fixed on the green silk tie with arabesque pattern at his throat. Dark red blood began to bubble above the knot as I stared.

"Hello, Ishtar. It has been a long time."

I couldn't avoid his eyes any longer. I took a deep breath and exhaled. "Hello, General."

CHAPTER 58 REVENGE

Rasheed arrived at my side in seconds. I didn't need to look at him to know his mood. His energy field was like the strobe of a pulsar.

The General smiled smugly at both of us and said, "Your lady friend is most charming, Rasheed. I envy you."

They knew each other! The shock of it slammed me. But it was in this life, not the other. River God and the General never met in the desert.

"We should go now." Rasheed took hold of my upper arm.

"Wait. Have a drink with me, Rasheed. You and your lovely friend." The General's tone sounded friendly, but it was clear he expected us to stay.

"Let us celebrate," he suggested in a somewhat teasing tone. He still had that smirk on his face.

The muscles in Rasheed's jaw clenched, but he didn't say no.

"Let us celebrate relationships—past, present and future," the General said, looking directly at me.

Rasheed nudged me, and I slid over. We sat so close our arms and thighs touched. As if by magic, a bottle of *Cristal* champagne arrived.

The hypnotic white noise of slot machines played in the background. A DJ tested his sound equipment. Herds of tourists streamed past. With a sudden rush, the early show at the Coliseum finished, and the crowd poured out.

Rasheed fixed his unblinking, hard, glittery eyes on the General.

"I sense that your beautiful friend and I have met before." The General sipped his champagne and gave me a knowing look.

I couldn't help my eyes widening. Surely the General wouldn't bring up what happened between us, not in front of Rasheed. I didn't want to think about what Rasheed would do if he realized this was the Persian who had tasted me—if he had the slightest hint of my ride on the comet. It would take more than bodyguards to pull him off.

"You have the most stunning eyes," the General continued, nodding his massive head at me in approval. "I have always had a weakness for emerald eyes like yours. They have been my downfall on more than one occasion."

He enjoyed himself, happily watching me squirm, waving a red cape in Rasheed's face. But it was the bull goading the matador.

Electric shocks ran from Rasheed's body into mine.

"Rasheed and I are business partners, did you know that, *ma bella*? You must find that a fascinating turn of events." The General's tone was far too intimate.

Did he want a war right here in Caesars Palace?

The impact of his words on Rasheed was obvious. He hadn't spoken; he barely breathed. He was like the cobra in the desert, eyes fixed, head almost swaying. I had to do something before he uncoiled and struck at the General's throat.

"What kind of business are you in?" I tried to sound polite and disinterested.

"The world is a dangerous place. Everyone feels he must protect himself. I help people do that. I am—what might you call it?—a broker."

He toyed with me. If the intent of his vague, taunting tone was to bring out my sharp tongue, he succeeded.

"What is it exactly that you broker?" I asked a little acidly. "Or is it a secret? Or maybe it's secrets that you broker?"

He threw back his head and laughed. It was the same laugh as in the tent when I accused him of not being a man of his word.

The General leaned over the table, closer to me.

"You've got guts, I like that. But then I've always liked that about you, Ishtar."

Rasheed turned his face to me, icy eyes narrowed with suspicion and distrust. *You didn't tell me about your plan with the Greek. What other silent lies have you told?*

The General stood out of the booth and spoke to Rasheed, who still stared at me. I couldn't look away from Rasheed's accusing eyes. I found myself wishing that he had River God's black eyes, convincing myself that the glint of hard obsidian would be easier to bear than this cold green glass.

"I look forward to doing business with you, Rasheed. I am confident of our mutual success."

"*Á vedeci, bella*. It was my pleasure to see you again. I am certain this is not the last time we will run into each other."

When I looked up at him, his smoky eyes were not unkind; they twinkled. They told me that we shared a secret and that he was willing to keep it that way—at least for now.

He walked away, his bodyguards around him, devastation in his wake. He'd gotten his revenge without raising a hand.

The bubbles in my glass rose in a continuous stream. I hadn't even tasted the champagne. I was afraid to look down at my dress, afraid there would be a lurid stain of bright blood gushing from my slashed throat.

Rasheed's aura had gone black. His left eyelid twitched in a wild spasm. Oh, how his dark side frightened me when his jealousy twisted his mind and hardened his heart.

He had no reason to be jealous now, but that didn't matter to Rasheed. His suspicions transcended time boundaries. There was something primal between the General and me, and Rasheed sensed it.

If he learned the truth, he might go after the General and not survive. I don't know if anyone could survive a frontal attack on the General.

With each heartbeat, he pulled back from me with the lightning speed of one of Tony's galaxies hurtling through space. The heat of his arm cooled as we sat. I was losing him, and there was nothing I could do.

I would gladly have lied, but my mind was a blank. I couldn't explain away the General. Rasheed's face was so frigid, the angles so harsh, that I thought his face would shatter with one flick of my finger. He always could turn his feelings from hot to cold like a shower faucet.

"I'm going home now." I said it quite simply, without much emotion in my voice.

He slid out of the booth and stood. I slid after him. He didn't help me. I hate a booth when you get out. It's so hard to be graceful, in control.

I folded my white mink coat carefully over my arm. I forced myself to relax the hand gripping my red clutch. Every movement was concentrated not to show my desperation.

But as hard as I tried, I couldn't stop my eyes from filling with tears. My three-inch heels put me on level with his once lush mouth. It seemed impossible that those hard lips had pleasured me and made my soul sing.

I wanted to kiss him, to warm him from stone to man, but his granite mouth was cold. Just like the night below deck on River God's ship, there would be no melting Rasheed. He refused to look at me, trying once again to make me a non-person. I didn't bother to summon the Power.

"Maybe you'll call me when you can let go of the past." My voice was soft and tinged with regret, but not particularly weak.

I think I sounded more resigned and sad than anything. But I'd decided Rasheed had to bend a little.

I walked away. He didn't try to stop me. He hadn't said one word since he first came to my booth and faced the General. I don't know how long his eyes followed me before I disappeared in the crowd.

The drive home was a fog. I was numb except for the ache in my chest where my heart used to be. My mind sped but went nowhere. I kept seeing faces, as they looked in Egypt, as they looked now, changing back and forth.

There seemed to be no rules about who remembered what. Hector had no memories until he saw me at Carla's party. I was a stranger to Tony, but Rasheed knew him instantly. I sensed the General knew much more than any of us. His few words severed Rasheed from me with the precision of a surgeon.

And I recognized everyone. Well, at least as far as I knew.

Barb called twice the next morning before I had the courage to answer. But instead of her usual "I told you so," she was sympathetic and supportive.

"I'm sorry. I know this guy has a hold on you that won't let go."

"Well, I'm pretty sure we can count on Rasheed and me being finished. There's no reaching him when he's like that."

"Want to have lunch?" she offered.

"Thanks, but I'm going to call Hector."

"That's one of the smarter decisions you've made in a while."

I was about to ring off when Barb stopped me with, "By the way, I've been thinking about these trips you take."

I waited.

"I mean, if Hector can go through the mirror, then anyone could. Right?"

"I suppose so," I answered cautiously. "I don't honestly understand how it works."

"I know that. It was just that—well—if you ever decide to go again, maybe I could go with you?"

Barb? No-nonsense Barb wanted to go through the Red Mirror?

"My love life's not all that great," she said. "And you did come back with two gorgeous men."

CHAPTER 59 FULL CIRCLE

Hector picked me up in his white Range Rover. He wore the straight-legged jeans with a pale yellow polo shirt and lizard cowboy boots. A worn bomber jacket lay on the back seat.

"*A donde vamos?*" he asked with his broad, white smile. "Your wish is my command."

He looked so like Hetmus-hor in that moment. The confident Hetmus on the morning of the hunt before he lost me in the sandstorm, and everything went wrong.

"You decide. I don't really care. I just needed company." What I needed was to be with someone who wanted me.

He smiled in a way that said he was pleased but didn't comment. We didn't talk for a while. I stared out the huge windows of the Range Rover and told myself that Rasheed didn't deserve me.

Hector focused on the traffic. Once, he reached over and squeezed my hand.

"You look beautiful today. I like you like this. Natural. Yourself."

"I thought you liked me as a blonde Greek," I teased.

"You were stunning, I admit. My Aphrodite."

Of course, I was reminded of that last devastating scene below deck with my three men. Rasheed filled me for a moment, but I pushed him out.

We rode for a few more minutes in silence before Hector said, "You have many beautiful things in your home. *Muy impresionante.* My mother would say you have an excellent eye."

I rarely brought men back to my condo, but when I did, they weren't much interested in the furniture.

"Show me where you find such treasures in Las Vegas."

"Seriously? Most men don't like shopping."

"I am not most men."

He was certainly not. For starters, he had gone through the Red Mirror.

I keyed the address into the GPS. The traffic thinned as we moved along Flamingo away from the Strip.

"You're not married, are you?" I asked.

I'd never asked Rasheed if he was married. I'd never asked Rasheed anything.

Hector laughed and beamed one of his smiles on me.

"No, Isis, I am not married. I have been waiting for you."

"I'm not very good at commitments, either," I answered.

"We will have to work on that," he said with a direct look that gave me a jolt.

His thighs stretched the tight jeans; his biceps stretched the band around his polo shirt sleeve. I looked at his strong hands on the steering wheel and his long, powerful fingers.

"What's Argentina like?" I asked, rather suddenly interested in exploring my options.

"Buenos Aires is full of life, like Las Vegas. But I grew up on an *estancia*, a ranch."

"So you're a cowboy. That explains the boots." *And those powerful thighs.* I envisioned his long legs squeezing the horse's flanks as he twisted and dipped in the saddle.

My boot comment wasn't funny, but we laughed. So easy between us, no effort at all.

"Where did you meet Carla?"

"Rio. At a polo match."

"You must have liked her a lot to come to Vegas."

"I told you that she means nothing to me. *Nada*, Isis."

I liked the way he mixed in a few words of Spanish when he talked. Charming. Yes, Hector was definitely charming.

"So, what is it that you actually *do*? I mean, besides play polo."

"I used to chase all beautiful women. Now I chase only you."

"Are you telling me that you're a playboy?"

"I prefer to think of myself as a man, not a boy."

We pulled into the parking lot of the antique mall on Eastern, the one where I bought the Red Mirror. Hector followed me down the aisles filled with armor suits, models of sailing ships, heirloom jewelry and embroidered Spanish shawls.

I should have known Hector would be an expert hunter. He went straight for quality and examined each piece carefully before going on to the next. He had a great eye himself.

"My mother has a wonderful collection of antiques—South American, European, some Asian. You will love it."

He had no doubts about us. Did he have a Red Mirror of his own that looked forward in time, instead of back?

"Here's where I found the Red Mirror. Over there, against the Chinese screen."

No one was in the stall at the end of the maze, exactly like the first afternoon I saw the Red Mirror, and like the day I bought it.

Hector pulled me back into him and, lifting me a few inches off the ground like I weighed nothing, carried me behind the yellow-flowered screen. He kissed my neck and my throat and nibbled at my ear. I whimpered as he stroked my breasts.

"I have wanted to do that since you first got in the car," he breathed into my neck as he turned me around.

"The security camera," I protested.

But his tongue went deep in my mouth and then in my ear. All the while his big hand with his strong cowboy fingers was between my legs. I was alive at his touch even through the thick denim.

He leaned me slightly backwards into a bookcase.

"You are so desirable, Isis. I want to touch you forever."

A vase fell first. Hector grabbed it in midair. But the bookcase kept swaying, and when I reached back to steady it, I knocked a shelf loose. A stack of dusty books tumbled to the floor. Then something heavy landed with a thud.

I stared in horror at the mess. Hector grinned.

"Look what you do to me," he teased and kissed me lightly on the lips.

I don't think the security camera worked, because no one came running.

"Nothing's broken that I can see, so we're saved," I said.

Then I thought, *It probably wouldn't matter to Hector.* He'd just write a check. He wouldn't even think of cleaning up.

But Hector bent to the floor and picked up a canvas-wrapped packet. I recognized the shape immediately. Luckily it had landed on a soft pile of books. He turned the crumbling fabric back and a glint of shiny green glass shimmered in the fluorescent light.

"I think this piece is really old," he said.

I could tell by his voice that he was a little awed.

"Is this something for you, Isis? Couldn't you read Greek on the other side?"

The neat rows of hand-etched Greek letters covering the hard, glassy surface formed words so familiar I could have been reading from today's newspaper.

the following to be the truth...

The Emerald Tablet.

I couldn't remember if I'd ever actually held it in my hands before. It was surprisingly heavy.

The Red Mirror and the Emerald Tablet. What were the odds of me finding them both here? Only I didn't believe anymore that I ever found anything but that fate found me.

I looked around the stall, half expecting Hermes *Trismegistus* to be there, smiling warmly from behind some screen. I even imagined his calming touch on my hand.

You are the chosen one, my daughter. It is your destiny to protect the Tablet.

Hermes wasn't finished. I wasn't finished. The circle of souls wasn't finished.

Hector slid his hand around my waist and pulled me back into him, not hot with passion but in a loving and tender embrace. He wrapped me in his arms, holding me close but not too tight. I could fly away and still come back to rest.

Leaning my head on his chest, letting him carry my weight, I relaxed into the cocoon of his warmth. Safe. Hector always made me feel so safe.

Happiness will come to Isis out of misfortune, after what she has undergone.

At first I was tempted to tell him everything. I thought of translating the Greek for him, of sharing the secret to cosmic power. He knew about the Red Mirror. Why not the Emerald Tablet?

Hector and I would have no secrets from each other. I would tell him everything. And he would tell me. Not like Rasheed.

"Go slow," warned my small inner voice. *"Hector has not quite proven himself."*

"But he'll do anything for me," I argued. *"He went through a mirror into a past life he didn't believe in."*

"What does Hector believe in?"

"I'm not sure," I admitted. *"Himself?"*

"What would Hermes say?"

Hermes had already said it. The world wasn't ready. It didn't seem any more ready today than it had 2,500 years ago.

So I didn't tell Hector and had my first secret from him. The first lie is the hardest. The next is easier. The third is no effort at all.

"This tablet is something quite special," I said cautiously. "More special than you could ever imagine."

"Then you must have it."

He grinned with the confidence of a man who has never known struggle. Life to Hector is like polo—a fast sport, based on swift maneuvers and quick response. Obstacles simply require shifts in the line of ball. He didn't fear losing one game. He looked forward eagerly to the next.

Happy Hector. Being with him was like watching Re rise on a clear morning.

When he saw how serious I was, he took my chin in his fingers and looked me deep in the eyes. His eyes were the warmest of browns freckled with those iridescent red specks that match the highlights in his hair.

"It's yours, Isis. *Cualquier cosa.* All you have to do is be you. I don't want anyone but you. And I want you just the way you are."

He leaned down and kissed me gently.

"Anything. And everything. It's yours if you let me give it to you."

Trouble is, now that I had the Emerald Tablet, couldn't I manifest everything myself? Couldn't I have River God?

EPILOGUE "HAPPINESS WILL COME TO ISIS..."

You might be wondering what happened after I sailed for Greece with Antinous, but I have no further memories of that lifetime. As real as the events are when I experience them, it's a bit like starting a play in the second act and leaving before the final curtain.

I don't know how the story ends, but I imagine that I have the courage to tell Antinous the truth.

We are close enough to the rocky coastline of Kos to see a red-roofed white village crawling up the hillside. The sea is calm and a deep shade of blue—almost the color of the Hathor ring I left behind.

"I am with child, Antinous. But not your child."

"Am I to be a father so soon? You are, indeed, a remarkable woman, Isidora. Life shall never be boring with you."

"Are you not going to ask who the father is?'

"You can tell me, but I cannot see the relevance. A child grows within you. It is a matter of biology. You are my wife. All that you are is now part of me."

He smiled, kissed me tenderly and then pulled me into his side.

"Everything comes from the One, Isidora. We are all one."

I try not to think about River God and the fate his Gods ordained. The Persians invade, and the Egyptians lose. I prefer to fantasize that River God escapes to Kush. But knowing his devotion to duty, I suspect he fights to the end. A noble death is the most I can hope for.

Hetmus-hor and his family had the kind of wealth that survives even conquerors. His father undoubtedly married him off to a Persian princess to secure the family's position.

As for the Crown Prince Psamtik, he became the last Egyptian Pharaoh ever to rule the Nile. Cambyses sold Psamtik's daughter into slavery and cut his son into pieces before his eyes. The Persians were neither benevolent conquerors nor kind masters.

The Isis incarnation is finished for now. I will go back—but not to her. I'm a different person because of Isis, and she was a different woman because of me. My future changed the past, as my past changed the present.

Three hundred years will go by in Egypt before I cross through the Red Mirror into the life of Athena of Korinth. My next incarnation is a tale of Alexandria, perhaps the greatest city in all ancient times. At the heart is the Library, a center of learning and repository of every book written.

The Egyptians welcomed Alexander the Great as the slayer of Persians and their savior. Little did they know the price. Egypt would become Greek.

I won't tell you who I meet in Alexandria, but you can probably guess. Hermes *Trismegistus* isn't finished; my role as protector of the Emerald Tablet isn't finished. The circle of souls continues.

The Emerald Tablet
Book Two of the The Isis Trilogy
One woman, four men, many lifetimes
One life is not enough...

AUTHOR'S COMMENTS AND GLOSSARY

The ancient story is *historically plausible*. Another term might be *faction*. Everything that happened in the book could have happened during this era of Egyptian history classified as 26th Dynasty of the Late Period. The date is 526 BCE. The introduction of camels to Egypt, coins to commerce, the influence of the Greeks, and the invasion of the Persians are facts.

I have fictionalized the personality of the real Psamtik III (*Psammetichus III*) who lost the battle of Pelusium and the siege of Memphis to Cambyses, King of Persia, within months of becoming Pharaoh.

Hermes *Trismegistus* or Hermes Thrice-Greatest is a legendary figure like Merlin of King Arthur fame. His life is shrouded in mystery and steeped in the myths of the Emerald Tablet popularized in the film and book "The Secret." The *Hermetica* (named after Hermes *Trismegistus*) is the foundation for alchemy. For more information about the Emerald Tablet and Hermes, you can read my research at:

www.SandraOfftheStrip.com/The Emerald Tablet

Names in Egyptian history can be quite confusing as both Egyptian and Greek versions are used interchangeably. The Greek names for cities are often more familiar to the general audience, so I have used *Thebes* over *Waset* and *Saïs* over *Sa*, among others.

I have included paraphrased translations of Egyptian poems, songs, sayings and proverbs from papyri, stelae and shards. I thank Miriam Lechtheim for her compilation of translations in "Ancient Egyptian

Literature, Volume III: The Late Period" and R.B. Parkinson for his compilation of translations in "Voices from Ancient Egypt." The toast by Hetmus to Isis on the day of the hunt is borrowed from an inscription on Tutankhamun's wishing cup.

The Egyptian characters with a pronunciation guide are listed at the end of the glossary.

Please visit my author website www.SLGore.com for photos of the Red Mirror, red sofa, a statue of Antinous and many other images from the Egyptian world of Isis, the Greco-Egyptian world of Athena, and the Roman-Egyptian world of Elektra.

GLOSSARY

CITIES:

Abydos. Greek for Egyptian *Abdju*. Abydos is one of the holiest places in all of ancient Egypt, and believed to be the burial site of Narmer the first Pharaoh and the head of Osiris, the god. The breathtaking Temple of Seti I with the List of Kings is one of the finest extant Pharaonic buildings in Egypt today.

Elephantine. Greek *Elephas* for Egyptian *Abu* or *Yeb*. The Greeks saw the island in the Nile at Aswan as having the shape of an ivory tusk, thus the Greek name for elephant. Sitting on the border between Egypt and Nubia, it was an ideal location for a military fort. Jewish mercenary soldiers likely started the Elephantine Jewish community with its temple to their one god circa 650 BCE.

Hermopolis. Greek for "City of Hermes;" Egyptian *Khmu*; Arabic *El Ashmunein*. A center of wealth and learning, Hermopolis was dedicated to the god Thoth, then to the Greek god Hermes.

Karnak. (Karnak Temple Complex). Egyptian *Ipet-isu*; named for modern village of *el-Karnak* near **Luxor**. The complex comprises a vast conglomeration of ruined temples, chapels, pylons and other buildings built over centuries of different dynasties. Karnak is part of the ancient city of *Thebes* and is the largest complex of extant temples in Egypt.

Khent-min. Also *Ipu* in ancient Egyptian; Greek *Khemmis, Chemmis* and *Panopolis*; Arabic *Akhmim*. Min, the God of Male Fertility is Khent-min's patron god. The city was known for magicians right up through the days of Arab conquest of Egypt in 641 CE. Very little exists today of once massive building projects.

Pelusium. Latin for Greek *Pelos*; Egyptian *Sena* and *Per-Amun*; Arabic *Tell el-Farama*. Located on the easternmost branch of the Nile near modern day **Port Said**, Pelusium was an ancient launching point for military and trade campaigns, and site of the battle where Persian Cambyses II defeated Psamtik III.

Rosetta. French *Rosette*, Arabic *Rashid*, Greek *Bolbitis*. In this book, Rosetta describes the point where the Bolbitine branch of the Nile meets the Mediterranean. Napoleon's men discovered the Rosetta Stone here, subsequently losing it in a sea battle to the British, who display the stone today in the British Museum.

Saïs. Greek name for Egyptian *Sa* or *Zau*; Arabic *Sa el-Hagar*. The capital city of the Saïte Dynasty in the Late Period (26th Dynasty), Saïs was located in the Nile Delta, 50 miles from the Mediterranean on the Rosetta (*Bolbitine*) Branch of the Nile. Virtually nothing of the ancient city exists today.

Susa. Capital of the Persian Empire under Cambyses at the site of the modern Iranian town of Shush close to the Iraqi border.

Thebes. Greek name for Egyptian *Waset* or *Niwet*; Arabic *Al-Uqsur* (palaces) and known today as **Luxor**. Thebes was a great political center during long periods of Egyptian history, but a religious center during the time frame of this book. Luxor is famous today for the Temple of Karnak, the Temple of Luxor and the Valley of the Kings.

COUNTRIES/REGIONS

Cyrene. The Greeks founded a colony on the Mediterranean coast of North Africa in 630 BCE. The ruins are located in modern day Libya near the Egyptian border.

Kemet. Ancient Egyptian name for Egypt meaning "Black Land."

Kush. An independent kingdom in ancient times established circa 1070 BCE, it covers roughly the same area as Nubia.

Libya. Greek *Libyes* for the region of Northwestern Africa. The name derives from *Libu*, Egyptian for a specific Berber tribe. The Greeks considered all Berbers *Libyans*, while the Egyptians differentiated between the many tribes.

Nubia. An independent kingdom in ancient times, Nubia refers to the region of southern Egypt along the Nile (25% of ancient Nubia) with the remainder (75%) extending into modern day northern Sudan. This area was also part of the Kingdom of Kush.

Punt. The exact location of Punt is unknown. Punt might have been located in modern day Somalia, Eritrea, or Yemen.

LANGUAGES

Berber. This group of ancient Semitic dialects of North Africa is still spoken today by native tribes in the mountains of Morocco and Algeria. It is considered a close relative to ancient Egyptian.

Elamite. A language spoken by the ancient Elamites adopted by the Persians as the official language of their aristocracy during the 6th to 4th centuries BCE.

Lingua franca. Italian for "Frankish language." This term refers to any language used to communicate between peoples over a large geographical area, who do not share a mother tongue. The *lingua franca* of the Persian Empire was Aramaic. Latin was the *lingua franca* of the Roman Empire and the Catholic Church. The *lingua franca* during the time of the Crusades was French, thus the term *franca* (Frankish). English is considered today's *lingua franca*.

Aramaic. Originally the native language of the Arameans, Aramaic became the *lingua franca* of the Assyrian and Persian Empires. It was adopted and spoken by many conquered peoples, including the Hebrews.

Demotic. Egyptian *sekh shat* or "writing for documents." The Demotic handwriting script form of Egyptian hieroglyphs developed from a variant of the Hieratic (priestly) script circa 660 BCE. It became the preferred form of writing during the 26th Dynasty for business, legal, scientific, literary and religious documents. It was written almost exclusively from right to left, in horizontal lines, and mainly in ink on papyrus.

GODS

Note: only small part of large and complex Egyptian Pantheon. Gods and goddesses merged over the 5,000 years of Egyptian history.

Hathor. Goddess of Love, Motherhood, Joy, Music, Dance. The Cow Goddess was associated with Ishtar by the Persians, Aphrodite by the Greeks, and Venus by the Romans. She is depicted as a woman with cow ears or with a crown of two horns with a solar disk. Isis of this book is a high-priestess in the cult of Hathor.

Horus. God of the Sky, War, and Protection. Horus was the male child of the god Osiris and goddess Isis. He is usually depicted as a celestial falcon. The Pharaoh was considered a manifestation of Horus in this life, and Osiris in the afterlife. Pharaohs had a Horus name among their five official names. The eye of Horus is a commonly known Egyptian symbol. The use of *hor* in a name indicates Horus, i.e. *Ankh-hor*.

Isis. The Goddess of the Moon, the Earth and Women eventually supplanted Hathor as the Queen of the Gods. Isis married her brother Osiris and gave birth to the falcon-headed god Horus. Her magical skills brought her husband back to life after gathering the parts of his body strewn over the earth by their evil brother Set, the god of destruction and chaos. She is depicted as a woman wearing a headdress shaped like a throne.

Min. The God of Fertility is depicted with an erect penis and upheld arm holding a flail (a kind of whip). His black skin represents the fertile black mud of the Nile Inundation. He was the patron god of Khent-min.

Osiris. The King of the Gods, God of the Underworld. Osiris was killed by his jealous brother Set, God of Chaos, who chopped him into pieces and spread them over the earth. Isis, the wife and sister of Osiris, used magic to bring him back to life and father their child Horus the Sky God. Osiris is depicted in white like a mummy with green skin symbolizing re-birth. The Pharaoh is Horus the god when he is living and Osiris after his death.

Re/Ra. The Sun God was considered the father of the gods. He is often merged with other gods, i.e. *Amun-Re* and Horus. He sailed each night in a boat on a journey through the twelve hours of darkness when he battled such creatures as *Apep*, the giant serpent of the Underworld. His nightly victories resulted in each day's new dawn. He is depicted as a man with a falcon head.

Set (Seth). God of Chaos, Destruction, Thunder, Desert. He killed his brother Osiris to usurp him as King of the Gods. Horus, the son of Osiris and Isis, became the new king. Set usually represents all that is evil. He is depicted as a man with the head of a jackal.

Thoth. God of Knowledge, Writing, Medicine, and the inventor of language. Thoth was associated with the Messenger God known as Hermes to the Greeks and Mercury to the Romans. His totem is the ibis or the baboon. He is depicted with a man's body and an ibis head.

ROYAL PERSONS and NAMES

Amasis II. Greek for *Ahmose II*. Father of Psamtik III. He fended off the Persian Cyrus the Great and succeeded in stopping an invasion of Egypt. The next generation clashed again; Cambyses, son of Cyrus, defeated Psamtik, son of Amasis, first at the battle of Pelusium and finally at Memphis, where Psamtik surrendered.

Akhenaton. A pharaoh of the 18th Dynasty (New Kingdom) who was crowned *Amenhotep IV* (Greek *Amenophis*), but changed his name to Akhenaton when he established his monotheistic religion worshipping the sun disk *Aten*. He moved the capital from Thebes to a city he built on the Nile called *Akhetaten*, today known as *el-Armana*. He ruled for 17 years until about 1335 BCE.

Cambyses II. The son of Cyrus the Great. Cambyses II expanded the Persian Empire into Egypt during the Late Period and defeated Psamtik III at Pelusium and Memphis, establishing the Persian Period in Egyptian history. He crowned himself Pharaoh and ended the long dynastic reign of Egyptians. His forces also unsuccessfully invaded the Kingdom of Kush located in modern Sudan.

Ramses the Great. Ramessses II was a 19th Dynasty pharaoh of the period known as New Kingdom and usually regarded as Egypt's greatest and most famous pharaoh. He was the Great Builder and financed massive building projects all over the kingdom, including his mammoth rock cut statues at Abu Simbel in Nubia. He ascended to the throne in his early 20's and ruled Egypt from 1279 BCE for a total of 66 years and 2 months.

Isenkhebe Nefrusobek. *Isenkhebe* was a Late Period name whose Greek form *Isis-in-Chimmis* means "Isis from Khent-min." *Nefrusobek* means "goodness or beauty of Sobek." Sobek was the crocodile god who came out of the waters of chaos to create the world. *Nefrusobek* was the first known woman pharaoh in Egyptian history and the last ruler of the 12th Dynasty in the Middle Kingdom Period. She ruled for four years from 1806 BCE.

-hor. The use of *hor* attached to other names indicates Horus, i.e. *Ankh-hor*.

ARCHITECTURE

Stela. (Latin plural *stelae*) A *stela* is a stone slab with an inscribed, carved surface used for dedication, commemoration, demarcation or burial. It can be free standing, or a tablet mounted or embedded in the facade of a building.

Lotiform: Egyptian style of abstract design representing the lotus. The columns usually have circular ribbed shafts with capitals (tops) in the form of closed buds or open lotus flower. This design was most often used in secular architecture.

Naos. Greek for "temple." It referred to the sanctuary or innermost chamber of a temple. Also known as Holy-of-Holies or inner sanctum.

Papyriform. Egyptian style of abstract design representing papyrus. There are several variations of this type of column, some with circular shafts of a single plant, others with ribbed shafts of a plant with multiple stems. Capitals (tops) can be closed buds or the open bell-shapes of the flowering plant.

Palmiform. Egyptian style of abstract design representing palm fronds. Palmiform fans and sunscreens were in the shape of single palm fronds. Columns were carved in a motif of eight palm fronds lashed to a pole.

Palisade. A defensive structure consisting of walls built around a stronghold.

Portico. A porch or walkway with a roof supported by columns, often leading to the entrance of a building.

Pylon. Greek for the monumental gateway to an Egyptian temple with two tapering towers topped by a cornice and joined together halfway up with a stone lintel over the gateway entrance.

OBJECTS

Akinaka. (Greek *Acinaces*). Persian thrusting sword or dagger adopted by the Greeks. It was double-edged and typically 14"-18" in length.

Amulet. Symbols or objects believed to have magical powers used as talismans against evil or injury.

Electrum. A naturally-occurring alloy of silver and gold whose color ranges from pale to bright yellow. Used in jewelry and chalices, it also coated the tips of obelisks and the pyramidions (small pyramids) that topped pyramids.

Incense. Incense was crucial to all Egyptian ceremony. The three preferred fragrances were frankincense, burned in the morning, myrrh in the afternoon, and *kapet* (Greek *kyphi*) for the evening. Incense came from aromatic woods and was imported from Arabia, Sudan, the horn of Africa, and later from India.

Lapis lazuli. This semi-precious stone has been prized since antiquity for its intense blue color. The finest quality was imported from Afghanistan and often combined in patterns with turquoise.

Menit. The *menit* is a ceremonial bead necklace associated with the goddess Hathor. Her priestesses transmitted the power of the goddess via the crescent frontpiece. A counterpoise hangs down the back to hold the necklace in place.

Naos of Amasis. Sanctuary carved from a single block of rose granite commissioned by the Pharaoh Amasis. The inside dimensions measured 30 ft high, 24 feet deep and 12 feet wide. Hollowed out, the massive block weighed 500 tons and took 2000 boatmen 3 years to bring it up the Nile from the quarries of Elephantine.

Osireion. Abydos burial tomb at the Temple of Seti I for the head of Osiris, god of the Earth and Underworld. According to legend, it was in Abydos that Osiris reclaimed his title as King of the Gods from his brother Set.

Ox Foreleg. Egyptian *Meskhetiu*. This constellation, known in the west as the Big Dipper or The Plough, was believed to be the Leg of Set cast into the sky by Horus, the son of the god Osiris and goddess Isis.

MISC TERMINOLOGY

Inundation. Egyptian *Akhet*. The annual flood of the Nile was between June and September and resulted from the heavy summer rains in the Ethiopian highlands that swelled the tributaries feeding the Nile. It brought rich silt and nutrients to fertilize the farmlands along the river. The Aswan Dam built by Nasser interrupted the cycle and the annual flood no longer exists.

Ka. The Ancient Egyptians believed that a human soul was comprised of five parts: the *Ren*, the *Ba*, the *Ka*, the *Sheut*, and the *Ib*. I have used *Ka* in this story for simplicity.

Wadi. Arabic for a valley, gully, or streambed in northern Africa and southwest Asia that remains dry except during the rainy season.

ᴸ

CAST OF CHARACTERS

Isis: (*Eye sis*) Isenkhebe Nefrusobek (*Egyptian*), Ishtar (*Persian*), Isidora (*Greek*).

Her four lovers (in order of appearance)
River God. Egyptian Commander. - Rasheed (*Ra sheed*)
Hetmus. (*Het-moose*) Egyptian Master of Hunt. - Hector
General Sher. (*Cher*) Persian general. - The General
Antinous. (*An tee no os*) Greek mathematician. - Tony

Rest of cast (in alphabetical order)
Aisha. (*Eye sha*) Las Vegas cat.
Amasis. (*Ah mass is*) Pharaoh & father of Crown Prince Psamtik.
Ankh-hor. (*Onk hor*) Nobleman and father of Hetmus.
Araxa. (*A rax a*) Persian second in command to the General.
Barb. Very Best Friend.
Carla. Friend.
Eben. (*EE ben*) Hebrew Kabbalist.
Ed. Boss.
Elaine. College friend and mentor.
Esperanza. (*Es pe ron za*) Latina TV hostess
Goliath the Nubian. Slave in service to Isis.
Harwa. (*Har wah*) Scribe to Pharaoh Amasis
Hermes *Trismegistus*. (*Err mees Tris me gis tus*) Creator of the
Emerald Tablet & Isis' father.
Kiya. (*Key ah*) Mistress of Chambers & Nursemaid of Isis.
Lars. Rasheed's Norwegian business associate
Maia. (*My ah*) Initiate to Isis.
Pasi. (*Pa see*) Guard in service to Isis.
Pehtes. (*Pay tes*) Egyptian Cat.
Psamtik. (*Sam tick*) Crown Prince of Egypt.
Qeb-ha. (*Keb ha*) Eunuch priest.
Setne. (*Set nay*) The Scribe & lover of Psamtik.
Sit-hathor. (*Sit hat hor*) High-Priestess & Isis' mother.
Ti. (*Tea*) Guard in service to Isis.
Wah. (*Whaw*) Guard in service to Isis.
Zavan the Merciless. (*Za van*) Persian master of torture.

ABOUT THE AUTHOR

Born with wanderlust, forever living in a fantasy world, S. L. Gore escaped the prairies of Kansas to follow the yellow brick road on an odyssey that took her to Europe, Africa, Latin America and the Middle East.

Starting with a one way ticket to Iceland, she returned with a Viking husband, an art degree and speaking five languages.

Years in North Africa, with months on the Sahara and hundreds of hours haggling in *souks*, set the stage for the *Isis Trilogy*. A love of adventure and romance combined with a fascination for exotic lands, classical history, ancient and modern languages, mysticism, and fine dining led Gore to create **The Red Mirror**, **The Emerald Tablet** and **The Black Scroll**.

Her non-fiction publications include the self-help manual **Sex and the Zen of Shopping:** *How to Live Rich by Shopping Smart* and memoir contributions to three **Life Choices** anthologies. She is a regular columnist for Life Choices Magazine with the food and table art feature **Beauty and the Feast**.

Gore is always actively engaged in her community and has served as a School Board Trustee, a Planning Commissioner and a Parks, Recreation and Beautification Commissioner. A frequent guest on the Dave Congalton Radio Show, she discusses international news and foreign policy.

The joyously married Nielsens have a grown daughter and son and divide their time between a California beach house and a Las Vegas condo.

S. L. Gore's Books

Isis Trilogy ~ *One life is not enough*
Published by Tajine Publishing in print and eVersion
The Red Mirror 🦢 (Book One)
 - Pharaonic Egypt, 525 BC
The Emerald Tablet 🦉 (Book Two)
 - Greek Egypt, 215 BC
The Black Scroll 🐊 (Book Three)
 - Roman North Africa, 130 AD

Lovers of Isis *Vignettes* 🐝 S. L. Gore
Published by Tajine Publishing in print and eVersion

Isis *Erotica* 🐕 Sandra Gore
Published by Tajine Publishing in print and eVersion

Isis Beach Read 🐝 Sandra Gore
Published by Tajine Publishing in print and eVersion

Sex and the Zen of Shopping: Live Rich by Shopping Smart
Sandra Gore Nielsen
Published by Tajine Publishing

Life Choices Anthologies
Published by Turning Point International
Navigating Difficult Paths: "A True Love Story"
Pursuing Your Passion: "The Muses Whisper"
It's Never Too Late: "Road to Vegas"

Tajine Publishing
Las Vegas NV
tajinepublishing@gmail.com
702-279-6556

Author website: **www.SLGore.com**